Rosie Goodwin h [barcode: D0512864] **d as a** fost   rer for mar   n, and live   Nuneaton with her husband, Trevor, and their fost   children.

Prais   for Rosie Goodwin:

'A g ed writer . . . Not only is Goodwin's characterisation . d dialogue compelling, but her descriptive writing is a j y' *Nottingham Evening Post*

'Goo win is a fabulous writer . . . she reels the reader in surpr ingly quickly and her style involves lots of twists and t   ns that are in no way predictable' *Worcester Evening News*

'Goodwin is a born author' *Lancashire Evening Telegraph*

'R ie is a born storyteller – she'll make you cry, she'll make ou laugh, but most of all you'll care for her characters nd lose yourself in her story' Jeannie Johnson

'Her stories are now eagerly awaited by readers the length and b   dth of the country' *Heartland Evening News*

05278930

Also by Rosie Goodwin and available from Headline

The Bad Apple
No One's Girl
Dancing Till Midnight
Moonlight and Ashes
Tilly Trotter's Legacy
The Mallen Secret

Forsaken

Rosie Goodwin

headline

First published in Great Britain in 2007
by HEADLINE PUBLISHING GROUP

First published in paperback in 2007
by HEADLINE PUBLISHING GROUP

14

ISBN 978 0 7553 3490 2

Typeset in Bembo by Palimpsest Book Production Limited,
Grangemouth, Stirlingshire

Printed and bound in Great Britain by
CPI Antony Rowe, Chippenham, Wiltshire

Headline's policy is to use papers that are natural, renewable and
recyclable products and made from wood grown in sustainable
forests. The logging and manufacturing processes are expected
to conform to the environmental regulations of the country of origin.

HEADLINE PUBLISHING GROUP
An Hachette Livre UK Company
338 Euston Road
London NW1 3BH

www.headline.co.uk
www.hodderheadline.com

This book is for John Thomas Churm, 'Jack,' a dear Grandad 1900–1970.
Never more than a thought away

Acknowledgements

To Trev, 'The manager!', who makes the time for me to write.

A big thank you to the following people:

My lovely children, Donna, Sarah, Christian and Aaron and their partners, Steve, Jason and Rachel, who offer endless encouragement and support.

Also to Nikki, Daniel and Charlotte, who light up my life.

And, of course, as always the team at Headline.

The staff at Waterstone's at Nuneaton. Not forgetting the staff at Nuneaton library.

To Janet and Geoff, who always believed in me and told me, *one day* . . .

And last but far from least, to all the readers who take the trouble to get in touch. It means so much . . .

Prologue

Blackpool 1947

'Come on, Sally. One more good push should do it.'
Beattie gently wiped a strand of damp hair from the forehead of the poor soul writhing on the bed.

'I . . . I can't.' Sally Winters' whimpers bounced off the walls as she thrashed about from side to side. She felt as if she were being rent in two and in that moment would gladly have welcomed death. What was there left to live for anyway? Soon the agony of birth would be over to be replaced by yet another agony as she struggled to feed one more little mouth. It certainly wasn't going to be easy, for even though the war was over, rationing was still as strict as ever and there never seemed to be enough food, or for that matter money, to go round.

Beattie pursed her lips as she glanced across the sparsely furnished room at the thin curtains covering the window. Where the bloody hell had that damn midwife got to? It must be all of two hours since she had sent Robbie, Sally's eldest, off to look for her. If this baby didn't put

1

in an appearance soon she would have no choice but to send for the doctor.

Downstairs she could faintly hear Sally's other children laughing and fighting, no doubt watched over by Bill, Sally's husband, who hadn't ventured up the stairs so much as once since Sally's labour had begun. It didn't really surprise her. Since returning from the war nearly ten months ago Bill was a changed man in all ways and had become almost reclusive; nothing at all like the happy-go-lucky chap that Sally had tearfully waved off. But then the war had changed them all and they could only hope that one day Bill would return to being as nice as he had once been. 'That's women's business,' he had told Beattie testily when Robbie had run to fetch her from next door, and here she had been ever since without so much as a swallow of tea to wet her throat.

As Sally groaned in the grip of yet another contraction, Beattie turned her attention back to the bed. Quickly wringing out the cloth that stood in the bowl of water on the bedside table, she wiped Sally's sweating brow and whispered soothingly to her. It was then that she heard footsteps on the stairs and when seconds later the door opened and Nurse Foss, the midwife, barged in, she let out a long sigh of relief.

'Thank God fer that. I were just beginnin' to panic,' she confided as the portly woman threw her coat off. 'She's bin pushin' fer hours but there ain't no sign o' the babby as yet.'

'Let's have a look then.' The midwife threw the thin

sheet from Sally's heaving frame and expertly began to feel around the swollen stomach. Seconds later she stood back up and shook her head.

'The baby appears to be breech.'

Beattie's brow creased in a frown that only added to the already numerous lines on her face. 'So what do we do now, then?'

Rolling up her sleeves the nurse told her, 'We have to turn it, though it won't be easy. Could you come and hold her arms down while I try?'

When Beattie faltered her voice became brisk. 'If you *don't* help me we could lose both mother *and* baby. They're obviously both deeply distressed and there's no time to call for a doctor now so it's up to you and me.'

Like a bullet from a gun, Beattie shot across the room and positioned herself at the head of the bed and as she gripped Sally's arms the nurse nodded with satisfaction and bent to her task. Within seconds Sally's screams were bouncing off the walls again as the woman inserted her hand into her womb and began to manipulate the child inside her.

Sally's body arched off the cheap mattress as Beattie held onto her thin arms for all she was worth. It seemed to go on forever but at last the nurse nodded and rose.

'That should do it. I've turned it as much as I can – now it has to be up to her.' Leaning over Sally she now said, 'Sally, can you hear me? Come on, love. Just one more good push when I tell you and it should be all over.'

Sally's head shook weakly from side to side. 'I've . . . no more strength,' she sobbed.

It was Beattie's voice that urged her on. 'Oh *yes* you have. Now just do as yer told an' let's get this over wi', eh? On the next pain push fer all yer worth.'

What seemed to be only seconds later the nurse gave Beattie a nod and leaning to the young woman on the bed she commanded, 'Push now . . .'

With the last of her remaining strength, Sally heaved her head off the pillow and pushed until she was red in the face, and suddenly the sound of a baby's cry was heard.

'Thank God fer that,' Beattie shouted joyously as the midwife quickly cut the cord and lifted the child from the bed. She gave it a resounding slap on the backside and the child cried out even more lustily as Sally dropped back onto the pillows, exhausted.

'Is it . . . another boy?' Her voice was weak.

The midwife grinned from ear to ear. 'Well, if it is there's a certain bit missing,' she teased. 'No, Sally, you've got yourself a beautiful baby girl and I have to say it's been many a long day since I saw a newborn as bonny as this. She's going to break a few hearts, you just mark my words.'

Sally stared at her incredulously, hardly daring to believe her ears. 'Did you say I had a little *girl*?'

'I most certainly did. But here – see for yourself if you don't believe me.'

After wrapping the child in a rough towel that Beattie

held ready, Nurse Foss now placed the child in Sally's arms and watched with satisfaction as a look of wonder spread across the young woman's face.

Just as the midwife had said, the child was truly beautiful. She had a mop of baby blond hair and eyes the colour of sapphires as she stared trustingly up at her mother.

Beattie began to sniffle into her apron. 'Well, I'll be. Four fine lads one after the other but now you've finally got the little girl you always wanted. An' just as Nurse Foss said, she's a beauty, though I don't know where she got her fair hair from when all the others are so dark. A Friday's child, eh? What is it they say – Friday's child is loving and giving? I've no doubt that will be the case wi' this 'un after all the years you've longed fer a little gel. I don't mind bettin' she'll be spoiled rotten, an' I wonder what Bill will have to say when we tell him he finally has a daughter? Do yer want me to send him up so as yer can tell him yerself?'

At the mention of her husband tears suddenly spurted from Sally's eyes to run in rivers down her pale cheeks. 'No, I . . . would you go an' tell him, Beattie?'

'Course I will, love, an' wi' the greatest o' pleasure if yer sure that's what yer want. But first give her to me an' I'll clean her up a bit an' make her fit to be seen.'

As Sally reluctantly handed over her precious bundle, Beattie asked, 'An' what were yer thinkin' o' callin' her?'

Sally frowned. 'To tell the truth, after having four boys I'd only thought of lads' names. I never dreamed I'd be lucky enough to have a little girl. But I think I'll call her . . . Sophie.'

Both Beattie and Nurse Foss smiled their approval.

'Well-chosen, I'm sure. She even *looks* like a Sophie,' Nurse Foss pronounced as she began the task of cleaning Sally up. And so it was decided.

Once Sally and the new baby were washed and comfortable, Nurse Foss departed and Beattie bustled away to make Sally a well-earned cup of tea. As soon as the door closed behind her, Sally gazed down at the new baby daughter nestling against her breast and tears squeezed from the corner of her eyes. Just as Beattie had commented, Sophie looked nothing at all like the other children. But then that was hardly surprising as Bill wasn't her father; not that she could ever tell him that, of course. A wealth of emotions swept through her but overriding them all was guilt as she pictured the child's father's face in her mind's eye. Sophie was like looking at a tiny carbon copy of him. The same blue eyes; the same fair hair, and yet he would never see her; never get to know her.

The short time they had spent together had resulted in this beautiful child that would always be a constant reminder of her adultery. She owed it to Bill now to try and be a faithful wife. Perhaps the changed man downstairs was her punishment for being unfaithful to him?

When the door inched open and Bill appeared as if her thoughts had conjured him up, she started. He approached the bed and she saw the frown that flitted across his face as he stared down at the infant.

She wanted to say so many things but the words lodged in her throat as she fixed her eyes on the child. It was too hard to look at Bill right now. If she did she was afraid he would see the truth written there.

Her thoughts raced back to the birth of their sons. Bill had been ecstatic with pride; but now there was no joy in his eyes. He looked at her strangely and in that second she knew he had guessed that this tiny little girl was not his.

'You finally got your daughter then?' His voice was flat and emotionless. Her head nodded weakly before he turned and strode from the room. Only then did she give way to the storm of tears that had built up inside her, for she knew that their marriage would never be the same again.

Chapter One

1964

'Are you sure you have everything you need then, Mam?' Sophie asked as she tied a brightly coloured headscarf under her chin.

'I'll be right as ninepence,' her mother replied with a smile. 'Now don't you let that old bugger you work for work you too hard.'

Sophie grinned. Since leaving school she had tried various jobs but was presently working in a café along the seafront. The hours were long and standing on her feet all day was tiring, but for all that Sophie enjoyed it, especially in the holiday season when the town came to life with holidaymakers.

The smile now slid from her face as she glanced back at her mother who was huddled in a chair at the side of the fire. Sally was only forty-four years old, yet she looked like an old woman. It was hardly surprising when Sophie thought of the life she had led with her father. Her eyes found him now, slumped across the table poring over the newspaper. As if he sensed her looking at him his eyes momentarily locked with hers and she quickly looked away as colour flooded into her cheeks. For some reason she had never got on with her father and had long since stopped trying to.

Her three oldest brothers had left home as soon as they were old enough and now only the youngest one, Matthew, who was four years older than her, and herself remained at home. Robbie, the eldest, had gone to live in Canada. Brian and Tony, the middle two, were both married and lived not too far away. Not that they bothered to visit much; they too found their father hard to get along with. But she and Matthew, or Mattie as he was affectionately known, were close, and many a time he had got between herself and her father when he had lunged at her in one of his numerous drunken rages. Her father had been harsh with all the children over the years but not nearly as hard on the boys as he had always been with her. It had always puzzled her why her father seemed to dislike her so, though she had long since given up trying to reason why. And her mother – why did she put up with his constant tempers and drinking as she did? Once she had asked her as much but her mother had simply taken her hand and looked at her with a wealth of sadness in her eyes.

'It was the war that changed him, love,' she had told her. 'Your father was in a prisoner-of-war camp for the last part of the war. They then moved him to a military hospital so it had ended well over a year before he came home and he's never been the same since. Men who ended up in those terrible places saw sights no man should ever see. It's only natural that it should have changed him.'

'But sometimes I get the feeling that he almost hates me!' Sophie had told her.

Sally had merely shrugged. 'Your dad has a chip on his shoulder about everyone. Try not to take it to heart. Happen age will soften him.'

With that Sophie had to be content, yet when she looked back now she realised that lately a subtle difference had occurred in his attitude towards her that made her feel slightly uneasy. It had started about a year ago when he had barged into the kitchen one night to find her washing her hair in the kitchen sink. Normally she would have done it upstairs but her brother had used all the hot water so she had boiled the kettle and washed it in the kitchen. She had removed her jumper and was standing in her brassière with a towel wrapped round her head.

On that particular night he had gone off to the local pub as usual, but then when he realised that he had forgotten his wallet, the door had suddenly burst open and he'd reappeared.

For a moment it would have been hard to say who was the more embarrassed of the two, but then to her mortification his eyes had sunk to her fast-developing breasts and a strange look had crept into his eyes. Hastily covering herself as best she could she had stuttered, 'Mam's upstairs having a lie-down . . . shall I call her?'

Never taking his eyes from her breasts, he had shaken his head. 'No, I only came back for this.' He had snatched up his wallet then to her relief headed back towards the door where he paused to look back at her.

'Turning into a proper little lady now, ain't you?'

Sophie had been too stunned to reply and hardly dared to breathe until the door had finally closed behind him. Ever since then she'd noticed the way his eyes would follow her and had avoided being in a room on her own with him for no reason that she could explain.

'Right then – I'd best get off else I'll miss the bus,' she declared now as she hurried towards the door. 'I get paid today so is there anything you want me to pick up on my way home, Mam?'

'No, love – thanks all the same. Our Mattie can pop down the corner shop when he gets in from work an' pick me up somethin' for dinner.'

'That don't mean to say you should spend all your money on fripperies on the way home,' her father cut in.

Ignoring him with the contempt she felt he deserved, Sophie focused her attention on her mother. 'All right then. You take it easy and don't get overdoing it while I'm gone. Remember what the doctor said,' she warned.

Sally grinned. 'This old ticker of mine will keep goin' for another few years yet. You just get yourself off an' stop worryin'.'

Sophie glanced at her father, whose eyes seemed to be burning into her, then she slipped out of the back door into the breezy March morning.

There was a nip in the air but it was bright and she found herself humming as she ran for the bus that was just trundling round the corner of the street.

Once alone, Sally frowned at Bill. 'That was a bit thoughtless, what you just said to our Sophie, weren't it? You know damn well that she tips up nearly every penny she earns. She hardly ever spends anything on herself, more's the pity.' She could have added that it was a sight more than he did but thought better of it. For the last few weeks he had been working as a barman at the local pub. The problem was that at least half his wages seemed to find their way back over the bar. Still, at least it gave them a break from each other, which was worth something, she supposed.

Shaking out the newspaper he was reading he glared at her. '*Sorry* I'm sure.' His voice was dripping with sarcasm. 'Fancy me havin' the nerve to have a go at your golden girl.'

Sally sighed as she stared at the glowing coals on the fire. It was getting harder and harder with each year that passed to remember the loving husband she had once waved away to war. But then *she* was hardly blameless. She had gone almost mad with grief and loneliness when he had first been called up, and over the years the loneliness had grown, which was probably why she had eventually been tempted into another man's arms. Not that that was any excuse for her infidelity. Sophie was a living reminder of the injustice she had done him, and although she adored her daughter, she was also the guilty tie that bound Sally to him.

As the bus rumbled towards Blackpool, Sophie gazed contentedly from the window. They had lived on the Grange Park housing estate for the last ten years. She could still clearly remember the day they had moved in as if it were yesterday although she had been only seven years old. After the slum terraced house that she'd been used to living in, the council house with its indoor bathroom and toilet had seemed luxurious.

She had grown to love the area even more when her brothers began to take her to the nearby Marton Mere nature reserve as a treat. Until then she had never known that such wide-open spaces existed and she never grew tired of going there. Even now that she was older she still loved to tramp around it whenever she could although now that her brothers no longer accompanied her it didn't seem to have quite the same appeal. She had missed them as they left home one by one. Not that she blamed them. If it wasn't for her mother and Mattie she too would have left like a shot. Being the only girl her brothers had spoiled her shamelessly, a fact that was not lost on their father, who pilloried them for it.

'Mornin', Sophie, love. Off to work are you?'

The bus conductor, who looked forward to seeing her cheerful face each morning as she travelled into work, dragged her thoughts back to the present.

She smiled up at him as he tore her ticket from the

machine strapped around his waist. 'I am that, Mr Dodds. But I'm not complaining 'cos it's pay day.'

Sophie had never been able to judge Mr Dodds' age. He had more lines on his face than the tramlines that snaked along Blackpool front and his wild wiry hair looked as if it had never been introduced to a comb. But for all that he was a lovely old man. 'You'll be off on the razzle tonight then,' he teased. 'An' no doubt with a handsome young bloke in tow.'

Sophie merely grinned. In actual fact she had promised her mother she would perm her hair for her. The Twink perm she had used on her hair the last time had worked a treat and she hoped it might cheer her up a bit. Since having a slight stroke two years ago, Sally rarely ventured from the house any more, so Sophie liked to treat her whenever she could.

Ten minutes later the bus turned onto the seafront and Sophie waved cheerily at Mr Dodds as she stepped down onto the pavement. The wind was whistling along the pavements and she had to bend her head against it as she ran the few yards to the café where she worked.

During her lunch hour she went along to the chemist's and bought the perm solution to do her mother's hair then she bought a bag of chips and sat on the seafront to eat them. In no time at all a flock of hungry seagulls were snapping around her feet as she tossed them morsels. Sophie never tired of watching the waves crash onto the beach. This was her favourite time of the year. As yet the holiday-makers had not begun to arrive in force and the beach was quiet; it seemed to be hers and hers alone. Soon they would gradually begin to trickle into the town, bringing it to life with their Kiss Me Quick hats and their toffee apples.

The café was quiet during the afternoon and so Sophie busied herself with cleaning, knowing all too well that once the holidaymakers began arriving she would only have time to do it if and when she could between cooking and serving.

It was mid-afternoon when Mr Harry, the café owner, decided to put in an appearance. During the slack times he was more than happy to trust Sophie with the running of the place. She smiled at him brightly as he entered and crossed to the till to check how much money she had taken during the day.

'It's been a bit quiet since the breakfast rush,' she told him cheerily. He perched on the edge of a table and watched her washing the windows. Sophie had been working for him for almost a year now and during that time he had watched her blossom from a girl into a very attractive young woman.

When she had finished she carried the bowl of water out back and he followed her.

'I've got your wages here.'

Sophie flashed him a grateful smile and reached out for the brown envelope he was holding. As she moved to take it from him he caught her hand and something about the way he was looking at her made the smile die on her lips.

'Off out with some handsome young feller tonight then, are you?' he asked.

She frowned. That was *two* men who had asked her that question today. 'No I'm not, actually.'

'*Shame.* A pretty girl like you shouldn't be staying in on a Friday night.'

It suddenly hit her like a blow where she had seen the look on his face before. It was the same look that her father had given her on the night he had caught her washing her hair in the kitchen sink. Her eyes fixed on his greying hair and his little pot belly and suddenly she felt nauseous.

'How is *Mrs* Harry?' She desperately wanted to remind him that he was a married man.

Her question had the desired effect and he dropped her pay packet onto a table.

'She's fine. Now, if you're sure you can manage I'll be off.' With that he moved away, leaving her more shaken than she cared to admit.

Despite the confrontation she'd had with Mr Harry she was in a good mood as she made the return journey home that night, but it was instantly shattered the minute she set foot through the door. Her mother was still sitting in the same chair she had been in that morning, looking for all the world as if she hadn't moved from it. She also looked extremely unwell.

'Had a bad day then, Mam?' Sophie strove to keep the concern from her voice as she hung up her coat at the back of the door.

'Not so good to be honest,' Sally replied though she kept a smile fixed to her face.

'Where is everyone?' Sophie glanced around the room as she struck a match and lit the gas ring beneath the kettle.

'Mattie's upstairs getting ready for a date an' your dad's already gone off to work.' Sally now confided, 'I reckon our Mattie's got it bad for this little lass he's steppin' out with. Wouldn't surprise me in the least if we didn't hear weddin' bells soon.'

Sophie nodded in agreement though the thought saddened her. Mattie was the last of her brothers still at home and she knew that she would miss him if he were to leave. Still, as she had heard her mother say each time one of her brothers had flown the nest, '*They can't stay tied to their mam's apron strings forever!*'

As she waited for the kettle to boil, Sophie began to unpack the things she had bought onto the table. 'I bought you a perm, though we needn't do it tonight if you're not feelin' up to scratch. Oh, an' I got you ten Park Drive and a bottle of Guinness an' all. It is Friday night after all, ain't it? So I thought I'd treat you.'

Sally felt a lump begin to swell in her throat as she looked across at her beautiful daughter.

'*Friday's child is loving and giving.*' She could still hear Beattie saying it on the night that Sophie had been born and her statement had proved to be true a thousand times over. So much so that she sometimes wondered how she would ever manage without her.

Of course she accepted that, some day, Sophie would meet a nice young man and leave home to begin a life of her own, which was just as it should be. But from a selfish point of view she couldn't help hoping that that day was still a long way off. She watched the girl moving about the room and marvelled yet again at how lovely she was, yet Sophie seemed completely oblivious to the fact, which only added to her charm.

It was then that Mattie burst into the kitchen and flashed Sophie a dazzling smile. At six foot four in his stockinged feet he was tall, dark and handsome just as his father had been when Sally had first met him.

With his hair slicked down with a generous amount of Brylcreem and the fashionable suit with drainpipe trousers and crisp clean shirt and tie he was wearing, he put his mother in mind of James Dean.

'*Blimey*,' Sally teased him. 'You'll have the lasses queuin' up for you tonight lookin' like that, lad.'

He laughed. 'I reckon I've found the only lass I want, Mam. Apart from you an' our Sophie that is.'

'Get off with you.' Sally blushed with pleasure as he planted a sloppy kiss on her cheek.

'Now is there anythin' you want me to do before I head off?'

'Not a thing. You just go an' have a good time. Me an' our Sophie will be just fine.'

The door had barely closed behind him when Sally heaved herself out of the chair. 'Do you know what, love? I reckon I'm goin' to treat meself to a nice early night. Why don't you get yourself ready an' get out with your mates for a bit o' fun?'

Sophie grinned. 'To tell the truth, Mam, I'm a bit done in meself after being on me pins all day. You get yourself off to bed and I'll bring you a nice cup of tea. Then I'm going to put me feet up and have a read and listen to the radio.'

Sally sighed. She wished that Sophie would get out and about a bit more with friends her own age. It didn't seem right that a lovely looking girl like her should stay in so much. But one thing that she *had* learned was that besides having a heart as big as a bucket, Sophie had also inherited her stubborn streak so there would be no sense in arguing with her. If Sophie had decided that she was staying in then wild horses wouldn't drag her out of the door tonight. Passing through the stairs door she closed it softly behind her.

Chapter Two

The sound of the back kitchen door opening brought Sophie springing awake. The room was in darkness save for the light of the fire that had now burned low. She cursed softly as she realised that she must have dropped off then, rubbing the sleep from her eyes, she whispered into the darkness, 'Is that you, Mattie?'

'No it ain't. It's me. What you doin' up so late?'

'Oh I er . . . I must have dozed off while I was listening to the wireless,' Sophie told her father uneasily as she sat forward in the chair. She could see him swaying, only feet away from her, and decided to go to her room before they got into an argument, which they invariably did when he had been drinking heavily.

As she made to go past him in the enclosed space he suddenly reached out and grasped the strap of her night-dress. Startled, she pulled away and they both heard the sound of ripping as the flimsy material tore.

Immediately her father's eyes dropped to her exposed breast as she hastily covered herself as best she could.

'*Now* look what you've gone and done,' she scolded him, trying hard to keep the panic out of her voice.

For no reason that she could explain her heart had begun to pound and sweat was forming on her forehead.

'Don't be in such a rush to be off. Stay an' talk to your old dad for a while, why don't you?'

Sophie slapped his hand away as he reached out to her and would have barged past him but he suddenly pushed her and she felt herself falling backwards to land in an undignified heap on the settee.

She stared up at him, her eyes blazing with anger that had swept away her fear. 'Why don't you just let me go to bed, Dad? You're that drunk you hardly know what you're doing. You don't want to wake Mam up, do you?'

He stepped closer; so close that she could feel his stinking breath on her cheek as he hung over her.

'No . . . I *don't* want to wake your mam. An' neither do you if I'm any judge. So why don't you just be nice to me for a change, eh?'

She started to tremble as she watched his hand drop to his belt. Was he going to get violent with her again? *Why* was it always her? She had never seen him so much as raise his hand to her mam, or her brothers for that matter, unless they tried to defend her that was, in all the years she could remember.

In horrified fascination she watched as he slowly drew his belt through the hooks on his trousers, but then instead of raising it as she had expected he dropped it to the floor and his hand went to his flies. In no time at all he had unzipped them and they slid down his hairy legs, leaving him standing there in just his underpants.

She saw the bulge through the white cotton and now panic began to flood through her as she realised his intentions. But no! She *must* be wrong. He was her father!

Pulling herself up onto her elbow she readied herself to spring past him but he was too quick for her and suddenly the breath was knocked out of her as he threw himself across her.

'Dad, *please*. Don't do this,' she implored.

'Why not? It's what you've been wantin', ain't it? You're nothin' but a little prick tease an' it's time you took what's been comin' to you.'

As she became aware of his hand sliding up her thigh she shuddered with revulsion. This couldn't be happening. Surely she would wake up in a minute to find it had all been a terrible nightmare?

She began to fight him, but her strength was no match for his. Strangely she didn't cry out. How would she ever explain what was happening if her mam were to appear in the doorway? Shame coursed through her as she felt his hand roughly fondling her breast and then he was parting her legs and all she could do was close her eyes as hot tears coursed down her pale cheeks.

When he finally entered her she screwed her eyes tight shut as a searing pain tore through her, and prayed for death. And all the time she was thinking, *How will I ever be able to face Mam again after this?*

When at last it was over he rolled his weight to the side of her and she lay there staring at the shadows on the ceiling. She heard his heavy breathing slowly begin to drop into a more normal rhythm and then he was standing and hastily pulling on his trousers as he kept his back to her.

'Sophie, I . . .' His voice trailed away as she painfully pulled herself into a sitting position and tried to cover herself. Strangely, he seemed sober now and stood there not knowing what to say. It didn't matter. The damage had been done and she knew in that moment that her life would never be the same again. She would take the shame of this night to the grave with her.

'Just go away.' Her voice was as dead as she felt inside.

He stood there for some minutes before shuffling away to disappear through the stairs door. It was then that the shock of what had happened set in and leaning over she vomited all across the new lino her mam had only recently had laid in the kitchen.

Staggering across to the sink she now filled it with water then grabbing a dishcloth she began to systematically scrub every inch of herself. It didn't occur to her that Matthew might appear at any minute, nor did she care. She only knew that she would never be clean again.

'So what's up with you then, love? You've hardly touched your breakfast. You ain't comin' down with somethin', are you?' As Sally leaned across the table to feel Sophie's brow the girl slapped her hand away.

'For God's sake. I'm not a child any more, you know?'
When Sally's face crumpled, Sophie was instantly apologetic. 'Sorry, Mam, I just didn't have such a good night, that's all,' she muttered.

Hiding her hurt, Sally nodded. 'Not to worry. We all have us off days. Why don't you go back to bed for an hour or so? You ain't got to go into work today, have you?'

The idea was tempting but then the thought of being under the same roof as her father for a second longer than she needed to be spurred Sophie on to lie. 'Actually, I *do* have to go in so I'd best get ready.'

She had the distinct feeling that her mam didn't wholly believe her. It was hardly surprising as she rarely worked on Saturdays but the need to get away from the house was so strong that the lie tripped easily from her lips.

Abruptly scraping her chair across the floor she headed for the stairs door as her mother watched with a look of bewilderment on her face. It wasn't like Sophie to be like this at all. Usually she was a ray of sunshine in the room.

Within minutes Sophie was back dressed ready for the outdoors with a bag holding the torn nightdress slung across her shoulder. She would have to get rid of that in a place where her mother would never find it. Perhaps in a dustbin somewhere?

'I'll see you later then. Expect me when you see me,' she threw over her shoulder then the door closed behind her. Sally looked thoughtful. It was the first time in

Sophie's whole life that she had ever left the house without kissing her goodbye and Sally's heart was heavy. Something had happened to upset her, that was for sure, but what could it be? Sophie had brought her a cup of tea in bed the night before and had appeared to be as bright as a button – so what could have changed between then and now?

Lifting Sophie's untouched breakfast, Sally carried it to the bin and scraped it away as her mind worked overtime. Could she and Mattie have had words when he'd come in the night before? She dismissed that idea almost immediately; Sophie and Matthew were as close as two peas in a pod and she could never remember them exchanging so much as one angry word.

Bill! Her mind moved on to her husband, who was still fast asleep upstairs, no doubt sleeping off the effects of the drink he'd had the night before. Could he have had a go at Sophie when he came in? This seemed the more probable answer, knowing how he always picked on the girl. She determined to ask him what had happened the minute he set foot out of bed.

An hour later, Sophie was shocked to find herself wandering along the seafront. She had fleetingly thought of visiting either Brian or Tony, her brothers who lived close by, but had dismissed that thought almost immediately. Knowing her as they did she knew that they would have guessed that something was wrong and what could she tell them? Should they ever find out what their father had done to her all hell would be let loose and the way Sophie saw it that could only make things worse. And so instead she had just kept her head bent and let her feet lead her where they would. It didn't matter. She could go to the ends of the earth and she knew that she would never forget what had happened the night before.

Moving to a bench that overlooked the sea she sank heavily down onto it. There was a cold wind blowing but the sky was bright and clear. The waves were crashing onto the beach below her and gulls circled in the sky overhead, ready to swoop for any morsel that might appear. Today, Sophie barely saw them. She was too wrapped up in misery to notice anything as she relived the shocking thing that had happened to her the night before. In her mind she could see her father leering down at her. Still feel the touch of his rough hands on her skin and smell his foul breath.

She shuddered involuntarily as she recalled the slobbering lips roving around her neck. The full force of what had occurred hit her and she lowered her head and wept bitterly.

How could she ever face him again, or her mother if it came to that? From now on she would never dare to be alone with him, not even for a second, unless . . . Sniffing loudly she gazed up at the fluffy white clouds scudding across the sky . . . unless she left home.

Tossing the pros and cons of the idea over in her mind she sighed. It was certainly appealing. But what would happen to her mother if she were to leave? Matthew would soon be gone. And if *she* went too her mother would find herself alone with him. Would he take care of her? It was a question she found she was unable to answer, yet although he had raised his hand to her many times she could never recall him being violent with her mother, or her brothers if it came to that.

As her gaze drifted out to sea and she pondered her dilemma she became so lost in thought that it was a shock when a voice suddenly asked, 'Are you all right, honey?'

Her head snapped round and she found herself looking up at one of the most handsome young men she had ever seen. As she realised what a mess she must look, her hand flew to her hair, which had become a mass of unruly curls in the spray from the sea. But then it dropped to her lap again; she didn't really care how she looked any more.

'No, I mean yes . . . I'm fine thank you,' she stuttered.

His eyebrows rose into his hairline and he continued to stand there although she was silently willing him to move on. Hastily swiping the tears from her face with the back of her hand she became surly. 'Look, haven't you got anything better to do than stand there watching me?'

He held his hands up as if to ward off a blow and grinned. 'Sorry. I don't mean to interfere but if you're all right then I wouldn't like to see you when you're not.'

Sophie shrugged and decided to ignore him, although she was intrigued with his American accent. She had never spoken to an American before but right now she was in no mood for idle chit-chat.

When he sank down onto the bench at the side of

her she pursed her lips in annoyance. They sat for some time gazing idly out to sea until he suddenly took a clean starched handkerchief from his pocket and held it out to her.

For a second or two she ignored it, but then she snatched it from him and after loudly blowing her nose she swiped at her damp cheeks again.

'Thanks.'

He nodded, though he made no attempt to look at her, for which she was grateful. After a time curiosity got the better of her and she peeped at him from the corner of her eye. His hair was so dark that it was nearly black and he had lovely almond eyes that reminded her of the colour of treacle. He was smartly dressed in a crisp white shirt and dark suit and his shoes were so shiny that she could see her face in them when she glanced down. She tried to judge his age and thought that he might possibly be in his mid-twenties though she had never been any good at guessing people's ages.

'I'm Ben Lewis,' he suddenly introduced himself and she felt herself blush before shyly replying, 'I'm Sophie . . . Sophie Winters.'

'Nice name.' Still he didn't attempt to look at her and she felt herself begin to relax a little.

'From round here are you?' he now asked conversationally.

Sophie slowly nodded. 'Not too far away,' she told him cautiously.

'Boyfriend trouble is it?'

Suddenly feeling very immature she snapped indignantly, 'No it is *not*! I don't have a boyfriend. Not that it's any of *your* business.'

'That surprises me.' He ignored her harsh tone. 'A good-looking broad like you? I'd have thought you'd have the guys queuing up to take you out.'

Before she could reply he smiled at her kindly and she felt her anger melt away. He obviously meant well, whoever he was. She shuddered as she wondered what he would think if she were to tell him of the terrible thing that had happened to her. No doubt he wouldn't be so keen to talk to her then, not that she *would* tell him, or anyone else for that matter. The way she was feeling she would rather die than confide in anyone let alone a complete stranger.

'It's just . . . family problems.'

As her voice trailed away he glanced at her sympathetically. 'Not something you care to talk about then?'

Again her head wagged miserably from side to side. 'No, I . . . No.'

'Fair enough. But if you're in some sort of trouble perhaps I could help you. What I mean is, Blackpool is full of runaways every year and if—'

'I'm *not* a runaway, and I'm *not* in any trouble,' Sophie gasped. 'And I don't need any help, thanks all the same. What I really need is some space to think.'

'I just thought that if you were . . . well, you know . . .'

The indignant look on Sophie's face said a thousand words and once again he held his hands out.

'How *dare* you?' she spluttered as she glared at him. 'What sort of a girl do you take me for?'

'Sorry. I was only trying to help but hint taken.' The grin was back on his face as he stood up and looked down at her. Holding out his hand he waited patiently while she eyed it dubiously. Eventually she shook it quickly before snatching her hand away as if it had been burned as he delved into his coat pocket. Producing a little card with a flourish he laid it on the bench at the side of her. Glancing at it curiously she saw the address and the phone number of a hotel on the South Shore printed on it.

'That's where I live,' he told her. 'My mother owns the hotel. If your problems don't sort themselves out and you ever need to talk to someone give me a call.'

With a cheery grin he began to walk away and Sophie watched him go. *Fancy that,* she found herself thinking. *An American owning a hotel in Blackpool?* After a time he crossed the road and turned into one of the numerous back streets that ran off the front, and once again Sophie's mind returned to her troubles. What was she going to do? How could she just go home and walk in as if nothing had happened?

As another thought occurred to her, her stomach did a somersault. What was it that Ben had said? *If you are in some sort of trouble . . .* What sort of trouble had he meant?

She felt vomit rise in her throat as a terrifying possibility occurred to her. What if she *was* pregnant? She would be carrying her father's child. It was too awful to contemplate and sweat broke out on her brow as panic set in. But then she tried to calm herself. It surely couldn't happen the very first time . . . *could it*? Of course it couldn't, she tried to convince herself. What had happened between her father and herself was bad enough, but if she were to be pregnant then she was sure that she'd have no alternative but to throw herself into the sea. What other course of action could there be? And how could she ever tell her mother of the shameful thing that her father had done? Just the thought of it brought colour stinging to her cheeks.

Dragging herself up from the bench she began to walk back the way she had come. There was a bite in the wind from the sea and she found that she was shivering, though she couldn't be sure if it was because of the cold or the fear growing inside her. The new wedge shoes that she had treated herself to only the week before made a clip-clopping sound on the pavements as she slouched along lost in thought, but she was oblivious to everything other than the predicament she found herself in.

She knew that eventually she would have to go home. With luck her father would have cleared off to his job at the pub by now and she could make some excuse and escape to her room away from her mother's prying eyes. She would say that she wasn't feeling too well. At least she wouldn't be lying.

All the way back she prayed as she had never prayed before and her prayer was answered, for when she pushed the door open she saw at a glance that her father's coat was gone from the hook.

'You're early,' Sally commented. She was leaning over the fire in the act of throwing some coals on when Sophie entered the room.

'I wasn't feeling so good so I thought I'd call it a day.' Keeping her eyes averted from her mother's, Sophie slid her arms out of her coat and hung it across the back of a chair.

'Huh! I'm surprised Mr Harry allowed you to,' Sophie huffed. 'Tight-fisted old sod usually keeps you there *beyond* your time if anythin'. Still — never mind that for now. What's wrong?'

Sophie felt her colour rise again as her mother crossed to her and felt her forehead. She longed to throw her arms round her waist and pour out all her troubles as she had as a child. But how could she ever tell her mother of what had happened between her and her father? With her mother's dicky heart the shock might bring on a heart attack and then she would have the guilt of that to live with too. So instead she sat stiffly staring into the fire as her mother fussed over her, longing for the moment when she could escape to the privacy of her room.

'You don't feel particularly hot,' Sally mused. 'I'll tell you what. I'll make you a nice cup o' tea an' put a bit of Indian brandy in it. That should do the trick, particularly if it's your monthlies that are due. They usually knock you about a bit, don't they?' As she hurried away to the sink she kept up her cheerful chatter. 'I were just the same at your age. Right through till I had our Robbie. Never mind, a drop o' this an' you'll feel fit to face the world again, you'll see.'

Sophie was so deep in despair that she doubted she would ever feel right again, but all the same she sat through her mother's kindly ministrations and even managed to swallow half a cupful of the foul concoction placed in her hand.

'There. Now give that time to work an' you'll soon be feelin' better,' Sally assured her as she carried the cup to the sink.

Seizing the opportunity to escape, Sophie rose hastily from her chair and headed for the stairs door. 'Thanks, Mam. I think I'll just pop up an' have a nice warm bath, then I'll have a nap if you don't mind.'

'O' course I don't mind, love,' Sally told her with a kindly smile. 'Stop up there till tomorrow mornin' if you've a mind to. Everythin's in order down here.'

Once in the quiet of her own little room, Sophie sank onto the edge of her narrow bed and buried her face in her hands. What was she going to do? How could she go on as if nothing had happened? Her mother had always been able to read her like a book and it could be only a matter of time before she realised that something was seriously wrong.

Slowly raising her head she looked around her bedroom. It was really little more than a boxroom and very sparsely furnished, but Sophie had inherited the trick of being able to make a place homely from her mother and had brightened it with cheap pictures on the walls and the pretty patchwork bedspread that she and her mother had lovingly sewn from any old scraps of material they could lay their hands on.

Since the day they had moved into the house, Sophie had loved this little room. But tonight it held no pleasure for her. In fact, she realised as she sat there that nothing held any pleasure for her at the moment, not even her chance encounter with Ben. Until now, Sophie had never really been that interested in boys, but she knew that if she had met Ben under any other circumstances he would have made her pulse race, for he was easily the best-looking young man she had ever seen. She screwed her eyes up tight at the injustice of it all and burying her face in her hands she began to sob bitterly. What man would ever want her now? She was soiled goods. Her father had seen to that.

Chapter Three

'Come on, our Sophie, we'll be late for work if you mess about in there much longer.'

Swiping her hand across the back of her mouth, Sophie leaned up from the sink and stared at her reflection in the small cracked mirror that hung above it. She looked dreadful, but not half as dreadful as she felt. Quickly pinching her cheeks and running a hand through her unruly curls she opened the bathroom door and flashed a weak smile at Matthew, who stood impatiently tapping his foot on the long narrow landing.

His face immediately altered as he took in her pale face and sunken eyes. 'Stone the crows. You look right rough. Should you be turnin' in to work today? You look like a day in bed 'ud do you more good.'

'I'll be fine, Matt,' she assured him. 'I reckon I must have picked a bug up from somewhere.'

Stepping past her he glanced at her before closing the door between them. 'Well, happen you know best.'

She slowly descended the stairs and once she'd entered

the kitchen studiously avoided looking at her father who was sitting in his usual position in the chair at the side of the fire.

Her mother was standing at the stove over a frying pan full of bacon and as the smell of it hit Sophie, she felt the vomit rise in her throat again.

'Would you like a bacon sarnie, love?' Sally asked kindly. 'I could always toss an egg in for you as well if you fancied one.'

Crossing hastily to the door, Sophie snatched her coat from the hook and started to struggle into it. 'I shan't bother with any breakfast this mornin', Mam. I promised the boss I'd be in early so I'll get something there.'

Sally frowned. 'This is the third mornin' on the trot you've gone out with nothin' inside you. I hope you ain't on one o' these silly faddy diets that's all the go? You certainly don't need to be. You ain't as far through as a line prop as it is. You'll end up lookin' like a washing line itself if you go on like this.'

'Of course I'm not,' Sophie assured her. 'I'm just in a rush that's all. Now you have a good day an' I'll see you later.' With that she let herself out into the yard as Sally watched her go with a look of concern on her face.

'There's summat not right with our Sophie,' she remarked. When there was no reply her voice became sharper. '*Bill*, did you hear what I said? You've allus got your head stuck in a bloody newspaper.'

'*What?* Sorry, love.' He glanced up guiltily then seeing her eyes were tight on him he studied his newspaper again. 'I were just readin' about these silly mods an' rockers fightin' in London. Arrested thirty o' the silly buggers yesterday they did. Makes you wonder what the world's comin' to. But what were you sayin'?'

'*I said* – there's summat as ain't right with our Sophie,' she repeated.

Bill shook his head as colour burned into his cheeks. 'She looks all right to me,' he answered gruffly. 'It's probably just you lookin' for problems where there ain't none.'

Sally stared thoughtfully off into space. There *was* something wrong. She knew it. Now that she came to think about it, Sophie hadn't been her normal cheery self for the last three or four weeks. Neither had Bill if it came to that and they'd been avoiding each other like the plague.

Casting her mind back she tried to remember when it had first started. It was the morning after Sophie had offered to perm her hair, but she had gone to bed early. Ever since then, Sophie had looked absolutely awful and had been creeping about the house like a ghost. But why? What could have happened to make her want to avoid her father? As a thought suddenly occurred to her, her eyes flew to Bill and she clutched at her heart. But she dismissed the idea that had just popped into her head almost immediately. It was just too awful to contemplate. Bill might have no love for Sophie, but he would never lay a hand on her. *Would he?*

Staggering to the nearest chair she sat down heavily, her eyes never leaving his face. Sometimes even now when she looked at him she could still glimpse the man she had waved away to war; the man she had sworn she would love forever. The war had affected him badly. But nowhere near as badly as Sophie's birth had, for she had known from the moment he clapped eyes on her that he knew what a terrible injustice she had done him, and every single day ever since he had punished her for it. Oh, not in a physical way, but in the way he looked at her and held the child at arm's length. And so through all the long years she had been trapped between them, feeling as if she were caught between the devil and the deep blue sea.

When Bill suddenly raised his eyes to her then looked guiltily away her fears grew. Something was indeed wrong. Now all she could do was wait until one of them decided to tell her what it was.

When Sophie arrived home from work that evening she looked even worse than she had in the morning and a cold hand closed round Sally's heart as she carried her daughter's dinner from the oven to the table. It was sausage and mash, which just happened to be one of Sophie's favourites, but tonight she merely pushed the food around the plate. Upstairs they could hear Bill and Matthew vying for the bathroom. Bill was getting ready for his shift at the local pub and Matthew was getting ready for a date with his latest girlfriend who he was still, much to Sally's shock, infatuated with. Up until now he had always been very much the love-'em-and-leave-'em type.

Matthew was the first to put in an appearance looking very dapper in skintight trousers and smelling, as Sally teased him, like a chemist's shop.

'Crikey, lad. You've gone a bit overboard wi' the old aftershave ain't you?' She grinned as she fussed with the knot of his tie.

'Give over, Mam. You wouldn't want me to go out smellin' like a sweaty sock would you?' He wriggled away from her and began to shrug his long muscular arms into his suit jacket.

He looked so like his father had as a young man that Sally's heart did a somersault in her chest. Why couldn't she have waited for Bill instead of betraying him as she had? But it was too late for regrets now. Over the years she had learned to take each day at a time and today would be no different. She had become so lost in thought that when she realised Matthew was hovering uncertainly at her side she started.

'What's up, love? Did you want me for somethin'?'

'Well, I er . . . I thought now might be as good a time as any to tell you that I popped the question to Becky last night. You know, the girl I've been seein'? I asked her to marry me. An' the thing is . . . she said yes, so from now on I'll be savin' up to get married.'

Tears sprang to Sally's eyes as she looked lovingly up at her youngest son. It seemed only seconds ago that he was a raggy-arsed little boy with a snotty nose and now here he was engaged. Yet another of her brood about to fly the nest.

'Why love. That's grand news. Congratulations. When do we get to meet this Becky then?'

He blushed a deep beetroot red. 'I could bring her round at the weekend if you like?'

'That's a wonderful idea. Make it Saturday an' I'll do you both a nice bit o' tea. I could perhaps bake you one o' my Victoria sandwich cakes you're so fond of, eh?'

'Thanks, Mam.' Matthew planted an awkward kiss on her cheek then, relieved that he had told her his news, quickly disappeared through the back door.

Bill chose that moment to make an entrance and Sally smiled at him wistfully. 'Our Matt has just informed me that he's got engaged,' she told him.

He shrugged. 'Ah well, at least we won't have to queue for the bathroom so long then,' he quipped and without so much as another word he disappeared the same way Matthew had.

'That's another one spoken for,' Sally commented, turning her attention back to Sophie. She was unable to keep the sadness from her voice. 'Looks like soon it'll be just you, me an' your dad.'

When Sophie hung her head, Sally crossed to her and put her arm round her slight shoulders. 'What is it, love? I know somethin's wrong. Can't you tell me about it?'

Suddenly the tears that Sophie had so bravely held back spurted from her eyes and she clung to her mother as if she were a lifeline. 'Oh, Mam. Everything's *such* a mess,' she sobbed as Sally cradled her in her arms.

'There's nowt that can't be sorted,' Sally comforted

her as she stroked her hair then deciding that it was time to take the bull by the horns she asked, 'Are you in some sort o' trouble, love?'

Sophie had decided that she would keep her terrible secret to herself but she felt so safe in her mother's arms that suddenly she just blurted it out. 'Yes, I am. I think I might be—' When the tears choked her and she couldn't go on, Sally finished her sentence for her.

'You think you might be pregnant . . . is that it?'

Sophie's head snapped up. 'How did you know?' she demanded.

Sally smiled sadly. 'I can pick out a pregnant woman from a hundred paces an' I've had me suspicions for the last couple o' weeks. But do you want to tell me who the father is? Will he stand by you?'

When Sophie shook her head and her chin dropped to her chest, Sally caught her breath and prayed as she had never prayed before that her suspicions might prove to be unfounded.

'*Why* won't he stand by you? Is he married?' Only silence answered her so she decided to take another tack. 'Is it someone I know?'

Sophie suddenly flung herself away from her mother and headed towards the stairs door but, arms folded, Sally placed herself in front of her in a pose that told Sophie she meant to get to the bottom of things.

'It's . . .' Her voice trailed away. How could she tell her mother that she might be pregnant by her own father? As things turned out she didn't have to, for Sally's shoulders suddenly sagged as she asked softly, 'Has your dad laid his hands on you?'

When the shock on Sophie's face told its own story she sank heavily onto the nearest chair.

'Oh, Mam.' Sophie dropped to her knees and flung her arms round her mother's waist as she sobbed into her lap. 'I'm not even sure that I *am* pregnant, but I've missed a period and my breasts are really tender. I didn't want to tell you. I feel so ashamed. It happened a few weeks ago when he came in late one night. I tried to stop him. I begged him not to. Honest I did, but . . . oh, Mam. *What* am I going to do?'

For a while Sally was too shocked to answer as guilt coursed through her. Why hadn't she realised that Bill might be capable of such a thing! The signs must have been there so why hadn't she seen them? Or *had* she seen them and chosen to ignore them? What sort of a mother was she anyway?

Eventually she pulled herself together enough to say grimly, 'You're pregnant all right. An' as fer what you're goin' to do . . .' Her mind was racing to match the thumping of her heart as she tried to think what would be best. 'You're going to get away. That's what,' she told her brokenly. When Sophie stared up at her incredulously she saw the pain etched on her mother's face and her heart broke afresh.

'But . . . but I can't just disappear an' leave you here all alone with *him*,' she gasped.

'He would never hurt me. At least not physically,' Sally

assured her. And as she looked into her daughter's eyes she knew that Sophie was finally paying the price for her deception all those long years ago. But even now she was too ashamed to confess all of her guilty secret. 'Sophie, there's something you should know,' she began hesitantly. 'What has happened isn't all your dad's fault. You see . . . I once did him a grave injustice.' As she slowly began to relay her sorry tale, Sophie's eyes grew as round as saucers.

'So what you're tellin' me is, you had an affair while me dad was away in the war?' she gasped when Sally was done.

Shamefaced, Sally nodded as Sophie struggled to take in what she had told her.

'So you see – I can't risk you stayin' here any more. If he's done it once he could try it again,' Sally told her. 'He's punishin' me through you and you don't deserve it. None o' this is your fault. There are places you can go to till the baby's born then you could have it adopted an' get on with your life.'

'I . . . I won't go without you!' Sophie declared as tears streamed down her pale cheeks. Sally gently wiped them away as she stared at the daughter who she had adored since the minute she drew breath.

'I *can't* leave him, love. Can't you see that? If it weren't for what I'd done he wouldn't be as bitter and twisted as he is now. I owe it to him to stand by him. I can take anythin' he cares to dish out. But I couldn't bear to stand by and see him taking it out on you. Please try and understand. You *have* to get away. But me . . . well, I can't go because you see . . . I *hate* him for what he's done to you but it's all my fault so I have to stand by him.'

'But . . . but where would I go?' The thought of being all alone in the world was terrifying and it sounded in her tremulous voice.

Forcing herself to be calm Sally frowned as she tried to think. Suddenly her head snapped up and she declared, 'I know where. I have an aunt and uncle in the Midlands somewhere. She was my mam's older sister. Aunt Philly we used to call her and she was the kindest woman you could ever wish to meet. I sort of lost track of her when I married your dad an' moved up here but I don't mind bettin' she'd take you in like a shot. From what I can remember of her as a child she had a really rotten time of it. All her and my uncle ever wanted was a family of their own but she lost one baby after another till in the end they gave up tryin', poor souls. I dare say that's why she always spoiled us so much.' Lost in happy memories her face creased into one of the rare smiles that Sophie had come to know and love. But then as her eyes settled on her daughter again the pain returned to them. Gently pressing Sophie aside, she went to a smart teak sideboard that the boys had clubbed together to buy her the Christmas before.

As Sally rummaged in the drawers, Sophie scanned her face and she tried to lock her every feature into her memory. If she did as her mother was suggesting she knew only too well that she might never see her again.

Sally suddenly let out an exultant cry and waved a

faded envelope in the air. 'I *knew* I'd kept one of her letters somewhere.' Crossing to Sophie she pressed it into her hand. 'There you are, love. That's got her address on it an' if you show it to her she'll be sure of who you are. I just pray she's still alive an' kickin', that's all. She must be well into her sixties now to my reckonin'.'

'Oh, Mam. I don't think I can do this.' Sophie was shaking with fear as her mother once again wrapped her in her arms.

'Oh yes you can, and you *must*. I don't ever want him to lay his hands on you again.' As Sally wiped the tears from her cheeks, Sophie heard the anger that was creeping into her voice.

'But why can't *you* come with me?'

'I've told you why an' that's an end to it. Now don't make this any harder than it already is. Run upstairs an' pack some things. You'll find a suitcase in the bottom of my wardrobe.'

Sophie dragged herself up from the floor and slowly made for the stairs door. Everything was happening so fast. She could hardly take it in. In no time at all the case was open on her bed and her clothes were packed. With the empty wardrobe seeming to leer at her she felt as if the room was already no longer hers. She then hastily scribbled a note for Matthew telling him that she had been offered a job in the Midlands and that she would be in touch in due course. It was a blatant lie but she couldn't bear to just disappear without giving him some excuse. Lastly she packed the small, framed photograph of herself, her mam and her brothers that she kept at the side of the bed and with a final glance around the room she slowly made her way back downstairs.

Sally was standing at the kitchen table with the tin she kept the bill money in, spilling its contents across the tablecloth.

Scooping the ten-shilling and pound notes into a pile she pressed them into Sophie's shaking hand. 'This will be more than you'll need for your fare an' there should be enough left to tide you over till you find yourself a little job. Spend it wisely, mind.'

They stood facing each other for long seconds and then suddenly they were in each other's arms, each with tears washing down their cheeks.

'But what about the lads . . . what will they think when I suddenly just take off?'

'Leave the lads to me,' Sally said. 'I'll think o' something to tell them. If they should ever discover the truth I reckon between them they'd kill him for what he's done, especially our Mattie.'

Sophie was sobbing as if her heart would break as Sally now whispered words of endearment into her sweet-smelling hair. Eventually they stepped apart and Sally helped her into her coat. And then it was time to go and neither of them knew quite what to say. Words seemed so inadequate for the pain they were both suffering.

'You take good care o' yourself now. An' just remember . . . I love you.'

'I love you too, Mam. Won't you *please* come with me?'

Too choked to speak, Sally shook her head and pressed Sophie towards the door. Lifting the small battered suitcase, Sophie turned to give her mother one last smile and then she opened the door and was gone, leaving Sally feeling as if her whole life had fallen apart.

For what seemed an eternity she paced the floor as tears blinded her. But then the tears dried up and cold hard anger took their place as she settled by the fire to wait for Bill to come home. It would be God help him when he did.

The fire had all but died away and the sound of the children kicking a can up and down the street had long since stopped when she heard the entry gate open and the sound of his footsteps in the yard.

Huddled in the dark in the chair by the fire she trained her eyes on the door and watched as he tentatively stepped into the darkened room. Fumbling for the light switch he clicked it on then stared at her. He sensed immediately that something was wrong and stood there wringing his cloth cap in his hands.

'What's up then?'

'*What's up?*' The words spat from her mouth with such venom that a trickle of saliva ran down her chin. 'Why – I don't know how you've the nerve to stand there and ask after what you've done, you dirty lousy *bastard*!'

In all the years of their marriage, Bill had never heard Sally swear and he gaped in amazement. She stood up painfully after the long hours of sitting there and advanced on him menacingly.

'You've punished me every single day since the day Sophie drew breath and I could live with that, God knows I deserved whatever punishment you decided to mete out. But to turn your hatred on *her* . . . I'll never forgive you for that, Bill Winters. She's just a girl and you've ruined her life.'

Bill seemed to shrink to half his size right before her very eyes as he realised that she knew what he had done.

'I . . . I don't know what she's told you but it wa—'

'*Shut up!*' Her eyes flashed fire as she confronted him. 'Don't you *dare* try to put the blame onto Sophie, because as sure as God's my witness I'll do for you if you do!'

They faced each other like two opponents in a boxing ring as his anger grew to match hers.

'She had it comin'. She were askin' for it. If it hadn't been me it would have been some other bloke,' he shouted. 'No doubt she's put it about anyway, an' it ain't as if she were *my* blood, is it? Don't you think I've known since the second I clapped eyes on her that she were nothin' to do wi' me? What do you think it's been like all these years knowin' that you were playin' the field while I were away fightin' for me country?'

The fight suddenly went out of her as her shoulders sagged. 'I ain't goin' to deny that I had an affair,' she said quietly. 'But what I will say in me own defence is that it only happened 'cos I was missin' you an' feared that you weren't comin' back. It were madness an' meant nothin' an' I'll tell you now there ain't been a single day since she were born when I ain't regretted what I did.'

'An' that puts everythin' right, does it?' he ground out as his fists clenched at his sides.

She shook her head. 'No it don't, Bill. An' all I can say is I'm sorry from the bottom of me heart. You've always been the only man I've ever loved. What I did was unforgivable but you should have taken your anger out on me, not her.'

For the first time in their married life he advanced on her threateningly and when he was within an arm's length he slapped her resoundingly on the face. The sound echoed round the room as she stared at him in disbelief. She opened her mouth to speak but then his fist was flying and she was doubling over as the blows rained down on her. All the pain and frustration he had felt over the years suddenly poured out of him and she knew that he had lost control. She would have to stop him before he killed her. Glancing to the side she saw the bread knife glinting on the table and almost before she knew what she had done her hand had flown out and grasped it. With a speed that surprised even her she raised it in the air and then everything seemed to happen in slow motion as she watched it plunging into his chest. The blows stopped as a look of astonishment lit his eyes and then blood spurted from his lips and he reeled away from her clutching at a dark stain on his shirt. He stood there swaying as a scream grew in her throat, then he was falling and she could only watch as he twitched convulsively before lying very still. When she finally came out of her trance-like state she dropped to her knees beside him.

'*Bill.*' She shook his arm gently but he merely stared sightlessly up at her and in that moment she knew that she had killed him.

'*Oh, Bill.*' Sobbing uncontrollably now she gently closed his eyes then slowly rose. The tears dried as if by magic as a strange sort of calm settled on her. Crossing to the small medicine cabinet over the sink she took out its contents. Slowly she tipped the assortment of tablets onto the vinyl tablecloth and spread them out. Her heart tablets, Bill's paracetamol tablets, aspirins. They almost covered the width of the table.

Her eyes once again turned to the man she loved. He had started on his final journey and it was only fitting that she accompany him. Lifting a half-empty cup of cold tea she swilled down the first handful of pills. They were bitter on her tongue and she shuddered, but even so she didn't hesitate and soon the table was cleared save for numerous empty overturned bottles.

Sinking back to the floor she lifted his head into her lap and then she closed her eyes and waited to join him.

When Matthew arrived home almost an hour later the sight that met him made him scream so loudly that he could be heard all down the length of the street. Within minutes doors were opening and closing as neighbours rushed to see what was wrong. One of them ran to phone an ambulance but as Matthew sat with his arms wrapped round his parents he knew that they were too late.

Chapter Four

As darkness cast its cloak across the windy streets, Sophie sat huddled on a bench on the seafront. She was so cold that she could no longer feel her fingers, or her feet if it came to that. But she was so miserable that she was beyond caring. An elderly man who was walking his dog, paused to stare at her, his thin grey hair blowing wildly in the wind.

'Are you all right there, love?'

'What?' Sophie raised tear-stained eyes to him and slowly nodded. 'Yes . . . yes I'm quite all right, thank you.'

The old man looked bemused as he hovered, uncertain what to do. She certainly didn't *look* all right if he was any judge and she was only a slip of a girl. Still, he decided, it was really none of his business at the end of the day. Probably just another runaway. God knows there were enough of them sleeping rough under the pier most nights. Shame though. She looked like a nice young thing. Shrugging, he whistled his old dog to heel and reluctantly moved on. His missus would have the kettle on and he didn't want to miss his last hot drink of the night.

Sophie watched him walk away, suddenly feeling more alone than she had ever felt in her whole life. The address of her aunt was tucked deep in her coat pocket but she wouldn't go there tonight. It was doubtful if she could have got a train even had she wanted to at this late hour. She again thought briefly of going to the house of one of her brothers but dismissed the thought almost instantly. What had her mother said? *I reckon they'd kill him for what he's done.* No, things were enough of a mess without making them worse.

Glancing up and down the seafront it suddenly occurred to her. The café! She still had the keys in her bag. There was an old overstuffed settee in the staffroom that she could sleep on. It was as hard as a rock and nothing like as comfortable as her old bed back at home but at least she would be warm and out of the wind.

With her mind made up she wearily lifted her case and headed off along the front till the café came into sight. It looked curiously uninviting at night with its windows staring like dark empty eyes. Sophie was too tired and cold to care any more. Fumbling with the key she managed to unlock the door and dragged the case inside. Her hand automatically reached for the light switch but she managed to stop herself just in time. Better not to draw attention to the fact that someone was in the premises. The last thing she felt like doing tonight was giving an account of why she was there to some policeman.

Feeling her way through the tables and chairs she eventually found the door that led to the staffroom behind the counter and hastily let herself in. Breathing a sigh of relief she dropped her case, which seemed to have grown heavier by the minute, onto the threadbare rug and flexed her fingers before crossing to the window at the back of the room. From here she could look out across the ocean and she stood for some minutes watching the lights of the ships far out to sea. Eventually she drew the thin curtains and risked turning the light on before setting the kettle on the gas ring and shrugging out of her coat. As her eyes swept the room she sighed. It was hardly what could be classed as a luxury hotel but she supposed that it was better than nowhere and at least it was reasonably warm and dry.

Half an hour later she curled up on the settee and pulled her coat across her legs. As she did so her aunt's address dropped out of the pocket and she stared at it almost as if it might pop off the page and bite her. How could she just turn up out of the blue and introduce herself to someone she had never even met? Her aunt could well be dead and buried by now and then she would have gone all that way for nothing.

As her thoughts went back to her mother tears welled in her eyes and ran unchecked down her cheeks. *Why* had she insisted on staying with her father when she *knew* what he had done to her?

A wealth of emotions swept through her. Regret at having to leave her home and her family; fear of what lay ahead; revulsion as she thought of the new life that was even now growing inside of her – but most of all a terrible feeling of betrayal. Why had her mother sent *her* away instead of her father?

No matter how long she thought of it no answer was forthcoming and eventually she fell into a fitful sleep as the first cold fingers of dawn brushed the sky.

By seven o'clock the next morning Sophie had washed in the tiny sink in the staffroom as best she could and was ready to leave. She surveyed the café regretfully as she stood there clutching her case in her hand. Mr Harry had never been the best of employers, but she had enjoyed her job, meeting the customers and being able to tip her wages up to her mother each week.

The money her mother had given to her was tucked deep down in her pocket and seemed a princely sum, but Sophie realised that it wouldn't last forever, so until the baby was born she would have to find some other way of making a living wherever she went. It was a daunting thought and once again loneliness overcame her as she placed the keys to the café on the counter and slowly left, closing the door firmly behind her for the last time.

Once outside in the chill morning air she looked to left and right and shuddered indecisively. She still had no idea at all where she was going. Somehow she dreaded turning up on some ancient relative's doorstep un-announced.

The seafront was slowly coming to life. Shop owners were busily unlocking their premises before arranging buckets, spades and brightly coloured windbreaks all along the front of their premises. The sight of them lent speed to Sophie's feet. If she stood there much longer Mr Harry might appear and the last thing she wanted was to have to embark on some lengthy explanation of why she could no longer work for him. Head bent against the bitingly cold wind, she hurried along until she came to Blackpool Tower, where she paused to rest.

Every instinct she had screamed at her to turn round and go home, but she knew that she couldn't. Just the thought of spending one more night under the same roof as her father made her flesh crawl. It was as she was standing there that she saw a figure walking towards her. Something about his walk was strangely familiar and as he drew closer she suddenly recognised Ben Lewis, the handsome young American who had spoken to her some weeks before. Hastily lowering her head she felt hot colour flood into her cheeks. She hoped that he would pass by and not recognise her, but as he drew abreast of her his footsteps slowed.

'Hi again . . . It's Sophie, isn't it?'

Sophie wished that the ground would just open up and swallow her as she raised her eyes and slowly nodded. Her heart was thumping so loudly that she was sure he must be able to hear it but if he noticed her discomfort he tactfully ignored it as he stared at the case she was clutching.

'Off on holiday are you?'

'No, I er . . .' Suddenly the tears were raining down her face again and in an instant he had thrown his arm about her slim shoulders.

'Hey, come on now, honey. Things can't be that bad,' he soothed. 'How's about we find somewhere out of the wind where you can tell me all about it, eh? You know what they say – a trouble shared is a trouble halved.'

Sophie knew that she should walk away. After all, she scarcely knew him. Then again, she felt that if she didn't talk to someone soon she would burst, and he *was* remarkably easy to talk to.

'All right then,' she sniffed somewhat dubiously. 'Thank you.'

Taking her case in one hand and her elbow in the other he led her through the back streets until they came to a small café where the owner was just placing a board with the day's menu written on it out on the pavement.

'Good morning, both.' He grinned jovially. 'Now *that's* what I call good timing. You'll be the first customers of the day and I can guarantee you a fry-up that will set you up till teatime.'

Just the mere thought of food made Sophie's stomach revolt but nevertheless she followed Ben meekly into the café where he ushered her to a table.

Once he had placed their order an awkward silence

settled between them until Sophie felt that she should say something.

'You're up and about early, aren't you?' she muttered self-consciously.

Throwing back his head he laughed and once again as Sophie looked into his twinkling eyes her heart did a little somersault in her chest. He was remarkably handsome. Not that he would ever look at her; what man would now?

'I like to stroll along the front every morning at this time,' he informed her. 'I always think it's the best time of day when the town is just coming to life, don't you?'

Sophie had always been too busy rushing to get to work on time to notice but she nodded out of politeness just the same. Seconds later, the cheerful café owner placed two steaming mugs of tea in front of them and she sipped at hers gratefully, very aware that he was watching her closely.

'So.' Ben's voice was gentle. 'It seems that every time we meet something has upset you. Would it help to talk about it? I'm a very good listener.'

Keeping her eyes fixed on the tablecloth, Sophie slowly nodded. 'I'm . . . I'm leaving home.'

'I see, and do you have somewhere to go?'

She shook her head miserably.

'Mm. Well, as I told you the last time we met, my mother owns a hotel on the South Shore. I'm sure she'd put you up until you decide what you want to do.'

'Why would she do that?' Sophie asked suspiciously.

The twinkle was back in his eye again as he grinned. 'Because you're my buddy,' he told her.

Sophie thought that two brief meetings hardly made them buddies but refrained from saying so. After all, he was only trying to be kind.

'It's very nice of you to offer . . . but the thing is, I can't really afford to stay in a hotel without getting a job. And I won't be able to work in a few months' time because I'm . . .' The word lodged in her throat as the full horror of the position she was in came home to her full force.

'Ah – you're pregnant? Is that it?'

She lowered her head, unable to answer for the great lump that was swelling in her throat.

'Is the father not willing to stand by you?'

When her head wagged from side to side she heard him sigh.

'Are you gonna keep the baby, Sophie?'

Again she shook her head as he leaned across the table and took her hand.

'No . . . I don't think so. My mam wants me to go to an aunt in the Midlands. I've nowhere else to go – but the thing is I've never even met her before and I'm not too happy about just turning up on her doorstep out of the blue. Perhaps there are homes for girls in my position? You know, where you can go until they're born and then give them up for adoption.'

Suddenly all the pent-up emotions poured out of her again and now the tears gushed from her eyes so quickly that she felt as if she were drowning in them. In a second he had rounded the table and had her head cradled against his chest.

It felt nice to be held and for a moment she gave herself up to the feeling of being safe as she drank in the clean smell of soap and aftershave. She longed to tell him the whole sorry tale but shame kept her silent as the tears spilled out of her like water from a dam. He continued to hold her until at last the tears subsided then he gently dried her eyes with a crisp white handkerchief.

'Feeling a bit better now?'

She nodded, reluctant to leave the sanctuary of his arms. So much had happened in such a short time that she could barely take it all in herself. Just a few short weeks ago she had been a part of a family. But now here she was all alone and pregnant by her own father. Despair washed over her and in that moment she wished that she was dead. Even her own mother had turned her away and although Sophie knew deep down that she had done it to protect her, still she felt abandoned and betrayed.

Once she had blown her nose noisily, Ben smiled at her. 'Right, why don't you come home with me while you decide what you wanna do, eh?'

When Sophie still hesitated he pushed his chair away from the table and stood up. Drawing the collar of his expensive coat tight around his neck he shrugged. 'It's entirely up to you, of course, but I guess you don't have an awful lot of options open to you, do you? *And* it just so happens that my mother has helped girls in your position before. Perhaps it was fate that we met? Mother has friends in the Welfare Department who could find a solution to your problem in no time.'

'*Really?*' Sophie could hardly believe her good luck. As he had quite rightly pointed out, there weren't an awful lot of options open to her apart from landing on the doorstep of an elderly aunt she had never even known existed until the night before.

Scraping her chair back from the table she nodded at him solemnly. 'Well . . . if you're quite sure that she wouldn't mind me turning up out of nowhere?'

He flashed her a smile that set her heart dancing as he lifted her case. 'Come on. Let's go and see what can be done.'

After tossing some coins onto the table he ushered her towards the door and looked left and right for a taxi. In the busy season they were everywhere but at this time of the year they were few and far between so he led her towards the nearest tram stop. They only had to wait for a matter of minutes before one drew to a halt and once aboard Sophie sat back in her seat and gazed out to sea as they travelled towards the South Shore. Surprisingly she had rarely ventured past the Tower, so for a while they sat in silence and she drank in the sights as they trundled along. Eventually her curiosity got the better of her and she asked, 'Have you lived here long? In Blackpool, I mean?'

He smiled before answering, 'Yeah, I have. For quite

a few years now, but I was born and brought up in New York.'

He laughed when he saw how impressed she looked. 'Hey, don't go running away with the wrong idea. We lived in Manhattan, in Hell's Kitchen, on Forty-third Street, and I don't mind telling you it was a *mean* neighbourhood. Why, you took your life in your hands if you so much as set foot out the door after dark. They'd cut your throat as quick as look at you there.'

'Is that why you came to England?' Sophie asked and he shrugged.

'I guess that was one of the reasons,' he admitted. 'When my father died there was nothing to hold us there. My mother is English, you see, so we just upped and left and came back here.'

Sophie was prevented from asking any further questions when the Pleasure Beach came into sight and the tram started to slow. Ben lifted her case and gallantly helped her down the steps.

'Come on,' he urged. 'Not far to go now. I think you'll get on well with my mother.'

She followed him through the back streets until he paused in front of a large hotel. 'The Ship Hotel' announced a beautifully painted sign that swung in the wind.

'This is it,' he told her cheerily as he climbed the steps to an elegant front door with stained glass panels and a huge brass doorknocker. Once inside Sophie glanced around, surprised at the luxuriousness of the surroundings.

A huge mahogany desk stood in the reception foyer and she felt her feet sink into a deep crimson carpet. Large gilt-framed mirrors and pictures adorned the walls and Sophie began to feel very out of place as she tried to comb her hair as best she could with her fingers.

'Morning, Mrs G.' Ben smiled at an elderly portly woman who appeared out of a green baize door at the back of the long hallway. The woman was enveloped in a voluminous white apron that was as white as snow and she nodded an acknowledgment before staring curiously at Sophie.

'This is a friend of mine come to meet Mother,' Ben told her as he swept past her, leading Sophie to another door along the hallway. The woman grunted and went on her way as Sophie nervously followed her new friend into the most beautiful room she had ever seen. She had no time to admire it, however, for a voice from deep in a fireside chair suddenly asked, 'Is that you, Ben?'

'Yes, Mother. I've brought a friend of mine to meet you. She's in a spot of bother and I thought perhaps you might be able to help her.'

The most regal-looking woman Sophie had ever set eyes on rose slowly from the chair and turned to eye her visitor. Sophie wrung her hands as she swept towards her.

'Hello, my dear. How nice to meet you. And your name is?' When she extended a perfectly manicured hand that was dripping in diamonds, Sophie shook it gently.

'Sophie . . . Sophie Winters,' she managed to stutter.

The woman smiled but Sophie was quick to note that the smile didn't quite reach her eyes. She also had an English accent, unlike her son. Sophie guessed that she must be somewhere in her mid forties, for tiny streaks of grey were spreading through her hair, which was pulled into an elegant chignon at the back of her head. She wore a pale blue suit that perfectly matched the colour of her eyes and round her throat was a string of pearls. Sophie was completely in awe of her and as she stared up at her she thought she had never seen such an attractive lady in the whole of her life.

'Right, my dear. Why don't you come and sit down here by me and we'll have a little chat while Ben goes off to bully the cook into making us a nice cup of tea?' Crossing to an elegant chaise longue she sat down, patting the seat beside her as Ben discreetly slipped from the room.

Once Sophie was seated she crossed her silk-clad legs and smiled again, that curious smile that seemed to rise no further than her mouth. 'So, my dear, how can I help you? Ben informs me that you are in some kind of trouble.'

Sophie gulped deep in her throat, so tongue-tied that the words stuck in her throat. She felt completely out of her depth and in that moment would gladly have given the moon to feel her mother's arms round her.

'I assure you there's nothing to be frightened of,' the woman told her softly.

Swallowing hard, Sophie decided to get it over with.

'The thing is I'm . . .' When she lowered her head, too ashamed to go on, the woman finished her sentence for her.

'You're pregnant. Is that it?'

Sophie nodded as colour flooded into her cheeks. She had slept fitfully the night before and although it was still only quite early in the morning she was bone tired.

'Right, well, that's hardly the end of the world in this day and age. You're certainly not the first and I can guarantee you won't be the last.'

Raising every ounce of courage she had, Sophie asked, 'Do you think you might be able to help me then?'

'Ah, now – before I answer that I need to ask you a few questions. Do you think you could be honest with me?'

When Sophie's head bobbed eagerly the woman smiled with satisfaction. 'Good. First of all then, where do you come from, Sophie?'

'I live on the Grange Park council estate on the other side of the town.'

'I see. And is there *no* chance of you returning home to your parents?'

It was all Sophie could do to stop herself from bursting into tears again as she miserably shook her head, so the woman continued, 'Are your parents aware that you are pregnant?'

'Me mam is. But I'm not sure if she's told me dad yet.'

'I see. And is there *any* chance at all that they might

come looking for you? You see, I don't want to put myself in the line of fire of irate parents.'

'There's no chance,' Sophie told her dully.

'Now for the most important question . . . Do you want to keep the child, Sophie?'

When Sophie shook her head vigorously, the woman smiled with satisfaction.

'In that case, I *may* be able to help you,' she told her cautiously. 'But if I do there are certain rules that you must be prepared to abide by. Are you still interested?'

When Sophie said she was, the woman went on. 'Good – then here's how it will be. I am prepared to give you a home here until the baby is born. In return you must promise to have nothing to do with anyone outside, nor any of the other people that work here until after the birth. You will have your own room and in return for your board and keep you will work around the hotel until near to the time the baby is born. When the child does arrive I have certain friends in the Welfare Department who will ensure that the child goes to a good home.'

'Will I have to sign lots of forms and things?' Sophie asked nervously.

'Not at all. It will all be done in such a way that when you walk away from here, which you will be quite en-titled to do once the baby is born, it will be as if this unfortunate accident never occurred. You will be free to go on with your life as you did before and forget all about it. How does that sound?'

The hope in Sophie's eyes was her answer as Ben came back into the room balancing a tray full of tea and biscuits precariously in his hand.

'Ah, Ben, Sophie and I have had a little chat and I may be able to help her. However, I do want Sophie to be quite sure that this is what she really wants, so how about she stays here for a while until she makes her mind up?'

'That's fine by me.' Ben beamed at Sophie, whose heart turned over as she looked into his twinkling blue eyes.

Ten minutes later, after Sophie had forced herself to drink a cup of tea out of a bone china cup and saucer that she was almost afraid to hold, Ben's mother rose from her seat and told him, 'Perhaps you could show Sophie to the room where she would be staying if she decided this is what she really wants?'

'Of course.' Ever the gentleman, Ben lifted Sophie's case and after nodding at his mother she started to follow him out of the room.

'Sophie – just one more thing.'

Sophie paused to look back at the stately woman who was standing watching her. 'If you *do* decide to stay I have to tell you that I don't like my staff getting overfriendly. There are two more girls here in the same position as you and I always feel that overfamiliarity breeds contempt. When this unfortunate incident is over with we want you all to get on with your lives with no links to the past. Do you *quite* understand?'

'Yes, Mrs Lewis.' Sophie was beginning to feel that she

was being admitted to a prison but held her tongue. After all – what other choice did she have?

Closing the door she followed Ben to another door at the other end of the passage and found herself climbing a steep narrow staircase. There were no luxurious carpets or pictures here and her shoes clattered on the bare wooden treads. By the time they reached the top, Sophie was out of breath. She found herself on a long low landing with four doors leading off it.

'This used to be the old servants' quarters,' Ben informed her as he led her to the third door along. Swinging it open he ushered her inside and she found that she was in an attic room with a high window set into its sloping roof. An old wooden wardrobe, a brass bed that must have been an antique, and an equally ancient chest of drawers were the only furniture in the room. Even so, Sophie saw at a glance that the bedding was clean, if somewhat faded.

'Not quite as grand as the hotel rooms,' Ben admitted. 'But even so you should be comfortable enough in here till it's all over. The bathroom is the last door on the landing.'

'Thanks.' Sophie hovered by the door like a bird about to take flight and sensing her nervousness he took her hand and drew her into the room. As his large fingers gently caressed her small hand her heart began to beat faster and she found herself gazing into his eyes.

'I hope you *do* decide to stay, honey,' he told her meaningfully. 'You see, the thing is, I knew you were special the second I set eyes on you. Who knows – perhaps when the baby is born you and I . . .' He stopped mid-sentence and grinned self-consciously. 'Sorry. I guess I shouldn't have said that. I don't want you to feel under any pressure. You have a rest today and you could perhaps tell us this evening what you've decided to do. We only want to help you. We don't want you to feel like a prisoner here. The rules and regulations Mother puts in place are all for your benefit once the child has been born.'

Crossing to the door he paused to look back at her. 'Right, I'm going to leave you now to have a think and get some rest. I'll have some dinner sent up for you in a couple of hours or so.'

After he had closed the door behind him Sophie sank onto the edge of the bed, which she soon discovered boasted a mattress that might have been stuffed with house bricks. Her mind was in complete turmoil as she thought back to what Ben had just said and the meeting with his mother. The woman had shown her nothing but kindness, so why then did Sophie feel that she didn't trust her? And Ben. Could it be that he had meant it when he insinuated that they might become a couple once the baby was born? But then he hadn't *exactly* said that – *had he?*

Sophie was so confused and tired that even the lumpy mattress was welcome as she curled up on it in a miserable heap. There was so much she needed to think about. But first she would get some sleep.

Chapter Five

Downstairs, Ben faced his mother as she paced up and down the sumptuously furnished day room. 'I'm not happy about this one,' she confided. 'She lives too close, and although she's upset at the moment she looks to me like she could have a mind of her own to be reckoned with.'

Ben shook his head. 'Her mother turned her out last night so they're hardly going to come looking for her, are they?' he pointed out.

'Just the same I have a bad feeling about her,' his mother told him. Crossing to her side he took her in his strong arms and gazed into her eyes. Ever since the day his father had died when he was just fifteen years old, Ben had become the man of the house. He was fiercely protective of her and there was nothing that he would not have done to please her. As his hands tenderly stroked her hair he felt her begin to melt into him. 'Trust me, Mother. She'll be putty in our hands.'

She sighed contentedly as she leaned against him and instantly forgot all about Sophie.

Late in the afternoon, after tossing and turning for most of the day, Sophie made her decision. She would go to her aunt in the Midlands and shame the devil. She didn't belong here with strangers, not even with Ben, to whom she felt strangely attracted. I'll tell them right now, she thought, and she had just finished tidying herself in preparation for doing just that when there was a tap at the door and Ben's head appeared. He looked very upset though she had no idea why.

'Sophie, could you come down to the drawing room, please?' A cold finger of fear began to inch its way up her spine as she looked back at him before obediently following him along the landing.

After the gloomy room she had spent the day in the bright crystal chandelier in the foyer made her blink and Ben had to take her elbow and lead her towards the drawing room.

They found his mother pacing the room like a caged animal, with a deep frown on her face. She crossed to them immediately they entered and led Sophie to the settee.

'My dear, I'm afraid I may have some very bad news for you,' she said without preamble.

Sophie's heart began to thump painfully against her ribcage as she stared fearfully back at her. Dragging her eyes away from the woman who had changed into yet

Rosie Goodwin

another smart outfit she tried to concentrate on the room: anything to avoid hearing what she was about to tell her. Silver and crystal glittered everywhere she looked and she felt as if she had stepped into the page of a magazine. She sat there feeling more out of place by the minute until the woman spoke again and dragged her attention back to what she was saying.

'Sophie, you *did* say that your name was Winters and you came from the Grange Park housing estate, didn't you?'

Sophie nodded numbly.

The woman sank down beside her and gently took her hand. 'Then, Sophie, you must prepare yourself for a terrible shock. Ben was just reading the newspaper in the kitchen while Cook made the tea when he read an article about something that took place on your estate last night. It seems that a woman by the name of Sally Winters stabbed her husband, Bill, and then took an overdose . . . Are they the names of your parents?'

Sophie felt the room swim around her as she stared back at her incredulously. Her mam and dad *couldn't* be dead. There must be some mistake.

As if reading her mind, Mrs Lewis patted her hand sympathetically. 'Ben, go and get Sophie a glass of water, would you? I'm afraid this must have come as a terrible shock to her.'

Ben melted quietly away as Sophie reeled from the shock of what the woman had just told her. If what she was saying was true then she was utterly alone in the world now with no home to go back to even if she wanted. She would never see her mam and dad again and it was all her own fault. The tears lodged in her throat were going to choke her, she was sure of it, and in that moment she prayed that they would. At least then she would be with her mam again. *Mam, Mam,* her heart was crying. She believed she had been the cause of the tragedy and the knowledge was almost more than she could bear.

'*No* . . . you . . . you must have it wrong! They . . . they *can't* be dead!'

The woman was trying to hold her but Sophie was lashing out, pushing her away.

'*Sophie . . . can you hear me?*' A voice was coming from a long way away but no matter how hard she tried she couldn't quite seem to find it. There was darkness creeping towards her and suddenly it swallowed her up and she fell in an undignified heap on the deep pile carpet.

'So how are you feeling today then?'

Sophie turned her head to see Ben standing in the doorway with a cup of tea in his hand. She watched him cross to the chest of drawers and place it down and wondered what she would ever have done without him.

It was two days now since they had told her the terrible news about her parents' death, but somehow it still wouldn't sink in. As she lay there in the lonely room she kept expecting to wake up and find that it had all been some sort of terrible nightmare. And then when she finally fell into an exhausted sleep and woke up again she would sob afresh when she realised that it wasn't. Ben had been wonderful, bringing her tea and food, which she left to go cold, and creeping in and out of her room like a ghost. She knew that she should be trying to pull herself together but somehow she didn't have the heart to.

Lifting herself onto her elbow she took the cup and sipped at the sweet tea as he gazed at her with concern written on his face. He had been so kind.

'Ben . . . I think it's time I went home to help sort things out,' she told him tremulously.

His face reflected his horror at her suggestion as he gazed at her. 'What's to be gained by you doing that?' he asked. 'You told me you had older brothers. Surely they'll see to all the arrangements for the funeral?'

'I'm sure they will,' Sophie admitted. 'But even so, I should be there . . . I can't just leave everything to them.'

He began to pace up and down the room with his hands clasped behind his back, his face creased with concern. 'I really don't think it's a good idea. What if they start to question you?'

Sophie shrugged. All she knew was that she longed to see her family – or what was left of it. It didn't feel right leaving everything up to her brothers when the whole tragedy was her fault.

'I know it's none of my business, and you haven't actu-ally told me why you left home so abruptly, but I have a feeling it might be something you might not like your brothers to know about, and . . . well, the thing is, it seems strange that this should happen to your parents so soon after your going.' He was looking at her pointedly. 'Are you quite sure that your brothers won't somehow think you might have had something to do with their deaths?'

Sophie hadn't thought of that and frowned. Suddenly, remembering the note she had left for Matthew, her frown deepened. Ben was right; it would look strange her turning back up when on the very same night her parents had died she had told him she had left to work away. Her shoulders sagged as despair washed over her. How could her life have gone so wrong in such a short time?

He came and took her hands and shook them up and down. 'You've got to trust me, Sophie. Mother and I only have your best interests at heart and to go back now could only cause yet more trouble. Your brothers would end up hating you if they thought the row you had with your parents had anything to do with their deaths. You have to think of yourself now, and the child of course.'

Dropping back onto the pillows she tried to absorb what he was saying – but it was so hard, she felt as if she was looking through a fog.

'Come on,' he urged, pressing the cup back into her hand. 'Drink the rest of this tea I've brought you and try to rest. You've had a terrible shock. It's no wonder you can't think straight.'

Obediently she drained the cup. Ben was right; she had had an awful shock, which was probably why she felt so tired all the time. As she stared miserably up at the ceiling he took the cup from her hand and tucked the blanket around her and in no time at all she was fast asleep again.

On the day of the funerals, Ben did everything in his power to help her through what was the most difficult time of her life. At one point she had considered attending but Ben and his mother had talked her out of it. As they had pointed out she was hardly in any fit state to go and it could only make things worse. She supposed that they were right. After all, how could she have stood in church knowing that her parents were being buried because of her? Now she knew it was time to repay Ben in any way she could. The next few months would not be easy but once they were over she would have to try and get on with her life and put the whole dreadful experience behind her.

'Would you tell your mother I shall be well enough to start my duties tomorrow?' she told him dully. The way she saw it, anything must be better than lying here. At least if she was busy she wouldn't have so much time to think.

'OK. But only if you're sure you're up to it,' he replied as he stroked a lock of stray hair from her forehead.

'I can't wallow in self-pity forever. That won't bring them back, will it?' She could have added that it was all because of her that they were both dead but she clamped her lips shut.

Sitting on the edge of the bed he told her, 'I have to go away tomorrow, Sophie, but only for a couple of days. Are you quite sure that you'll be all right until I get back?'

'Of course I will,' she answered. 'But *somebody* wasn't all right in the night. I heard someone crying and I could have sworn it came from one of the rooms along the landing.'

He grinned as he played with her fingers. 'You probably heard some drunk on the seafront. Things tend to echo and get distorted up here in the gods.'

She shrugged. She had been so locked in her own little world of grieving that her mind had no doubt played tricks on her.

'Anyway, what jobs has your mother got in mind for me?' She was keen to change the subject.

'I'll get her to come along and see you later on. It will probably be chambermaid. The hotel is beginning to get busy now, though not half as busy as it will be in another few weeks. During the summer season we hardly know if we're on our heads or our heels.'

Sophie welcomed the thought. The busier the better as far as she was concerned; then she wouldn't have so much time to dwell on things.

'Thanks for being so good to me through all this,' she said awkwardly.

He rose from the bed and smiled down on her. 'Think nothing of it. That's what friends are for.'

Plucking up her courage she suddenly asked, 'Have you been in the hotel for long?'

'Yes, we have as a matter of fact. As I told you, I was about fifteen when my father died and shortly after that we left the States to come over here. We bought the hotel soon after that.'

She'd intended to ask more but suddenly the need to know was gone as she thought of her mother again and she leaned back against the pillows and stared off into space.

Long after he had gone she lay gazing at the skylight and as she did so she thought she heard someone crying again. Curious, she clambered from the bed and inched the door open before peering cautiously up and down the landing. She listened for some minutes then deciding that she must have been mistaken she made her way to the bathroom at the end of the landing. It was a cold bleak-looking room and as she slowly undressed she shuddered. A large white bathtub took up the whole of one wall; opposite it a cracked sink with a broken mirror hanging above it leaned drunkenly sideways. A toilet surrounded by drab grey tiles stood next to it. Not wishing to spend a moment longer than was necessary in the grimy little room, Sophie hastily bathed and washed her hair.

It was as she was making her way back to her room with a towel wrapped round her head that the door at the end of the landing opened and a girl with fiery red hair and striking green eyes appeared. They surveyed each other in silence for some seconds but then the girl came forward and held out her hand. Sophie noticed that she wore a shapeless navy dress with a white collar and cuffs and wondered if this might be some sort of uniform, but her mind was distracted when the girl introduced herself.

'Hello there, you must be the new recruit. I'm Tilly Trent.'

'Sophie. Sophie Winters.'

'Pleased to meet yer I'm sure. When did you arrive?'

'About a week or so ago,' Sophie informed her solemnly.

All the while they were standing there, Tilly's eyes kept dancing towards the door. She knew how strict Mrs Lewis was about her staff becoming friendly and had no wish to be caught gossiping.

'Well, nice to meet yer. I'd berra gerron though.' Tilly was visibly nervous. 'I've still got three more rooms to do afore the guests arrive an' Mrs Lewis will have me guts fer garters if they ain't done to her satisfaction. That's my room on the end there an' Cathy, that's another girl that's stayin' here, is in the room next to yours. I just came back to get me hankie. I've gorra rotten cold on me. Ta-ra fer now then.'

She flitted away like a butterfly leaving Sophie to stare after her open-mouthed. From her accent, Sophie guessed that she was from London, for she sounded like a right little cockney sparrow. She would have liked to talk to her for longer but Tilly had obviously been too busy. Perhaps later, she thought to herself, then hurried on to her room. Ben had told her that his mother sometimes helped girls in her predicament out and Sophie briefly wondered if Tilly and the other girl she had mentioned faced the same dilemma as herself. She began to rub at her hair and the thought vanished.

It was quite a surprise when Mrs Lewis tapped on the door some time later. 'Sophie,' she said abruptly. 'Ben tells me that you are feeling well enough to begin work.'

Sophie nodded slowly, very aware of her cheap off-the-peg clothes as she looked back at Mrs Lewis who was impeccably turned out as usual. The woman looked satisfied.

'Good. Then perhaps you feel up to eating your meal in the kitchen this evening and I can go through the list of your duties with you.'

Again Sophie nodded and now Mrs Lewis handed her a dress that was folded across her arm. Sophie saw that it was identical to the one Tilly had been wearing.

'I'd like you to wear this while you're working,' the woman informed her. 'It looks so much nicer if the staff are all dressed the same, don't you think?' Before Sophie could answer she beckoned to her, so flinging the dress onto the bed Sophie hastily left the room. After the steep descent down the curving staircase the woman led her towards the kitchen where Sophie saw the woman Ben had called Mrs G stirring a large saucepan at the stove. Tilly was there too, sitting at a large scrubbed table, but she kept her eyes downcast and never said so much as a word as her employer swept into the room. Sophie saw with a little shock that Tilly was heavily pregnant and wondered why she hadn't noticed at their meeting earlier on. She had no time to dwell on the fact, however, for Mrs Lewis was already reeling off a list of jobs that she wanted Sophie to do the next day.

'So – are you quite clear about what is expected of you then?' she finished.

Sophie nodded numbly.

'Good, then be down here for six thirty sharp in the morning. You will help Mrs G prepare breakfast for the guests then when they vacate their rooms by ten o'clock you will be responsible for the cleaning of the rooms on the third floor *only*. Make sure you remember what I said about the fourth floor though. No one, but *no one*, is allowed on that floor except Mrs G, my son and myself. Should you disobey my wishes on this matter I shall have no choice but to ask you to leave. Do you *quite* understand?'

'Perfectly,' Sophie told her with a trace of irritation. All she really wanted was for the next few months to be over with so that she could get on with her life, or what was left of it. But how could it ever be the same now that she had lost her mother?

Thankfully, Mrs Lewis turned her attention to Tilly. 'Tilly, you will show Sophie where all the cleaning equipment is before she starts in the morning. Also where the clean bedding is and where she should put the dirty bedding.'

'Yes, Mrs Lewis.'

'Good, now do proceed with your meal. And girls.

Remember what I said about idle gossip. When you return to the top floor I expect you to go straight to your own rooms. Have I made myself quite clear?'

When both heads nodded in unison she turned and swept from the room like a ship in full sail.

It was Mrs G who broke the silence that settled over them when she carried two plates laden with food to the table and placed them down in front of the girls.

'Come on, get that down you,' she urged. 'You'll be surprised how much better you'll both feel on a full stomach.'

Sophie seemed suddenly to have lost her appetite again but while she pushed her food around the plate Tilly fell on hers with a vengeance as if she hadn't eaten for a month.

'Mrs G,' she said between mouthfuls. 'You ain't seen owt of Cathy today have yer?'

Mrs G scowled at her, setting her many chins wobbling like a jelly. 'You should know better than to ask that, Tilly,' she scolded. 'You know the rules here by now. You ask no questions and you'll be told no lies.'

Shame-faced, Tilly hung her head though Sophie thought she detected a note of concern in her eyes. Who was this Cathy? Was she yet another girl in the same unfortunate position as she and Tilly?

The rest of the meal was eaten in silence with only the sound of the coals popping on the fire to break it. When it was done the girls carried the pots to a deep stone sink where Tilly washed them while Sophie dried them.

When they were all put away to Mrs G's satisfaction she nodded towards the door. 'Right then, Tilly. Show Sophie back to her room, would you? And don't forget. No idle chit-chat on the way.'

'Yes, Mrs G.' Tilly left without a word and Sophie followed her until they were on the steep staircase that led to the attic. Only then did Sophie dare to whisper, 'Who is Cathy?'

'Ssh . . .' Tilly fearfully put her finger to her lips and Sophie followed her until at last they were on the landing that led to their rooms.

Once there, Tilly let out a sigh of relief as she turned to face Sophie.

'Cathy is another girl that Mrs Lewis is helpin'. She's due to have her baby in a couple o' weeks or so an' then she's goin' to head back to Ireland where she come from. Her family are strict Catholics an' told her they'd have nuffin' more to do wiv her until she'd got rid o' the child she were carryin'. The worst of it is she confided to me that it were the bloody father o' the church she attended who *put* her in the family way. Not that her family would believe her, o' course. Lovely timid little fing, she is. When I saw her the night before last she were in terrible pain. That's why you ain't seen her doin' no jobs around the place. I reckon she were in labour meself. Mrs Lewis has let her stay in her room. Soon as ever she's had the kid, Cathy told me she's out o' here like a dose o' salts an' I can't say as I blame her. I'll tell yer what – we'll pop in an yer can meet her fer yerself.'

Some seconds later, Tilly tentatively tapped on the door next to Sophie's and poked her head into the room.

'S'all right, Cathy,' she soothed. 'It's only me. I've brought Sophie, the new recruit, to meet yer.'

After glancing along the landing to make sure that they weren't being watched she quickly drew Sophie into the room and shut the door behind her.

'So how yer feelin' then?' Tilly asked as she looked across at the mousy-haired girl lying on the bed.

'Not so good . . . I think it's started,' Cathy muttered miserably.

Tilly's eyes almost popped out of her head. 'Why, yer lucky bugger. Not much longer an' you'll be headin' back home then. But ain't it a bit early?'

'In answer to your first question, wild horses wouldn't stop me,' Cathy declared as she rubbed at her back. 'An' in answer to your second question – sure, 'tis a bit early according to my calculations, but Mrs Lewis reckons it's normal for a first baby to be a couple o' weeks either way.' Screwing her eyes tight shut with pain she looked away and Sophie looked on helplessly until at last Cathy took a deep breath and looked back up at them.

'You two had better make yerselves scarce. Mrs G an' Mrs Lewis have been checkin' on me all through the day an' they're due back any time. I wouldn't want either of 'em to catch you in here else sure heads will roll.'

Seeing the sense in what she said, Tilly grabbed Sophie's elbow and hauled her towards the door. 'Good luck, Cathy. It will probably be all over the next time I see yer so all the best. Be sure to come an' say ta-ra before yer go, won't yer?'

'Sure I will,' Cathy promised as she bent over with yet another pain.

Once out on the landing again, Sophie stared at Tilly fearfully before asking, 'Shouldn't she be in hospital?'

Tilly shrugged. 'How should I know? I ain't a nurse, am I? I dare say Mrs Lewis knows what she's doin'.'

Sophie frowned as she pondered her words. 'Has she had a lot of girls in our position here then?'

'Well, there were one other girl here when I first arrived about three months ago. But she must have had her babby an' then scarpered 'cos she suddenly just didn't show up fer her meals any more.'

Sophie's frown deepened. 'Don't you think this set-up is a little . . . strange?' she asked after a moment or two.

'In our position it pays yer *not* to bleedin' think,' Tilly told her firmly. 'All we need to know is we can walk away wiv no fuss an' palaver when it's all over an' go on as if nuffin' had ever happened.'

'But what about the babies? Don't we get to know what happens to them?'

Tilly sighed in exasperation. 'Why do we need ter know? If we were that bloody worried about 'em we wouldn't be here in the first place, would we?'

'I suppose not,' Sophie admitted miserably. 'But poor Cathy. I bet that's who I heard crying.'

'Huh! Hark at the pot callin' the kettle black! I've heard enough sniffles comin' from your room over the last few days. You ain't bin cryin' over the fact that you'll be givin' the baby up, have yer?'

Looking up into Tilly's heavily made-up face, Sophie shook her head. 'No . . . I lost my mam an' dad the night before I came here.'

'Bloody 'ell!' Tilly's face creased into a mask of concern as her hands joined and twisted into a knot and just for a second Sophie caught sight of the kind heart beneath the brash front she presented to the world.

'Would it help ter talk about it?' she whispered gently, but Sophie shook her head.

'No – not really . . . not that I don't appreciate your concern. It's just that it's still a bit raw at the moment and I . . .'

'I understand. Just remember though – when yer do need someone to talk to I'm here, all right? Now we'd berra get back to us own rooms else we'll both get chucked out on us ears if Ma Lewis finds us here. Night, Sophie.'

'Night, Tilly.'

Sophie watched Tilly slip into her room before making her way to her own bedroom door. Strangely she didn't feel quite so alone any more and she decided that in Tilly she had found a friend.

Chapter Six

It was the following evening when Tilly complained, 'I just can't understand why Cathy hasn't come to see me afore she left if she's had the baby? She *must* still be here somewhere, 'cos I snuck into her room today an' all her clothes are still in the wardrobe. Mrs Lewis would go mad if she knew what I'd done but I was worried about her.'

'I should think the most likely thing is that she's in hospital,' Sophie told her wisely. 'After all, they'd hardly have the facilities to deliver babies here, would they? And it was more than obvious when we saw her yesterday that the baby was coming.'

Tilly shrugged, setting her fiery red curls dancing. 'Mebbe yer right. It's probably me just frettin' fer nothin'. I'd like to hear from her, that's all. She's a good kid, is Cathy.'

Suddenly realising that they'd been standing there talking for some minutes she set off at a fair old trot across the landing. 'Berra say goodnight now,' she muttered in a low voice as if the walls had ears. 'Mrs Lewis would skin us alive if she were to find out we'd been standin' here chattin'.'

'Goodnight, Tilly.' Sophie stood there and watched until she disappeared into her room along the landing then she let herself into her own room and sank down onto the edge of the bed. This was turning out to be a very strange set-up from what she could see of it. Mrs Lewis was either an angel in disguise or there was something not quite right here. But what could it be? And then there was Mrs G. Why did everyone call her that? What was her real name? In fairness, Sophie had to admit that she had been nothing but pleasant to her since the minute she had arrived. But all the same she seemed totally devoted to Ben and Mrs Lewis and if Sophie had even so much as tried to ask a tentative question about them or the hotel the older woman had closed up like a clam and barked at her to get on with her work.

Too tired and disheartened to think about it any more, she undressed and fell into bed where she slept like a log until the next morning.

By three o'clock the following afternoon, Sophie felt as if her back was about to break. She'd spent the entire day stripping beds and cleaning bedrooms on the third floor where the guests stayed, as Mrs Lewis had ordered. Oddly enough, Sophie had soon discovered that she rarely got to see the guests because the staff were made to use the back staircase. Sometimes she would enviously eye the possessions that the lady guests left lying about the rooms. It was more than obvious that the hotel catered to a high-class clientèle, for the hotel was a far cry from the seedy bed and breakfast places that could be found farther back from the seafront in the back streets. Each room on the third floor was decorated in a different colour scheme and everything coordinated. One was painted in a delicate blue, with lovely dove-grey curtains and bedding covered in tiny blue flowers. On the floor was a darker blue wall-to-wall carpet and even the ornaments and framed pictures dotted here and there had been bought with the particular colour scheme in mind, as had the towels.

Today Sophie was particularly pleased when she had finished the last room, which was painted in soft shades of lemon. She collected all the dirty laundry from the length of the elaborately decorated landing then with her arms full she made her way downstairs to a laundry room at the back of the large hotel where Tilly was pushing washing down into a bubbling copper with big wooden tongs. This, Sophie had discovered, was Tilly's job and each time she saw the girl with her hands red raw and sweat pouring from her brow she thought that perhaps she had the best job of the two of them after all, even if every bone in her body did ache. Tilly, however, was used to it and greeted her each time she appeared with a smile. Today was no different and when Sophie appeared she grinned at her before telling her, 'Just drop 'em down there.'

Sophie did as she was told as Tilly manhandled a load of washing from the copper to a large stone sink where she would rinse everything. They would then be carried outside to the most enormous mangle Sophie had ever seen and after being fed through that they would be pegged onto lines that stretched from side to side of the yard to flap and dance in the wind.

Tilly rubbed her hand across her sweating brow. 'Stone the crows, it's like a furnace in here,' she complained. 'Yer wouldn't nip along to the kitchen an' ask Mrs G fer a drink fer me, would yer?'

'Of course I will.' Without hesitation, Sophie went through the door into the hall that led to the foyer where she saw a smart-looking couple standing at the desk with two expensive leather suitcases at their feet. She smiled at them and the woman smiled timidly back. The man at her side looked the other way and Sophie noticed that he seemed nervy and on edge. Not at all as if he was about to start a holiday. And then she grinned as a thought occurred to her. Perhaps they were on honeymoon and the man was feeling a little embarrassed?

Mrs Lewis was smiling at them disarmingly but when she saw Sophie approaching she turned slightly to glare at her.

'Get along then, girl,' she snapped. 'The work won't get done if you stand there gawking, now will it?'

Turning her attention back to the couple she flashed them a charming smile. 'Would you like to follow me, Mr and Mrs Hamilton? I'm sure you'll be ready for a rest after your long journey. I've put you in a room on the fourth floor.'

'Thank you.'

Sophie noticed that the man had an American accent as she scuttled past. Seconds later she burst into the kitchen, which was deserted, and after hastily filling a glass with orange squash she hurried back to Tilly with it.

'Cor, that'll go down a treat.' Tilly took the glass and drained it in seconds as Sophie nodded towards the pile of laundry she had deposited at the side of the copper minutes before.

'That's the lot for today,' she informed Tilly and the fiery-haired girl sighed with relief.

'Thank God fer that,' she remarked, running the back of her hand across her forehead. 'Yer could melt in here wiv all this bleedin' steam.'

Sophie frowned as she hovered uncertainly in the doorway. 'I just heard Mrs Lewis telling a couple that they've been given a room on the fourth floor. They were Americans I think. But I thought that was where Mrs G, Ben and Mrs Lewis had their rooms?'

'It is,' Tilly agreed nonchalantly. 'Best not to question it though – perhaps they're friends o' the family.'

'I don't think so because she called them Mr and Mrs Hamilton. Surely she'd have called them by their first names if they'd been friends? I got the impression that they might be on their honeymoon.'

Tilly shrugged, not much bothered one way or another who Mrs Lewis had in her private quarters. 'Just fink yerself lucky. We ain't allowed on that floor so at least yer won't have their room to clean, will yer? I bet me bottom dollar their dirty bleedin' sheets end up in here fer me to wash though.'

'Mm, there is that,' Sophie agreed. 'But who does do the cleaning up there?'

'They have this woman come in most mornin's from what I can make of it,' Tilly told her. 'I've seen her a couple o' times but I've never got to speak to her 'cos she don't live in.'

'I see.' Sophie stared thoughtfully off into space for a moment before then saying, 'Don't you think it's strange that Mrs G lives on the fourth floor too? I mean, she's only the cook at the end of the day so you'd think she'd get to be on our landing with us, wouldn't you?'

'I dare say yer would now yer come to mention it,' Tilly said as she stabbed at the bubbling water with her tongs. 'Though between you an' me I don't much care if the miserable old cow sleeps in the back yard. She's gorrit in fer me.'

Sophie grinned before changing the subject and asking, 'So what am I to do now then?'

Tilly nodded in the direction of the kitchen. 'Berra go through an' help Mrs G wiv the evenin' meals fer the guests.'

Sophie did as she was told and as she passed through the foyer again she glanced up at the grand staircase. There was no sign of Mrs Lewis or the young couple who had just arrived. She'll probably be settling them into their room, she decided, before moving on to the kitchen. This time when she entered she saw Mrs G basting a huge leg of lamb and in no time at all, the woman had her peeling potatoes and scraping enough vegetables to feed an army. After the backbreaking work she'd been doing all day, Sophie didn't mind. In fact, it was nice to be able to stand in one place for a time instead of rushing from room to room like an idiot. As she and Mrs G worked in companionable silence the older woman was impressed with Sophie's knowledge of cooking.

'Helped your mother with the cooking at home then, did you?' she asked eventually as she watched Sophie expertly whipping up some eggs and flour to make Yorkshire puddings. At the mention of her mother, Sophie's eyes flooded with tears. The pain she was feeling still cut so deep that the answer lodged in her throat and all she could do was nod.

Sensing the girl's distress the woman chewed on her lip. She knew that she shouldn't become involved with the girls who stayed here from time to time. But even so, there was something about this girl that she found strangely endearing and made her want to protect her. 'Kick you out when she found out you were in the family way did she?' she asked softly.

Sophie's head snapped round as her hand automatically flew to her stomach. Surely it couldn't be evident that she was pregnant already? She was barely two months gone.

'*No* . . . she didn't. My mam would *never* have turned me out,' she snapped indignantly.

Mrs G wished she could have bitten her tongue out and cursed under her breath. What had she had to go prying for? It would only need this young slip of a girl to have a word in the madam's ear and she would find herself in serious trouble. 'Sorry,' she muttered. 'I shouldn't have gone sticking my nose in where it wasn't wanted. I was only trying to be friendly. There was no offence meant, I'm sure. Let's forget I ever asked, shall we?'

At that moment, Tilly appeared in the doorway and sensing the tense atmosphere looked from one to the other of them with her eyebrows raised.

'Missin' summat, am I?' She fixed her gaze on Sophie who was already regretting snapping at the woman. Normally she was very even-tempered but the happenings of the last few weeks had stretched her nerves to the limit.

'I'm so sorry I bit your head off, Mrs G,' Sophie apologised. 'I'm not normally so rude but the last few weeks have been so . . . so . . .' When her voice trailed away and fresh tears spurted from her eyes the red-faced woman immediately forgot all her good intentions and hurried across the highly polished tile floor to wrap her in a warm embrace.

'There, there, love,' she soothed as Tilly watched in amazement. She had been at the hotel for over three months and in all that time the cook had barely said more than a dozen words to her, though she could understand why she felt drawn to Sophie. She had an air of vulnerability and innocence about her that was strangely touching. *A bit like Cathy really.* Thoughts of her errant friend caused her to frown and suddenly she could hold her concerns inside no longer.

'Mrs G. Have you seen Cathy?' she blurted out.

The colour drained from the elderly woman's face and dropping her arms from Sophie as if they had been burned she turned away and busied herself at the stove. 'You know how Mrs Lewis feels about the staff gossiping,' she scolded, but her voice was laced with fear. 'Now come on the pair of you. The guests will be sitting down to dinner in an hour or so and it will be God help us all if it's not ready to dish up.'

Sophie and Tilly exchanged a glance then scuttled away to do as they were told.

Long after the girls had retired to their rooms that night, the old woman sat on in the kitchen with her feet propped on the fender and a glass of sherry in her hand as she gazed into the flames of the fire. She had lived at the hotel for more years than she cared to remember, though she often threatened to leave. But deep inside she knew that she never would. While Ben and his mother needed her, as they surely did, she was as much of a prisoner there as the young girls that came and went. As pictures of their faces flashed before her eyes she lowered her head and wept. *I'm getting too old for this game,* she thought, and wished with all her heart that she could be stronger or at least find the courage to walk away and leave Ben and his mother to it. *Still,* she consoled herself, *it can't be for much longer now.* And a little voice in her head whispered, *It mustn't be.*

Upstairs, Sophie was standing on the landing keeping a watchful eye on the door while Tilly crept once more into Cathy's room. She was gone for only seconds and when she emerged her face was ashen.

'Everyfin's still there,' she muttered fearfully. 'An' I mean *everyfin'*! Surely she'd have taken *some* of her fings if she'd gone into hospital?'

Sophie thought about Tilly's words and was just about to answer when the door at the end of the landing suddenly swung open and Mrs Lewis appeared closely followed by Mrs G, whose face was the colour of bleached linen.

'Just what the hell do you think you're doing?' Mrs Lewis thundered.

At once, Tilly's face became the picture of innocence. 'Why, we ain't doin' nuffin', Mrs Lewis. It's just that Sophie an' I just wanted to use the baffroom at the same time.' Turning to Sophie she flashed her a disarming smile. 'Go on, you go first.' She smiled politely and only too glad of a chance to escape, Sophie shot into the bathroom and locked the door behind her.

Slightly placated, Mrs Lewis sniffed. 'Very well then. I suggest you go into your room until the bathroom is free,' she told Tilly coldly. 'Mrs G and I need to get a few things for Cathy.'

'Has Cathy had her baby then?' Tilly dared to ask.

'I hardly think that is any of your business, though if you must know, she hasn't, not yet,' Mrs Lewis replied in a voice that was as cold as ice. 'Now will you *please* go to your room?'

There was a lot Tilly would have liked to ask but seeing the expression on the older woman's face she decided not to push her luck and reluctantly entered her room. Once inside she pressed her ear to the door and after a while she heard their footsteps on the landing again. She waited till they had died away before cautiously inching the door open. Everywhere was as quiet as a grave so she hurried along the landing and without even bothering to knock she slipped silently into Sophie's room.

'So what do yer make o' that then?' she asked breathlessly as Sophie's startled eyes flew to her.

'Seems innocent enough to me,' Sophie remarked. 'You'd only just said yourself that Cathy would need some of her things, so that's obviously what they'd come for. No doubt she'll be back to say goodbye in a day or two when she's had the baby.'

Tilly was not at all convinced and began to pace up and down. Suddenly she turned about and went towards the door. 'I'm goin' to see what they've taken,' she declared. Before Sophie could object she disappeared only to appear again seconds later looking as if she had seen a ghost.

'All her stuff is piled into carrier bags by her bedroom door,' she told Sophie solemnly.

'So? Didn't you say that Cathy was keen to get home to her parents? Mrs G and Mrs Lewis have probably just packed them ready for her to collect.'

Seeing the sense in what Sophie said, Tilly relaxed a little. 'Yer probably right. It's just me bein' nervy again. Cathy promised as she wouldn't leave wivout sayin' goodbye so no doubt she'll be here to collect her stuff in the next couple o' days or so.'

When she saw that Sophie had her coat on she frowned. 'What the bleedin' hell do yer fink you're doin'? We ain't allowed out, you know that.'

Feeling that she could trust Tilly, Sophie decided to confide in her. 'You know I told you that I'd recently lost my mam an' dad. Well, Ben and his mother decided that it wouldn't be wise for me to go to their funerals. But the thing is . . . I need to pay my respects so I'm going to go to the churchyard to say my goodbyes.'

'Ma Lewis will scalp yer alive if she knows yer goin' out,' Tilly warned then, her voice softening, she told Sophie, 'If yer *must* go, foller me. I know a way as yer can gerrout wivout 'em knowin' you've gone.'

Once again she inched the door open and peered up and down the landing before beckoning Sophie to follow her.

In no time at all, Sophie found herself standing in the middle of Tilly's room, which looked as if a bomb had dropped on it. Seeing Sophie's expression, Tilly blushed.

'I ain't the tidiest o' people as yer can see,' she admitted, sweeping a pile of clothes from the chair onto the floor. 'But never mind that fer now. Look 'ere.'

Sophie went to stand beside her as Tilly wrestled with the sash-cord window, which she eventually managed to prise halfway open. She found herself looking out onto a fire escape that dropped away to the back of the kitchen, from which a light was still shining.

'You'll have to be as quiet as a mouse,' Tilly warned. 'Mrs G has got ears like an elephant an' if she hears yer an' knows you've come from my room my head'll be on the block good an' proper.'

A rare smile spread across Sophie's face. 'Do I take it you've used this as a form of escape before?'

Tilly folded her arms. 'It just so happens I have,' she admitted, then unable to keep her secret for a second longer she confided, 'I've got me a boyfriend.Yer needn't look so surprised. I've told him I'm pregnant an' why I'm here but he's a good lad an' soon as ever this is over wiv we're goin' to make a go of it.'

Sophie was intrigued. 'And what's his name then?'

Tilly's face took on a dreamy look. 'His name's Alfie. He works on the pleasure beach an' I met him the first week I came to Blackpool. He's just about the nicest bloke I've ever met. He even told me he don't care about the baby. He says he'd take it as his own but I want . . . well, I want this to be special. Forever like. An' I want us to start wiv a clean slate so I've asked him to wait till it's born an' then we'll start afresh.'

'Oh, so the baby isn't Alfie's then?'

'Ner,' Tilly looked slightly ashamed. 'That's anuvver story. But if yer goin' you ought to be makin' tracks. Come on. I'll help yer out.'

In no time at all, Sophie was standing on the metal rungs of the fire escape, which to her horror she soon discovered seemed to sway more than a ballroom dancer.

'You'll be all right,' Tilly assured her as she looked into Sophie's panic-stricken face. 'Just hang onto the handrail an' take it slow.'

Taking a deep gulp, Sophie nodded and began the perilous descent.

'Are yer sure as yer wouldn't like me to come wiv yer?' Tilly offered when Sophie had gone no more than a few steps down but she shook her head.

'All right then. Watch how yer go then an' when yer get back just tap on the winder an' I'll let yer back in.'

Sophie nodded as with her heart in her mouth she concentrated on the steps. She had always had a fear of heights and the ground below seemed to be a dangerously long way away, but at last her feet touched solid ground and she breathed a sigh of relief. Creeping past the kitchen window she peeped inside but it seemed to be empty so she crept on across the darkened yard and felt her way along the wall until her hand connected with a tall wooden gate. After fumbling in the darkness for what seemed an eternity her cold hand finally found the latch and within seconds she had let herself out into the street beyond where, with head bent, she lost herself amongst the crowds.

A short tram ride and forty minutes later she found herself outside the church where Ben had told her her parents had been buried. The beautiful old church of St Michael was in darkness as she stumbled through the lych-gate and entered the deserted churchyard. She stood for a while letting her heart steady and her eyes adjust to the darkness before she began to work her way amongst the tombstones. A mist was creeping across the ground and the headstones seemed to be leaning towards her but she forced herself to go on. Now that she had come this far she was determined to find their resting place before leaving. The wind was whipping through the yew trees that surrounded the graveyard and her imagination began to play tricks on her as she imagined that someone was calling her name. And then just as panic began to engulf her the moon sailed from behind a great black cloud and she found herself standing at the foot of a freshly dug grave. It was little more than a great mound of black earth covered in wreaths with a simple wooden cross standing to attention beyond the flowers.

Moving towards it she peered at the name that was engraved there, but it was so dark that she couldn't make it out.

Fumbling in her coat pocket her fingers closed around a box of Swan Vestas matches and after hastily lighting one she shielded it with her hand against the bitterly cold wind and leaned closer. WINTERS. The name seemed to jump out at her and as the match suddenly burned her hand she let out a cry and flung it away. So Ben had been telling the truth then? All the way there she had been praying that he'd been mistaken or even played a cruel trick on her, for even that was preferable to knowing that her parents were dead. But now she could deny it no longer. Her mother and father had gone from her forever. Running her hand across the name on the cheap wooden cross she began to cry bitterly. She supposed that the cross had been placed there while her brothers had a nice marble one engraved. Knowing them as she did, she felt confident that they would never settle for this cheap wooden affair. And so she sat there, talking to them and reliving in her mind every happy memory she had of her mother and even of her father as hot tears coursed down her cheeks.

Time passed but she wasn't aware of it until the church clock suddenly chimed eleven o' clock, shocking her out of her memories. Rising blindly to her feet she knuckled the tears from her eyes and blew a kiss to their resting place before staggering away. Somehow for her life had to go on.

It was almost midnight when she finally tapped at Tilly's window. The curtains flicked aside almost instantly and within minutes Tilly was hauling her across the windowsill.

Sophie noticed that without the heavy make-up Tilly usually wore she looked much younger.

'Bleedin 'ell!' Tilly exclaimed in alarm as she noted how exhausted Sophie looked. 'Yer look totally knackered. P'raps it weren't such a good idea you goin' there after all?'

'It was,' Sophie told her dully as Tilly tried to rub some warmth into her blue fingers. 'At least I've said my goodbyes. But apart from my brothers I haven't got a single soul in the world now.'

Never good with words, Tilly stood helplessly by until suddenly the tears gushed from Sophie's eyes again. When she hesitantly stepped forward and wrapped her in her arms, Sophie clung to her.

'It's all right,' Tilly soothed as she stroked her hair. 'The worst is over now. As yer say, you've made yer peace. An' as fer you havin' no one apart from yer brothers . . . well, that ain't strictly true. You've got me now an' we'll get through this together . . . you'll see.'

Chapter Seven

The following day the girls clattered down the stairs side by side. It was not yet six o'clock in the morning and Tilly was barely awake, so Sophie stayed silent, knowing that she would get no sense out of her new-found friend until she had drunk at least two cups of hot sweet tea.

As they were approaching the kitchen door Tilly placed her hand on Sophie's arm and warned her to stay quiet.

Stopping abruptly, Sophie frowned and followed Tilly's eyes to the door through which they could hear raised voices.

'I *knew* something like this would happen sooner or later.' They recognised the voice of Mrs G and glanced at each other as they held their breaths. She sounded distressed.

'Look, stop worrying both of you, will you? It's just a little setback, that's all. She can't go much longer can she, for goodness' sake?'

As Sophie heard Ben's deep voice her heart leapt. He

must have come back late last night, or surely he would have come up to see her?

'As soon as breakfast for the guests is out of the way I'll go back up to her,' they heard Mrs G say. 'Meantime, you'll have to take her back to her room.'

'I'm not so sure that's a good idea,' said Mrs Lewis. 'What if she gets chatting to the other two? That Tilly is a little too loose-tongued for my liking. I told you that on the day you brought her here, Ben.'

'Look, Tilly will be no trouble. Neither will Sophie,' they heard Ben reassure her. 'They'll both just think that Cathy is back upstairs because it was a false alarm, which it was. Where's the harm in that?'

As the girls heard footsteps in the kitchen, Tilly suddenly grabbed Sophie's elbow and propelled her forward. The last thing she wanted was for them both to be found eavesdropping. Thrusting the kitchen door open she burst into the kitchen so unexpectedly that Mrs G almost jumped out of her skin.

'Mornin' all,' she said cheerily. Sophie's eyes immediately sought Ben's but to her disappointment he merely started towards the door without so much as a glance in her direction.

Before he left the room he paused to look back at the two girls. 'Cathy will be coming back to her room today,' he informed them shortly. 'It seems that she wasn't in labour after all. It was just a false alarm. Could you please make sure that she's left alone? As you can imagine she's feeling rather tired so we want her to save her energy for the birth.'

Tilly sniffed. 'If that's what yer want.' Her voice was as cold as marble and Sophie saw Ben flush with annoyance.

'It sure *is* what I want.' He glared at her as if to add emphasis to his words then slammed out without so much as another word.

'Huh! Sounds like he got out o' bed the wrong side this mornin',' Tilly quipped, which brought Mrs G bristling to his defence.

'You just mind your lip, my girl, and get that kettle on. This is not a holiday camp!'

'Don't I bleedin' know it!' Tilly muttered as she snatched up the kettle and stamped towards the sink.

Mrs Lewis, who was looking decidedly uncomfortable, edged towards the door and Sophie was shocked to see that for the first time since she had met her she was looking less than perfect. In fact, she looked very tense.

'I'll . . . see you all later then,' she said nervously and hastily followed Ben.

Breakfast was a dismal affair with little said, so much so that the girls were relieved when it was over and they could go about their duties.

It was nearly eleven o'clock before Sophie lugged the first load of dirty washing into the laundry room where she found Tilly ironing with the coppers all on the boil and ready to begin.

'So . . . what do yer make o' that lot this mornin' then?' she whispered the second Sophie set foot through the door.

After quickly glancing over her shoulder to make sure that they were alone, Sophie shrugged. 'I'm not sure, to be honest. It sounded to me like Cathy had a false alarm, that's all.'

'Yer right. So why had they got themselves so worked up?'

'I've no idea,' Sophie admitted as Tilly began to throw the sheets into the bubbling water.

'I reckon soon as ever I get the chance I'm gonna nip upstairs an' see what's goin' on.'

Sophie didn't think this was such a good idea but already knew Tilly well enough to realise that it would be useless to try and put her off if her mind was made up. She made her way upstairs where she soon put the morning's happenings to the back of her mind as she wrestled with the sheets on the beds.

It was early in the afternoon when she suddenly began to feel nauseous, so much so that she knew she would have to risk going back to her room for a few minutes to rest. It was either that or risk being sick all across the clean beds, she decided, so clamping her hand across her mouth she scuttled away. The second she reached the top-floor landing she scurried into the bathroom where she was violently ill. When she emerged looking pale and drained some minutes later she was just in time to see Tilly disappearing into Cathy's room, and despite the fact that she felt as if she were dying, her curiosity got the better of her and she hastily followed.

They found Cathy lying huddled on the bed looking, as Tilly tactlessly put it, like death warmed up.

'So what's goin' on then?' she asked abruptly.

Cathy shrugged. 'Unfortunately it was a false alarm.'

Tilly shook her head sympathetically. 'Never mind, mate. It can't be much longer now. The little bugger's gorra put in an appearance sooner or later, ain't it?'

To their dismay, Cathy suddenly burst into tears. 'Oh Tilly, I'm so scared,' she sobbed as Tilly dropped down at the side of the bed and grasped her hand.

'Well, that's nowt to be ashamed of. I can't say as I'm much lookin' forward to the birth bit meself.'

'It's not that I'm afraid of, it's . . .'

'What then?' Tilly prompted.

Looking fearfully towards the door Cathy's voice dropped to a whisper. 'They put me in a room on the fourth floor.'

'*Yer what?* Yer mean they never took yer to a hospital?' Tilly was horrified and it sounded in her voice.

Cathy shook her head. 'I never even got to see a nurse or a doctor. When I asked them when they'd be takin' me to the hospital they just fobbed me off an' told me to stop worrying and then the pains just suddenly stopped. I've got an awful feeling that the baby will be delivered here when it does decide to come. But what if anything goes wrong?'

Tilly chewed on her lip as she tried to take in what Cathy was telling her. 'Yer must have it wrong,' she assured her eventually. 'Happen yer weren't far enough gone fer 'em to take yer in?'

Cathy's eyes were fearful as she stared up at the cracked ceiling. 'I hope you're right, Tilly. All the same I've got this bad feeling, so I have. There was a cot an' baby clothes all ready in the room. Why would they have them there if they intended me to give birth somewhere else? An' there was a young couple came to see me. Americans so they were.'

Tilly could find no answer and for a time they all fell silent until Sophie, who could sense that Cathy was close to panic, suddenly whispered, 'I think you're getting yourself into a state over nothing, Cathy. Really I do. Try to calm down. *Lots* of women have their babies at home. They were probably just waiting until you were well on your way before they brought the midwife in to you. But now we ought to be getting back to work, Tilly. What if Mrs Lewis decides to come and check on Cathy?'

Reluctantly rising from the side of the bed, Tilly gave Cathy's hand one last squeeze. 'I'll be back up as soon as I can,' she promised.

'Tilly . . . before you go could I ask you a favour?'

Turning back, Tilly nodded, 'O' course yer can. Ask away, mate.'

After fumbling in a drawer at the side of the bed Cathy withdrew her rosary beads and held them out to her. 'Would you mind looking after these for me until I'm ready to leave? 'Tis terrified I am that they'll go missing. I've had them all me life an' I'd hate to lose them, so I would.'

Feeling strangely honoured, Tilly looked down at the beads in her hand. The pearls that formed the main chain of the necklace had been fingered so many times that they were as smooth as silk and glinted in the glow from the lamp. Although she was no jeweller she saw at a glance that the cross and the clasp were made of solid gold.

'They'll be here waitin' for yer,' she promised as she slipped them into the deep pocket of her apron. Then the two girls hurried from the room and went back to work in a very subdued mood.

The atmosphere was no better in the kitchen later in the day as Sophie helped Mrs G to prepare the vegetables for the guests' evening meals. The woman seemed subdued and unusually snappy so Sophie went about her jobs silently. It was a relief when Tilly eventually breezed into the room like a breath of fresh air.

'Blimey, summat smells good,' she commented. 'I'm that bloody hungry I could eat a scabby horse.'

'Less of your swearing in my kitchen if you don't mind,' Mrs G scolded and Tilly winked at Sophie.

It was blatantly obvious that Mrs G hadn't taken to her, to say the very least, but her disapproval rolled off Tilly like water off a duck's back. The way she saw it she'd only be there for another couple of months at most and then the moaning old sod could go and take a running jump for all she cared. Her worries would be over then and she could go and start a new life with her Alfie. As Tilly thought of him a dreamy expression settled on her face and Sophie found herself grinning. Tilly was a right card by anyone's standards but Sophie liked her and wished with all her heart that she could be more like her. Nothing seemed to worry Tilly for long whereas she seemed to do nothing *but* worry.

When Mrs G slapped Tilly's dinner down in front of her, Tilly tucked into it as if she hadn't a care in the world and it was all Sophie could do to stop herself from laughing aloud. They were almost halfway through their meal when Mrs Lewis swept into the kitchen in a very agitated state.

Beckoning to Mrs G to follow her she led her to the far corner of the kitchen where they couldn't be overheard and started to whisper rapidly into her ear. In no time at all the cook had whipped off her apron and thrown it haphazardly across the back of a chair, then addressing the two girls at the table she barked at them, 'You two finish your meals and wash your pots up. Then you get yourselves away to your rooms and get yourselves an early night. I've something to do so I'll see you both down here in the morning and mind you're not late.'

With that she hurried from the room with Mrs Lewis close behind her, leaving the two girls to stare at each other in amazement.

'So, what were all that about then?' Tilly asked as she looked at the door that had just slammed shut behind them.

'I've no idea,' Sophie admitted and then as a thought

occurred to her, she muttered, 'Do you think it's anything to do with Cathy again?'

'I certainly bloody hope not, but then in this place yer never know what's goin' on, do yer? I mean, fink about it – this here fourth floor. There's Mrs G has a room there, Ben and his mother have their living quarters up there and that's where they took Cathy when they thought she was goin' into labour, not to mention that couple that arrived. Mr and Mrs Hamilton didn't yer say their name was? They've put *them* up there an' all—'

She would have said more but at that moment the door swung open again and Ben barged into the room with a face like thunder. When he studiously avoided Sophie yet again, her heart sank into her shoes. Not so long ago he had hinted that there might be some sort of future together for them once she'd had the baby, yet now it seemed that he could barely bring himself to look at her. It was all very confusing. Tilly's eyes followed him with unconcealed dislike as he fetched himself a glass of water from the sink. He drank half of it then flung the glass into the bowl before stamping back out of the room without so much as a word to either of them.

Seeing Sophie's downcast expression Tilly glared at her. 'Don't tell me he give *you* the old chat-up line an' all?'

The tears that sprang to Sophie's eyes were her answer; sighing, Tilly reached across the table and squeezed her hand. 'Oh love, yer didn't fall fer it, did yer? He does that to *all* the girls that end up here. Or them I've known of at least – includin' meself. He's a right smarmy, smooth-talkin' little bastard, you make no mistake about it. Don't get me wrong. I'm glad to be here 'cos it suits me to have the baby an' just walk away wiv no fuss an' palaver – but think about it. Why does he go wanderin' about the streets early every mornin', eh? It's to look fer girls like us who've fallen on hard times an' got theirselves into a mess. If you've lived here you'll know that Blackpool is full o' runaways all tryin' to find a way out. An' then along comes Ben an' he's like an answer to a prayer.'

Sophie pondered Tilly's words. She had to admit that there might be something in them, for hadn't she felt uneasy about the situation ever since she'd arrived? There was something not quite right here, although it was nothing that she could quite put her finger on.

'So, if you feel like that why are you here? Why don't you just get out?'

Tilly lowered her head as if she was struggling with something then suddenly she raised her eyes and Sophie was shocked to see the raw pain in them.

'I'm here 'cos till I've got rid o' this it's me best option,' she confided, patting her stomach. Seeing Sophie's confusion she decided to be honest with her. 'I suppose fer yer to understand I ought to start at the beginnin',' she said softly and then hesitantly she went on. 'As yer know I come from the East End. Me mam an' dad lived in a flat barely big enough to swing a cat round in. It didn't stop 'em churnin' kids out though, which is why I ended up wiv three bruvvers and three sisters. To be fair I'd have to say I didn't have an awful childhood but then when I were nearly ten me dad had a bad accident at work. He were a builder an' he come off a scaffold an' broke his back. He couldn't work after that an' that's when things started to go wrong. There were never enough money fer anythin' an' me mam an' dad seemed to be at each other's throats from mornin' till night. It got to the point when things were so bad I thought o' doin' a runner but then suddenly me mam started tartin' herself up an' goin' out of a night an' suddenly there were food on the table again an' things seemed to get easier. Round about the same time she started hittin' the bottle an' all, which weren't so good, but bein' so young I didn't put two an' two together. Then one night I woke up wiv a ragin' thirst on me so I got up to get meself a drink o' water an' caught me mam at it wiv a bloke right there in the middle o' the rug in the livin' room. Young as I were it all fell into place then an' I realised she were on the game. I tell yer I were so ashamed I thought I'd die, but then I got to thinkin', what choice did she really have? Our neighbourhood were rife wiv prostitutes an' after all me mam were doin' it fer us, weren't she?

'So, after that I just sort of accepted it an' it seemed natural when I got to me teens fer me to go on the game too. Everythin' were fine till I slipped up an' landed meself wiv this.' She stabbed a finger at her swollen stomach. 'I decided then it were time to get away so I waited till me mam had gone out one night an' headed fer the bus station. It just so happened that there was a bus there ready to pull out so I hitched a ride wiv the driver an' eventually I ended up 'ere. The rest yer can guess. I spent the first night here sleepin' under the pier an' the very next mornin' Ben comes strollin' along the beach and asked me if I needed any help.'

Sophie was horrified as she stared back at her friend. 'It must have been awful for you,' she muttered softly but Tilly merely grinned.

'No more so than it is fer you,' she pointed out. 'When I first got here I thought Ben was the best thing since sliced bread an' I'd have jumped through hoops fer him if he'd asked me to. But the nicey-nicey soon wore off an' that were when I started sneakin' out of a night an' met Alfie. An' now fer the first time in me whole life I really feel that I've got a bright future ahead o' me. I've told him everyfin' but he's happy to accept me as I am, warts an' all. Alfie is the kindest bloke I've ever met an' I just *know* we'll be happy together soon as this is over.'

Her eyes bright with unshed tears, Sophie went and hugged Tilly soundly. For all she made herself out to be a little hard nut she was as soft as butter underneath and Sophie knew that they would become firm friends. She was what her mother would have termed a rough diamond. 'Come on,' she urged. 'Let's get this washing-up done and hit the sack. I don't know about you but I'm about dead on my feet.'

'Not bloody likely, you can hit the sack if yer like but I've got other plans fer this evenin'.' Swiping her runny nose along the sleeve of her cardigan, Tilly rose and started to carry the dirty pots to the sink and there for a time they worked side by side in a companionable silence.

Outside in the hallway out of earshot of the girls, Mrs G rounded furiously on the other woman. 'Haven't I told you time and time again that I want nothing to do with what's going on up there?' she barked, jabbing a plump finger towards the ceiling.

Amanda Lewis's hands twisted together convulsively as she looked back at her imploringly. 'And nor do I involve you but . . .' She struggled for the right words. 'There's something wrong. She started again a couple of hours ago, pains every few minutes but nothing seems to be happening.'

Arms akimbo, Mrs G glared at her. 'Then you'll have to get the poor lass off to the hospital, won't you, Amanda?'

Mrs Lewis loked horrified. The older woman only ever called her by her first name when she was greatly agitated, which she clearly was now. She had no time to answer however, for now the woman was leaning towards her with her eyes flashing fire.

'I will not, do you hear me? *Not* be drawn into this.'

'But the baby? Mr and Mrs Hamilton were expecting to leave today with it.'

'Well, they won't be able to, will they? And whose fault is that, eh?'

At that moment, Ben appeared from the deserted dining room, and just as they always did at the sight of him the older woman's eyes softened. 'I was just telling your mother that she'll have to think of getting Cathy off to the hospital,' she informed him.

As his mother had moments before he shook his head. 'We can't do that – you *know* we can't.' His voice became wheedling as he draped his arm about her broad old shoulders. 'Couldn't you come upstairs and take a peep at her . . . just for me?'

When indecision showed in her wrinkled face he played on her emotions. 'If you don't, we could lose the baby.'

It seemed for a moment that he had won her over but then suddenly she shook her head and headed for the stairs as if the devil himself were after her. 'You know I'd do anything for you, Ben. But not this. I told you I'd never be involved and I meant it. I'm sorry – you're on your own.'

As Ben and his mother watched her walk away, his mother's shoulders sagged. 'What are we going to do now?'

'Whatever has to be done,' he replied coldly, then pushing his mother in the direction the older woman had just taken, he told her, 'Get yourself off to your room. I'll deal with it and I'll fetch you when it's over.'

'But, *Ben*—'

'*Go.*' His voice brooked no argument and without a word she hurried away as he squared his shoulders and prepared himself for what was ahead.

As Sophie and Tilly entered the landing that led to their rooms, they were just in time to see Cathy emerging from her room leaning heavily on Ben's arm.

Keeping her eyes downcast, Cathy allowed him to lead her past them without a word and when the door at the end of the corridor had closed behind them, Tilly whistled through her teeth. 'Bleedin' 'ell. Did yer see the state she were in? She were as pale as a bloody ghost, poor little cow. She must have gone into labour proper this time.'

Sophie nodded in agreement. 'It did look that way, but she didn't have a bag or anything with her. Where do you think he's taking her?'

'Back to the fourth floor if what she said earlier were anyfin' to go by.' Tilly's voice was heavy with concern as they stood looking at each other helplessly.

'Oh well, at least it should be over soon,' Sophie said. 'Perhaps they have a midwife who'll come in to see to her?'

'Let's bloody hope so. Anyway, I'm off to get ready. I'm meetin' my Alfie tonight an' if I don't get a move on I'll be late.'

'Do you think that's wise? What I mean is – Ben and Mrs Lewis could be coming up to fetch things that Cathy might need. What if they check on us and you're not there?'

'Tough. If they do an' they start a ruckus then I'll be out of here like a shot,' Tilly replied firmly. 'To tell the truth I'm seein' things as I ain't too keen on an' the way I'm feelin' at the minute I could walk away from this set-up wivout a second thought, baby or not.' With that she flounced off to her room leaving Sophie to gaze thoughtfully after her.

It was the early hours of the morning when Sophie was wakened by someone gently shaking her arm. She blinked in the darkness and then started when she saw Tilly leaning over her.

'*Sssh,* and listen.' Hearing the note of urgency in Tilly's voice, Sophie pulled herself up onto her elbow and did as she was told.

'I can't hear anything,' she murmured after a few moments and Tilly straightened and started to pace up and down the room.

'I could have swore I heard someone screamin',' she fretted.

Swinging her legs out of the warm bed, Sophie padded across to her and placed her arm comfortingly round her shoulder.

'It's probably just your mind working overtime,' she soothed.

Tilly's head wagged from side to side in denial. 'I ain't lost me marbles yet, an' I'm tellin' yer, I heard someone. Yer don't fink it's Cathy, do yer?'

'I shouldn't think so. Though even if it was from what

I've heard it's quite normal for some women to scream when they're giving birth.'

Tilly's shoulders sagged. 'I suppose yer right. But I just feel so bloody useless stuck up here. Do yer think she's all right?'

'I'm sure she will be,' Sophie reassured her, then glancing at the small clock on her bedside table she gave a rueful grin. 'Why don't you go back to bed and try to get some sleep? I hate to tell you this but in three hours' time we've got to be at work all bright-eyed and bushy-tailed.'

Seeing the sense in what she said, Tilly reluctantly headed for the door. 'I s'pose yer right. I'll see yer in the mornin' then.'

Once the door had clicked softly closed behind her, Sophie leaned back on her pillows and strained to listen in the darkness. What if Tilly had been right and she *had* heard Cathy crying out? She sighed; there was nothing she could do even if she had so perhaps it would be best if she followed her own advice and got back off to sleep. Turning onto her side she pulled the blankets tightly about her, but she was on edge and try as she might sleep eluded her.

Eventually she got out of bed again and crossed to the window where she gazed across the rooftops to the sea in the distance. She had thought that coming here would be the answer to all her problems, but as time passed she realised more and more that her life would never be the same again. She would never get over the dreadful thing that her father had done to her, and she would have to live with the consequences of it for the rest of her life, because even when she had given the baby she was carrying away, it would always be there, somewhere, to haunt her. It was a daunting thought.

Chapter Eight

At ten to six the following morning, Sophie tapped lightly on Tilly's door and when there was no response she tentatively pushed it open. Instantly, her face broke into a grin. Tilly was lying fast asleep in a tangle of bedclothes with her swollen stomach reaching into the air like a mini mountain. So much for her concern, Sophie thought to herself; it certainly hadn't stopped her from going out like a light!

Tiptoeing across the room she gently shook her friend's arm and urged, 'Come on, Tilly, it's nearly six o' clock.'

'Whaaa . . . ?' Tilly yawned and stretched before yanking the bedclothes over her head again. 'Go away, I ain't had a lorra sleep an' I'm dead on me feet.'

Sophie chuckled. 'Well, you shouldn't be out till all hours then tripping the light fantastic. I'll go down and put the kettle on and if you know what's good for you you'll be joining me before the tea's mashed.'

When there was no response she let herself back out onto the landing before beginning the long descent down the stairs. It was as she reached the fourth-floor landing and was turning the twist in the stairs that she heard something that made her pause with her foot in mid-air. Leaning heavily on the banister rail she stared back at the door that led to the rooms there and sure enough there it was again, but unmistakable this time: the sound of a baby crying.

Her breath caught in her throat, but at that moment the door was suddenly flung open and Ben appeared. Unshaven, with his clothes dishevelled, he glared at her. 'What do you think you're doing standing there?'

'I . . . I was just on my way to the kitchen,' she stammered.

'Right, well get to it, then.'

Nodding, she almost fell down the stairs in her haste to get away from him.

She found the kitchen deserted so after clicking the light on she filled the kettle then set it on the gas ring to boil. Next she raked out the ashes and threw some coal onto the dying fire before beginning to lay the enormous scrubbed pine table that dominated the centre of the room for the staff's breakfast.

She was halfway through her task when Mrs G appeared, and it was soon very evident that, just like Ben, she was very far from her usually good-humoured self. Ben followed her into the room seconds later; from the corner of her eye Sophie saw him nod almost imperceptibly at her. The colour immediately drained out of Mrs G's face as if by magic and she clung to the edge of the table with one hand while making the sign of the cross on her chest with the other. Sophie frowned. What was wrong with everyone this morning? Thankfully, Tilly burst into the kitchen at that moment and an air of normality returned.

'Where the hell have you been?' Mrs G snapped.

Flashing her a cheeky grin, Tilly retorted, 'I've been puttin' me slap on. Yer wouldn't want me lookin' anyfin' less than me best would yer? Christ, if the guests saw me wivout it they'd run a mile.'

Tutting, Mrs G flung herself away from the table. It was more than obvious that she didn't like Tilly at the best of times but this morning she made no attempt to hide it.

'Just get the frying pan out an' make yourself useful for a change can't you?' she snapped, then with a swish of her voluminous white apron she disappeared into the huge walk-in pantry. Letting out a long sigh, Sophie began to carve the large crusty loaf on the table. One thing was for sure – it didn't look set to be a very good day at all.

By late morning, Sophie's assumption had been proven true a dozen times over. Every time she so much as looked at Mrs G, the cook snapped her head off and Sophie began to wish she could just walk away from her and the hotel and never see either of them again. In fact, by lunchtime she was in two minds to do just that, but common sense prevailed. After all, where would she go?

Matters had been made worse by the fact that she

hadn't had a chance to talk to Tilly alone all morning. On the two occasions when she had gone to the laundry laden down with dirty washing, either Mrs Lewis or Ben had been there, both in as bad a mood as Mrs G.

Lunch was a solemn affair with just herself and Mrs G in the kitchen. For some reason Tilly had failed to put in an appearance, which was strange in itself. As Sophie had discovered very quickly, Tilly had an appetite that would have done justice to one of the donkeys on the beach.

At one point she nearly asked Mrs G where her friend might have got to, but then she thought better of it. It could only make things worse if Mrs G found out that they were becoming close. So she sat there, moving her food around the plate until Mrs G suddenly stood up and snatched the plate away.

'Oh, just *leave* it for goodness' sake. It's more than obvious that you're not going to eat it. I sometimes wonder why I bother to cook for you at all!'

Sophie rose from the table without a word and quietly left the kitchen. The instant she had gone, Mrs G slammed the plate back onto the table as tears flooded her eyes. Why had she had to go and take her bad mood out on Sophie? She pushed the answer away immediately. She was becoming too fond of the girl and that was dangerous. She could shut her mind to what went on in the hotel with most of the girls who arrived there. Most of them got what they asked for, like that little trollop, Tilly. But Sophie? She seemed different somehow; naïve and innocent.

Sinking down onto the hard wooden chair, Mrs G buried her face in her hands and sobbed. If only Amanda wasn't so . . . she searched for the right word. Unstable: that was it. Sometimes it was as if Ben was the parent and Amanda the child. Oh, she was good at coming across as the efficient landlady, but Mrs G knew the truth. She could be bright as a button one minute and raving like a March hare the next. Again she wondered, *When is it all going to end? When will they call a stop to what is going on here?*

Sophie's steps were heavy as she climbed the stairs. Her shoulders were stooped and in that moment she would have given anything for a glimpse of her beloved mother's face. Her loss was still uppermost in her mind and she still would often cry herself to sleep as she thought of her. Each time she did, her thoughts moved on to the child growing inside her; somehow she was beginning to feel that what had happened was all the child's fault. Common sense told her that it had all started on the night her father had raped her, but he was gone now and so the blame had shifted to the baby. If she could have torn it from inside her she would gladly have done so. But she knew that was impossible so she was trying desperately to get through the next few months until she could be shot of it and all that it stood for.

As she pushed the door to her room open her eyes rested on the chest of drawers that housed her few meagre possessions. Beneath her underwear was the address of her aunt, which her mother had given her on the night she had left home. Sometimes she wondered if she shouldn't just run away, turn up on her doorstep and throw herself on her aunt's mercy? But pride always stopped her. So, the only sensible alternative was to stay here until it was all over. Perhaps then she would have the courage to go and introduce herself. The way things were going she was aware that she might not have much choice, for any thoughts of a future relationship with Ben had flown out of the window. Sometimes it seemed to be all he could do to speak to her civilly, but then if what Tilly had told her was true she was just one of many young girls he had lured here. Now that she had got used to the fact, it no longer hurt her. After all, weren't they both using each other?

Sighing heavily, she rinsed her face in the ceramic washbowl on the chest of drawers then after tugging a comb through her thick hair she made for the door again. There were still three bedrooms on the second floor waiting to be made up and the sooner she started them the sooner she would be finished.

She had just reached the fourth floor when the door to the rooms suddenly swung open and she almost collided with someone. Hands reached out to steady her and she looked up into the eyes of the young woman she had seen arrive with her husband some days ago. Sophie had forgotten all about her but now she smiled at her hesitantly.

'I'm so sorry.'

'No, please don't be.' The young woman's eyes were kindly. 'It was my fault entirely. Are you all right?'

'Perfectly, thank you.'

The young woman dropped her hands and now glanced nervously across her shoulder to the closed door. 'I . . . I was just on my way to the foyer,' she told Sophie, as if she owed her some sort of explanation. Sensing the tension in the air Sophie nodded and stood aside to let her pass. The woman clattered away down the stairs and after a moment Sophie followed at a more leisurely pace on her way to the second-floor bedrooms.

By mid-afternoon the bedrooms were all done and dusted so, heaving the pile of dirty laundry into her arms, Sophie manoeuvred it downstairs and headed for the laundry room.

'This is the last lot for today, Tilly.' She frowned as she gazed around the empty room and deposited the washing in an untidy heap on the floor next to the copper. The door into the yard was swinging open in the breeze and as she looked towards it the frown was replaced by a grin. I bet she's nipped out for a crafty fag, she thought to herself, and hesitantly approached the door and peeped into the yard. Seeing no sign of her, Sophie crept to the corner and looked towards the gate; sure enough there was Tilly, deep in conversation with a good-looking young man who put her in mind of a gipsy. He was holding the hand of a copper-haired little girl.

As she watched, Tilly sank to her knees and wrapped the child, who appeared to be no more than two years old, in a firm embrace, then when she stood back up, Sophie saw her slip something into the man's hand.

Sophie hovered uncertainly. She had no wish to appear as if she was spying on her, but if she turned now and Tilly saw her it would look all the more suspicious.

'Tilly . . . is everything all right?'

Tilly's head snapped round and when she saw Sophie standing there a mixture of emotions flitted across her face: firstly fear closely followed by a look of sheer relief.

Turning back to the man she whispered something urgently to him, then after hastily bending to kiss the child, who Sophie saw now was absolutely adorable, she closed the gate and hurried over to Sophie.

Seeing the questions in Sophie's eyes she held up her hand. 'Look, please don't ask me to explain right now. I promise I'll tell yer everyfin' tonight when we're back in our rooms. Fer now though we'd better get about our business afore we're missed, eh? An' Sophie . . .' She grasped her arm and Sophie was shocked to see how pale she was. 'Yer won't get sayin' owt about what yer just saw, will yer?'

'Of course I won't,' Sophie snapped indignantly as side by side they hurried back into the laundry room.

Mrs Lewis was just entering from the other door with her arms full of yet more dirty sheets and when she saw the two girls enter together her cheeks flamed with anger. 'Just *what* the hell is going on here?'

'It's all right, missus. She were just helpin' me to hang out some o' the sheets seein' as she's finished her jobs,' Tilly gabbled.

Accepting her explanation Mrs Lewis's colour receded a little. 'Well, I'm sure that Mrs G will find her something to keep her busy in the kitchen,' she snapped. 'Or is the job becoming too much for you, Tilly?'

'Oh no, missus,' Tilly assured her quickly.

'Very well then. Get yourself off, Sophie. And I do *not* expect to find this happening again. Have I made myself quite clear?'

'Yes, missus,' the two girls chorused as Sophie scuttled towards the door like a frightened rabbit. As she rushed into the foyer she was just in time to see Ben disappearing out of the hotel entrance with the young woman she had bumped into earlier in the day. Her husband was close behind her carrying a large suitcase in each hand and Sophie was surprised to see that the woman was carrying a bundle closely wrapped in a snow-white shawl. She realised with a little shock, as she saw the woman glance down adoringly at it, that it was a baby. But surely they hadn't had a baby when they arrived? She would have seen it.

She slewed to a halt as a possibility occurred to her. Could it be that the baby she was holding was Cathy's? Was this the couple who were going to adopt it? If she was right then Cathy might well be back in her room packing ready to leave right now.

Changing direction with no thought of the roasting she would no doubt get from Mrs G for being late she charged up the stairs two at a time. By the time she reached the top she was breathless but without pausing she raced to Cathy's door and firmly rapped on it. Only silence answered her, so cautiously she inched it open and peeped inside. It was empty, exactly as Cathy had left it. Her half-packed bags were still placed at the side of the door and the sheets were thrown back as if she had just climbed out of bed. Sophie stared around. Every instinct she had told her that something was wrong, but then if Cathy had only recently given birth she was probably still resting.

Closing the door softly, she made her way back to the kitchen. This was turning out to be a funny old day one way and another.

After their evening meal the girls, who were both glad of a chance to escape the gloomy atmosphere, excused themselves from the kitchen and retired to the top floor. Once they were there and sure that they were alone, Tilly sneaked into Sophie's room and quickly closed the door behind her.

There was so much to discuss that neither of them quite knew where to begin but Tilly started the conversation when she blurted out, 'That last load o' beddin' that the missus brought in while you were in the laundry room were sheets, an' they were *covered* in blood. There were no amount o' scrubbin' would get 'em clean so I've left 'em to soak in some bleach in the copper till mornin'. Do yer reckon that Cathy's had the babby an' it were *her* blood?'

Tilly's voice trembled with fear and Sophie noticed that her hands were shaking.

Solemnly, Sophie nodded. 'Yes I do. This afternoon I saw Ben disappearing out of the hotel with the Hamiltons, that American couple that Mrs Lewis put on the fourth floor. He was carrying their cases so they were obviously leaving, but the thing is . . . she was carrying a baby, which is strange because I saw them arriving too and they didn't have a baby with them then. In fact, if you remember, I thought they might be on their honeymoon.'

'Do yer fink it might have bin Cathy's baby?' Tilly choked.

When Sophie nodded, Tilly crossed her arms tightly about her chest and began to pace back and forth in the confines of the small room, a habit Sophie had noticed she adopted when she was nervous. 'So where the bleedin' hell is Cathy then?'

'Well, she's probably still resting somewhere. If what she told us when she had her false alarm is anything to go by then she could be right here in the hotel on the fourth floor.'

'But do you think she's all right?'

'I can't see why not,' Sophie replied, not wishing to panic Tilly any more than she already was. 'It's normal for someone who's just given birth to stay in bed and rest for a few days, so all being well we should see her up here again soon when she comes to collect her things.' For the moment her thoughts turned from Cathy to the man and the child she had seen Tilly talking to at the gate and now she asked, 'Who was that man you were talking to outside earlier on?'

Tilly's cheeks flamed until they matched the colour of her hair and for a while she hesitated. But there was something about Sophie that made her feel she could trust her so dropping onto the edge of the bed she sighed.

'It were my Alfie.' Just the mention of his name made her face momentarily light up, but then she became sombre again and crossing to the window she stood gazing out, unable to meet Sophie's eyes.

'And the little girl?' Sophie probed gently.

'That . . . was Rachel.'

Sophie waited patiently until eventually Tilly turned from the window and told her, 'Rachel is my little girl.'

'*What?*' Shock made Sophie's voice uneven as she stared incredulously back at her.

Tilly had the good grace to blush. 'The thing is . . .' she stammered, 'I ain't bin entirely honest wiv yer. Or what I should say is, I ain't exactly *lied*, I just didn't tell yer everyfin'.'

Turning away from the window she went and sank onto the side of the bed as she sighed heavily. 'I told yer that when I lived in London I were on the game an' that much was true. When I found out I'd fallen fer Rachel I looked at me mam an' I saw meself in a few years' time wiv a string o' kids round me neck all to different blokes. I knew then that I wanted better than that so I cleared off an' fer a time I lived in this awful dingy little basement bedsit. I decided that as soon as the baby came I'd give it up fer adoption an' start a new life somewhere else. Trouble was, the minute I set eyes on her I knew I couldn't part wiv her, so I was as bad burnt as scalded. I had to feed her an' put a roof over our heads but there ain't many jobs you can do when you've got a babby to care for so in the end I had no choice but to go back on the game.

'I started savin' every penny I could so that by the time she were a bit older I could move to somewhere nicer an' give her the sort o' life she deserved. But then I went an' got pregnant again an' I didn't know what to do fer the best. I couldn't very well go to the Welfare an' ask fer help, could I? Once they discovered I was a prostitute they'd no doubt have taken Rachel off me an' I couldn't bear that so I got on a train an' brought her to Blackpool where no one knew us. I didn't *really* sleep under the pier when I first got here.' She glanced at Sophie apologetically. 'I actually landed on me feet 'cos I found lodgin's wiv this lovely widow lady, Mrs McGregor, in Waterloo Road. She took to Rachel like a duck to water an' soon after I met Alfie. I'd gone out for a stroll one evenin' an he were outside the Pleasure Beach an' he chatted me up. I knew straight off he were the one fer me. He didn't mind me havin' one nipper but he wasn't too keen about takin' on another one so when I bumped into Ben it were like an answer to a prayer. The lady I were lodgin' wiv agreed to take care o' Rachel till this is all over. Out o' the money I saved in London I pay her her keep each week an' that's where I go every night. To see her, yer see? An' sometimes Alfie too, o' course.'

'Oh, Tilly!' Instead of being disgusted with her as Tilly had feared she would be, Sophie's heart went out to her. 'What a *rotten* time you've had of it.'

Tilly shrugged. 'No more than most I suppose. Trouble is this is the only way out fer me now. If I go to the Welfare Department an' tell 'em I don't want this baby they might try to take Rachel away from me too an' if I lost her I fink it would kill me. I love her so much, Sophie.'

Sophie could see the sense in what she said. 'But how will you feel when this baby is born if you couldn't part with Rachel? Isn't there a chance that you might want to keep this one too?'

Tilly shook her head. 'No. When I had Rachel I had no one else in the whole world, but now I've got her an' Alfie an' a whole new life waitin' fer me. If I keep this one an' all . . . Well, I won't be able to do me best fer Rachel an' I have to make her me priority. It won't be easy though.'

Sophie put her arms about her and kissed her soundly on the cheek. 'I hope everything works out for you,' she told her and she meant it from the bottom of her heart.

Downstairs in the kitchen, Mrs G had her feet propped up on the brass fender and a glass of sherry in her hand. As far as she was concerned, this was the best time of the day, when all the work was done and she had the kitchen to herself. It didn't last for long, however, for Ben suddenly strode into the room and put the kettle on to boil before beginning to prepare a tray.

Instantly a feeling of dread settled around her like a thick black cloud.

'That for your mother, is it?'

When he shook his head the feeling intensified. Without a word she watched him spoon tea leaves into the pot then place a cup and saucer on the tray. She so wanted to talk to him but panic kept her silent. Once the kettle was singing on the hob he poured the bubbling water into the pot. Then just as she had feared he took a small glass bottle from his pocket and shook a few drops into the tea before stirring it vigorously and placing the lid and the tea cosy on it.

'How is Cathy doing?' She knew that she shouldn't ask but suddenly the words just popped out anyway.

When he glared at her sullenly her heart sank. 'Ask no questions and I'll tell you no lies.'

'Oh, Ben, *please*—'

He silenced her with a glance as he began to carry the tray towards the door. 'We shall need you to watch the hotel for a time this evening,' he told her coldly over his shoulder. 'Mother and I have to go out.' Then he was gone and she was left there with tears streaming down her cheeks as she made the sign of the cross.

It was about to happen again and she didn't know how she would bear it.

Almost an hour later as Sophie lay on her bed staring at the ceiling pondering Tilly's confession, there came a tap to the door and Ben looked into the room.

'I've just come up to tell you that Mother and I will be going out this evening,' he informed her shortly. 'If you need anything Mrs G will be downstairs.'

'I'm sure I won't, but thank you for telling me,' Sophie replied equally coolly and he disappeared the way he had come without so much as another word.

It was funny, now that she came to think about it, that she had ever found him attractive in the first place. All she saw when she looked at him these days was a very spoiled, mammy-pampered, self-centred young man. Even his American accent grated on her nerves now. Not that it mattered. Like Tilly, she now had no intention of staying here a second longer than she had to. Just as soon as the baby was born she would be gone and good riddance to the place. After the long days of being confined to the hotel the walls felt as if they were beginning to close in on her and she longed to walk along the seafront and feel the wind in her hair and the rain on her face.

That wish at least was soon to be granted her when only minutes later Tilly appeared in the doorway. She had backcombed her hair until it almost stood on end and her face was covered in a heavy layer of panstick make-up, which in contrast to her ruby-red lips made her look desperately pale.

Despite her bold appearance she looked at Sophie with apprehension. 'Are we still mates then?' she ventured timidly.

'Of course we are. Why wouldn't we be?' Sophie re-assured her.

Tilly visibly relaxed and in a second the twinkle was back in her eye.

'How's about that fer a bit o' good luck then, eh?' she piped chirpily. 'Now they're out o' the way we could go out fer an hour. Yer know what they say, while the cat's away the mice will play.'

'Oh yes, and where is it we could be going?'

Tilly hesitated before blurting out, 'I thought yer might like to come an' meet Rachel. Proper like?'

Sophie was deeply touched and somehow felt that an honour had just been bestowed on her. 'I'd love to,' she admitted. 'But won't we be pushing our luck? I mean – what happens if Mrs Lewis and Ben come back early?'

'They won't do that,' Tilly replied confidently. 'I weren't thinkin' o' bein' gone fer hours anyway – so what do yer say?'

Faced with yet another night of staying in staring at the walls, Tilly's offer was too tempting to resist. Getting off the bed, Sophie hastily tidied herself up and pulled her coat on. 'You're on,' she laughed and like partners in crime the two girls hurried along the landing to wrestle with the sash-cord window that led to the fire escape in Tilly's room.

In no time at all they were on the pavement outside. Sophie took a great gulp of the bracing air and sighed with relief then Tilly grabbed her elbow and started to haul her along.

'You'll like Mrs McGregor,' Tilly told her. 'She's got loads o' kids of her own, poor cow. Her husband died last year an' between you an' me I reckon she finds it hard to make ends meet, which is why she's so glad o' the money I give her to keep Rachel.'

Avoiding the seafront for fear of being seen she led Sophie through a labyrinth of back streets as if she had lived in Blackpool all her life and soon they emerged into Waterloo Road.

'Not much further now,' she said breathlessly. 'Mrs McGregor lives in one o' the flats above the florist's.'

A little further along the road she skirted round the shops to the back of the buildings before beginning to climb a metal staircase that led up from a very dark yard. Once at the top of it she banged on the door and seconds later it was flung open by a petite, fair-haired woman who had a child hanging on her skirt and a toddler in her arms.

'Ah, Tilly. Come away in. It's right pleased Rachel will be to see you, so it will. An' who's this lass then?'

'This is Sophie, me mate,' Tilly introduced them but there was no time to say any more, for suddenly the little copper-haired girl that Sophie had seen at the back gate of the hotel appeared in a doorway behind the woman and hurtled towards Tilly on stocky little legs.

'*Mammy.*'

For a moment it was hard to tell who was kissing who and Sophie was touched as she saw the child's genuine delight at seeing her mother. Tilly swung her up into her arms and held onto her as if she was never going to let her go until the woman scolded them. 'Will you get yerselves in out o' the cold now? You're lettin' all the heat out, so you are.'

'Sorry.' Tilly came forward then kicked the door shut with her foot before beckoning Sophie to follow her into the living room. For a moment, Sophie thought she'd stepped into a kindergarten, for there seemed to be children of all ages, shapes and sizes, and toys wherever she looked.

'Excuse the mess, lass,' Mrs McGregor said.

Sophie smiled at her. 'Please don't apologise. It's lovely, all sort of cosy and lived-in.'

'Oh, it's certainly that.' The woman swiped a stray lock of hair from her eyes and grinned ruefully. ''Tis not much point in tryin' to tidy till I've got them all off to bed though why I bother I'll never know. Come the mornin' when they all get up again it's as untidy as ever in no time. Not that I'm complaining. Sure, I wouldn't have it any other way.'

As Sophie looked around she saw that it was in fact a charming room and absolutely huge. Easy chairs were dotted here and there and a welcoming fire, protected by a large fireguard, was roaring up the chimney.

All the while the interchange was going on Tilly held Rachel close and as Sophie looked across at them she saw why Tilly loved the child so much. She was absolutely beautiful with great green eyes that could have charmed the birds from the trees and hair that hung to her chubby little shoulders in copper-coloured curls.

''Ere, missus. Will you help me wi' me jigsaw?'

Sophie found herself looking down into the face of a little boy who appeared to be about six or seven. He was dressed in little pyjamas and his face was freshly scrubbed.

'Now Jimmy. Don't go being rude to our guest now,' Mrs McGregor scolded.

'Oh, he isn't,' Sophie assured her. 'And yes, Jimmy. I'd love to help you with your jigsaw.' She flung her coat off and in no time at all she was down on her knees helping him fit the puzzle together. For the next hour she enjoyed herself more than she had for ages.

It was Tilly who eventually told her, 'I reckon we'd better be thinkin' o' gettin' back now, Sophie.'

Reluctantly, Sophie stood up and smoothed her skirt over her hips.

Rachel clung to her mother as tears started to her eyes. 'No go, Mammy.'

Instantly Mrs McGregor took control of the situation when she swung the child up into her arms and kissed her soundly. 'Now then, Rachel. Mammy has to go to bed an' so do you. But sure, she'll be back to see you again tomorrow, won't you, Mammy? An' in the meantime we've a story to read, so we have.'

Slightly placated, the child jammed her thumb in her mouth as Sophie struggled into her coat.

'Thank you so much for having me, Mrs McGregor,' she said. 'You've got a lovely family here.'

'Aye, well I won't be arguing with that, lass, so I won't,

an' make sure you come to see us again. It seems you've found an admirer in my Jimmy here.'

Sophie grinned as she tousled Jimmy's hair then reluctantly she and Tilly made their way to the door.

As they clattered away down the metal stairs making enough noise to waken the dead, Sophie sighed contentedly. 'Rachel is lovely,' she said and Tilly's chest puffed with pride. 'Yer don't need to tell me that,' she agreed. '*Now* do yer see why I need to get this over wiv?'

'Of course I do.'

They ceased talking as they hurried through the back streets. The wind had picked up and was howling down the alleys and a misty drizzle had begun to fall that soon had them wet through.

Sophie was relieved when they silently let themselves in through the back gate and crept up the fire escape. The net curtain was flapping out through Tilly's partially open window and Sophie held it aside as Tilly clumsily climbed back into the room, then she followed, her cheeks glowing from the time spent in the fresh air.

'I'll see you in the morning,' she whispered as she headed for her own room. 'And thanks, Tilly, for taking me I mean. Mrs McGregor is a lovely woman and Rachel is absolutely adorable.'

A wide smile was Tilly's only answer as she began to peel off her wet clothes.

Once she was back in her own room, Sophie quickly changed into her nightshirt and climbed into the lumpy bed, shuddering as the cold cotton sheets settled around her legs. And there she lay reliving every happy moment she had spent at Mrs McGregor's home before finally falling asleep feeling contented for the first time since she had been there.

Chapter Nine

'Come on sleepy'ead. It'll be dinnertime at this rate.'

As Sophie's eyes struggled open she became aware of Tilly standing in the doorway with her arms wrapped round her chest. 'It's enough to freeze the 'airs off a bleedin' brass monkey up here,' she complained. 'Nobody would ever believe it were nearly the end of April. Get yerself dressed an' I'll go an' get the kettle on. I've had an awful night. This one 'ere has bin kickin' the livin' daylights out o' me since the early hours. Thank Christ I've only got a few more weeks to go. I must be black an' blue on the inside.'

Sophie yawned and stretched. She had slept soundly for a change and was reluctant to get out of the warm blankets. When Tilly had gone she got out of bed and shrugged her arms into her thick candlewick dressing gown. Just as Tilly had said, it *was* cold up here. The wind seemed to find every opening it could and the curtains were moving faintly in the draught from the window. Grabbing her wash bag she hurried along the landing and had a hasty wash.

On her way back a thought occurred to her and she paused outside Cathy's room. Would she be back in there yet? Deciding that there was only one way to find out, she tapped softly on the door. Only silence answered her so, shrugging, she went on her way.

There was no sign of Mrs G when she entered the kitchen some minutes later, which was strange to say the least. Usually she was the first one up in the morning.

A large pot of tea was mashing in the middle of the table and Tilly was bent over the fire toasting bread on a long wooden toasting fork.

'So where do you think Mrs G has got to?' Sophie asked as she spooned sugar into two cups.

Tilly shrugged. 'I ain't got the foggiest idea an' I don't much care if yer want the truth. It takes the miserable old cow all her time to be civil to me anyway. Not like you, you're her blue eyes.'

'I am *not*,' Sophie told her indignantly but then seeing the amusement in Tilly's eyes she softened.

'Well, I suppose she can be a bit hard on you,' she admitted and then they fell silent as Tilly joined her at the table and they started to spread home-made jam onto their toast.

'At least the snap here is good,' Tilly muttered as she licked away a dribble of butter that had slid down her chin. Leaning towards Sophie she glanced at the door before asking, 'So, you enjoyed yerself last night then?'

'Oh yes. I really did. And Rachel is absolutely lovely. I can see why you love her so much. You must be counting the days until you can be with her again. I know I would be if she were mine.'

'You ain't wrong there.' There was such a wealth of sorrow in Tilly's voice that Sophie's kind heart went out to her. Life can be cruel, she said to herself as she thought of their situation. Neither of them wanted to be here and yet they both were through no fault of their own.

As if talking of Mrs G had conjured her up out of thin air, she suddenly appeared in the doorway and at a glance both girls saw that she looked absolutely dreadful. Her eyes were sunk deep into their sockets and there were bags under her eyes that they could have done their shopping in.

'Not had a good night, Mrs G?' Sophie asked sympathetically as she pulled another cup towards her and started to pour the woman some tea.

'Huh! That's an understatement if ever there was one.'

Dropping heavily onto a chair, Mrs G took the tea without a word and stared morosely into the fire. The rest of the meal was eaten in silence. The girls washed their dirty pots up then, glad of an excuse to escape the gloomy atmosphere, they left the room to start their jobs, closing the door behind them.

'I wonder what's up wiv her then?'

Sophie shook her head. 'Probably just had a bad night?'

At the bottom of the stairs they parted company, Tilly off to the laundry room and Sophie up the back stairs to begin the rooms on the second floor. Soon they were so busy that for the rest of the morning they forgot about Mrs G.

At lunchtime Tilly went to her room to fetch a clean handkerchief and while she was up there she looked into Cathy's room. Everything she owned was now packed in brown paper carrier bags with string handles and placed at the side of the door. The sight lifted her spirits. She must be comin' back to collect 'em today then, she thought, and hurried down to dinner intent on telling Sophie the good news.

The mood in the kitchen was no better and Sophie flashed her a warning glance the second she set foot through the door, evidently cautioning her to watch what she said. Mrs G was stamping about like a bear with a sore head and almost snapped the girls' heads off every time they so much as opened their mouths. In the end they both fell silent and kept their eyes fixed on their plates.

As they were leaving the room Tilly plucked up her courage to innocently ask, 'Will Cathy be comin' to collect her things today, Mrs G?'

The colour suddenly drained from Mrs G's face as she leaned heavily on the table while she composed herself. 'How should I know? I'm not her keeper, am I? And anyway, what business is it of yours? You just worry about yourself, my girl, and keep your nose out of what doesn't concern you!'

'*Sorry*, I'm sure,' Tilly sniffed indignantly, then flounced out of the room slamming the door resoundingly behind her.

Mrs Lewis entered the kitchen some time later to find Mrs G in a right old state. 'What's the matter with you?' she asked, taking in her red-rimmed eyes at a glance.

'What the hell do you *think* is the matter with me?' Mrs G hissed. 'I'll tell you now, Amanda. I don't know how much more of this I can take. It's playing on my nerves something terrible. It's not right! When is it going to end? You and Ben told me that you almost had enough money to retire on months ago, so when are you going to call a stop to it? You're not well, you know you're not . . . and all this stress can't be doing you any good at all.'

A finely plucked eyebrow was raised to the ceiling as Mrs Lewis sighed deeply. Her first instinct was to shout back but then she decided to try another tack. After all, they needed to keep the woman sweet at all costs. Amanda wasn't sure how she would cope without her.

'I'm quite well at present, I assure you,' she said quietly. 'I can't help it if I live on my nerves, can I? But I suppose you're right. We'll just let the other two girls that are here have their babies and then as you quite rightly say, perhaps it's time to say enough is enough?'

Relief washed across the older woman's features as she stared back at her.

'Oh, love, thank the Lord for that. Do you *really* mean it?'

'Of course I do. Now pull yourself together or you'll be getting us all hanged.'

'Tilly was asking earlier on if Cathy would be coming back for her things today,' Mrs G now confided. 'It might be best to get them out of her room before Tilly starts to get suspicious as to where she's gone.'

Amanda nodded in agreement. 'I'll ensure Ben sees to it straight away,' she promised then went across to plant a gentle kiss on Mrs G's cheek.

'Don't worry, things will be fine . . . you'll see.'

'God knows I hope you're right,' Mrs G muttered as the younger woman exited the room in a waft of expensive perfume.

Once in the foyer she beckoned Ben, who was behind the desk, to her side. 'She's getting edgy again,' she whispered, thumbing across her shoulder towards the kitchen. 'Could you go in and have a word with her? You can always calm her down.'

Stepping from behind the desk he nodded. 'For you, Mother – anything.'

She glanced at him trustingly from beneath lowered lashes. He bent his head to kiss her gently on the cheek and Sophie, who had just rounded a corner in the hallway, stepped back round the corner, so shocked that she almost deposited the dirty laundry in her arms onto the floor.

Her heart began to hammer inside her chest. Had they seen her? Common sense took over and she knew that they couldn't have, otherwise they'd have been screaming at her by now. Still confused about what she had just witnessed she waited for seconds that seemed like hours before cautiously checking round the corner again. They were standing slightly apart now, but the look Ben was bestowing on his mother was the indulgent kind that a parent might bestow on a child. It was all very strange, but then Sophie had noticed how erratic Mrs Lewis's moods could be and for the first time she started to wonder if perhaps the woman had some sort of mental illness. That would explain why her son seemed so fiercely protective of her and why sometimes she would shut herself away in her bedroom for days at a time without venturing out.

Suddenly realising that she shouldn't even be there, Sophie quickly retreated. There would be ructions if they were to see her using the staircase reserved for the guests, so she headed for the backstairs that led to the laundry room at the rear of the house.

Once in the warm steamy atmosphere she dropped the bedding and leaned heavily back against the wall as Tilly stared at her curiously. 'So what's up wiv you then? You look as if you've just seen a ghost,' she stated.

'I've seen *worse* than that,' Sophie told her as she looked nervously back at the door. Seeing Ben and his mother together like that had stirred up painful memories that she was struggling to forget. It just didn't seem right somehow the way Ben fussed over his mother. Not sexual exactly but . . . unnatural was the word that sprang to mind, almost as if Ben were the parent and Mrs Lewis was the child. 'I can't tell you about it now,' she muttered. 'Wait till we get up to our rooms this evening, eh?'

Disgruntled, Tilly sniffed. 'Looks like I ain't got a lot o' choice in the matter.'

Sophie didn't even bother to reply; she simply scuttled back the way she had come leaving Tilly to scratch her head in bewilderment. Just what the bloody hell could have happened now? This day seemed to be going from bad to worse. Still, she comforted herself as she scooped the sheets Sophie had just dropped into the copper, at least she would be seeing Alfie tonight.

Sophie didn't go down to dinner that evening and when Ben stuck his head round her bedroom door to ask why it was all she could do to stop herself from screaming at him. She looked back at him with open contempt on her face as he stepped into her room.

'Mrs G wondered why you didn't come down for your meal?'

'*Did* she? Well, tell her I've lost my appetite.'

He hovered uncertainly. 'Are you feeling unwell, Sophie? I mean – is everything all right with the baby?'

'I wouldn't know, would I, seeing as we're not allowed to have medical checks.'

Ben seemed completely at a loss as to how he should handle the situation. Sophie had always seemed such a compliant little thing; nothing at all like the young woman who was staring at him now with open hostility bright in her eyes.

'Right, I'll . . . I'll go then. Give me a shout if you need anything.'

A curled lip was Sophie's only answer as he left, closing the door behind him. He stood for a moment, his brow creased in confusion. What the hell was wrong with her? He had thought she was putty in his hands until her little outburst. Shrugging, he squared his shoulders and strode away. He was probably worrying about nothing. After all, it was a well-known fact that pregnant women were prone to mood swings. Something to do with their hormones, he believed.

A smile returned to his face as he fingered the bundle of notes in his jacket pocket. First thing in the morning he would go and buy his mother the sapphire necklace she had admired in the jeweller's shop behind the tower. He liked her to wear sapphires; they matched the colour of her eyes. As he took the stairs two at a time he was softly humming to himself.

Half an hour later Tilly found Sophie curled into a ball on her bed. 'What's up?' she asked as she entered the room after making sure that no one was on the landing.

'*This* place is up.' As Sophie stretched and stared up at the ceiling Tilly saw that there were tears in her eyes. Instantly the bright façade was gone and she was all concern.

'What's happened now then?'

Sophie tried to banish from her mind the picture of her father dragging her to the floor on the night he had raped her. Ever since she had seen Ben kiss his mother it had been haunting her.

'This is a *bad* place, Tilly; in more ways than one.'

Tilly felt a shiver run up her spine as she looked at Sophie for an explanation. 'An' what's that supposed to mean?'

Suddenly Sophie could hold back the tears no longer and they gushed from her eyes. Up until now she had held the hurt inside her but she felt as if she didn't talk to someone about it soon she would burst.

'Oh Tilly, everything is such a mess. I wish I were dead, and this thing I'm carrying.'

'Don't you *dare* say that.' Tilly was horrified as she rushed to her side and wrapped her in her arms. 'Come on,' she urged softly. 'I think it's about time yer spilled the beans. Yer know what they say – a trouble shared is a trouble halved. An' don't go thinkin' yer can shock me. After the life I've led I'm unshockable.'

'Well . . .' Sophie began hesitantly. 'It started a few months ago when me dad came in from the pub late one night.' As Sophie tearfully related her sorry tale, Tilly's face crumpled in horror.

'Yer poor little cow,' she muttered when it was finally told. 'An' that dirty old bastard! But yer shouldn't blame yerself. It were him at fault, not you.'

'If it hadn't happened, me mam would still be alive an' I wouldn't be here,' Sophie sobbed.

'That's true. But the thing is it *did* happen, an' now you have to make the best of it an' get on wiv yer life,' Tilly soothed philosophically. 'How do yer think I felt when I found out I'd fallen fer Rachel? Why, I can't even

153

tell the poor little sod who her dad *is*, but it didn't stop me lovin' her from the minute I clapped eyes on her. In fact, she's turned out to be the best thing that ever happened to me. I'm not sayin' you'll feel like that when this 'un is born, but I am sayin' you have to go on. Look at what's happened to me. When I left London to come here I felt exactly as you do now, but then I met Mrs McGregor an' Alfie an' suddenly the future looked bright again.'

She continued to hold Sophie till her sobs had subsided to dull hiccuping whimpers then she asked, 'How about we go out fer an hour again later on, eh? It cheered you up no end last night an' I know Rachel would love to see yer again. She took to yer straight off, which is unusual 'cos she's usually shy around strangers. Then yer could come wiv me to meet my Alfie. I know you'll love him.'

Sophie suddenly realised that she hadn't told Tilly about the way she had seen Ben and his mother fussing over each other earlier in the day. She opened her mouth to start but then for some reason clamped it firmly shut again. After all, what was there to tell apart from the fact that Ben seemed to be obsessively protective towards his mother? Perhaps she had read too much into it. Instead she asked Tilly, 'Won't we be pushing our luck if we sneak out again so soon?'

'Ner.' The smile was back on Tilly's face. 'It's very rare anyone ventures up here after eight o'clock. 'Specially when there's no one about to give birth.'

Her words made them both think of Cathy and for

a second they fell silent until Tilly exclaimed, 'I shall really start to worry if Cathy don't put in an appearance by the end o' the week.'

Sophie nodded in agreement before declaring, 'I *will* come with you tonight. But can we wait till after eight though? Just in case someone does come to check on us. I was rather rude to Ben earlier on and he might decide to come back to see if I'm all right.'

'Huh! Fat chance o' that,' Tilly quipped.

Clambering off the bed she arched her aching back before heading for the door. 'Right, I'm off fer a nice hot soak in the tub. Me back feels as if it's breakin' an' me ankles are that swelled I can barely get me shoes on. Be ready fer eight an' we'll get off an' sod the lot of 'em, eh?'

With a cheery wink she let herself out of the room, leaving Sophie with a smile on her face. She liked Tilly. In fact, she was turning out to be the best friend Sophie had ever had and it felt as if she had known her forever. She hoped that they would stay friends once the ordeal they both had to face was over. She couldn't imagine her life without Tilly now, or little Rachel for that matter. The smile broadened as she thought of Tilly's little girl. One day she hoped she would have one just like her.

The visit to Mrs McGregor's went as well as it had the night before and this time, when they arrived, Rachel sidled up to Sophie and shyly took her hand.

The journey there had not been without incident, for Tilly was getting so big now that she'd had to struggle to climb from the window onto the fire escape. Sophie had wound up in fits of laughter, which threw Tilly into a complete panic with one leg in and one leg out of the window. '*Shurrup*, will yer?' she had implored. 'Else you'll have Ben an' the missus down on us like a ton o' bricks. I shall 'ave to find some uvver way o' gettin' out soon else you'll need a crowbar to get me out o' here.'

By the time they left Mrs McGregor's that night, Rachel and Sophie were firm friends and the little girl clung onto her hand as if she never wanted to let her go.

'I'll come back again, sweetheart. Just as soon as I can,' Sophie promised and with that Mrs McGregor swept Rachel up into her arms and they waved her off from the door.

'Right, now you'll get to meet my Alfie,' Tilly told her as they headed through the back streets towards the pleasure beach.

Sophie wasn't quite so sure about this. 'Won't I be in the way?' she asked falteringly.

'Why would yer be?' Tilly chuckled. 'He's hardly gonna get his leg over this lot, is he?' She patted her swollen stomach. 'Poor bugger's on ration now till it's all over.'

When they reached the Queen's Hotel, Tilly popped her head round the bar door and sure enough there was Alfie having a game of darts with his mates. When he'd finished he swaggered across to them with a smile on his face. Just as Tilly had said, he was a handsome chap with thick black hair that curled over his collar, and deep blue eyes. He wore a gold earring in one ear and a kerchief tied round his neck, so that Sophie was once more reminded of a gipsy. Despite all the glowing things that Tilly had told her about how wonderful he was, Sophie took an instant dislike to him.

'Evenin', doll. I don't suppose yer've got a few bob on yer ter to treat yer old man to a pint, have yer?'

At once, Tilly delved deep in her handbag and produced a ten-shilling note, which she handed to him.

'Ta, doll. An' who's yer friend then?' As he eyed her appreciatively up and down, Sophie squirmed.

'This is me mate, Sophie,' Tilly told him, pushing Sophie forward.

Sophie reluctantly shook hands with him before telling Tilly, 'Right, I'm going to get off now. I'm not feeling too good so I think I'll go back and have an early night.' It was the best excuse she could come up with at short notice but Tilly seemed to accept it. 'Ah, that's a shame. Are yer sure yer can't stay an' have a drink wiv me an' Alfie?'

'No, thanks all the same. I'll see you in the morning, shall I?'

'That yer will,' Tilly told her then she turned adoring eyes back to Alfie and Sophie knew that she was already forgotten.

Once back in the confines of her room, Sophie sighed sadly as she watched the moon riding high in the sky through the window. Alfie hadn't turned out to be at all what she had expected and she hoped that Tilly wasn't about to let herself in for another load of heartache with him. She wished for a happy-ever-after, fairy-tale ending for Tilly, but somehow she doubted she would find it with Alfie. Fairy-tale endings didn't happen to girls like them.

She must have slipped into an uneasy sleep but some time later a noise on the landing woke her up. Rubbing the sleep from her eyes she strained her ears in the darkness before deciding that it was probably just Tilly on one of her many nightly trips to the toilet. Snuggling back down she was soon fast asleep again.

The following morning as she slipped from her room she was surprised to see Cathy's bedroom door swinging open. Even as she watched, Tilly suddenly waddled out of it with an expression of deep concern on her face.

'Everyfin's gone,' she blurted fearfully.

'What do you mean . . . everything's gone?'

'Just what I say. Here, look fer yerself if yer don't believe me.'

Squeezing past her, Sophie let her gaze travel round the little room. What Tilly said was true. Apart from the sparse furniture that was dotted here and there it was empty.

As her eyes moved to Tilly's the girl shook her head. 'Somefin' ain't right. Didn't I tell yer so? She would never have left wivout sayin' goodbye to us.'

'Perhaps she went while we were out last night?' Sophie suggested.

'She wouldn't have gone anywhere wivout these.'

Taking Cathy's rosary beads from her pocket, Tilly dangled them in Sophie's face. 'Yer know how much they meant to her. An' besides – if Ben an' the missus had come up with her an' found us missin' all hell would've broken loose. Somefin's amiss, I can feel it. She promised she wouldn't leave wivout sayin' goodbye an' Cathy weren't the kind of girl to break her word.'

Sophie was inclined to agree with her but seeing how distressed Tilly was she decided not to admit it.

'I'm sure there's some logical explanation,' she said instead. 'Now come on. We'll try to get to the bottom of this later. Let's get downstairs else heads will be rolling if we're late.'

With a last concerned glance into Cathy's empty room, Tilly followed her on feet that felt as heavy as lead.

Sophie, meantime, was feeling as concerned about Cathy as Tilly was. Every day spent at the hotel now was becoming an ordeal and the thought of just clearing off and turning up on her great-aunt's doorstep in the Midlands was becoming more appealing by the minute. But then she thought of Tilly and she knew that she couldn't just abandon her. She would have to stay at least until Tilly had had her baby, otherwise she would never be able to live with herself. All the same, she found herself wondering what Aunt Philly would be like; that was if she was still alive.

Chapter Ten

'So what have you got planned for today then?' Adam Bannerman asked as he spread a thin coat of butter onto a slice of toast.

His wife pulled her expensive negligee more tightly about her and shrugged as she examined her manicure. 'I thought I might go and get my hair done then go and see a film. That is unless *you* could spare some time for me?'

'You know there's nothing I'd like better, but I have a surgery this morning.'

He sighed before dropping his eyes. The kitchen that he had recently had installed at great expense and at her insistence looked as if a whirlwind had swept through it. But then he supposed he shouldn't complain. He had known that Celia wasn't the domestic type when he'd married her. Still, the cleaner would be in today, so at least he might come home to a tidy house tonight even if it was an empty one; no doubt Celia would have made plans that didn't include him. He supposed that he couldn't really blame her. His job as a doctor meant working unsocial hours, a fact that Celia had never been able to adapt to. In the days of their courting she had loved to boast that she was engaged to a doctor, but the novelty had soon worn off after their marriage when she realised that he couldn't be there at her beck and call every minute of the day.

Rising from the table she now headed towards the door that led into the spacious hall and disappeared through it without so much as another word.

Resting his elbows on the table he dropped his head into his hands. After a while he rose and adjusted his tie then headed for the door carrying his black bag. Pausing to glance up the stairs he shouted, 'Goodbye. I'll see you this evening.'

There was no answer though he could hear the water gurgling into the bath. No doubt she would be beginning her beauty regime and that as he knew only too well was a very lengthy process. Quietly he let himself out.

'What's up with you today then, lad? Not feeling so chipper?'

Adam smiled at his partner, Dr Leonard Beech. He was just collecting some papers from Miss Finch, the receptionist, who smiled at Adam adoringly as he approached the desk.

A tiny twittery woman with wispy grey hair, Miss Finch lived up to her name and was like a second mother to Adam, who she shamelessly fussed over. She had worked at the Maples Surgery for more years than she cared to remember and had taken to Adam the second he joined the practice fresh from medical school. It was a fact that was not lost on Dr Beech, who found it highly amusing. If he were to be honest, he too had a huge soft spot for his young partner, though he couldn't say the same for Adam's wife. She was a flighty little piece if ever he'd seen one; but then she was Adam's choice and he never interfered, although the younger doctor sometimes looked as if he had the weight of the world on his shoulders.

'I'm fine, Leonard,' Adam now assured him as he ran his eye down the list of morning patients. It looked like he was going to be busy, not that this was unusual. The practice seemed to grow by the day and at this rate they might soon need to enlist yet another doctor to help them with their increasing workload. It was something that they had often discussed though, as yet, they hadn't done anything about it.

'How about we pop out and grab ourselves a bit of lunch after surgery?' Dr Beech suggested kindly.

'I'd love to, Leonard, but I've got a few things that need doing back at home.'

The older man frowned. 'Well, don't burn yourself out, man. You're on call tonight so you should get some rest where you can.'

At that moment the waiting-room door swung open and a harassed-looking woman gripping the hand of a loudly protesting child appeared.

'Looks like your first patient, Dr B,' Miss Finch told him with a twinkle in her eye. She always sent the children to Adam and often scolded him for the sweetie jar that she knew he kept in his desk drawer. She'd lost count of the number of times she had told him how bad they were for his patients' teeth, but they always came out of his room gripping one in their little hand anyway. Sometimes she would feel a lump growing in her throat as she watched the way Adam waved goodbye to them. There was a longing in his eye that broke her heart. He would have made a wonderful father; not that there was much chance of it happening from where she was standing. That tarty little piece he was married to would never risk losing her figure to give him a child.

'Give me a couple of minutes and then send the first one in would you, Miss Finch?'

'What . . . Oh, yes, yes of course, Doctor.' Miss Finch pulled her thoughts sharply back to the present and instantly became the efficient little receptionist who kept the surgery running like clockwork.

Much later that morning Adam closed the file on his last patient and left his room. He found Miss Finch and Leonard deep in a conversation that immediately stopped as he approached the reception desk.

Cocking an eyebrow he grinned at them as he realised that they had been talking about him. 'Don't let me interrupt you. Do carry on,' he told them sarcastically.

Miss Finch had the good grace to flush and drop her

eyes but Leonard merely grinned back at him totally unabashed.

'Right, well if you must know I was just saying that you look nearly dead on your feet. Why don't you take a couple of weeks off? I could always bring a locum in to deal with your patients while you're away.'

'Thanks Leonard, I know you mean well, but I'm fine, honestly.'

'Then why don't you at least take me up on my earlier offer and let me take you out for lunch? You look like a scarecrow on legs, man. If you lose any more weight you'll slip down a drain.'

Adam grinned ruefully as he lifted his bag from the desk. 'As I told you earlier I have things to do before I start my rounds. But thanks, Leonard, for caring I mean.'

He gave them a final salute before stepping out into the bitterly cold wind. Turning up the collar of his coat he hastened to his car and in no time at all he was on his way home.

The second he pulled up outside his smart Victorian town house in Manor Court Road he saw Mrs Springs' old bicycle propped up against the conifer tree that took pride of place in his small front garden. Cursing beneath his breath he threw himself out of the driver's seat and shot up the path as fast as his long legs would take him. As he let himself in through the stained-glass door he almost bumped into her in the hallway and she laughed.

'Slow down, lad. Where's the fire? You'll do yourself an injury rushin' around like that.'

'Sorry, Mrs Springs. I was hoping to get back to tidy up a little before you started.'

She threw her head back and laughed aloud. 'Eeh, lad. You're a strange 'un, make no bones about it! You pay *me* to do the cleanin' so why should you worry about doin' it before I get here?'

'Because . . . well, I know Celia isn't the tidiest person in the world and you are . . .' When he stopped abruptly she giggled like a woman half her age.

'I'm knockin' on a bit. Is that what you were about to say? Well, let me tell you something – the day I'm too old to earn me money will be the day they put me in me box. This house will be sparklin' from top to bottom afore I've done today, you just mark my words.'

'Oh, Mrs Springs, I know that and I certainly wasn't trying to imply—'

'I know you weren't, lad. An' don't look so worried, there's no offence taken I'm sure. Now . . . will you get out o' me way or are you goin' to pay me to stand here gabbin' to you all day?'

'Sorry,' he muttered as she swept past him into the kitchen. Once there the smile slipped from her face as, hands on hips, she surveyed the room.

Dirty little madam, she found herself thinking as she thought of Celia. She fixed the smile back in place as he came to stand shame-faced beside her.

'I'm so sorry it's such a mess, Mrs Springs,' he gabbled, obviously deeply embarrassed. 'I *did* mean to clean it up before I left for the surgery this morning but I've had two nights of call-outs so far this week and—'

'Oh stop harpin' on,' she interrupted him as she threw her old coat across the back of a chair and rolled her sleeves up. 'Put the kettle on an' make yourself useful, eh? This wind is enough to cut a body in two so we'll have a cup o' tea before I get stuck in. An' while we're at it I'll make you some sandwiches to keep you goin' till tonight. I don't suppose you've eaten yet, have you?'

He shook his head as he filled the kettle at the deep stone sink, which was piled high with dirty pots. Meanwhile, Mrs Springs crossed to the bread bin and wrinkled her nose in distaste as she withdrew a mouldy loaf.

'Ugh, well happen we'll forget the sandwiches. Let's have a look what you've got in the cupboard instead.' After a certain amount of fumbling she produced a tin of soup, which she proceeded to pour into the only clean saucepan in the room.

'Looks like her ladyship could do with doin' a good shop to fill them cupboards up. I ain't seen one so empty since the end o' the rationin',' she remarked.

Adam was instantly on the defensive. 'Celia's had a lot on lately,' he told her lamely, and tongue in cheek she nodded. Probably too busy havin' her hair an' her nails done, she decided, but didn't voice her thoughts. The poor chap looked mortified enough as it was.

Soon he was seated at the table, which she'd had to clear for him, and now she looked around wondering where she should start. Every single surface was cluttered with dirty pots, nail varnish and make-up. And this was only the kitchen; no doubt the rest of the house would be equally bad. Still, she had all afternoon to do it so she wasn't complaining. Dr Bannerman paid her well and she liked to think that she earned her money. Not that it was as easy as she had made out to him any more. Philly Springs was approaching seventy years old and the last winter had taken its toll on her, though she would never have admitted it.

Leaving the young doctor to eat his meagre meal in peace she crossed the hallway and entered the front room, which she saw at a glance was in total chaos. Clothes were strewn about here, there and everywhere. Shoes were discarded all over the floor and ashtrays overflowing with cigarette ends were balancing precariously on the arms of the smart velvet three-piece suite.

Despite the mess, every single stick of furniture was quality and not for the first time she wondered how the young lady of the house could neglect it so. She thought of her own little cottage up in Bermuda village and sighed. It was full of stuff that her Jim had bought for her over the years from second-hand shops and rummage sales. Even so every piece was polished until you could see your face in it and the floor was so clean that her Jim had always used to tease her he could have eaten his dinner off it.

Thinking of him now, a wave of loneliness washed over her. Jim had been dead for three long years yet she still missed him every single day. They'd never had a lot apart from each other, and that had been enough. It had needed to be, for despite their yearning for a family they had never succeeded in producing a child. In the earlier days of their marriage she had suffered nine miscarriages one after the other and each time she lost an unborn child a little bit of her had died with it. Eventually, Jim had put his foot down and told her enough was enough. They had stopped trying after that and slowly as they grew old together the yearning had died away and they had accepted their lot.

She was all alone in the world now although she did still have family somewhere that she had somehow lost touch with over the years. At one time she had been very close to her sister, Miriam, but she had moved up north somewhere long ago and, caught up in their own lives, they had somehow stopped communicating. She wondered how her children would be, realising with a little shock that Sally, her niece, would be all grown up, probably with a family of her own.

Still, it was no good crying over spilt milk; gathering the dirty clothes into a bundle she mounted the ornately carved staircase and entered the main bedroom at the front of the house where the doctor and his wife slept. It was a magnificent room full of matching mahogany furniture that reeked of quality. Dumping the clothes onto a chair, which was already loaded high with discarded outfits, Philly caught sight of herself in the full-length mirror on the door of one of the wardrobes and paused.

Grinning, she lifted her hands to try and tidy the greying bun that was escaping from its clips on the back of her head. In her earlier days Jim had always told her that her hair was her crowning glory. It had remained thick and had a tendency to do as it pleased but the beautiful auburn colour had faded to silver-grey and she saw an old, old woman staring back at her. She had been well-built in her time but now she looked slightly frail and her clothes hung loosely off her. Not that it worried her. Philly had never been vain, which was why she found the doctor's young wife so hard to understand. How could she have such a lovely home and such a wonderful young man for a husband and think so little of them?

Shrugging, she crossed to the unmade bed and began to yank the dirty sheets off it. She'd just finished remaking it with crisp clean bedding when Adam appeared in the doorway.

'Oh dear, I'll tell you what, Mrs Springs. That looks *very* tempting.' He grinned. 'I could just crawl into that and drop right off. Better not though. I don't think my patients would be too impressed if I didn't put in an appearance this afternoon, do you?'

'I dare say they wouldn't be,' she replied with a smile. 'Though if you don't mind me saying, you look like a good nap would do you the power of good.'

'Oh, don't *you* start,' Adam laughed. 'I've had Miss Finch and Dr Beech down at the surgery on at me already this morning. At this rate I'll start to think there's something wrong with me.'

She would have liked to say that there was nothing wrong with him that the love of a good woman wouldn't put right, but feeling that it wasn't her place to be so personal she kept her lips clamped shut as he hastily changed his tie, down which he had somehow managed to spill soup.

Seconds later he was ready to go. At the door he paused to look back and tell her, 'Your money's on the table in the kitchen, Mrs Springs. But don't get doing more than your three hours. What doesn't get done today can wait until the next time.' Even as he spoke he knew that he was wasting his breath. Mrs Springs wouldn't leave until the whole house was gleaming, if he knew her, even if it meant staying on till bedtime.

Once he'd gone she set to with a will and an hour later the whole of the upstairs was gleaming and smelling of lavender polish. She then moved on to the dining room and systematically worked her way through the house until eventually she found herself back in the kitchen. By then it was late afternoon and she was beginning to tire so she decided to treat herself to a cup of tea before tackling the sink full of dirty pots.

After putting the kettle on she sank down onto a chair at the kitchen table and it was then that she heard a key in the front door.

Seconds later, Celia appeared loaded down with shopping bags, which she threw onto the table.

'Still here, are you?' she asked unnecessarily. 'I thought you were supposed to be here at one?'

'I *was* here at one,' Mrs Springs retorted indignantly.

'Mm, well, perhaps if you didn't have so many tea breaks you'd get your work done in the allotted time.'

Philly's lips pursed into a grim straight line. If it wasn't for the young doctor she would have told the little madam where to stick her rotten job there and then. In fact, she would have told her long ago. As it was she simply replied icily, 'In actual fact this is the first break I've had since the doctor was here at dinner time.' She would have liked to add that if the house hadn't been in such a state she would have been long gone, but for his sake she swallowed that retort too.

'Do you want me to stay an' finish the kitchen or what?' she asked shortly instead as Celia began to withdraw her purchases from the various bags to admire them.

'What . . . Oh yes, just carry on. I have to be out again in two hours' time. I certainly don't have time to do it, which is why we pay you.'

As Philly looked at her she wondered how anyone so beautiful could be so very selfish. And Celia *was* beautiful, she had to admit; at least on the outside. Her blond hair curled on her shoulders and she had a figure that turned heads wherever she went, of which she was very aware. Never once in all the time Philly had been working there had she ever seen Celia without her make-up on. Nor had she ever seen her in the same outfit twice, if it came to that. But there any claim to beauty ended, for when Philly looked beyond Celia's appearance she saw that she was as cold as a fish and selfish to the core.

It was a well-known fact that she led the doctor a hell of a life but he was so besotted with her that it seemed he would put up with anything.

Sighing, she hoisted herself up from the chair. She had gone off the idea of a cup of tea now and just wanted to get home, so she set to with a vengeance. The sooner she started the sooner she could be gone. Not that the thought of returning to an empty cottage gave her much joy.

Chapter Eleven

'And Tilly, when you've got that next lot of washing onto the line, empty that rubbish into the bin, would you? The dustcart is due today.'

'Yes, Mrs Lewis,' Tilly replied respectfully then when the woman turned to stride from the room she stuck her tongue out at the retreating figure. 'Miserable old slave-driver,' she murmured, before once again bending over the mangle.

Half an hour later with the freshly washed sheets flapping in the breeze she collected the litter from the laundry room and dutifully carried it out to the enormous bin on wheels that served the hotel. Struggling with the heavy metal lid she tossed the rubbish inside and was just about to close it again when something tucked deep down beneath a load of vegetable peelings caught her eye.

After glancing over her shoulder to make sure that no one was watching she heaved herself higher and leaned as far down as she could until she grasped what she had spotted. As she withdrew it her breath caught in her throat and she broke into a sweat. At that moment she heard Sophie's voice calling to her and she was so startled that she almost fell headfirst into the enormous bin.

'Pssst,' she hissed urgently and the next second Sophie's head popped round the corner. Her face immediately broke into a smile as she saw Tilly hanging precariously across the bin.

'What *are* you doing now? Don't expect *me* to haul you out if you fall in. We shall have to call the fire brigade.'

Ignoring the teasing note in Sophie's voice, Tilly beckoned her over, all the time keeping a watchful eye on the laundry-room door.

''Ere, what do yer make o' this? It's Cathy's cardigan an' if I ain't very much mistaken there's some more of her stuff in there. Look fer yerself if yer don't believe me.'

Her face solemn now, Sophie did as she was told and sure enough, just as Tilly had said, she could make out some clothes spilling from brown paper carrier bags that were rammed deep down in the bin.

She gazed at Tilly in consternation. 'What do you think it means?' she asked fearfully.

Tilly gulped deep in her throat and for the first time since Sophie had known her was lost for words.

'Look, we'd better get inside,' Sophie said eventually. 'If Ben or Mrs Lewis catch us out here there'll be hell to pay. Push that cardigan back down where you found it.'

Tilly did as she was told without argument before

following Sophie back inside where they looked at each other with fear in their eyes.

'Somefin's happened to her. She'd *never* have gone off wivout her clothes.' Tilly was trembling and although Sophie didn't immediately answer her she was inclined to agree.

'We can't talk about it here,' she told Tilly in a hushed voice. 'The best thing we can do is to carry on as normal for now and we'll have a word tonight.'

Turning away she left Tilly wringing her hands in consternation.

By the time they reached the privacy of their rooms that evening Tilly had worked herself into a terrible state and was barely coherent as she gabbled her fears out to Sophie.

'I just *knew* summat were amiss here,' she said for what must have been the twentieth time that evening. 'But what can we do?'

'Nothing from where I'm standing,' Sophie told her sensibly. 'What we have to do now is keep a look-out for each other.'

Tilly's head wagged furiously in agreement. She looked very pale and drawn and Sophie noticed that her hand constantly went to her back.

'Are you in pain?' she asked with concern.

Tilly sighed heavily. 'Not pain exactly. It's just this dull ache in the bottom o' me back. It'll probably go away in a while. I've probably spent too long hangin' over the copper today. Now the hotel is gettin' busier the bleedin' washin' seems endless.' She suddenly looked at Sophie appealingly. 'I don't suppose I could ask yer a big favour, could I?'

'Of course you could. What is it?'

'Well . . . the thing is – I ain't feelin' too chipper an' I don't really feel up to goin' out tonight but I promised to meet Alfie after I'd popped to see Rachel. He'll worry if I don't turn up, an' besides I'd told him I'd lend him a bit o' cash just to see him through to the weekend. I don't like to think of him wi' nowt in his pocket.'

'Is that wise? You ought to be hanging onto your money till you get out of here. The way I look at it, if you and Alfie are going to make a go of it, it should be *him* looking after *you*!'

Hearing the note of disapproval in Sophie's voice, Tilly flushed. 'He will once I'm away from this place, you'll see. He's promised to find somewhere fer us all to live an' everyfin'. We'll be just like a real little family. But meantime . . . well, do yer think *you* could go an' see Rachel an' just meet him to hand the money over fer me? To be honest, I ain't feelin' so good at all an' I really don't know if I'm up to traipsin' about tonight.'

Sophie's first instinct was to refuse Tilly's request or at least the last part of it. Going to see Rachel could only be a pleasure, but then seeing her friend's hopeful face she sighed.

'All right then. I'll meet him just this once.'

Flashing her a brilliant smile, Tilly crossed to the chest of drawers and withdrew a small wad of notes from beneath her underwear, which Sophie saw with amusement was thrown into the drawer anyhow.

She passed four ten-shilling notes to Sophie before tucking the rest back where it had come from. 'I'll be glad when this little 'un decides to put in an appearance now,' she confessed. 'What wiv' the money I give Mrs McGregor fer Rachel's keep an' wiv slippin' Alfie a bit here an' there the money I saved is dwindlin' fast.'

Sophie swallowed the hasty retort that sprang to her lips. The way she saw it, the money would last for a whole lot longer if she didn't keep giving it to Alfie, but then she supposed that it wasn't her place to say so. Tucking the money deep into her pocket, Sophie raised a smile. 'I'd better go and get ready then. What time were you supposed to be meeting him?'

'Well.' Tilly squirmed uncomfortably. 'I weren't *meetin'* him exactly. I were goin' to the Queen's bar. It's easier, yer see? I don't like to put him to the bovver o' havin' to come an' meet me. Just stick yer head round the door an' give him the money an' tell him I'll get there tomorrer if I'm feelin' a bit more lively, eh?'

Sophie nodded and hurried from the room before her temper got the better of her. It looked to her like Alfie was simply using Tilly, but how could she tell her and shatter her dreams of the future she so longed for? She prayed as she got ready to leave that she was wrong, for Tilly was overdue a bit of happiness. Only time would tell.

★ ★ ★

During the next week, Sophie went to see Rachel almost every night in Tilly's place. Her friend's ankles were so swollen now that she could barely walk on them and she got breathless just climbing the stairs. Each time she saw the little girl the bond that was forming between them strengthened and Sophie came to love her. It would have been hard not to because, as she soon discovered, Rachel had the temperament of an angel. More and more, Sophie came to realise just what a good job of raising her Tilly had done and what sacrifices she must have made. Rachel's clothes were all good quality, not at all like Tilly's own off-the-peg market outfits, and her manners for a child who was not yet two years old were impeccable. The realisation only made her pray all the harder that Alfie would do right by her friend because the way Sophie saw it Tilly deserved happiness now.

Her hopes were squashed when Tilly once again asked her to take some money to Alfie the following week.

'Just this *once* more,' she pleaded, seeing the disapproval on Sophie's face.

Sophie took the money without a word and that night after visiting Rachel she kissed her soundly and set off very reluctantly for the Queen's Hotel. As usual she found Alfie slouched across a table engrossed in a game of dominoes with an equally unsavoury-looking character.

The instant he saw her standing hesitantly in the doorway he rose from the table and hurried across to her.

Without a word she took the money from her pocket

and held it out to him, intent on getting back to Tilly, but Alfie seemed to have other ideas.

Gripping her hand, he eased her into the smoky atmosphere. Sophie stifled the urge to smack his hand away, reluctant to cause a scene, but the look she gave him was withering.

'There's really no need for me to come in,' she told him curtly. 'Tilly asked me to give you this and now I have I'd like to go, please.'

Flashing her a smile that could have charmed the birds from the trees he held onto her hand. 'Now don't be like that, luv. A nice-lookin' girl like you should have a bit o' fun from time to time an' I'm yer man.'

'I'm not interested.' Sophie glared at him as her patience began to wear thin. 'So now, if you don't mind, I'd like you to let go of my hand so I can get back to Tilly, who you *might* like to know isn't at all well.'

'Let's just forget about her fer now, eh? I reckon you an' me could have a real good time. What do yer say?' He was so close that she could feel his breath on her cheek and she had to fight the urge to lash out at him. How could he stand there saying these things to her when he'd promised Tilly they had a future together?

Sophie was trembling with rage now and her voice was scathing as she spat, 'You don't deserve Tilly. She's worth a dozen of you – do you know that? It would break her heart if I told her what you were saying. Doesn't that bother you at all?'

He grinned but then as it occurred to him that she

might repeat what he'd said to Tilly he realised that he might lose his latest source of income and his manner changed.

'Course it bothers me. Yer've just misunderstood me – that's all. I were only askin' if yer might like to have a drink before yer go back. You give her my love an' tell her I hope she's feelin' better soon, eh?' Jamming the money she'd given him down into his trouser pocket he watched her leave before shrugging his shoulders and returning to his game of dominoes. Stuck-up little cow, he thought, before dismissing her – and Tilly – from his mind.

Sophie's heart was heavy as she made her way back to the hotel that night. The streets were becoming busier now as the holidaymakers began to arrive in droves. She barely noticed them; her thoughts were on Tilly and what would become of her once she'd had the baby if Alfie let her down, which Sophie had no doubt at all he would. He was scum in her opinion, but there was no question that Tilly was looking at him through rose-coloured glasses.

When the Ship Hotel came into sight she stood back in the shadows and stared up at it. With its windows brightly lit it looked warm and inviting like any of the other hotels in the street but Sophie suspected now that the hotel was just a front for something far more sinister. What had happened to the girl who had been there when Tilly first arrived? And why had Cathy left without so much as a single word, leaving all her belongings behind her when she had promised them faithfully that she would say goodbye first? The more she thought of the arrangement she had made with Ben the more suspicious it now seemed and she wondered if she shouldn't just have gone to her aunt in the Midlands as her mother had asked her to. But then she would never have met Tilly and Rachel and they had come to mean a lot to her. Tilly had somehow become like the sister she had always longed for.

The shudder that now ran up Sophie's spine was nothing to do with the cold wind tunnelling along the street and she had the urge to turn and run as far away from the place as she could. But she knew that she wouldn't. Tilly was in there somewhere and Sophie suspected that in the next few weeks she would need her more than ever. It certainly didn't look like she could rely on Alfie. Then there was Rachel to worry about. What would become of her if anything happened to Tilly? Mrs McGregor was lovely, but it was more than obvious that she wouldn't be able to afford to keep her without the money that Tilly gave her.

Sighing heavily, she slowly made her way round to the back of the hotel and crept up the fire escape as quietly as she could.

Tilly was hovering by the curtains waiting for her and almost dragged Sophie through the window. 'So how was Rachel an' Alfie then?' she gushed before Sophie had even had time to pull down the sash-cord window.

Seeing the love alight in her eyes, Sophie's heart sank. How could she tell her that Alfie was a two-timing philanderer who only wanted her for her money?

Taking a deep gulp she crossed her fingers behind her back. 'They were both fine and Alfie said to tell you he hopes you'll be better soon.'

Tilly's radiant smile lit the room up. 'Ah, bless him. It must be awful fer him sittin' there waitin' fer me night after night. Still, not long to go now an' then I'll be able to make it up to him, won't I?'

Lowering her head, Sophie nodded before making for the door. 'Right, I'm off to bed then. Goodnight, Tilly.'

'Goodnight. An', Sophie – thanks . . . I don't know what I'd do wivout yer an' that's a fact.'

As Sophie slowly trailed back to her own room her cheeks were wet with tears. Tilly would be broken-hearted if Alfie let her down and she'd been through so very much already. Unfortunately, there was not a thing she could do about it.

By the middle of May the hotel was buzzing with visitors and it was all Sophie and Tilly could do to keep up with their work. Sophie was alarmed to notice that Tilly no longer bothered to apply her thick layer of panstick make-up and each morning she now appeared in the kitchen looking totally worn out before she had even started.

She dared to mention it to Mrs G one morning before Tilly had put in an appearance and to her consternation she saw the older woman's lips set in a grim line.

'Well, it isn't me you should be telling, is it?' she snapped peevishly. 'It's up to Ben and his mother who does what in this place. I'm just an employee here the same as you. Why doesn't Tilly open her mouth and tell them herself if she isn't feeling well?'

'I don't think she dare,' Sophie admitted. 'You must agree that Mrs Lewis can be a little . . .' She sought for the right word before finishing lamely, '*Formidable?*'

Instantly on the defensive, Mrs G spat back, 'I hardly think it's your place to comment on that!'

At that moment the subject of their conversation entered the room looking as if she had just stepped out of a beautician's.

'What are you doing up so early?' Mrs G asked in astonishment.

Mrs Lewis looked slightly disgruntled. 'Anyone would think I lay in bed till dinnertime every day to hear you. I *do* have a hotel to run, you know.'

Flinging a rasher of bacon into a huge frying pan, Mrs G sniffed disdainfully. 'So, what was it you were wanting? It isn't often you show your face in here unless you want something.'

Mrs Lewis looked slightly uncomfortable. 'Now you know that isn't true.'

The door opened yet again and this time Tilly appeared looking decidedly pale. Avoiding Mrs Lewis she skirted the table and looked across at Mrs G who was haphazardly stabbing the bacon sizzling in the pan.

'I was wondering if I could perhaps have a word with

you . . . in private?' Mrs Lewis looked pointedly at the two girls before turning and marching from the room.

Mrs G cursed softly beneath her breath before wiping her hands on her apron and beckoning Sophie to her side. 'Keep your eye on this, would you? I shan't be more than a couple of minutes.' She stamped round the table as the girls exchanged a bewildered glance then disappeared into the corridor, slamming the door so loudly behind her that it danced on its hinges. For a while all was silent then suddenly the sound of raised voices reached them, although they couldn't hear what was being said.

'Seems Mrs G ain't scared of her, don't it?' Tilly commented sarcastically.

One thing was for certain – Mrs G certainly wasn't pleased about something. This was borne out when she flounced back into the kitchen some minutes later looking as if she could have committed murder. 'It seems you'll be having a new room-mate up on the fifth floor today,' she announced in a voice that was heavy with disapproval. Tilly glanced at Sophie as her eyebrows rose into her hairline but both girls wisely stayed silent.

It was only when breakfast was over and they were out in the hallway that they dared to comment on what Mrs G had told them.

'Some other poor unsuspectin' little bugger must have fell into Ben's trap then,' Tilly muttered quietly.

Sophie nodded in agreement. But what could they do? And why had Mrs Lewis told Mrs G about it? After all, as she had taken the trouble to point out only that morning, she was only an employee. It was all very strange.

Leaning towards Tilly she suddenly asked, 'Do you want to get away from here?'

Tilly looked astonished. 'Well, o' course I do – but there ain't no chance o' that, not till I've shifted this.' She patted her bloated stomach. 'Think about it, Sophie. Where would we go and what would we do wiv Rachel *an'* two more babies to look after? We ain't hardly got two penny pieces to rub togevver between us.' She shrugged despondently. 'Ner . . . much as I hate it here I'm goin' to see it through now. It would be daft to walk out when I'm so close to bein' rid o' this.'

Sophie fiddled with the buttons on her cardigan before suddenly blurting out, 'Is Ben or Mrs Lewis aware that you already have a child?'

'Not on your nelly!' Tilly looked horrified at the very thought. 'They have the right to do what they want wiv this 'un once it decides to put in an appearance. I could never afford to support two little uns so I don't have no choice but to give this one up. But they ain't gettin' their hands on my Rachel. Why do you ask?'

Sophie stared off into space as she tried to put her thoughts into some sort of order. 'It's just that I've realised that the girls that have stayed here seem to have no one else. Or if they do, Ben and his mother seem very keen that they won't know where they are staying. Take yourself for instance. As far as they know you've run away from London and no one knows where you are. Then there was Cathy: her family had virtually disowned her and had no idea at all where she was; and then there's me . . . until Mrs Lewis discovered that my parents were both dead she seemed very reluctant to let me stay. Don't you find that a little strange, especially after the way Cathy just disappeared into thin air after the birth?'

'Look.' Tilly's voice was fearful. 'Neither you nor me is thick. I think we've both clocked onto the fact that things ain't exactly kosher around here. But they've got us over a barrel, ain't they? Strikes me that we don't have much choice but to see it through. O' course, my baby will be born well afore yours. But don't worry. We'll keep in touch an' soon as you've had yours you can come an' stay wiv' me an' Alfie.'

By now they had arrived at the door that led to the laundry room and Tilly opened it with a feeling of dread. The thought of slaving over a hot copper all day was daunting feeling as she did, but then she really didn't have much choice.

'Look, try an' keep yer pecker up,' she encouraged. 'It ain't forever, is it? Afore yer know it we'll be out of here an' livin' the life o' Riley an' we'll be able to forget all about this place.' With a last smile she slipped into the room and Sophie sighed before climbing the stairs to begin her own job.

Once the sound of her footsteps had died away, Mrs Lewis appeared round the corner and stared after her deep in thought. She had heard every single word of the conversation Sophie and Tilly had just held and her worst fears were confirmed. That Sophie was too bright for her own good. Hadn't she told Ben so on the day he had brought her here? What would they do if the girl decided to leave now? Worse still, if she told anyone of their arrangement? Deeply troubled, she went in search of her son. Something would have to be done about that little madam. She was getting far too inquisitive for her own good.

Chapter Twelve

By the time the Whit weekend arrived, Tilly was walking about like a bloated zombie. The weather had turned warmer, which only added to her discomfort. Sophie kept teasing her and telling her that if she got any bigger she would explode, but Tilly's sense of humour was sadly lacking at the moment.

'You should think yourself lucky you can stay in here in the cool,' Mrs G scolded her one morning when Tilly was moaning. 'It's safer inside at the moment. There were ructions in loads of holiday places yesterday according to what I heard on the radio earlier on. Those mods and rockers have been on the rampage again. Seventy-six arrests in Brighton there were apparently, then yet more trouble in Margate, Southend, Bournemouth and Clacton. Let's just hope the idiots don't decide to target Blackpool next, eh? It won't be safe to walk the streets soon, not that you look like you'd be up to it anyway. How much longer have you got to go?'

Tilly scowled at her. 'Not more than a couple o' weeks

now accordin' to my reckonin' an' I'll tell yer now, I don't think I'll manage another whole day leanin' over that copper. Me back feels as if it's goin' to break afore I even start.'

Before Mrs G could answer, Sophie piped up. 'I could always come down and give you a hand when I've finished the bedrooms. That is if Mrs G can manage on her own in here?'

Mrs G looked from one to the other of them before reluctantly nodding. 'I suppose I could if push comes to shove. After all, we don't want her going into labour too early, do we?'

Amy, an attractive dark-haired girl who had joined them on the fifth floor landing a couple of weeks before, kept her head bent over her breakfast and her mouth firmly shut. As Tilly and Sophie had soon discovered she was a very private girl who liked to keep herself to herself. She was extremely well spoken and her clothes were all of excellent quality, a fact that had led Tilly to declare she was a downright snob.

'Perhaps she's just shy?' Sophie had suggested tentatively when Tilly first stated that she didn't like her. Tilly had snorted in derision.

'Huh! If she's shy then I'm a monkey's uncle. She's stuck-up more like. Still, stayin' here'll soon knock her down a peg or two. I've an idea the missus has got her in mind to take over my job in the laundry.' This caused her to chuckle wickedly as she thought of Amy's lily-white hands. Sophie tried hard to look stern but Tilly's chuckle was so infectious that soon she was laughing too.

The rest of the meal was eaten in silence and the girls were just clearing away the dirty dishes when the door opened and Ben came into the kitchen looking very cool and handsome in a crisp white short-sleeved shirt.

His eyes immediately settled on Amy, who gazed back at him adoringly as Sophie and Tilly exchanged a knowing glance. In that moment they felt almost sorry for her, for hadn't they both fallen under Ben's spell too when they had first arrived? Amy would soon learn that his devotion didn't last long. Not that either of them had any intention of warning her. Let her find out for herself the hard way as they'd had to.

'Amy, I was wondering . . . could I have a word?' Ben asked and Tilly had to stifle a giggle. Anyone hearing him would have thought that butter wouldn't melt in his mouth.

'Of course,' Amy flushed a becoming shade of pink as she hastily rose from the table and followed him into the hallway.

The two girls continued with the washing-up until Ben reappeared seconds later with Amy, who wasn't looking quite so pleased with herself any more.

Addressing Tilly now, he said, 'Tilly, Mother and I have decided that for the last couple of weeks before your confinement you should take things easy, so Amy here will be taking over your duties in the laundry room.

Would you mind just spending the day in there with her today to show her the ropes?'

Tilly flashed Sophie a glance that seemed to say 'I told you so' before nodding eagerly. 'Not 'alf. It'll be my pleasure. 'Specially as the weather's gettin' hotter. You'll certainly sweat the fat off you in there, girl,' she teased a resentful-looking Amy.

Waddling across the kitchen she beckoned Amy to follow her, looking like a cat that had got the cream. 'Come on,' she ordered bossily. 'Let's show you where everything is then.'

Amy reluctantly followed looking none too pleased as Sophie suppressed a smile.

Once in the laundry room, Amy looked around disdainfully. 'It's rather *stuffy* in here, isn't it?'

Tilly giggled as she hurried to throw the door into the yard open. 'If yer think this is bad just wait till yer've bin hangin' over the copper fer a couple of hours. I warn yer, it gets like an oven in here at times an' that's through the winter – so God knows what it'll be like through the summer. Rather you than me, that's all I can say. But now, down to business, eh?'

Pointing across to a huge wooden clothes horse in a far corner of the room she told Amy, 'All them sheets folded over that have to be ironed. But first you've to fill that big copper wiv buckets o' water from the sink over there an' put it on to heat up. By the time Sophie comes down wiv the first lot o' sheets an' pillowcases it should be hot enough – then here's what yer do.' First she showed Amy the procedure she was to follow with the washing. 'Then, yer have to get 'em all out o' the copper when they're clean an' rinse 'em thoroughly in the sink over there. Mind they ain't got no marks left on 'em though. The missus insists that the sheets are as white as snow so don't say as I didn't warn yer if yer try to get away wiv half measures. Next yer takes 'em out to the yard and feeds 'em all through the mangle, an' finally yer hang 'em out to dry on them lines strung up there. If it's rainin' yer have to dry 'em over the clothes horse, which takes twice as long.'

By now Amy was looking positively tearful and despite the fact that Tilly hadn't really taken to her she smiled at her encouragingly. 'It ain't so bad once yer get used to it,' she said kindly. 'An' the good thing is that yer always so busy the day passes in a flash. You'll soon get used to it, you'll see.'

'I doubt I will,' Amy mumbled sullenly. 'In the private school that I attended my washing and ironing was done for me. I never dreamed there was so much to it.'

At a loss for words, Tilly shrugged as she settled herself onto the only hard-backed chair in the room. 'Right, you'd best make a start then. I'll stay here till yer sure you've everyfin' in hand.'

Amy rolled her sleeves up and slowly began to fill bowls of water, which she carried to the copper as Tilly looked on. She then turned on the iron and under Tilly's guidance began to iron one of the crisp white sheets that Tilly had washed and dried the day before on the enormous wooden ironing board. She had barely ironed more than a few inches when she squealed with pain and dropped the iron.

'Oh, I've burned myself,' she wailed.

Tilly lumbered across to her and sure enough there was an angry red weal already beginning to show on her fingers. 'Clumsy sod,' she muttered. 'I'll nip off to the kitchen an' get some butter from Mrs G fer you to rub on. That should help it.'

Amy's eyes flooded with tears. 'I don't think I'm going to like it here,' she whimpered. 'Ben never told me that it would be like this.'

Tilly snorted. 'Huh! I shouldn't take too much notice of anyfin' he tells yer. He's as two-faced as they come an' the sooner yer realise that fact the happier you'll be. Don't go runnin' away wiv the idea that he brought you here to help yer whatever yer do, 'cause you'll be settin' yerself up fer a fall. Ben only has his own interests at heart, you believe me – an' yer don't mean that much to him.'

When Tilly snapped her fingers in front of the girl's bewildered eyes, Amy promptly burst into tears. Tilly suffered a pang of guilt before heading for the kitchen. But why *should* she feel guilty? She'd only told Amy the truth, hadn't she? She'd probably done her a favour, for once Amy stopped looking at Ben through rose-coloured glasses she could start to settle down.

When she arrived back in the laundry room minutes later she found Amy sitting on an upturned laundry basket sobbing as if her heart would break. Tilly's hard front melted and she gently lifted her hand and began to rub the pat of butter she'd fetched from the kitchen onto Amy's burn. Poor little sod, she thought. She can't be no older than sixteen.

Amy winced with pain but held her hand steady until Tilly had finished then, rising, she made her way back to the ironing board.

'I suppose I'd better get on,' she muttered forlornly. Tilly could think of nothing to say so she merely nodded.

Sophie was on her way downstairs with the first bundle of dirty washing when Mrs Lewis appeared round a corner. 'Ah, Sophie. I've been hoping to bump into you,' she greeted her. 'I was wondering – do you think you could come up to the fourth floor when you've finished the other rooms? The chambermaid who usually comes in to clean up there is off sick and I want you to make up a double room for me. We have visitors arriving who will be staying on that floor with us later today.'

Sophie was so surprised that she almost dropped the bundle she was holding. The woman that usually cleaned that floor came and went and kept herself very much to herself. Apart from catching the odd glimpse of her neither Sophie nor Tilly had ever even spoken to her; and now here was Mrs Lewis telling her that she was to clean up there when before she had made such a point of insisting that that floor was totally out of bounds.

Her stomach started to churn sickeningly. The last

young couple who'd stayed on the fourth floor had arrived alone and left carrying a baby. Cathy's baby, she was sure of it now. Could it be that the couple arriving today were coming to wait for the birth of Tilly's baby?

Hastily pushing the thought away she managed to nod politely. 'Yes, Mrs Lewis. I'll be there as soon as I can.'

Mrs Lewis nodded before leaving Sophie standing there chewing on her lip in consternation. After a time she shrugged. What did it really matter? Tilly had already made her mind up to give the baby away so she supposed that the sooner it was over the better. Hoisting the washing higher into her arms she hurried on.

It was mid-afternoon before she finally tapped tentatively on the door that led to the fourth-floor bedrooms. Almost instantly Mrs Lewis opened it.

'Ah, Sophie.' She pointed to a door. 'You'll find all the clean linen is in that cupboard there and I want you to clean the last room along the landing.' The woman was dressed in a smart two-piece costume and was just drawing her gloves on, which suggested that she was about to go out. This was borne out when she told her, 'Ben and I have an appointment this afternoon, so when you've finished here you may knock off for the day and go to your room until teatime.'

'Yes, Mrs Lewis.' Sophie stood aside for the woman then after she had listened to her clattering away down the stairs in her high-heeled shoes she slowly walked onto the landing.

She saw at a glance that this floor was even more

luxurious than the other landings in the hotel. There was a thick wall-to-wall carpet, and a gilt mirror and various rich paintings hung on the walls that separated the rooms. Crossing to the linen cupboard that Mrs Lewis had pointed out, she took out some clean sheets and pillowcases and made her way along, her feet making no sound as they sank into the thick floor covering.

When she entered the room Mrs Lewis had indicated it almost took her breath away; it was so beautiful that she could almost imagine she had stepped into the pages of a magazine, or a palace. Rich heavy chintz curtains hung at the window, and the matching furniture was all carved in mahogany, which had been polished until she could see her face in it. An enormous brass bed dominated the centre of the room and Sophie sighed with envy as she saw the thick feather mattress on it. It was at least three times thicker than the lumpy old thing that she had to sleep on each night, but then she supposed that she shouldn't complain. After all, she was hardly a paying guest.

Shaking out the fresh sheets across the mattress she quickly began to make the bed up and half an hour later she stood with her hands on her hips and contentedly surveyed her work. The whole room was spotless. Even Mrs Lewis wouldn't be able to find fault with it, she was sure. Gathering together her cleaning things she made her way back onto the landing, softly closing the door behind her; it was then that her curiosity got the better of her.

Glancing up and down she saw that the landing consisted of five rooms. The fifth room, which was the one that she had just cleaned, was obviously the one that Mrs Lewis kept for special guests. Moving on to the next one she hesitated. She knew that she should leave now that she'd done what she'd been requested to do but her curiosity was eating away at her. She tried the handle of the door and when it turned she slowly inched it open. At a glance she surmised that this must be Mrs G's room, for a pile of clean aprons was folded neatly across the foot of a single bed. Nowhere near as big as the room she had just cleaned, it was nonetheless a very pleasant room.

The third room she peered into puzzled her. It was so bare that it was almost clinical. A single bed with a starched white sheet stood against one wall and next to it was a hard-backed chair with a large number of towels neatly folded on it. On the other side of the bed was a table on which stood a large jug and bowl. But the thing that most drew her attention was the small crib standing in the far corner next to the window, which was covered in heavy white net curtains.

Instantly her thoughts turned to Cathy. This, then, must be the room where Cathy had given birth. Shuddering as a cold finger snaked its way up her spine she hastily shut the door. If she were right then *she* would be lying on that very bed in a few months' time when she gave birth to her baby. She tried not to think of it as she tried the next door. This was much like the end bedroom that she had prepared for the guests; again, very luxurious, boasting two single beds that dominated the room surrounded by beautiful wardrobes and drawers in a soft cream colour. Her eyes were drawn to a fine dressing table on which stood a heavy ornate gilt mirror. As she was admiring it she noticed a pair of gold cufflinks standing next to a cut-glass perfume bottle: they were Ben's. He wore them regularly and she would have recognised them anywhere, but what were they doing in here? Checking over her shoulder to make sure that she was still alone she stole into the room and quietly opened one of the wardrobe doors. Amanda Lewis's clothes were neatly arranged inside. She opened the next door and her heart did a somersault in her chest. It was full of Ben's clothes. She suddenly had to swallow the vomit that rose in her throat as her mind reeled. Ben and his mother were sharing a room! In separate beds, admittedly, but even so it felt unnatural.

Staggering back out onto the landing she stood there until her heart had settled into a steadier rhythm. It was then that she reached her decision. As soon as Tilly had given birth to her baby and was safely away from this ungodly place, Sophie was going to follow her. Reeling from the shock she glanced into the last room as she passed it and saw that it was a bathroom. Two more minutes and she would have been gone, but it was her bad luck that at that moment the door swung open and Ben appeared. Taking in her pale face at a glance he frowned then as his eyes travelled the landing he saw that the door to his room was slightly ajar and comprehension dawned on his face.

'Been poking about where we shouldn't, have we?' he asked as he gripped her arm cruelly. Sophie shook her head as panic pulsed though her.

His lip curled as he bent his head to hers. 'Perhaps I should have listened to Mother after all, eh? She said you were going to be trouble.'

She could feel his fingers biting into the soft flesh of her upper arm and whimpered in pain.

'Right, perhaps it's time you and I had a little talk.'

Before Sophie could stop him he had slammed her against the wall, chasing the breath from her lungs.

'Now you listen to me. You will go about your business as if it was just another day and you will *not* talk about what you have seen up here to anyone. Do you understand me?'

Sophie nodded in terror, never taking her eyes from his face.

'Good. The sooner you make your mind up that you're here until after your confinement the better. Don't get thinking of running to the Welfare or the police either if you know what's good for you. Think how it would look. It's always seemed very strange to me that on the very night you left home both of your parents died. You wouldn't want anyone delving too closely into why, now would you? That would give the newspapers something to write about, wouldn't it? Your name would be splashed about everywhere. You'd never be able to hold your head up again. My mother and I run a highly respectable business here so who do you think they would believe if you went to them with some cock and bull story? We would simply say that we'd given you somewhere to work and stay because we felt sorry for you. You could even find yourself chucked into a loony-bin. It wouldn't be the first time they'd stuck an unmarried mother in one of those places to rot. And of course you won't even *think* of running away, will you? After all . . . it would be a terrible shame if I had to come and find you. *And believe me I would!* There is nowhere on this earth that you could hide from me. We made an agreement and until you've fulfilled it you'll do as you're told. My mother has times when she is slightly . . .' He hesitated before finishing, 'Unwell, which is why I sleep in the same room as her in case she should need me. There's nothing wrong in that, is there?'

Seeing the light of madness in his eyes Sophie shook her head. Satisfied, he released her arm and she slumped down the wall as shivers of fear ran through her. She had thought of going to the police but Ben was right – who would believe anything she had to say against him?

'Now get out . . . and remember what I said. If you breathe so much as one single word of what you've seen up here today I promise you you'll live to regret it. Or what I should say is . . . you *won't* live to regret it. Now go!'

Sophie lurched unsteadily towards the door on legs that had suddenly turned to jelly and then she fled upstairs where she collapsed onto her bed as she tried to still her beating heart and put her thoughts into some sort of order. It was him that was mad. He *must* be! And Mrs Lewis; how could she sleep in the same room with her own son? Hurrying across to the bowl, Sophie vomited until her stomach was empty. Eventually she returned to the bed where she collapsed, feeling totally spent. Despite the promise that she had made to Ben her mind was made up. The second that Tilly had safely delivered her baby and was away from here she would run away. Nothing would keep her in this unholy place a second longer than was absolutely necessary any more. She felt like the poor rabbit she had seen caught in a snare on the Marton Mere Park when Matthew had taken her there once after school when she was a child. She had sobbed all the way home and been totally inconsolable, but as Matthew had told her gently, 'Life ain't always fair, Sophie.'

How right he had been proved to be! She did briefly consider what she would do about her own baby if she plucked up the courage to run away but then pushed the thought to the back of her mind. She would have to cross that bridge when she came to it. One thing was for sure: nothing could be as bad as having to stay here. As she lay there she toyed with the idea of telling Tilly about what she'd discovered but eventually decided against it. She had enough of an ordeal ahead of her and what she didn't know wouldn't hurt her. This was one burden she was going to have to bear alone.

★   ★   ★

That evening, Sophie once more prepared to visit Rachel. Tilly was feeling out of sorts and looking decidedly uncomfortable. 'Thanks, Sophie,' she muttered as Sophie headed for the fire escape. 'I do appreciate this. Really I do. You're seein' more of her than me lately. At this rate the poor little mite will be thinkin' you're her mam.'

'It's all right. I enjoy going to see her.'

'Are you feelin' all right?' Sophie had seemed very subdued this evening and Tilly was concerned about her. She felt guilty for asking her to go and see Rachel yet again, but if she didn't have word of the little girl daily she found it hard to sleep for worrying about her. The birth couldn't come quickly enough for her now because she didn't know how much longer she could bear to be apart from her daughter. And something else was troubling her too.

'I'm fine,' Sophie assured her dully as she prepared to clamber through the window.

'Sophie . . . Before yer go, there's sumfin' I need to tell yer. I've been tryin' to decide whether I should or not but I think you have a right to know.'

'Yes?' Sophie paused to look back over her shoulder.

'The thing is, while it were quiet this afternoon I decided to take a peep in the guest book. Yer know, the one they keep under the desk in the foyer?'

'Whyever would you do that?'

''Cos I got to thinkin'. I've had a lot o' time to think since I stopped workin' in the laundry. Anyway, I were curious to see if that American couple that left wiv the baby were registered in there an' they weren't.'

Sophie was confused now. 'So . . . what about it?'

'Well, don't yer see? *All* the guests are registered in the book but the Hamiltons were shown straight up to the fourth floor. There were no invoice in the book for 'em, no payment slip, nuffin' at all, which got me to wonderin' again. We've both said that we thought there might be sumfin' fishy goin' on here an' now I'm pretty sure of it. Think about it – Ben told us both when we first came here that his mother had sumfin' to do wiv the Welfare – but has anybody ever been to see us? The answer to that is no. An' then the fact that we ain't bin allowed any medical check-ups, don't yer find that strange? An' Cathy deliverin' her baby here in the hotel?'

'What are you trying to say?'

'I'm tryin' to say that I think Ben an' the missus are runnin' some sort of an illegal baby farm here. Yer know, sellin' the babies to couples who can afford to buy 'em.'

Sophie had to admit, it did seem to add up.

'That ain't all,' Tilly went on. 'The more I think about the way Cathy just disappeared the worse I feel about it. You know as well as I do that Cathy would never have just upped an' gone wivout comin' back fer her things, so where is she?'

Sophie had no answer to the question as she stared back at Tilly. After a short time Tilly shrugged. 'Look, don't get worryin' about it now. We can talk about it later. You'd berra get off else Mrs McGregor will think you ain't comin' an' she'll put Rachel to bed.'

Sophie nodded solemnly as she started to clamber through the open window.

'Yer won't forget to drop that money off to Alfie in the Queen's on yer way home, will yer?'

'No – of course not.' Sophie was wondering yet again why her life had suddenly become so complicated and the last thing she needed at the minute was another meeting with Alfie. Even the thought of him made her flesh crawl, although of course she couldn't tell Tilly that. Just this week the waistbands on her skirt had begun to get a little tight but apart from that no one would have known she was pregnant as yet if she hadn't told them, which was why she supposed Alfie had shown an interest in her. She stifled a grin as she wondered what his response would be if he should find out though she suspected that he would run a mile.

'I'll be back as soon as I can,' she promised now and taking her shoes off she stole quietly down the fire escape and tiptoed towards the back gate.

Once in Waterloo Road she climbed the steps to Mrs McGregor's flat and in no time at all Rachel hurtled towards her and flung herself into her arms. A wave of love washed over Sophie as she cuddled the sturdy little body to her and for no reason that she could explain she suddenly felt like weeping. Mrs McGregor seemed to pick up on her despondent mood and once Rachel was happily playing with her dollies some minutes later she led Sophie to the kitchen and made her a cup of tea.

'Come on then, spit it out,' she said gently. She had always prided herself on keeping her nose out of other people's business but Sophie looked so downhearted that she felt sorry for her. When Sophie didn't immediately answer her a terrible thought occurred to her and she pressed, 'Nothing's happened to Tilly, has it?'

'Oh, no. It's nothing like that,' Sophie quickly assured her.

Mrs McGregor sighed with relief. She was aware that the birth of Tilly's baby was imminent and already she was wondering how she would cope when she came to take Rachel away. Over the months that the child had been there she had come to love her as her own, but she also knew that Tilly adored her child, so the sooner they could be together again the better. She had often wondered exactly where Tilly was staying and why, but seeing as it was none of her business she had never asked. Not that she hadn't wanted to! Sensing that Sophie wasn't going to talk she urged her back into the lounge where she spent another half an hour with Rachel before saying her goodbyes.

Once back out on the road, Sophie's footsteps slowed. She knew that she should go to the Queen's Hotel and pass over the money that Tilly had sent for Alfie but feeling as low as she did she somehow couldn't face it. She decided that instead she would tell Tilly a white lie and say that she must have missed him. Suddenly she needed to see the sea and have a little time to herself.

Within minutes she was standing on the seafront gazing

out at the ships far out on the ocean. A solitary tear slid down her cheek as she thought back over the day's events. How had she come to be in such an awful position? It was as she was leaning across the railings looking down onto the deserted beach that she heard a familiar voice and her heart began to thump. Stepping back into the shadows of a hot dog stand her eyes searched the hordes of holidaymakers passing by and then sure enough – there he was. It was Matthew, her brother, and he had his arm tight about the waist of his fiancée. She watched them pass within a few yards of her and fought the urge to run out and throw her arms about him and beg him to take her home. But she knew that she never could now. Matthew looked happy and she had to leave him to get on with his life. He was in the past now and she had to be strong enough to face the future alone.

When he eventually disappeared into the crowd she dragged herself away from the railings and slowly made her way back to the hotel. Tilly would be waiting for her, eager to have news of Rachel and Alfie. Ah well, she consoled herself, at least she could assure her that Rachel was well. She was almost there when she had yet another shock, for as she rounded a corner she nearly collided with Alfie who had his arm round the shoulders of a young girl as he laughed down into her face. He looked up and for a moment it would have been hard to tell who was the more shocked of the two of them, but then Alfie grinned resignedly. He had been caught in the act good and proper.

Sophie's hands clenched into fists of rage at her sides as she glared at him. 'Couldn't you have waited for just another couple of weeks until Tilly had had the baby?' she snapped. 'Do you have *any* idea at all of just how much she loves you?'

Shock registered on the face of the young girl and she moved away from him. ''Ere, what's all this about a babby then?'

'It's all right. It's nothing to do wi' me,' Alfie quickly assured her. 'It's just her mate went an' got a crush on me an' I couldn't get rid o' the silly little tart.'

'You didn't think she was so silly when you promised her a future and took her money off her every chance you got!' Sophie flared.

He shrugged. 'Come on, doll. You ain't daft. You saw who it were doin' all the chasin'. I'm hardly goin' to turn it down when it's bein' offered on a plate, now am I?'

Sophie had to resist the urge to slap his face as white-hot rage bubbled though her veins but then as suddenly as it had come the rage ebbed away and she felt tears stinging at the back of her eyes.

'I'll tell yer what. Now's as good a time as any, so when yer get back yer can tell Tilly that I've found me someone else, eh?'

Her shoulders sagged as she watched him walk jauntily away without a care in the world, his arm once again slung round his latest girlfriend. If she were to be honest with herself she knew that a lot of what he had said was true. Tilly *had* done all the chasing. In all the time that

Sophie had known her she had only ever seen Alfie put himself out for her once, on the day when he had taken Rachel to the gate of the hotel to see her. But then, Sophie could understand why Tilly had done it. She had suffered so much that she'd seen Alfie as a means of escape from the life she had known. He was going to be the knight in shining armour who would take her away and make everything right with the world. And then they would all live happily ever after. As Sophie was discovering, fairy-tales didn't have happy endings in real life. But how was she going to tell her?

Chapter Thirteen

As Sophie approached the bottom of the fire escape she saw that Tilly's window was in darkness and a little worm of unease began to wriggle its way around her stomach. Usually, Tilly would be hanging out of the window, eager to hear news of Rachel and Alfie. But tonight there was no sign of her. Slipping off her shoes, Sophie began to climb the cold metal steps. Once outside Tilly's window she levered it up and climbed silently into the room then stood awhile waiting for her eyes to adjust to the darkness.

'Sophie, is that you?'

Tilly's voice made her jump and as she peered into the gloom Sophie saw the outline of her curled up into a ball on the bed. Dropping her shoes to the floor she hurried over to her.

'Yes, it's me. But what are you doing lying here in the dark?' Crossing to the light switch she snapped the bare electric light bulb on before looking back at Tilly. What she saw made her gasp with concern. Tilly was as white as a sheet and her skirt was wet and sticking to her legs.

'Tilly, what's happened?'

Tilly grinned ruefully. 'Me waters have broke an' the pains have started but I didn't want to tell the missus or Ben till you got back an' I knew Rachel an' Alfie were all right. They *are* all right, ain't they?'

As tears sprang to Sophie's eyes she wrestled with her conscience. How could she tell Tilly now that Alfie had finished with her? Making a hasty decision she nodded solemnly.

'They're both fine,' she muttered tearfully. It was so hard to see Tilly like this and to be unable to do anything to help her.

'What's my Alfie have to say then?' Tilly asked eagerly. 'Is he missin' me?'

'Y . . . yes, I'm sure he is. But let's not talk about him now. What can I do to help you?'

Tilly looked back at her with affection shining from her eyes as she gently took Sophie's hand and squeezed it. 'You can wish me luck an' then get back to yer room so I can go an' get this over wiv. An' don't look so frightened. I've bin dreamin' of this day. Very soon now I'll be free to go an' start a brand new life. But Sophie . . .' She hesitated; she had never been one to show her true feelings, except to Rachel and Alfie. 'Sophie, I want yer to know that you've bin the best friend I've ever had,' she said shyly. 'I'll never forget what you've done fer me an' the way you've allus stood up fer me. There's just one more thing I need you to do for me now though . . . if you would?'

'Of course. Anything – just name it.' A big fat tear slid down Sophie's cheek and plopped onto the bed as she returned the pressure of Tilly's hand.

Tilly was unable to answer for a moment as a pain ripped through her but then when it had passed she took a deep breath and pointed to the top drawer.

'In there you'll find an envelope. I want yer to take it an' keep it safe. I intend to be out o' here wivin the next couple o' days but if fer any reason I don't show up to collect me stuff an' see yer before I go, then yer to open it. *Please* say you'll do that for me. You're the only one here I can trust.' She could have added that only that very night she had decided to pack her bags and get out of there, but it was too late now. The baby was coming and she would have to stay and see it through despite her misgivings.

'Consider it done.' Sophie fetched the envelope then crossing back to Tilly she helped her climb off the bed. For a moment they gazed at each other, then suddenly they were in each other's arms and clinging together.

'Do yer know, if I could have had a sister I'd have wanted her to be just like you,' Tilly told her softly.

'Oh, Tilly, I'll miss you so much.' Sophie was sobbing now and it was Tilly who was doing the comforting.

'Yer daft ha'porth. You'll have me blartin' an' all in a minute. Now go an' put that envelope somewhere safe an' wish me luck, eh?'

With Tilly leaning heavily on Sophie's arm the girls emerged onto the landing and Sophie walked her to the top of the stairs. 'Do you want me to come down with you?' she asked anxiously.

'Berrer not. Yer know what the missus is like if she thinks we're becomin' overfamiliar. Can't fault the timin' though can yer? I reckon that couple who arrived this evenin' that the missus put on the fourth floor have come to wait fer the baby. I just hope they'll be good to it, that's all.'

Sophie tended to agree with her but was so choked with emotion that for now she couldn't say anything.

Leaning towards her, Tilly pecked her softly on the cheek then taking a deep breath she slowly began to descend the stairs. Sophie watched until she was out of sight before going into her room. And suddenly the loneliness closed round her yet again.

That night sleep eluded her. She sat for some time trying to read one of the newspapers that had been discarded in the dining room but nothing seemed to hold her attention. She had a long hot soak in the bath and stood for hours gazing from the window across the Blackpool rooftops; still she couldn't sleep, so she paced up and down her room until she was worried she would wear a hole in the cold linoleum underfoot as she fretted about Tilly and thought on the things that she had told her earlier in the evening.

Eventually she turned off the light and climbed into

the lumpy bed, where she tossed and turned until she saw the first signs of dawn struggling through the gap in the thin curtains.

When she emerged from her room the next morning she almost collided with Amy, who was on her way to the kitchen too. She nodded at Sophie then hurried on as Sophie followed at a more leisurely pace.

Once again they found Mrs G in a black mood as she slammed the sausages into the frying pan. She looked tired and seemed to be a bag of nerves, jumping at her own shadow.

'You'll be on your own in the laundry room today, Amy,' she informed her shortly.

Amy looked horrified. 'Won't I even have Tilly there to tell me what to do?'

'I just *said* not, didn't I?'

As colour stained Amy's cheeks she lowered her head and stared at her plate and despite the fact that Sophie didn't find her particularly easy to get along with she found herself feeling sorry for the girl.

Throughout the day, Sophie returned to her room at every opportunity she got, hovering outside the door that led to the fourth-floor landing each time, hoping to hear something – anything. More than once she was tempted to sneak in and see if she could catch a glimpse of her friend but she was too afraid to. Each time she was disappointed and went back to work with her heart a little heavier. Perhaps they had taken Tilly into hospital. She hoped so, for as she thought back to the tiny little room where Cathy must have given birth it filled her with dread. What if complications arose during the birth? Did Mrs Lewis get a trained midwife in to assist? The questions ran round and round in her head until she had worked herself into a rare old state and it was all she could do to stop herself from storming onto the fourth floor and demanding to see her friend. But common sense prevailed and she managed to resist the urge.

It was as she was lying in bed that night lost in thought that a noise dragged her back to the present. Leaning on her elbow she strained to listen and sure enough there it was again: very faint, but quite unmistakably the sound of a baby crying. Tears of relief washed across her face. It *had* to be Tilly's baby, which meant that it was all over. Despite the fact that she knew Tilly had no intention of keeping it, she found herself wondering what it was. Had she given birth to a little girl or a little boy? And did it have the same lovely red hair as Rachel? Thoughts of Tilly's baby made her hand drop to her own stomach. Although she hadn't told Tilly yet, she was still determined to get away from here before the birth. Even the prospect of throwing herself on the mercy of the Welfare was preferable to staying here now and with every day that passed she was more determined to escape. But first she must know that Tilly was all right and reunited with Rachel.

She wondered how she would tell Tilly about Alfie's betrayal. She had no doubt at all that Tilly would be absolutely broken-hearted but what choice did she have? Deep down she supposed that she shouldn't have lied to her on the night she'd gone into labour, but comforted herself with the knowledge that she had done so for Tilly's own good. At least she had faced the birth with a dream in her heart to keep her going.

Eventually she fell asleep from sheer exhaustion and slept like a top until the cacophony of early morning traffic outside awakened her the next morning.

When she entered the kitchen she found Amy slouched at the table with her lips in a pout and Mrs G in a towering rage.

'Bacon or sausage?' Mrs G barked at her and, to Sophie's surprise, Amy flung her chair away from the table and shouted back at her.

'Neither! I don't care for all this fatty food. *Nor* do I care for being treated like a skivvy. At the private school I attended everything was done for me. Tell Ben if he wishes to speak to me I shall be in my room but I certainly won't spend another single day in that *awful* laundry!'

'Well, you're not at your private school now, and I think I can safely say it will be a cold day in hell before Ben comes running after the likes of *you*,' Mrs G retorted as Amy stamped towards the door with murder in her eyes. 'And furthermore – perhaps you should have thought of where you might land up before you went and got yourself into trouble, my girl!'

The last words were lost as the door slammed

resoundingly behind her and Sophie stood there with her mouth open.

'Stuck up little madam!' Mrs G snapped furiously. 'Just who the hell does she think she is anyway!'

Sophie edged nervously towards the table and twiddled with the fringe of the tablecloth. She'd been hoping to get Mrs G alone to see if she could wheedle any news of Tilly out of her but it was abundantly clear that now was not a good time so she stayed tight-lipped and wide-eyed as the portly woman rampaged around the room. Within seconds her anger ebbed away and she leaned heavily against the large wooden dresser as her shoulders sagged.

For a time it seemed that she hadn't even noticed that Sophie was there but then when she looked up, Sophie saw that tears were streaming down her cheeks.

'Mrs G . . . Are you all right?' With her hand outstretched, Sophie took a hesitant step towards her.

Mrs G sniffed loudly as she lifted her apron and wiped it across her face.

'I'm tired, Sophie,' she replied quietly with such a wealth of sadness in her voice that Sophie was sorry for her.

'Why don't you think of retiring then?' she asked innocently.

'Huh! If only it were that simple.'

'But it *could* be. Couldn't you buy yourself a little place somewhere and take it easy for a change? Haven't you got any savings?'

'Money isn't the problem. It's those two up there. How could I leave them? They need someone to keep an eye out for them, because—' Mrs G suddenly clammed up. What was she doing letting her mouth run away with her like that?

'Let's get this breakfast on the go, eh?' she suggested briskly. 'The guests will be coming down soon and the missus will raise the roof if it isn't ready. We'll deal with that little madam later.' Once again her usual efficient self, she set to with a will and Sophie had no choice but to help her.

It was mid-morning before she entered the room again to find Ben and Mrs G close together deep in conversation, but the second she walked in they sprang apart and Ben headed for the door. Sophie might not have even been there, for he barely glanced in her direction. Not that it bothered her. She had stopped looking at Ben through rose-tinted glasses long ago.

'Amy will be leaving us later today,' Mrs G informed her, keeping her eyes on the loaf she was slicing.

'Oh . . . where will she be going?' Sophie found it hard to keep the surprise from her voice, especially when she saw colour flood into the older woman's cheeks and her hands begin to tremble.

'I've just told you all you need to know,' Mrs G answered shortly and refused to say so much as another single word on the subject. Sophie helped herself to a drink of water then quietly left the kitchen, but the second she shut the door behind her she heard Mrs G burst into tears. Sighing, she went back to work already beginning to count the hours until she too could leave this cursed place.

That evening she heard someone on the landing and when she inched the door open she was just in time to see Ben and Amy disappearing through the door that led to the stairs. He was carrying a large bag, which contained Amy's possessions, and Amy was gazing up at him flirtatiously.

Best of luck, Sophie thought, then went back to the newspaper article she was reading about Nehru, India's Prime Minister, who had died that day.

Two days later as Sophie was on her way to the laundry room she saw the couple who had been staying on the fourth floor descending the guests' stairs with Mrs Lewis. The man was carrying a huge suitcase and the woman had a baby in her arms. Sophie crept silently along the landing and after hitching the pile of dirty laundry more comfortably into her arms she peered down into the foyer below. As she was standing there she caught a flash of red hair as the crystal chandelier shone on the baby's head.

That must be Tilly's baby, she thought, and her heart sank. How must Tilly be feeling now? It was all very well preparing yourself to give a child away, but would it really be so easy once you'd seen it and held it in your arms? Knowing how much Tilly adored Rachel she guessed that right now her friend would be in a terrible state. She longed to go and comfort her but knew that she couldn't. Her thoughts moved on and she found herself wondering how she would feel when the time came to give *her* baby up. But then she thought back to the child's conception and shuddered. If she kept it, it would always be a constant reminder of the night her father had violated her.

Pushing the depressing thoughts away she tried to cheer herself. Tilly must be very close to leaving now if the child had already gone. She might even appear upstairs tonight to collect her things. Or she could even be there already. Impulsively she dropped the bundle of washing and took the stairs two at a time.

Once on the fifth-floor landing she ran along the corridor and threw Tilly's door open only to find Ben bundling her things into bags.

Skidding to a halt, she glared at him. '*Where's* Tilly?' she demanded to know.

He paused before telling her, 'She'll be up here tonight to collect these. Obviously she's still recovering from the birth so I thought I'd come up and pack for her to save her the trouble. Now . . . haven't you got work to do?'

Sophie's brow furrowed in a frown. How could she know if he was telling the truth?

'May I see her?' she blurted out before she had a chance to stop herself.

'Certainly not! You know the rules here. Now get back to work.' His voice was threatening now and a shudder ran up her spine.

'Look, I . . .' She gulped before forcing herself to say, 'I really don't feel happy with this arrangement any more. Amy has gone and Tilly has had her baby, so I would like to leave too.'

Was it her imagination or did she see fear flash in his eyes before he said firmly, 'I'm not prepared to discuss this with you. We made an agreement and you know what will happen if you should try to break it. Now go about your business before I get angry.'

She backed towards the door and hurried away. If Tilly returned tonight she would leave with her and just let him try to stop her. There *was* something going on here that wasn't quite right. If he made any more threats she would tell him she was informing the police. That would put a stop to his gallop.

For the rest of the day she found it hard to concentrate on anything and she was grateful when she could excuse herself from the kitchen and go to her room. First, though, she would check and see if Tilly was back. The second she opened her bedroom door her worst fears were realised, for she saw at a glance that all of Tilly's things had gone, just as Cathy's had after the birth of her baby.

Clattering back down the stairs she rushed through to the kitchen and flung the door open, then without preamble she snapped, 'Where's Tilly? And where are Mrs Lewis and Ben?'

Mrs G's hand flew to her throat. 'They've gone out,' she mumbled fearfully. Without a word Sophie rushed from the room again. She ran through the darkened laundry room and after fumbling with the key in the lock she flung the door open and stumbled into the yard where she opened the huge metal lid of the bin and stared down into it; sure enough there were some bags tucked deep down beneath the rubbish. Leaning precariously over the edge she pulled one towards her and gazed in horror as one of Tilly's miniskirts fell out of it.

'Oh, dear God, *no*. Please don't let anything have happened to her,' she sobbed into the gloom. It was then that a pain had her doubled over and she sank to her knees as she clutched at her stomach. When it had passed she slowly rose and headed back to the kitchen where she stared coldly at Mrs G.

'They've done something to her . . . haven't they?'

Mrs G's mouth worked, but for a while no words came out until suddenly she blurted out, 'You have to get away from here, Sophie – *NOW!*'

Hurrying round the table she took Sophie's two small hands in her own and gently shook them up and down. Sophie was a good girl, she had somehow known it since the first time she'd met her, and suddenly she could stand no more.

'Listen to me,' Mrs G told her urgently. 'I want you to go upstairs and pack your bags right this minute. They'll be gone for a good couple of hours yet. But once you've left you must promise me that you'll *never* let on to anyone that you were ever here. Do you understand? Get as far away as possible an' keep your lips sealed else I can't be responsible for what might happen to you.'

Her fear was contagious and Sophie felt herself nodding as the old woman led her towards the door. Once there Mrs G hugged her with tears streaming down her face.

'Will you be all right here all on your own?' Sophie asked fearfully.

'Don't you get worrying about me. I can handle those two,' the old woman assured her and then as a thought occurred to her she crossed to a large ceramic jar on the dresser and took a small bundle of notes from it. Hurrying back to Sophie as fast as her swollen feet would allow she pressed them into her hand. 'Take this and get as far away from here as you can on it. And may God go with you . . . Now hurry – there's not a moment to lose.'

Sophie hesitated just long enough to drop a kiss onto her wrinkled cheek, then she fled from the kitchen and clattered away up the stairs as if the devil himself was on her heels. Once in her room she dragged the battered suitcase she'd arrived with from the bottom of the wardrobe and began to fling her clothes haphazardly into it. It was as she was emptying her drawers that the next pain gripped her and she felt a flood of warmth between her legs. Gritting her teeth, she tried to ignore it as she flung the envelope Tilly had entrusted to her onto the clothes and snapped the lid shut.

Seconds later she stood at the door with her coat over her arm and her case gripped in her hand. She cast one last glance around the room then without even stopping to turn the light off she left the door swinging wide open for the very last time. Ignoring the back staircase that the staff were normally encouraged to use she stumbled down the main one that led into the foyer. All the way down the stairs her heart was in her mouth and she expected Ben or his mother to leap out in front of her, but the only people she saw were a family of guests returning to their room on the third floor. At the bottom of the stairs she paused. If she went out of the front door and Ben and his mother were returning she would bump straight into them. Turning, she barged back into the kitchen where she found Mrs G sitting at the table sobbing as if her heart would break.

'Why don't you come with me?' she asked softly.

The old woman sadly shook her head. 'I can't, love. They need me, you see? But don't worry, they would never hurt me. Now go and make the best of your life while you have the chance.'

Sophie hovered for the merest of seconds wondering what it could be that made the old woman so very loyal to Ben and his mother. But then she let herself out into the yard and took a deep breath before cautiously moving towards the back gate.

Once out on the pavement panic lent speed to her feet and she began to run until she had put some distance between herself and the hotel. It was then that she had no choice but to rest, for the pains were coming in great waves that took her breath away. Leaning heavily against a wall she clutched at her stomach. What was happening to her? Was she having a miscarriage? She'd been so intent on getting away that she hadn't considered where she was going but now she tried to gauge her bearings. Glancing around she found that she was in South Street, which meant that she wasn't far from Waterloo Road and Mrs McGregor. She would help her, Sophie was sure of it – she would go there.

Gripping her case again she started towards the lights at the end of the road but suddenly the floor started to come up to meet her and the light from the street lamps grew dim. She shook her head as she tried to clear the fog that was forming, but it was no good: the lights were going out. Pictures of Tilly and her mother flashed in front of her eyes and she felt the tears on her cheeks though she hadn't been aware that she was crying. She called out to them but they seemed to be drifting further and further away from her as her panic increased. As it grew darker, the overwhelming pain seemed to fade away, so instead of fighting it any more she gave herself up to the welcoming oblivion and sank to the ground.

Chapter Fourteen

'Are you sure that you didn't see Sophie leave last night?'

'No, no I didn't – honestly.' Mrs G twisted her fingers together as Ben paced up and down the kitchen in front of her. He was so enraged that for the first time she feared him. His mother stood to one side listening to all that was being said with her left eye twitching uncontrollably, a habit she always adopted when she was nervous.

'Look, why don't you just try to forget about the girl?' Mrs G implored him. 'She's not going to spout about being here, is she? She'd be too afraid of the repercussions after the way you frightened her.'

'I'd like to think you were right but the trouble is she got too damn close to Tilly for my liking! And furthermore – *how* did she escape? I don't think she'd have dared to walk out through the front door and if she'd left via this room you'd have seen her.'

'There's the laundry-room door at the back,' Mrs G pointed out, terrified of him guessing her part in Sophie's departure. All the time they were talking Amanda Lewis was watching the older woman closely. Suddenly she asked pointedly, 'Are you *quite* sure that you didn't see her leave?' The suspicion in her voice brought the colour flooding into the older woman's cheeks.

'Of course I didn't! I would have stopped her if I'd known she was going, wouldn't I?'

'Would you? I always got the impression that you'd rather taken to Sophie.'

'Well, I have to admit she was a cut above the girls that usually end up here but I don't interfere in what is none of my business. Not that I condone it. I've told you before and I'll tell you again, I reckon you're both skating on thin ice now. Enough is enough and if you've got any sense you'll let this be a lesson to you both!'

Ben's pacing continued, up and down, up and down, until Mrs G's nerves were stretched to the limit. 'For God's sake, Ben. Calm down. What's done is done. And carryin' on like this certainly won't fetch her back. What's the matter with you? Were you more than a little fond of her as well then? Is that what this is all about?'

Jealousy flamed in his mother's eyes as Ben furiously rounded on Mrs G. 'Don't be so stupid. You know perfectly well where my affections lie.' Crossing to his mother he took both of her hands in his and gently shook them up and down as if to add emphasis to his words. 'You know I love *you*, don't you, Mother? I would never leave you for some stupid little slut.'

'Sophie wasn't a slut,' Mrs G declared. 'And it's about time you did find yourself a nice girl. Someone your own age. I'm here to take care of your mother should she need it. Though why any of us is still here is beyond me. It's greed, that's what it boils down to. You two are never satisfied, are you? You never have enough, and you just mark my words, that will be your downfall.'

Ben tossed his head in annoyance. Why did she have to keep going on about him finding someone his own age? He was perfectly happy with the way things were. He knew that she wasn't happy about the fact that he shared a bedroom with his mother, but he himself could see no harm in it, so why should she?

She meantime was having thoughts of her own. Sometimes at night she would lie awake in bed listening to them talking in the next room as tears streamed down her face. Amanda was totally dependent on her son, to the point that he wasn't allowed a life of his own, which to Mrs G's way of thinking was unhealthy. But what could she do about it? *You could leave*, a little voice in her head whispered to her, *just pack your bags and go*. But then what would happen to them both without her to look out for them?

Thankfully, Ben's temper seemed to have burned itself out for now so she waited until she had composed herself a little and turned back to them. At that moment the bell in the foyer sounded.

'You'd best go and see who that is. We've three families due to book in for today.' Her words were addressed to Amanda, who slowly ran her sweating hands down the skirt of her smart costume.

'I'll go.' So saying she lifted her head high and walked regally from the room.

Instantly, Mrs G addressed Ben. 'I want you to promise me that you'll not go looking for Sophie, Ben.'

He ignored her but she took that as a good sign, for at least he hadn't disagreed with her. 'Is . . . Tilly all right?' she now asked hesitantly. She had promised herself that she wouldn't ask but the words had slipped out before she could stop them.

He shook his head. 'Far from it. In fact, she's being *very* uncooperative.'

'So . . . why don't you let her go too then and let this be an end to it once and for all? If you did she'd no doubt join Sophie, wherever she might be, and you could start again. Buy a little hotel of your own somewhere else where no one knows you. I'd stay here and look after your mother – you know I would.'

When he looked across at her with raw pain bright in his eyes it was all she could do stop herself from dragging him into her arms. 'Think about it,' she gently encouraged him. 'I saw how you looked at Sophie from time to time. You're a young man with your whole life before you. This obsession you have with your mother is unhealthy. You should be with someone your own age who could give you children and a normal life.'

He studied her intently for a moment before suddenly turning to go. 'Mother needs me,' he told her dully and as the door closed behind him she lowered her head and wept.

'Oh, dear God,' she sobbed to the empty room. 'When is all this going to end?'

'Hello. *Hello* . . . can you hear me?'

The comforting darkness was receding and someone was calling to her. But Sophie was reluctant to leave the warm, dark place she had found. She blearily opened her eyes, blinking in the harsh light, and slowly a face in a starched white cap swam into focus.

'Ah, so you're back with us are you?' The voice was kindly and Sophie wondered who it was. And where was she? What had happened?

Suddenly the events of the previous night flooded back and her hand settled on her stomach. It felt much flatter again and the terrible pains were gone; in their place was a dull, throbbing ache.

As she tried to rise from the pillow gentle hands pressed her back down. 'Don't try and sit up just yet,' a voice advised. 'You're in hospital and you've had a little oper-ation. But don't worry about it. You'll be fine now and the doctor will be round to see you in a minute. In the meantime can you tell me your name?'

Sophie turned her head away from the voice as a soli-tary tear slid down her cheek and plopped onto the starched white pillowslip.

'It's all right. You don't have to talk now if you don't feel up to it. Just lie there and rest. How about a cup of tea? You must be as dry as a bone.'

When she heard footsteps move away she slowly began

to look around her. She found she was in a small ward with whitewashed walls and a locker standing at the side of the bed. Everything looked very cold and bleak and smelled faintly of stale disinfectant but she was beyond caring as she stared dully up at the ceiling. Pictures of Tilly's laughing face and fiery red hair danced in front of her eyes and a feeling of despair washed over her. But she didn't have long to wallow in self-pity, for just then an older woman in a navy uniform that reminded Sophie of the one she had been forced to wear at the hotel walked briskly into the room. She was closely followed by an elderly man in a white coat with a gold pince-nez perched precariously on the end of his nose.

'Ah, she's awake at last, Matron.' The doctor smiled at Sophie. 'You gave us a bit of a scare back there, young lady. It's a good job you were found and brought in when you were or you would have been in very serious trouble indeed. How are you feeling now?'

Sophie's lips set in a grim line as she stared resolutely at the ceiling. She hated to appear so ungrateful but was determined not to tell them her name.

Lifting her charts from the end of the bed the doctor began to study them as he said, 'Ah well, perhaps you'll feel more like talking when I do my rounds tomorrow and you're a little more rested? Meantime I can tell you that you've been very lucky indeed. What I mean is − there's no permanent damage done. Sadly you did lose the baby, of course. That was gone before you arrived here. But I've had you in theatre and after a couple of days of bed rest you should be as good as new.' He looked pointedly at the third finger of her left hand and when he saw that it was without a wedding band he tactfully asked, 'Is there anyone you'd like us to contact?'

Sophie shook her head as a wealth of emotions coursed through her. So the baby was gone? She would be able to get on with her life now. She supposed that she should feel sad for the life that was lost, but in all honesty her overriding feeling was one of relief.

'Very well then. I shall be back to see you in the morning. Meanwhile don't hesitate to ask if there's anything you want.' He hooked her charts back onto the end of the bed and with a final nod left the room with Matron in hot pursuit.

Sophie lay there trying to put her thoughts into some sort of order. So very much had happened in such a short time that they were in turmoil. As her focus returned to Tilly panic took hold. Where was her suitcase? Tilly's envelope was inside it and because she had left the hotel in such a rush she hadn't had time to open it. Heaving herself up onto her elbow she looked round the room and to her relief she saw it on the floor next to the locker. As she swung her legs out of the bed and her feet connected with the floor a wave of dizziness swept over her and for a moment she thought that she was going to faint. She took some deep breaths then shakily crossed to the case, amazed at how weak she felt. After fumbling with the catch the lid finally fell open and she withdrew the precious envelope with shaking fingers and carried it back to the bed.

Once she was settled against the pillows again she slit the envelope and to her amazement a bundle of notes fell onto the counterpane. She looked at the money anxiously. This must be every single penny of the savings that Tilly had had left. Sweeping it aside for now she opened out the letter that was with it and slowly began to read:

My Dear Sophie,

If you ever get to read this letter I might be dead. There is nothing else that could ever stop me coming to say goodbye to you. I've enclosed the rest of my savings, which I'd like you to see Rachel gets. Please Sophie, if I don't return get out of here! This is a bad place. I know it's a lot to ask of you but will you make sure that Rachel is going to be cared for? I would love you to take her because I know Mrs McGregor can't afford to keep her without the money I give her each week. If you feel unable to I'll understand. Involve the Welfare if you have to but please, please make sure that she's all right for me. Also, will you get word to Alfie that I won't be seeing him again? Don't tell him too much or you might put yourself in danger if Ben finds out.

Lastly I want you to know that I love you as the sister I never had and always wanted. Don't know why 'cos we're as different as chalk from cheese. Life is a cruel bugger at times, ain't it?

Have a good life, dear friend. Mine was better for

having known you. Now please get away and take care,
and never let Rachel forget how much I love her.
  With love, your friend
  Tilly xxx

As the letter dropped from her hand harsh racking sobs
shook Sophie's body. Deep down she had known that
nothing would keep Tilly away from Rachel but she'd
hoped that she was wrong and her fears would prove to
be unfounded. Images of Tilly's belongings tucked deep
down in the hotel dustbin flashed in front of her eyes
and her hands balled into fists of rage. Why had this had
to happen? Tilly had never been a bad person, not deep
down. Misguided certainly, but she'd had a heart as big
as a bucket and had adored her little girl.

Thoughts of Rachel brought a fresh torrent of tears.
What would happen to her now? If she involved the
authorities as Tilly had suggested, she would probably be
adopted. But what if the people who adopted her didn't
love her? The questions whirled round and round in her
head. Rachel was such a precious little girl. How would
she ever live with herself if she didn't do right by her?

As the tears slowly dried on her cheeks she made a
hasty decision. *She* would take Rachel. She had thought
that now her own baby was gone she would be free to
carry on with her life and here she was about to take
on the commitment of someone else's child. Her heart
told her that she had no other option so she decided
that she must be practical. Lifting the bundle of notes

from the counterpane she slowly counted them. Altogether they totalled thirty-six pounds and ten shillings. Added to the money her mother had given her on the night she left home it meant she had almost fifty-five pounds. It seemed like a lot of money but Sophie was sensible enough to know that if it was going to feed herself and Rachel it wouldn't last for long. And where would they live? It certainly couldn't be anywhere around here for fear of bumping into Ben or his mother, which meant that she would have to take a train or bus fare out of the money for a start. She would have to get a job too. But what job could she do with a toddler in tow? The problems seemed insurmountable; then as she thought of Tilly she knew that she *must* find a way for her sake.

Once again she considered going to the police but as she thought back to the night Ben had pinned her against the wall she shuddered. *They could lock you away in a loony-bin*: his words echoed in her head. She knew that he was right. After all, who would take her word against his? By now he would have removed every scrap of evidence that she or Tilly had ever been there. And what would happen to Rachel?

Aunt Philly! As the idea formed she looked towards the case where the address her mother had given her was tucked down below her clothes. Perhaps she would help? Of course, Sophie realised that it was many years since her mother had seen her relative. She might go all the way to the Midlands only to find that the aunt was dead now. What a wild goose chase that would prove to be. But then what other choice did she have? With luck it *was* far enough away to escape Ben.

Glancing at the clock above the door she saw that it was mid-afternoon. Somehow she had to get out of here without being seen before too many questions were asked. At the moment the chance of that seemed highly improbable. Visitors bearing huge bunches of flowers and grapes were streaming past the door to disappear into the main ward. Nurses were flitting to and fro and the whole place was like a hive of activity. An idea suddenly occurred to her. If she were to get dressed and wait until the bell heralded the end of visiting time she might just be able to mingle with the visitors as they left and escape that way.

Deciding that it was worth a try she struggled into her clothes. Her arms and legs felt like lead and she was as weak as a kitten but she was also determined and eventually she managed to get her shoes and coat on. After snapping the lid of the case shut again she popped back into bed and pulled the covers up to her chin so that if anyone looked through the glass in the door they wouldn't see that she was dressed.

The next hour was one of the longest of her whole life. She lay there dreading a nurse coming in to check her blood pressure or something. Thankfully no one did and slowly the minutes ticked away.

When the bell finally sounded, Sophie almost jumped out of her skin. This was it then. Climbing weakly from the bed she took up her suitcase and crossed to the door, fighting off the waves of nausea that washed over her. After scanning up and down the corridor to make sure there were no nurses about she waited for the first visitors to start leaving and soon enough they began to file along the corridor in a straggly line of all shapes and sizes.

She pulled up her coat collar and when what appeared to be a family group passed her room she inched the door open cautiously and with her head bent began to follow them as closely as she could, keeping her case tucked in tight to her side. As they neared the large double doors at the entrance to the ward her heart leaped into her throat. The nurse who had tended to her earlier in the day had just entered with a doctor and was coming straight towards her. Sophie held her breath but thankfully the doctor and nurse were deep in conversation and sailed past her without so much as a glance.

Silently she began to count her footsteps, expecting to feel a restraining hand on her shoulder at any moment, and then a large woman member of the family ahead of her was pushing the doors open with a hand as big as a spade and she was outside the ward and could see the doors in front of her at the end of a long corridor that led to freedom.

Within minutes she was outside the hospital but still she didn't slow her steps until she was sure that no one was following her. She turned one corner then another with no idea at all of which direction she was going in until at last the hospital was some distance behind her. Only then did she stop to lean heavily against a wall. Already she felt as if she had walked miles. There was a dull ache in her stomach and her mouth felt dry but now that she was free she was intent on getting to Rachel. Moving on to the end of the road she stood for a second to get her bearings then as a bus rumbled towards her she got onto it, lugging her case behind her.

'Waterloo Road, please.'

The weary-looking bus conductor peeled a ticket from his machine and took her money without a word before swaying away down the aisle of the bus. Sophie stared from the grimy window, glad of a chance to be able to sit down for a while.

'Nice day, ain't it, ducks?' An elderly woman who was holding a large wicker basket on her lap smiled at her but Sophie merely nodded and looked away. She was in no mood to start a conversation.

When the bus drew to a halt at the end of Waterloo Road she climbed down and glanced up and down the road. So far so good. It was only yards now until she was at Mrs McGregor's and then she would see Rachel again.

At the bottom of the steep steps that led to the flat, a thought suddenly occurred to her and her footsteps slowed. What was she going to tell Mrs McGregor, or Rachel for that matter? She was still unsure by the time she knocked at the door but the second she saw Rachel scampering towards her with a cry of delight she stopped worrying. There would be time to think about explanations later.

'Why, Sophie.' Mrs McGregor's voice was laced with surprise. 'And what are you doing here in the day? You and Tilly usually visit at night, to be sure.'

Buying herself time, Sophie smiled over Rachel's shoulder as she swung her up into her arms. 'I'll explain in a minute; but for now I'd kill for one of your lovely cups of tea. I don't think anyone makes one quite like you, Mrs McGregor.'

'Well, that's a simple enough request and soon sorted, so it is,' the pleasant woman replied affably as she trundled towards the kitchen. 'Sit yourself down, lass, if you can find a chair that isn't covered in toys, that is, an' I'll be back in two shakes of a lamb's tail.'

As Sophie did as she was told and cuddled Rachel to her she felt as if her heart would break. Rachel was so like her mother that she could see Tilly every time she looked at her. But now was not the time to go to pieces. Very soon, Rachel would be her responsibility and she must be strong for her.

When Mrs McGregor appeared from the kitchen holding a tray of tea and biscuits, Rachel slid off Sophie's lap and happily pottered away to play with her toys. Sophie refused the biscuits that were offered but gratefully sipped at her tea as she chose her words carefully.

'Actually, Mrs McGregor, I've come to settle up with you what Tilly owes you and take Rachel.'

Mrs McGregor's tea slopped all down her skirt as she

stared at Sophie in amazement. She had known that Rachel wasn't going to be with her for very much longer, but now that the day had arrived she was filled with sadness.

'So, Tilly's had the wee baby then?' she asked tentatively.

Avoiding her eyes, Sophie nodded. 'Yes, she has, which is why I've come for Rachel.'

Mrs McGregor would miss her, and Tilly and Sophie too if it came to that. She'd come to look forward to their visits. It was a lonely life being a widow. And then of course there was the money she had earned for caring for Rachel. It had helped tremendously and she would miss that too.

Even so, she put up no argument. It had always been a bit of a funny arrangement now that she came to think of it and she'd quickly learned that the less she asked about Tilly's circumstances the better. Not that she could fault the girl; she was a good little mother. She obviously adored Rachel and her love was returned, for Rachel's little face would light up every time she saw her. In all the time she had cared for Rachel, Tilly had never been late with her board so much as once. She sighed before rising from the chair.

'What time were you thinking of taking her? She's due for a nap any time now and she tends to get grumpy if she doesn't have it.'

'Oh, that's all right,' Sophie assured her. 'If she has her nap it will give you time to pack her things.' Secretly she was pleased that they didn't have to leave straight away. In a few more hours it would be dark and she would be less conspicuous. It would also give her a chance to rest for a while because she was feeling so tired now that she could barely keep her eyes open.

If Mrs McGregor thought it strange that Tilly hadn't come for the child herself she wisely kept quiet. What she did comment on was the fact that Sophie didn't look at all well.

'Are yer not feeling so grand, lass?' she asked with concern.

Sophie opened her mouth to tell her that she was fine but then snapped it shut and grinned ruefully. 'I'm not feeling all that brilliant to be honest,' she admitted instead.

'In that case then, a little rest would do you no harm either. James, move those toys from the end of the settee and let Sophie put her feet up for a bit, there's a good bairn.'

Four-year-old James obediently did as he was told and Sophie swung her legs up. I'll just shut my eyes for half an hour, she thought to herself but in no time at all she was fast asleep.

Almost an hour later the sound of cutlery brought Sophie springing awake and she turned her head to see the children all seated at the table impatiently tapping their spoons as Mrs McGregor filled their dishes with a delicious-smelling beef stew.

'Come on now,' Mrs McGregor urged. 'There's a place

set here for you too. You look as if a decent meal inside you would do you the world of good, so you do.'

Sophie hadn't given food so much as a thought but suddenly she was hungry and she took a seat at the side of Rachel who smiled up at her adoringly. In that moment Sophie knew that she was doing the right thing. She would never have forgiven herself if she'd abandoned the child.

The meal was a merry affair with the children all chattering and giggling and Sophie found herself wishing that she could have stayed there to be a part of this close-knit family. Of course, she knew that it was impossible. Very soon now she and Rachel would have to begin a journey into the unknown. They would be travelling to another part of the country to find an aunt who might not even still be alive. She tried hard not to think of that. From now on she would take things a step at a time. She really had no choice.

The parting was tearful. Mrs McGregor kissed both Rachel and Sophie soundly as she said her goodbyes. Sophie had slipped her a little bit extra when she settled up what Tilly owed her, knowing how hard it must be for the woman to make ends meet with a growing family and no man to support her.

'Bless you, lass,' Mrs McGregor told her. 'And be sure to keep in touch. I want to know how you're all going on from time to time. Remember, my door is always open to you.'

'I will,' Sophie promised as she strapped Rachel into

her little pushchair. It was going to be no mean feat juggling two suitcases and the pushchair but somehow she would have to manage.

Eventually she balanced the smaller of the cases on the back of the pushchair and carried the other while she steered with the other hand.

'Why don't you leave one here for tonight? Or better still why don't you go wherever you're going in the morning? The weather has turned and the wind's enough to cut you in two out there. I wouldn't be at all surprised if we didn't have a thunderstorm,' Mrs McGregor fretted, but Sophie shook her head.

'I'll be fine, honestly. You go back inside now or the children will be crying for you. And thanks for all you've done. I know Tilly appreciates it.'

A final hug and they were on their way. There was no going back now. This was the start of a new life for both of them.

Chapter Fifteen

Rachel stared up at Sophie trustingly then clamping her thumb back in her mouth right up to the knuckle she leaned back in her pushchair. The streets of Blackpool were still alive with holidaymakers and Sophie was glad of the crowds as she hurried along as best she could. It was no easy task, burdened as she was not to mention her aching stomach and her tender breasts.

Every now and then she glanced nervously back across her shoulder but thankfully no one seemed to be following her. Having lived in Blackpool all of her life she knew the labyrinth of streets like the back of her hand. Tonight she was grateful for the fact, which meant that she also knew all the short cuts to take. After a while she steeled herself and turned onto the street that ran along the seafront. Despite the heat of the day the wind was now howling across the pavements and she could hear the sea pounding on the beach. Every now and again spray would hurtle over the sea defences and in no time at all her long dark hair was whipping about her heart-shaped face in damp wispy curls.

She paused just once to glance at the myriad coloured lights overhead that were strung for as far as she could see and to tuck the blanket more tightly about Rachel's sturdy little body, grateful to see that the child was slipping into a doze.

As if the wind and salt spray wasn't enough to soak her through a drizzle began to fall and she cursed beneath her breath. Rachel should be tucked up all warm and cosy in bed now, instead of which she was about to embark on a journey that had no guarantee of a home at the end of it.

Casting a last glance at the sea, Sophie again turned off into one of the side streets and headed towards the train station. She had almost reached her destination when she paused. Wouldn't the train station be the first place Ben would go when he discovered that she'd fled?

As she considered, she decided that it probably would be. Making a hasty decision she now changed direction and headed for the bus station instead. If she were to change buses two or three times it would mean there was less chance of her being found. She was quite aware that she was probably being paranoid but she wasn't prepared to take any unnecessary chances.

At last she reached the ticket office and fumbled in her purse as the man inside raised his eyebrows.

'Where you heading then, love?' he asked, as he glanced at Sophie curiously.

She felt colour flame in her cheeks. Hadn't he ever seen a woman with a child before?

'I want to get to Nuneaton in Warwickshire,' she told him shortly.

'Right . . . let me see now. Ah, you'll need the one going through to Coventry then. Once you arrive you can get one from there into Nuneaton. Taking the last of the holidaymakers home it is. You're lucky. Another half an hour and you'd have missed it.'

She slipped the money across the counter to him. 'I'll have a one-way ticket to there then please.'

Without a word he took her money and pushed the ticket across to her. If he were any judge, this young woman looked as if she was in some sort of trouble. She was so nervy that she was almost jumping at her own shadow. But then, he supposed she knew what she was doing. Probably had a ruckus with her old man and decided to clear off for a while, he guessed. She certainly didn't look the type though. She was very young and he noticed that she wasn't wearing a wedding ring although she did have a child. Deciding that it was really none of his business, he told her, 'Terminal two.'

Nodding her thanks she grasped the handles of the pushchair with one hand and juggling the cases in the other she turned away. He sighed before lifting the newspaper he had been reading to continue where he had left off.

Thankfully, Rachel slept for most of the way curled up in a tight little ball on her seat with her head in

Sophie's lap. Sophie stayed alert as she gazed from the bus window, wondering what life had in store for them both and missing Tilly more than she could say.

It was getting late when they arrived in Coventry and Sophie was glad of the kindly bus driver who transferred the pushchair and her cases from the bus onto the one that would take them into Nuneaton. When they finally arrived there she looked around with interest but it was dark and she couldn't see much.

'Could you tell me which stand I need to get a bus to Bermuda village?' she enquired of the same kindly driver as he unloaded her luggage and deposited it at her feet.

'That'll be stand number two over there, love, an' yer might just get it if yer lucky. But be quick though. It's just about to pull out an' there'll not be another one tonight,' he told her affably.

Nodding her thanks she gently deposited Rachel, who was still fast asleep, into her pushchair before following his pointing finger. By now she was tired and it was all she could do to keep her eyes open as the bus took her on the final part of her journey.

'Nearest you'll get to Bermuda village is Heath End Road,' the conductor told her when he came along with his ticket machine. 'But don't worry. It's not far to go once you get there. I'll point you in the right direction and tell you where to get off.'

She leaned back in the seat with Rachel cuddled close to her chest. Her greatest fear was that Aunt Philly might no longer be at the address her mother had given her, but she decided not to worry about that until the time came. It had been a long journey and all she wanted now was to close her eyes and sleep.

She almost did just that but suddenly she became aware of someone gently shaking her arm. 'Sorry to disturb yer, love, but we're comin' up to your stop.'

Sophie blinked up at the bus conductor who was leaning over her, his face concerned.

'What . . . Oh, thanks.'

She slithered along the seat then shifted Rachel to a more comfortable position in her arms before standing up in the aisle.

'I take it yer not from round here then?' he asked as he lugged her cases to the door for her.

'No, I've come to stay with an aunt in Bermuda village, though I don't have the foggiest idea where it is.'

'Not to worry.' He took her elbow and steadied her as the bus drew to a shuddering halt then after depositing the cases on the pavement he lifted down the pushchair before Sophie joined him.

'Take that road over there, look. That's Bermuda Road an' if you follow that it'll take yer straight down into the village.'

'Thank you. You've been very kind,' Sophie told him as he hopped back aboard.

'It's my pleasure. You take care now.' He smiled and gave her a friendly wave as the bus pulled away.

Sophie watched until the bus's tail lights had disappeared

around a corner. After laying Rachel back into her pushchair again she tucked her blanket tightly around her then standing back up she looked around. Luckily it wasn't raining here and she was thankful for small mercies. She found she was standing outside a public house called the Hare and Hounds and gazed at the windows curiously. She could see some men engrossed in a game of dominoes and stared enviously at the huge fire roaring up the chimney behind them. It had turned cold now and every single bone in her body seemed to ache. In fact she had never known she *had* so many bones to ache.

Wearily turning the pushchair in the direction the conductor had pointed she soon found herself in what resulted in little more than a lane. It was full of potholes and more than once she cursed softly as the suitcase she was balancing on the handles of the pushchair almost jolted off. She had gone no more than a few yards down it when the street lights stopped abruptly and she found herself making her way by the light of the moon. On either side of her were open fields with not a light to be seen anywhere and she began to grow nervous. After living so long in Blackpool she wasn't used to such wide-open spaces and she found herself straining her eyes into the darkness and glancing fearfully back across her shoulder. The hedges that bordered the lane whispered and leaned towards her as the wind gently shook them and when a fox suddenly darted across in front of her, her heart leaped into her throat and she let out a startled cry. The fox stopped abruptly, his bushy tail standing to attention as he stared back at her, then he shot off and disappeared through the hedge as she leaned heavily on the handles of the pushchair. It was as she was standing there that the enormity of what she was about to do hit her and she started to cry. How could she possibly just turn up unannounced on the doorstep of a great-aunt she had never met . . . and how would she explain Rachel away? And Tilly, what if she was after all unharmed somewhere and trying to find Rachel? Despite the letter that Tilly had written, Sophie clung to the hope that she *was* still alive. Perhaps Ben had locked her away?

Taking a deep breath she dragged her thoughts back to her present situation. This wasn't the time for worrying about anything but finding herself and Rachel a bed for the night. As her hand dropped to her coat pocket she fingered the piece of paper with her aunt's address written on it as if it would give her courage. She had read it so many times throughout the journey that she knew it off by heart now.

Mrs Phyllis Springs,
No 8 Claypit Cottages,
Bermuda Village,
Nuneaton,
Warwickshire

In her mind she had an image of a tiny little thatched cottage with hollyhocks growing in the garden in gay abandon and roses climbing round the door. The image was so strong that she could almost smell the flowers in the garden when she thought of it. Her aunt would turn out to be a slim, gentle woman, tall and stately with a beautiful smile. Beyond that Sophie didn't dare to think. What if she sent her away with a flea in her ear? Deciding that there was only one way to find out what her welcome would be she moved on again. After coming so far it seemed silly to turn back now.

She reached the top of a hill and as she looked down she saw lights twinkling in a valley below her. This then must be Bermuda village? It wasn't at all as she had expected it to be, for instead of being the picturesque, chocolate-box vision she had imagined, from up here it looked like a huddle of little terraced houses.

She began to practise an introductory speech in her mind as she started on the downward slope, but nothing sounded right even to her own ears. It must be almost eleven o'clock at night by now and her aunt could well be tucked up in bed, which meant that she probably wouldn't be too thrilled to be disturbed. Particularly by a great-niece she had never even met who had just decided to turn up out of the blue.

As she looked down on Rachel's sleeping face the responsibility of the child weighed heavy on her. With her eyelashes curled on her cheeks and her chubby thumb jammed in her mouth she looked like a little angel. But would an elderly lady want a toddler rampaging around the place? Aunt Philly, as her mother had affectionately called her, would probably be set in her ways. And what about her uncle? What would he be like? So many questions were whirling round in her head but she had the answers to none of them and the nearer to the village she got the more nervous she became. She longed to turn tail and run. But where would she run to? Even if her aunt wasn't pleased to see her she could only hope that she would let them stay at least for the night. Then tomorrow she would have to rethink where they might go.

By now the houses were looming nearer and soon she found herself walking along the main street through the village. Many of the windows she passed were in darkness but here and there a light shone out onto the cobbled road. She peered at them as she passed and soon realised that each terrace had a separate name.

Myrtle Cottages, Brick Cottages, Blue Lagoon Cottages and then suddenly – Claypit Cottages. She stopped outside the door of number eight with a frown on her face. There were no hollyhocks or roses; in fact, there wasn't even a garden and each front door opened directly onto the narrow little street. Even so Sophie breathed a sigh of relief. The curtains on the tiny downstairs window were tightly drawn but there was a light faintly shining through them, which told her that her aunt or whoever now lived there was at least still up and about.

She stood there uncertainly but then as she looked down at Rachel she knew she really had no choice but to swallow her pride and knock at the door. The poor little soul should have been tucked up in a warm bed hours ago.

Dropping the heavy case to the ground she sighed with relief as she flexed her fingers before lifting the other one down from the handles of the pushchair. She was sure that her arms must be at least six inches longer after all the carrying she had done. Tentatively she tapped at the door and her heart began to pound as a voice shouted, 'All right. I'm comin'. Hold yer horses.'

She heard footsteps approach and the sound of a bolt being drawn and then the door was inched open and a shaft of light flooded out into the street.

'Who is it – an' what do yer want at this time o' night, eh?'

The second image was shattered when she found herself confronted by a little grey-haired old lady who was wrapped in a voluminous candlewick dressing gown, which she clutched about her as she peered into the darkness.

'I . . . I'm sorry to bother you so late at night but . . .' The speech Sophie had so carefully rehearsed fled and for a moment she was speechless.

'Are yer a gypsy?' As the old woman stared suspiciously at the pushchair Sophie found her tongue again.

'Oh no, no, I promise I'm not a gypsy. I think I might be your great-niece . . . if your name is Phyllis Springs, that is.' There – it was said now and she stood back and watched as the old woman's mouth stretched in amazement.

'I'm Sally Winters' daughter,' Sophie babbled, fearful of the door being slammed in her face, 'and I believe my grandma, Miriam, was your sister. I'm Sophie.'

'Well . . . I'll go to the foot of our stairs,' the old woman uttered and then suddenly remembering her manners she held the door wide and ushered Sophie inside. 'Come on in, love. An' it's right welcome you are. Though I have to admit you've took me completely by surprise turnin' up like a bolt from the blue.'

Sophie manoeuvred the pushchair through the doorway, then turned back to drag the cases into the small room before closing the door behind her. She then looked at her aunt apologetically. 'I'm so sorry to turn up unannounced like this. My mam gave me your address some time ago and I know I should have asked if it was all right to come but I . . . I . . .' Suddenly everything caught up with her and tears spurted from her eyes. In a flash her aunt had taken her arm and led her towards a cosy chair by the fire.

'Never mind about that fer now. Yer look totally worn out. Take your coat off an' sit yerself down while I make yer a nice hot drink. Will this little one want anythin'?' When she thumbed towards Rachel, Sophie shook her head.

'No, I doubt she'll wake till morning now. Poor little thing is all in. It's been a very long journey for her.'

Her aunt nodded then yanking on the belt of the faded old gown she was wearing she shuffled away through a door leaving Sophie to take off her coat. She folded it and placed it neatly over the back of the chair before sinking gratefully into it. Her arms felt as if they were about to drop off and it was all she could do to keep her eyes open, particularly with the warmth of the fire lulling her. I'll just rest until she comes back, she thought as her eyes fluttered shut but within minutes she was sound asleep.

A shaft of watery sun streaming though a gap in the pretty curtains woke Sophie the next morning. In the room next door she could hear someone clattering about and the smell of sausages frying wafted temptingly on the air, making her stomach rumble with anticipation. She saw that her feet were resting on a low stool and someone had thrown a warm blanket across her. She lay there for a moment in that warm place between sleep and wakefulness, reluctant to leave it, but then once again the events of the last days caught up with her and she sat bolt upright. Where was Rachel? She swung her feet off the stool and looked around her curiously. When she'd arrived at her aunt's the night before she had been so exhausted that she'd barely noticed anything, but now she saw that while the outside of the cottage had proved to be something of a disappointment the inside was quite charming. A cottage suite covered in a gay floral fabric was arranged round a pretty tiled fireplace, in front of which stood a shining brass fender, and the window was hung with flowered curtains that almost matched the pattern on the suite. By the wall behind the settee stood a finely carved oak dresser with brightly painted plates displayed along its shelves. Old black and white photographs and pictures of landscapes in heavy gilt frames adorned the walls and the ceiling was heavily beamed. Sophie peered more closely at one of the photos, a family picture. The closer she looked the more certain she was that the little girl in it was her mother.

As Sophie's eyes swept the rest of the room she was enchanted with what she saw. However, there was no time to admire her surroundings for now, for Rachel was uppermost in her mind, so after folding the blanket neatly and laying it across the arm of the chair she tentatively approached the door from which the sounds were coming.

Her aunt was standing at a cooking range, which looked as if it might have been an antique, and as she saw Sophie enter the kitchen she flashed her a smile.

'Feelin' better after your sleep are yer?' she enquired kindly.

'Yes thank you, I am. But where's Rachel?'

Her aunt laughed. 'Well, the last I saw of her she were snorin' her head off in the boxroom at the back. You went out like a light last night so I got her undressed an' tucked her in.'

'Thanks.' In the cold light of day, Sophie was beginning to wonder if coming here had been such a good idea. After all, her aunt was bound to ask questions and she was in no position to answer any of them without lying.

Sensing her unease, Philly gestured towards the table. 'Sit yourself down then, an fer God's sake don't look so scared. I ain't the wicked witch o' the West, yer know? Now, how do yer like your bacon cooked?'

'Well done, please. Isn't your husband joining us for breakfast?'

A look of sadness settled on her aunt's face. 'I lost yer Uncle Jim some time back, more's the pity. Life ain't never been quite the same since, which is one reason I was so pleased when yer turned up last night. Will yer be able to stay for a while?'

Sophie hesitated before answering her. 'Well actually, I . . .' she floundered, suddenly feeling guilty for dumping herself and Rachel on this kind old woman.

'I'll take that as a yes then. Now – get yourself to the table an' get some o' this inside yer. I've seen more flesh on a scarecrow than there is on you. We'll hear the little 'un if she wakes.'

Sophie hesitantly lifted her knife and fork but then hunger overcame her and she fell on her food as if she hadn't eaten for a month as her aunt looked indulgently on. When her plate was cleared she smiled apologetically. 'Sorry, you must think I have no manners at all but I didn't get to eat much yesterday and—'

'You don't have to apologise to me, love. It's nice to have someone to cook for again. Nine times out of ten I don't bother now there's just meself to see to.' As her aunt was speaking she was refilling Sophie's cup with freshly brewed tea, which Sophie sipped at gratefully. She was beginning to feel almost human again now that she'd eaten, although she was aware that she must look a frightful mess. As if her aunt could read her mind she told her, 'Soon as you've had that you can go upstairs an' get washed an' changed if yer like. I've put your case in the room next to mine. The bathroom is the last door on the landin', though I'm afraid you'll have to manage with an outside privy. We're only one step away from still bein' in the dark ages in the village. It's through that door there next to the coal house when yer need it.'

Sophie nodded. It was then that they heard something scratching urgently at the door and her aunt leaped from her seat with a speed that would have done justice to a woman half her age.

'Bugger me, that's our Lily. I'd forgotten to let her in,' she exclaimed. When she opened the door a tiny little dog launched itself at her with its tail wagging furiously and the old woman laughed as she scooped it into her arms and kissed the top of its head affectionately. 'This is Lily,' she told Sophie. 'Don't ask me what breed she is 'cos the answer to that is I ain't got a clue, though I know her mother was a Yorkshire terrier. I got her to keep me company just after I lost your Uncle Jim an' she's as daft as a brush. You ain't scared o' dogs, are yer?'

Sophie smiled and shook her head as her aunt pottered away to get a dish for Lily, which she then loaded a spare sausage into. A silence fell for a time as they both watched the curious little animal scoff her treat down.

The questions are sure to start soon, Sophie thought to herself, and sure enough her aunt suddenly turned her attention from the dog back to her and smiled before remarking, 'Eeh! Yer look so like our Sally did at your age, it's almost uncanny. How is your mam, love?'

Sophie's heart started to thump so loudly that she was sure Aunt Philly must hear it. Gulping deep in her throat she opened her mouth to reply but at that moment a kitten-like wail floated down from upstairs and both pairs of eyes flew to the ceiling.

'That'll be Rachel and no doubt she'll be frightened waking up in a strange bed. You go on up to her, love. Your legs are younger than mine – she's in the third door along. Bring her down. I've got a nice pot o' creamy porridge bubblin' away on the stove all ready for her.'

Sophie flashed her a grateful smile before taking the stairs two at a time. She found Rachel wide-eyed and looking totally bewildered in a tiny room that was only just big enough for a single bed, but as soon as she saw Sophie she held her arms out trustingly to her.

Sophie kissed her soundly as she turned back the blankets and lifted her warm little body into her arms, and once again sadness overcame her. She couldn't bear to think that Rachel might never see her mother again. Tilly had loved her so much. She *must* be still alive somewhere. There and then Sophie promised herself that if she was, she would find her. The thought of returning to Blackpool filled her with dread but then she thought, what does it matter now? She was no longer pregnant so what could the police or the Welfare Department, for that matter, do to her?

The answer came with sickening speed. They *could* still take Rachel away. After all, she was only just turned eighteen and legally she had no claim to the child. They might decide that Rachel would be better off in a foster home, or they might even put her up for adoption and then she would have let Tilly down and she could never do that.

Her new-found courage deserted her as a picture of Ben's face swam in front of her eyes. What was it he had said? *There is nowhere on this earth where I wouldn't find you!*

She shuddered as she remembered and clutched Rachel more tightly to her. For now, she would just worry about keeping Rachel safe. But somehow in the near future she must find out what had happened to Tilly.

Hoisting Rachel onto her hip she slowly negotiated the steep staircase as she carried the child downstairs for her breakfast.

Aunt Philly was waiting for her and covered the little girl in kisses the second Sophie carried her into the room. Sophie smiled to herself. It looked like Rachel was in grave danger of being spoiled if they stayed here for long.

Within an hour she had eaten her breakfast and had been washed and changed. With her hair all brushed and her face scrubbed clean she was now giggling and rolling around the floor with Lily.

'Looks like them two are goin' to be the best o' friends,'

Aunt Philly remarked with a smile that stretched from ear to ear.

Sophie nodded in agreement but then her aunt glanced at the clock and hurriedly stood up. 'Bloody Nora, look at the time. I do a part-time cleanin' job at a young doctor's house in Manor Park Road an' if I don't get a move on I'll be late. Will yer be all right till I get back, love?'

'Of course I will.' Sophie struggled to keep the surprise from her voice; her aunt appeared to be well into her sixties and she was shocked to hear that she was still working. But there was yet another shock in store, for after Sophie had watched her rushing around the room getting ready she then stepped into the yard and dragged an old bicycle from a lean-to shed. Sophie's mouth fell open.

'Keeps yer fit,' her aunt said with a wink, seeing Sophie's bemused expression. 'Now you help yourself to whatever yer want till I get back. I'll only be gone three or four hours. Ta-ra fer now.'

Philly moved towards a gate that led into an alley that separated the houses, then swinging her leg across the ancient bicycle she set off, leaving Sophie to stare after her in amazement. One thing was for sure; her aunt was certainly an extraordinary woman, and at least now she'd been granted a temporary reprieve from the inevitable questions that were sure to come. She would use the time while she was away deciding how best she would answer them and also to write a letter to Brian, her second eldest brother. It was time she let him know that she was safe and well. Just thinking of her brother brought all the heartbreak and loneliness of the last few months pouring back.

Chapter Sixteen

Celia Bannerman was just about to leave the house when Philly arrived. As usual she was immaculately dressed and as she swept past Philly in the hallway she left a waft of exotic perfume in her wake.

'Aren't you a little late?' she asked somewhat caustically.

Philly pursed her lips. *The stuck-up little madam*, she thought to herself. Normally she always arrived early and very often she left late, though Celia didn't bother to comment on that fact, of course. Still, her voice was civil when she answered her. The unexpected arrival of her great-niece had thrilled her so much that she was determined nothing would spoil today.

'If I am it's because I had visitors arrive unexpectedly last night an' I wanted to get 'em fed before I left home. It's me great-niece,' she explained with a measure of excitement in her voice.

Celia curled her lip as she adjusted the little concoction of a hat perched on top of her head in the hall mirror. 'Oh, it's just awful when people turn up unexpectedly, isn't it? They can be *so* inconsiderate, with never a thought as to what you might have planned.'

'Actually, I was chuffed to bits to—'

'Oh, and while I think about it . . . I shall be out for the whole day and probably won't be back till late this evening. Could you rustle Adam something up to eat for when he gets home and tell him not to wait up for me?'

Celia had stopped Philly in mid-flow and once again the old woman found herself thinking, *Whatever does he see in her?* She was thoroughly self-centred. Not at all like Sophie, who seemed to be a caring sort of girl. The smile returned to her face as she thought of her back at home with Rachel, and then it immediately wavered. There was something not quite right from where she was standing. She had a sneaking suspicion that Rachel wasn't Sophie's child, though as yet she hadn't had time to question her. They certainly looked nothing alike and she'd noticed that Sophie wasn't wearing a wedding ring. Not that that could stop her having a child, of course. Philly was very aware that children were born out of wedlock. Yet something told her that Sophie wasn't that sort of girl, so if Rachel wasn't hers, whose was she?

She had become so lost in thought that she started when the door slammed shut heralding Celia's exit. She'd gone without so much as a by-your-leave. Not that it worried Philly. She preferred the stuck-up little madam to be out of the way when she was working. Moving on into the kitchen she paused in the doorway and frowned. As usual it looked like a bombsite and any hopes she'd had of finishing a bit early immediately flew out of the window. Sighing heavily, she rolled her sleeves up and set to.

When Adam Bannerman arrived at lunchtime he found her just lifting a steaming dish from the oven. Sniffing the air appreciatively he grinned. 'Smells good enough to eat. What are you making?'

'I popped down the butcher's an' picked up some steak an' kidney. Then I made some pastry an' baked you a pie. There's some nice crispy roast potatoes to go with it an' all; will that do yer?'

'Do donkeys like strawberries?' He laughed and threw his black bag onto a chair, then plonked himself down at the table as she began to pile his plate high.

When she had finished the whole lot off with thick gravy he lifted his knife and fork and licked his lips in anticipation.

'You spoil me, Mrs Springs. I shan't be able to see to my patients after I've tackled this lot.'

She smiled at him then eager to tell him her good news she joined him at the table. 'I had a visitor arrive last night. Me great-niece all the way from Blackpool.'

'Why, that's wonderful. It must have been a nice surprise. Will she be staying with you for long?'

'Well, I ain't too sure yet. But I'm hopin' so. She's a lovely girl.'

'Then why don't you knock off now and get back

home to her? There's nothing here that can't wait and you must both have a lot of catching up to do.'

Once again she was struck by the difference between this kindly young man and the selfish young woman he had married. She flashed him a grateful smile that transformed her wrinkled old face, giving him a glimpse of the lovely woman she must once have been, before shaking her head.

'That's really kind of you, lad, an' I appreciate the offer. But I wouldn't dream of shirkin' me duties. The missus wouldn't like it. By the way, she asked me to tell you she didn't know what time she'd be back tonight an' not to wait up fer her.'

His face fell and once again she found herself feeling sorry for him. He deserved so much better but then it wasn't her place to comment. Instead she heaved herself up from the table and waddled towards the door. He watched her go with a frown on his face before asking, 'Is your arthritis playing you up again, Mrs Springs?'

She sniffed. 'Well . . . it is a *bit*,' she admitted reluctantly.

'Are you quite sure that all this cleaning isn't getting too much for you?'

'Why – are yer tryin' to get rid o' me?'

Horrified to hear the trace of fear in her voice he hastened to reassure her, 'Of course I'm not. But . . . well, the thing is, you're not getting any younger and I'd hate to think you were making yourself worse by coming here. I would understand if you wanted to say enough is enough, though I admit I'd miss you. In fact, I'd miss you very much indeed. And if it's money you're worried about, then don't. I'd never see you short.'

Her indignation fled as she looked at him. 'That's very kind of you, lad. But I ain't quite a charity case just yet an' I reckon there's still a bit more work left in me.'

'All right then. But don't overdo it, eh? If you didn't do such a good job, Celia would have to pull her finger out a bit more.'

Philly opened her mouth to tell him she doubted there was very much chance of that happening but then hastily clamped it shut again. There were times when she would dearly have loved to, but she knew deep down that he already knew and the last thing she wanted to do was pour salt onto his wounds.

'Right,' she said instead. 'I'll go an' make a start on the bedroom then. You enjoy your dinner, eh?'

'Oh, I think we can quite safely say I'll certainly do that.'

As she climbed the ornately carved staircase her heart was light. She wouldn't be going home to an empty cottage with just the dog for company tonight.

It was mid-afternoon before she clambered onto her bicycle and started the journey home. *I wonder if the distance is gettin' further or if it's just me gettin' older?* she thought, as her legs pumped the pedals up the Cock and Bear hill. The going got a little easier when she reached Croft Road and she found herself smiling as she thought of Sophie and Rachel.

When she wheeled the bicycle into the little shared yard she found them playing with Lily on the pocket-handkerchief lawn at the back of the cottage. Although the child had only met her that morning she ran to her and Philly's heart swelled as she bent to plant a kiss on her forehead.

'Me play,' Rachel informed her solemnly as she pointed back towards Sophie, who was also walking towards her.

Sophie's breasts were so swollen today that she could barely put her arms to her sides. Even so, she forced a smile as she said, 'I wasn't sure what time you'd be home else I'd have had a cup of tea ready for you. Not to worry, you sit down and have a rest and I'll make you one in a jiffy.'

Philly beamed, warming to the girl even further. 'Blimey. Look after me like this an' I'll not let yer leave,' she told her playfully.

Sophie's face became solemn as they trooped into the tiny kitchen. 'Actually, I've been thinking about that and I realise I owe you an apology. It was really thoughtless of me to just land us both on you so unexpectedly. But I promise we won't impose on you for long. I've got a little money, so perhaps you could recommend some-where Rachel and I could stay till I find a job?'

Philly bristled with indignation. 'You'll do no such thing, my girl! Why – you turning up is the best thing that's happened to me for ages. I'm at heaven's door and don't know how long it will be till I pass through it, so it's nice to have family about me. I've always had a dread of bein' alone when Him up there summons me. So . . . no more talk of leavin', eh? At least not for a while. You've only just arrived an' I reckon you an' the little 'un have given me a new lease o' life.'

Sophie dropped her eyes. Aunt Philly was a dear old woman, but would she still want her if she knew the truth? She had wrestled with her conscience all day wondering just how much she should tell her of the circumstances that had brought her here. But already she had decided that Aunt Philly was to be trusted so she would tell her as much as it was safe for her to know when the time was right.

That time came that evening when Rachel was tucked up in bed and she and her aunt were enjoying a cup of cocoa in front of the empty fire grate. Lily was curled up fast asleep in a ball on Sophie's lap and she was feeling so at home that she felt as if she had been there forever.

Never one to beat about the bush, Philly suddenly asked 'So – do yer want to tell me what brought you here so unexpectedly then?'

Sophie had known that the question must come sooner or later so she was prepared for it, yet somehow she didn't quite know where to begin.

Once again her aunt seemed to be able to read her mind and asked, 'Let's start with your mam. Is she well?'

After a moment's hesitation, Sophie shook her head and as the pain returned she had to blink away the tears. 'Both my mam an' dad died a short while ago.' Shock drained the colour from Philly's face, but she didn't press the girl for details straight away, for she saw that she was struggling to hold herself together. After a time she asked softly, 'Was it an accident? A car crash or somethin'?'

Sophie took a deep breath. There was no point in lying; she didn't want their relationship to be built on falsehood so she told her, 'No . . . My mam stabbed me dad then took an overdose.'

'Good God in heaven!' Philly felt as if she might be sick but she held herself together for Sophie's sake. Eventually she had rallied enough to ask, 'Whatever drove yer mam to do that?'

'I can't tell you that right now, Aunt Philly,' Sophie told her brokenly. 'But . . . I promise I will tell you everything . . . eventually.'

Philly felt stunned. What could have driven Sally to do such a thing? She remembered her as a placid kindly-natured girl. But then she had never met Sally's husband so no doubt he had driven her to it. Perhaps he'd been a wife-beater or a drunkard or a womaniser? She longed to ask more questions but sensing the girl was almost at breaking point the old woman decided not to press her and instead asked, 'So what did you do then?'

'I went to work at a hotel and it was there that I made a friend. Her name was Tilly and she was, or I should say is, Rachel's mother. She was pregnant, so she'd left Rachel with a carer. The woman who owned the hotel and her son were going to arrange for the new baby to be adopted after it was born. Tilly couldn't afford to care for two children, you see, because she wasn't married.'

Seeing her aunt's brows draw together, Sophie hastened to defend her friend. 'Tilly wasn't a bad girl, honestly she wasn't, and she adored Rachel. But she'd been brought up in London and she'd had a really hard life.'

'So why is Rachel here with you then?' Philly asked bluntly.

Sophie lowered her eyes. 'She . . . she had the baby and then disappeared.' The explanation sounded lame even to her own ears so she wasn't altogether surprised when Aunt Philly leaned forward in her seat with a deep frown on her face.

'But why would she do that if she loved the child so much?'

'I'm not sure.'

'Haven't you asked the woman who owned the hotel where she is? Surely she would know if she was arranging an adoption? And *where* is the baby?'

As Sophie bowed her head, Philly guessed that there was more to this than Sophie was telling and alarm bells began to ring in her head.

'And *why* would this woman be finding adoptive parents? Was she something to do with the Welfare Department? Did she run a home for unmarried mothers?'

Sophie wrung her hands miserably. Aunt Philly was clearly no fool and this was turning out to be even harder than she had expected it to be.

As a frightening possibility suddenly occurred to Philly she stared at Sophie in horror. 'What were you doing working at that place? Was it just coincidence or . . . are *you* pregnant too?'

'I . . . I was,' Sophie admitted in a small voice. 'But I lost the baby a few days ago.'

Philly's hand flew to her mouth and for a while she was speechless as she stared at her niece's bent head.

Sophie expected to be ordered from the house at any second as shame washed over her in waves but, instead, Aunt Philly suddenly reached across and squeezed her hand encouragingly.

'You poor little love. What a rotten time you've had of it. But who was the father of your child? Wouldn't he stand by you?'

Sophie longed to throw herself into her aunt's arms and sob out the whole sorry story but it was more than she dared do. With his threats still ringing in her ears she knew only too well just how dangerous Ben could be and she had no wish to involve her aunt in anything that might bring harm to her.

'Look, Aunt Philly. I can't tell you everything just yet but please trust me. I've done nothing wrong, I promise. If Rachel and I can stay here for just a few days till I find somewhere for us to go you can forget you ever saw us.'

'You'll do no such thing,' Philly retorted indignantly. 'Like I told you before you're goin' nowhere. We're family an' families stick together. Whatever's goin' on I'm behind you so don't even think o' leavin', do yer hear me? By the way, were you the only one? In the family I mean?'

'No, I have four older brothers but I can't let them know where I am either,' Sophie mumbled. 'I have written to Brian, he's the second oldest, to let him know that I'm safe though I haven't given him a forwarding address.'

Philly's head wagged from side to side as she said, 'Sophie. I have a feelin' that you've somehow got yourself mixed up in somethin' a little underhand. Answer me one question – could you not go to the police an' tell 'em about whatever it is yer runnin' away from?'

Sophie miserably shook her head. 'If I did the Welfare Department would become involved an' they could take Rachel away. I couldn't bear that 'cos her mother was my best friend an' I need to look after her till I can find Tilly.'

'In that case then, fer the time bein' at least we'll pass Rachel off as your child should anybody ask.'

Sophie blinked in surprise. She had been expecting her aunt to show her the door but here she was supporting her even though Sophie hadn't told her the whole story.

Meanwhile, Aunt Philly's old eyes filled with tears as she thought on what Sophie had told her. 'Fancy our Sally bein' gone. She were no age at all an' she were such a beautiful child. Many a time I've envied our Miriam fer havin' such a lovely family. But anyway, you're still here so we'll just worry about you an' Rachel fer now, eh?'

Gratitude shone from Sophie's eyes as she looked back at her. Just as her mother had told her, Aunt Philly truly was a lovely woman and somehow she felt for the first time in months that she just might get through this terrible time.

'If you're quite sure you don't mind us staying for a while I can give you some money for our keep,' Sophie told the old woman. It was more than obvious that her aunt wasn't wealthy. Otherwise why would she still be working?

Again her aunt seemed to read her mind when she replied, 'There's no need to worry about that. I've got a few bob tucked away but I like to keep meself busy, which is why I still do for the young doctor an' his wife. Not that I've got time fer that stuck-up little madam. Between you an' me he could have done a lot better fer himself. A more selfish, self-centred little hussy yer could never wish to meet. Still, I suppose it were his choice at the end o' the day.'

Sophie remained silent until her aunt suddenly asked, 'Will yer just answer me one question if yer can?'

A nod was her answer so she went on, 'Is there anyone likely to come lookin' fer you?'

'No, there isn't. No one knows where I've gone, or Rachel for that matter. But at some stage I will have to go back to Blackpool. You see, knowing Tilly as I do I know she would never just up and leave Rachel. Something must have happened to her and somehow I've got to find out what it is. Otherwise I'll never be able to live with myself. Every single time Rachel asks for her mammy it nearly breaks my heart. But trust me,

Aunt Philly – *you* are in no danger at all. I would never bring trouble to your door, I promise.'

'I do believe you, love. And when and if you decide you have to go back you can leave the little 'un here with me while you go. How's that, eh? She'd be well looked after, I can assure you.'

Sophie smiled her thanks and the next minute Aunt Philly had her locked in a tight embrace. 'The only thing I'll ask of you is this. Don't get thinkin' about goin' back to Blackpool just yet awhile. You've gone through the mill over the last few months what wi' one thing an' another from what you've told me an' I want you to be strong before you venture back there. Will you promise me that at least?'

It seemed very little to ask under the circumstances so Sophie nodded her agreement. 'I promise, but I can't leave it too long. Tilly must be in trouble if she's still alive and if she is I have to help her.'

'I understand, but fer now have a good rest an' let's get to know one another properly, eh? You turnin' up wi' a little 'un in tow is like havin' all me birthdays an' Christmases rolled into one, though I have to admit I'm shocked to the core to hear of yer mam an' dad bein' dead.'

As Sophie looked across at her with gratitude shining in her eyes she knew instinctively that she and her aunt were going to be the very best of friends.

Chapter Seventeen

Once it was dark that evening, Ben climbed into his car and cruised through the streets of Blackpool. He was visiting his other business, which only his mother and Mrs G knew about. Soon he had left the bright lights behind him and entered back streets that had long since seen better days. A row of factory units stood with their broken windows staring out into the night like great dark empty eye sockets and he parked his car in front of one of them.

Slightly further up the street was a row of old three-storey terraced houses that looked to be on the brink of dereliction and it was to one of these that he made his way.

He rapped sharply at the door; seconds later a woman long past her prime opened it and peered out at him. Seeing who it was she opened the door wider and ushered him into a surprisingly well-decorated hallway. A thick plush red carpet was fitted from wall to wall and lamps with red shades that were strategically placed here and there cast a soft glow about the place.

'How are things, Carol?'

The woman shrugged, setting her sagging breasts wobbling like jellies. She raised a hand to her bleached blond beehive and patted it. 'That last 'un yer brought is givin' me trouble,' she confided as he followed her along the hallway. 'Although Amy's settled down a bit now. It's took a few good hidin's though.' The sound of laughter and music wafted down the stairs as she led him into a comfortably furnished lounge where three young girls, all heavily made up, were sitting in various stages of undress on chairs. In a far corner stood a huge bear of a man with his arms crossed across a great gut of a belly. He nodded at Ben as he passed but said not a word.

'These three are bein' as good as gold, ain't yer, me lovelies?' the older woman praised the girls as he followed her through yet another door that led to a kitchen at the back of the house. The bright light there did her no favours at all and Ben found himself dropping his eyes in repugnance from her brightly painted lips and thickly powdered face. Going to a cupboard she took out a tin and extracted a bundle of notes from it, which she then placed in his hand.

'Not such a good week this week. But then yer have to understand wi' two new 'uns to prepare I've had things on me mind.'

He nodded in understanding as she rattled on. 'That Tilly is a right little wildcat. Look at these.' She dropped her top even lower than it already was and he was horrified to see long scratches etched into her sagging skin.

Clucking her disapproval she then smiled slyly. 'Needless to say she won't be tryin' *that* again in a hurry. Not after the pastin' Walter give her. Huh! It'll be a week before any punter would want her anyway wi' the shiners she's got on her. But don't worry. She'll see sense in the end. Most of 'em do. Meanwhile I've got her that drugged up she barely knows what time o' day it is. One thing though – who the fuckin' 'ell is Rachel? She keeps callin' fer her all the time.'

Ben frowned. 'I've no idea. She assured me she had no one so it might be a good idea to try and find out who it is she's on about. We don't want any irate relatives crawling out of the woodwork.'

The woman shrugged and nodded before leading him back the way they had come. 'Did yer want to see her? She should be awake by now.'

He nodded. 'Yes, I might as well while I'm here.'

At the bottom of the steep staircase she pointed before passing a key into his hand. 'Second floor, last door on the landing. Be careful though. Like I told yer if she's awake she'll likely go fer yer. And make it snappy. We've got punters due any time.'

As he climbed the noises from above became louder and he smiled as the sounds of lovemaking drifted from the bedrooms as he passed. Carol and Walter had run the whorehouse for him for years and made him a nice tidy profit. Most of the girls that worked there had come willingly but others who had previously stayed at the Ship Hotel with him and his mother sometimes had to be persuaded into their new way of life. That was where Walter excelled. It only usually took a few beatings from him and they were putty in his hands. Of course, there had been the odd exception over the years, like Cathy, but he wouldn't think about those for now.

When he came to the bedroom that Carol had directed him to he paused to listen before inserting the key into the lock. All was silent. As he inched the door open he saw that it was in darkness and he fumbled for the light switch. It was then that someone suddenly launched themselves at him and he felt sharp fingernails rake at the soft skin on his cheek.

'*Ouch!*' Instinctively he lashed out and whoever it was went hurtling away from him as he snapped the bare overhead light on and raised his hand to his face. Tilly was on all fours glowering up at him like a wild animal with a look of madness in her eyes.

'Let me out o' here, you bastard,' she spat as saliva trickled unheeded down her chin. Her unbrushed hair stood out on her head like snakes' tails and she looked dirty and dishevelled.

'Calm down, Tilly. There's nothing to be gained from behaving like this,' he told her. Never once did he dare to take his eyes from her, for she looked as if she was ready to launch herself at him again.

'It'll take more than the likes o' you *or* them to keep me here,' she screamed as she stabbed at the metal bars on the window. Her eyes were purple and black with bruises and he saw that the weight seemed to have dropped off her to the point that she appeared almost skeletal.

Moving his hand from his face he saw that it was red with blood and anger coursed through him. Even so he managed to keep his voice light as he told her, 'This can be as hard or as easy as you like. The sooner you make your mind up to behave and do as you're told the sooner you'll get to come out of here.'

She glared at him. 'Hell will freeze over before I do as you tell me,' she spat. 'An' don't think that yer can keep me here against me will because yer can't. My Alfie will find out I ain't gone fer Rachel an' he'll come lookin' fer me, then it'll be God help yer.'

'Oh yes . . . and just who are Alfie and Rachel?'

Seeing the concern on his face she now sneered at him contemptuously, 'Ah, yer thought I were all alone in the world, didn't yer? But yer were wrong, see. Alfie's me boyfriend an' Rachel is me little girl. Don't yer think they'll come lookin' when I don't show up?'

'You . . . you have a *child*?'

When she saw the shock register on his face she laughed. 'Oh yes, I have a child all right. I left her with a carer while I were at the hotel an' she'll soon have the cops on yer if I don't show up. That's if Sophie ain't already.'

'What do you mean? What does Sophie know about all this?'

'Everythin',' she told him with an air of defiance, delighted to see the fear in his eyes. Crossing to her he slapped her resoundingly across the mouth. Her head rocked on her shoulders and when she looked back at him he saw that blood was trickling from her split lip to mix with the saliva that dripped down her chin.

'You lying little bitch! You told me that you had no one.'

'An' *you* told me that once I'd had the baby I'd be free to go – so we're both liars, ain't we?' She watched with satisfaction as he began to pace up and down the room then while his attention was diverted she looked about for something to hit him with. Her eyes settled on the tray that Walter had brought up for her earlier. The food on it was untouched and the mug of tea was stone cold, but her eyes were directed at the fork lying next to the plate. A knife would have been better, she thought to herself, but seeing as they hadn't given her one the fork would have to do. If she could get to it, that was.

Still on hands and knees she began to crawl towards it and she was almost there when he suddenly turned to look at her. Realising her intention he ran to the tray and slapped it into the air, sending congealed food and cold tea splattering everywhere. The fork clattered away under the bed and when she dived for it he lifted his foot and kicked her hard in the ribs, driving the air from her lungs and causing her to cry out in pain.

As she lay there in a quivering heap he glared at her with contempt. 'You dumb broad. You've made things very hard for me if you did but know it,' he rasped. 'And believe me you're going to regret crossing me. So is your little friend Sophie when I get my hands on her.'

'Ben, no. Don't take it out on her, please. None o' this is her fault.'

The only answer was the sound of the door as it slammed and the key turning in the lock. Tilly curled herself into a tight ball and began to sob as if her heart would break. How could she have let her mouth run away with her like that? If Sophie was still at the hotel Ben would go back and take his temper out on her now and then Tilly would never be able to forgive herself.

Once downstairs, Ben slapped Carol's hand away as she raised it to the scratches on his face.

'She *already* has a little girl. That's the Rachel she keeps on about. Find out where it is before I come next. And see if she knows where someone called Sophie has gone. I need to find them. Do you understand?'

In all the time she had known him, Carol had never feared Ben before, but now as she stared back at him she thought she detected a look of madness in his eyes and she shrank away from him as she nodded numbly.

'Good. Make sure that you do.'

He stormed away along the hallway slamming the door resoundingly behind him as Carol and Walter exchanged a worried look.

Back at the hotel in her room, Mrs G unashamedly listened to the conversation taking place in the bedroom next to hers. Ben had returned some hours before like a bear with a sore head and he didn't yet sound to be in any better a frame of mind.

'I have no choice but to find her now,' she heard Ben tell his mother. 'It seems that Tilly and Sophie were closer than we thought and if that's the case then Sophie will probably know where Tilly's child has been staying.'

'But how will knowing that solve anything?' This was from Amanda.

'There are people who want children, aren't there?' he replied caustically. 'Not *everyone* wants a baby. And it can't be that old, can it, looking at Tilly? She's little more than a kid herself. Apparently the child is a girl called Rachel.'

'Oh, Ben, didn't I tell you on the very first day that she arrived that I had a bad feeling about that Sophie? What are we going to do now?'

'I've told you. I'm going to find Sophie and hopefully that will lead me to the child. That will kill two birds with one stone. Then I just have to find out where this guy, Alfie, lives. Walter will help me sort him out.'

Appalled, Mrs G listened and her heart beat faster. Thank God she had sent Sophie away when she had. But what if Ben were to find her? And the little girl – what would become of her? Sinking onto the bed she buried her face in her hands. Something deep down told her that this was one mess Ben might not be able to get himself out of.

In the sparsely furnished bedroom Tilly managed to crawl painfully to the bed and haul herself onto it. When she came to think about it, the position she found herself in was ironic. Ben wanted her to become a prostitute, which was what had got her into this mess in the first place. She could have taught the girls downstairs a trick or two if she'd had a mind to. But that had been in the days before Alfie came along. Now she wanted nothing more than to turn her back on that way of life. All she wanted was to live in peace with Rachel a part of a loving family and to put the past behind her.

Her thoughts now turned to Sophie, who she prayed had done as she asked in the letter she had left for her. If so, then both she and Rachel should be long gone by now to Sophie's elderly aunt in the Midlands. Tilly's heart ached as she thought of her little girl. Would she be missing her and thinking that her mammy had abandoned her? The thought was almost more than she could bear, but somehow she trusted Sophie to tell her differently and one day she would be reunited with her. After all, she reasoned, they couldn't keep her locked up here forever, could they? Perhaps it was time to try a different tack and do as they told her. Then once she'd gained Carol's and Walter's trust they would be bound to let their guard down and she could escape and blow the whistle on what Ben and his mother were up to. As pain throbbed through her she wrapped her arms tight about her knees and fell into an exhausted sleep.

Chapter Eighteen

In no time at all, Rachel's cheeks were glowing with health from the happy hours spent playing in Aunt Philly's pretty little garden and she had the old woman wrapped well and truly round her little finger.

Sophie looked much better too, although sometimes when her aunt looked at her Philly would see the haunted look in her eyes and know that she was far from settled; this was impossible until she had discovered what had become of Tilly.

Each day, Philly dreaded Sophie telling her that she was going back to Blackpool, but she knew from Sophie's increasingly unsettled behaviour that the day was drawing closer.

On this particular day the sun was riding high in a cloudless blue sky as Philly wheeled her bicycle towards the entry gate.

'Right, I'll be back mid-afternoon,' she promised as she paused to plant a kiss on Rachel's rosy cheek.

'Me come,' Rachel implored as she held her chubby arms up to her.

Aunt Philly laughed delightedly. 'There'd be nothin' could give me more pleasure than to take yer, me darlin'. But I think you'd be bored where I'm goin'. No, you stay here wi' Sophie an' Lily an' when I come back I'll bring yer some sweeties, eh?'

The child now toddled happily away with Lily in hot pursuit as Sophie opened the gate for her. 'You'll melt having to clean in this weather,' she told her, a note of concern in her voice.

Aunt Philly chuckled as she manoeuvred her bicycle down the narrow entry.

'It shouldn't be too bad today. The missus was about to take herself off on holiday wi'out the doctor an' seein' as it's her as usually makes all the mess I doubt there'll be that much to do.'

She waved as she pedalled off down the road, leaving Sophie with a broad smile on her face. 'Why don't you take Rachel for a splash in the edge of the Blue Lagoon?' she called to Sophie across her shoulder.

Sophie considered it. The Blue Lagoon was an old clay pit that was now full of water and a favourite swimming place in summer for the young people who lived hereabouts. She'd taken Rachel there a few times since living with her aunt and the child loved it but today she didn't feel in the mood for an outing; possibly because with each day that passed her concern for Tilly grew.

The opening words of Tilly's letter flashed in front of her eyes as she thought of her. *If you ever get to read this letter I might be dead . . .* But she *couldn't* be dead. Sophie refused to believe it. Once again she thought of taking her concerns to the police but as she spotted Rachel rampaging amongst the flowerbeds in her aunt's garden she knew that she wouldn't. If the Welfare Department became involved and took Rachel away to be brought up by strangers she would never be able to live with herself.

Sighing, she closed the gate and joined the child in the bright sunshine. But she would have to go back to Blackpool . . . and soon.

Humming softly to herself, Philly lifted the heavy cut-glass vase and headed in the direction of the kitchen. Dead flowers drooped over the sides of it and the water smelled foul, but it was nothing that couldn't be remedied with a good clean-out. The lounge was spotless now and she gave it a last approving glance before setting off across the hallway. Sadly, the same couldn't be said of the kitchen as she saw at a glance when she opened the door. Celia was fixing a wide-brimmed straw hat onto her shining blond hair with an ornate hatpin as Philly headed for the sink. She paused to comment, 'I thought you were off on your holidays?'

'Oh, it's been delayed for a couple of weeks,' Cellia informed her coldly, then studiously ignored her, which suited Philly just fine. In fact, she could hardly wait for her to go out so that she could get on with her work in peace without the untidy little madam mucking everything back up as soon as she'd done it. She was halfway across the room when she heard the front door open and shut and the next instant she heard the doctor's pleasant voice. 'Hello, darling. Hello, Mrs Springs.'

Still balancing the heavy vase in her two hands she half-turned to answer him and it was then that her foot stood on something slippery and shot out in front of her. The vase flew out of her hands as she went down like a ninepin and a searing pain shot up her leg as the vase crashed to the floor, shattering into a million pieces.

In a second all hell had broken out. Adam flung his case down as he raced to her while Celia cried, 'Oh no. That was the vase my aunt bought us for a wedding present.'

'*Sod* the bloody vase,' Adam cursed as he dropped onto his knees at Philly's side.

In all the time that Philly had been working at the house she had never heard him raise his voice to his wife so much as once but now he looked furious. 'Come and help me get her onto a chair, can't you?'

Celia pouted. 'I can't bend in this skirt. It's brand new and you wouldn't want me to split it, would you? It cost an absolute fortune. Can't she get up by herself?'

He glanced at her with disgust then turning to Philly he gently manoeuvred her onto a chair. He then stooped to lift something from the floor. 'This looks to be the cause of all the trouble,' he growled. 'Who had a banana for breakfast, I wonder?'

'I did,' Celia admitted sullenly.

'Well, perhaps next time instead of throwing the skin in the general direction of the bin you might like to dispose of it safely. Look what's happened through your carelessness now!'

Unused to being spoken to in such a way, Celia glared at him as she snatched up her bag and gloves. 'I *refuse* to stay here for you to shout at me. I'm going out and by the time I get back you'd better be in a happier mood or I shall go straight back out again.' With that she tossed her head and stormed from the room in a tantrum that would have done justice to a two-year-old.

As the front door slammed resoundingly behind her he then turned his full attention back to Philly and told her, 'Oh, Mrs Springs, I'm so very sorry about this. I really don't know why Celia can't be more careful. Are you all right?'

She had paled alarmingly and he hurried away to get her a glass of water before asking, 'Where does it hurt, Philly?'

'It's me ankle,' she told him in a small voice as pain washed over her.

'All right then. I'm going to rest it on this chair here while I take a look at it.'

Philly almost cried out as he carefully swung her leg up onto a chair and then she blushed as red as a beetroot when he told her, 'You'll have to take your stocking off I'm afraid. Can you manage it on your own?'

'I certainly can,' she flustered, horrified at the thought of him helping her. Who had ever heard of such a thing, indeed?

Seeing her embarrassment he discreetly turned his back on her while she fumbled with the penny piece that held her stocking up, then after a while she muttered, 'That's it then.'

He gently began to examine her ankle, which was already swelling up like a balloon. 'Well,' he declared after a time. 'There's good news and bad news. The good news is that nothing appears to be broken. The bad news is that it looks to be badly sprained, which means you're going to be out of action for a while I'm afraid.'

'B . . . but who will look after you?' she exclaimed in horror.

He laughed softly and once again, as she had many times before, she found herself thinking what a genuinely nice young man he was.

'I'm more worried about you at the minute.' His voice rang with sincerity. 'And as it was Celia's fault that it happened I shall be paying you your wages until it's better and you're fit to come back again.'

'You'll do no such thing,' she sputtered indignantly. 'It will be a cold day in hell afore I take money as I haven't earnt as yer should well know! It were an accident – it's as simple as that. But how am I goin' to get home? I don't think I'd manage me bike just yet awhile.'

'You're not going anywhere until I've made you a nice cup of hot sweet tea,' he informed her. 'It's good for shock and a fall like that at your age must have badly shaken you, so just sit still and do as you're told for a change. When I've made the tea I'll bandage the ankle up for you while you drink it and then I shall be taking you home in my car.'

Philly wasn't too sure about that. She'd occasionally taken a trip into town on a Midland Red Bus but she'd never been in a motorcar before. Even so she kept her concerns to herself and remained silent. He had his doctor's hat on now and she somehow guessed that it would do no good at all to argue.

Wetting a towel at the sink he now placed it round her ankle before filling the kettle and bustling about as he got the teapot and the mugs ready.

As he fussed over her she eventually asked, 'Won't you be late back to surgery?'

'Don't you get worrying about that; I'll phone Miss Finch and she'll get Dr Beech to cover for me till I get back.'

When her ankle was duly bandaged he began to collect her things together. 'I shall put your bicycle round the back of the house and it will be quite safe until I can deliver it to you. I might even ride it there,' he grinned. 'The exercise would certainly do me good. But now – you're going to have to keep this off the ground for at least a couple of days. Didn't you say you had a niece staying with you, or has she left?'

'No, no, she ain't left. Our Sophie is still there an' she's a right good girl,' she informed him proudly.

'Good. Then perhaps she wouldn't mind keeping her eye on you until you can get about again?' Relief washed over his face when she nodded.

'Right, let's get you out to the car then. Put your arm round my neck and lean on me. Hop if you have to but don't put any weight on that ankle or you'll wish you hadn't. The problem with sprains is they have to heal themselves and it doesn't happen overnight.' Seeing the disgruntled look on her face he grinned. Knowing Philly as he did he had an idea she wasn't going to make the best of patients and he felt almost sorry for Sophie before he had even met her.

By the time they pulled up in front of the neat little cottage she was shaking and he wasn't sure if it was from the shock of the fall or her first car ride, which she obviously hadn't enjoyed very much at all.

'I'll just go in and tell your niece what's happened. You wait there,' he told her as he climbed from the driver's seat, but he had no need to because at that moment the front door of the cottage burst open and Sophie, who had seen them arrive from the window, ran out.

'What's happened?' she cried as she saw how pale her aunt was.

'I'm afraid your aunt had an accident in my kitchen,' he told her apologetically.

As she stared at him quizzically he found himself blushing in a most unprofessional manner. She really was a remarkably attractive girl. Not in the same glamorous sense as his wife, but in a more natural way. And those eyes; they were the colour of bluebells.

'I'm afraid she, er . . . slipped on a banana skin on my kitchen floor,' he told her thinking how ridiculous it sounded even to his own ears.

'And *what* was a banana skin doing on the floor?' Two spots of colour had risen to her cheeks; he could see that she was angry, quite rightly so.

'My . . . wife dropped it.'

'Then your wife should be more careful. Do you know how old my aunt is? Why, a fall like th—'

'Eh, I'm still able to speak fer meself, yer know?' Aunt Philly declared as she pushed the car door open. 'Now would yer both kindly stop squabblin' like a pair o' school-kids an' get me inside, please?'

Shamefaced, they hurried to help her, almost colliding in their embarrassment. Sophie ran to fetch a blanket and fussed over her like a mother hen as the doctor settled her comfortably on the settee.

'Do yer know, I reckon I could get used to bein' waited on like this,' Aunt Philly teased as she looked at the two of them hovering over her.

'What exactly has she done?' Sophie now asked with concern as she tucked the blanket round her aunt's legs.

'Badly sprained her ankle I'm afraid, which means she isn't going to be able to get out and about for a while. She'll probably be able to potter around home after a couple of days but it could be a couple of weeks before she's able to go further than that.'

'It doesn't matter. I'll make sure she's all right,' Sophie assured him and somehow although he had only just met her he felt that she would.

'It's you I'm more concerned about,' Philly fretted, addressing the doctor. 'Yer know what an untidy little bugger that wife o' yours is. The house will go to rack an' ruin if I ain't there to keep on top of it.'

Sophie now surprised them both when she told them, 'No it won't. As soon as you're well enough to keep an eye on Rachel I'll take over your cleaning job until you're well enough to do it yourself again. That is if neither of you have any objections, of course?'

Swallowing her surprise, Philly smiled. 'I think it's a grand idea an' yer need have no fear. She's as good at cleanin' as I am,' she told the doctor. 'An' speakin' o' Rachel. Where is she?'

'I've just put her upstairs for a nap. She's been up there for over an hour so it shouldn't be long be—' A piercing wail from above stopped Sophie mid-sentence and she flashed them both an apologetic look before scurrying away.

The glance that the doctor cast to the clock on the mantelshelf was not lost on Philly and she told him, 'Why don't yer get yerself away an' back about yer business, lad? I shall be fine now. Our Sophie will look after me.'

Aware that he was already desperately late for afternoon surgery, Adam was longing to do just that. But at the same time he felt guilty about leaving her, particularly as the accident had occurred in his house because of his wife's negligence.

He hovered uncertainly and as he did so Sophie reappeared with a little girl in her arms. The child eyed him uncertainly for a moment as she kept her head glued to Sophie's shoulder but then she flashed him a smile that seemed to light up the room. He smiled back before making his way to the door.

'Are you quite sure that there's nothing I can do for you before I go? Do you need anything from the shop?'

Philly nestled further down into the chair, quite enjoying all the attention. 'There's nothin' we need. An' even if we did, Sophie would go an' fetch it so will yer *please* just get on yer way?'

'Very well. But I shall be back tomorrow to check on that ankle and in the meantime I want you to promise me that you'll rest it and put no weight on it.'

'I promise,' Philly told him solemnly, though he thought he detected a twinkle in her eye. 'An' thanks fer bringin' me home, lad.'

A final nod and he was gone; seconds later they heard his car start up and drive away.

Sophie left Rachel with her aunt while she bustled away to put the kettle on. Then she crossed to the table where she bowed her head and fought back the tears stinging at the back of her eyes. There would be no chance of returning to Blackpool to look for Tilly now until her aunt was up and about again, and that could be weeks away. And what had she been thinking of when she offered to take over her aunt's cleaning job? As a picture of the young doctor's handsome face swam before her eyes she found herself blushing. Here I go again, she scolded herself. The last man who had made her pulses race was Ben and look where *that* had got her! Angrily, she spooned tea into the pot then laid a tray with cups and saucers and a plateful of fancy biscuits that Rachel would no doubt polish off before anyone else even got a look-in.

Thinking back to the night she'd arrived here she instantly felt guilty. Her aunt had shown her nothing but kindness from the second she opened the door to her and now it was Sophie's turn to pay her back. In a slightly better frame of mind she carried the tray into the cosy parlour.

Chapter Nineteen

As Walter placed the untouched tray down on the kitchen table, Carol frowned. 'She's still not eaten nothin' then?'

'Not so much as a bean,' Walter informed her with a shrug. He didn't much care if the mouthy little cow upstairs wasted away after the abuse she slung at him every time he so much as set foot in the door.

Carol tapped a scarlet-painted fingernail on the table top as she mulled over what he had told her, then heaved herself out of the chair and made towards the kitchen door, pausing to hold her hand out to Walter as she went. 'Give us the key. I'll go up an' see if I can't talk some sense into her.'

'Please yerself, though I think you'll be wastin' yer breath. Now if you'd just say the word I bet *I* could make her talk . . . an' eat for that matter.' Ignoring the cruel light in his eye she marched past him and negotiated the steep staircase in her ridiculously high-heeled shoes.

It was mid-afternoon so the house was quiet; many

296

of the girls were still asleep or preparing themselves for the night ahead. On Friday night they all expected to be kept busy.

Once on the top-floor landing she paused to catch her breath. 'It's no good, gel, yer goin' to have to lay off them Park Drives a bit,' she scolded herself as she approached the door at the end of the corridor. Pressing her ear to it she listened but it was as silent as a grave within so tentatively she inserted the key in the lock and inched it open. The smell of sweat and stale urine met her full force and she felt her eyes smarting. Through the gloom she saw that Tilly was curled up in a foetal position on the unmade bed. Clicking the light on she slowly advanced towards her.

'Tilly . . . don't yer think yer takin' this a bit far now?' She had come to threaten and do battle if necessary but something about the girl touched a chord deep down inside her, probably because Ben had informed her that Tilly had a child.

'Look, this can be as easy or as hard as yer want to make it,' she said sternly but still there was no response whatsoever from the curled figure on the bed. Glancing across at a bucket that was overflowing with urine she wrinkled her nose in distaste and when she looked back at the bed she was shocked to see Tilly staring back at her with hatred blazing in her eyes.

'Decided to come an' do yer dirty work yerself, have yer?' Her lips drew back from her teeth in a feral snarl. 'Where's yer little errand boy? He ain't touched me in that way yet but if the other whorehouses I've worked in are anythin' to go by no doubt he'll get to have the first go, won't he?'

'Huh! You should be so lucky. No, love; I'm afraid yer've got it all wrong there. Yer see, Walter bats fer the other side if yer know what I mean. Yer don't think I'd risk a red-blooded male in here wi' all me girls, do yer?'

One to me, thought Carol, as she saw shock settle across Tilly's face. Feeling that she was now at somewhat of an advantage she edged closer to the bed.

'Why don't yer just tell me where yer little girl is?' Her voice was as sweet as sugar but she hadn't reckoned on Tilly being no fool.

'Oh yes. I'm really gonna tell yer that, aint I?' Tilly spat contemptuously. 'Then yer boss can get his hands on her an' sell *her* an' all like he did the one I've just had.' As she thought of the child she had so recently given birth to her eyes burned with tears. She had never wanted the child for a second for the whole of the time she had been carrying it. It had been a mistake, an accident. And yet the moment she had heard its first little cry she had felt differently. She could remember closing her eyes so that she wouldn't have to look at it because she had known in that moment that if she did she would have ended up fighting tooth and nail to keep it.

Within minutes a young couple had entered the room on the fourth floor where the child lay in a crib at the side of the bed and with her back to them she had been forced to listen to them billing and cooing over it before they took it away. Every time she thought of it, it was like a knife piercing her heart. But she couldn't allow herself to think of that child now. She must concentrate on Rachel and Alfie and the whole new life waiting for her beyond the locked door.

Once again she briefly toyed with the idea of pretending to go along with Carol's wishes and joining the other girls downstairs until she could make her escape, but she knew that she couldn't. That part of her life was over now and she was determined never to go back to it.

As Carol now looked at Tilly she saw herself many years ago and despite her resolution to bend the girl to her wishes she again felt pity for her. After all, hadn't *she* once had a child taken off her and then been forced into a life of prostitution? It seemed a lifetime ago now, yet she still ached every time she thought of it. The child would be twenty-two or -three now and she wondered how she would have turned out. Of course, many of the girls who'd worked for her over the years had also given babies up at birth. But to be in Tilly's position was unthinkable. She tried to imagine how much more traumatic it would be to actually grow to love and care for the child only to be torn away from it, and failed dismally.

Forcing her thoughts back from the road they were taking she again turned her attention to Tilly and her voice was soft now as she asked, 'How would yer like a bath?'

Tilly eyed her suspiciously. Was this another ruse to get her out of the room and into another part of the house? The offer was tempting, though, for the smell in the room was beginning to make her feel sick.

'Why would yer let me do that?'

'Because the stink in here is goin' to start spreadin' to the rest o' the bleedin' place soon an' I have a reputation to keep up,' Carol told her briskly. 'There's one thing I pride meself on an' that's the fact that my girls are always clean.'

As Tilly leaned up on one elbow her stomach rumbled with hunger and Carol abruptly headed back towards the door.

'I'll be back wi' a tray in a minute an' when you've eaten I'll take yer to the bathroom,' she informed her shortly. Then the door closed behind her and Tilly's shoulders sagged. For the first time she began to wonder if she would ever escape. Was Rachel still with Mrs McGregor? And had Sophie managed to get away . . . and if so had she taken Rachel with her? Was her little girl in care somewhere? Round and round the questions went in her head until she felt that she was going mad. Her stomach rumbled again but she knew that she must stay strong. For the briefest time she had sensed a softening in Carol, but if she went along with what she wanted in no time at all she would end up doing as she was told and then she might never get away.

With her resolution strong again Tilly lay back on the

bed and stared at the bars on the window. Somehow she would get out of here if it were the last thing she did.

'Remember what I said: don't let that little madam rile yer.'

Sophie grinned. 'Aunt Philly, I'm going to clean her house, not befriend her. I don't care if she doesn't even look at me. In fact, from what you've told me I'd rather she didn't.'

Philly watched Sophie wheel her bicycle from the outhouse where Sophie had put it when the doctor had kindly returned it some days ago.

'Now remember what I said. Straight to the top o' the hill then cut across past the Hare and Hounds pub into Croft Road an' after you've gone down the Cock an' Bear hill, Manor Court Road will be right in front o' yer. Yer can't miss it. But I really ain't so sure that this is such a good idea now,' she fretted.

It was now a week since she had taken her fall and the doctor had called to see her every single day. She could now potter about the house again with the use of a walking stick, which he had thoughtfully brought for her, but much to her frustration she still needed to rest.

'I'm quite capable of doing a bit of cleaning,' Sophie reassured her, 'and anything will be better than having to listen to you keep worrying about the doctor. But are you quite sure you're going to manage Rachel?' She glanced down the garden to where the child was busily picking buttercups with Lily close on her heels before continuing, 'I've left you both some sandwiches for your dinner and once she's eaten if you settle her down on the settee she should sleep for an hour.'

'I'll be absolutely fine. An' if I should run into any trouble Flo next door will be round to help me out like a shot,' Philly assured her.

Sophie planted a kiss on her cheek before climbing clumsily onto the bike. It was years since she had ridden one and Philly watched with amusement as she wobbled away down the road. It'll be *her* who needs a doctor at this rate, she thought to herself. Then she settled herself into the deckchair that Sophie had placed in the yard for her and soon became engrossed in the newspaper.

Once Sophie arrived at Dr Bannerman's house she propped the bicycle up against the front wall and tentatively tapped at the front door. There was no answer so after tapping again she opened the gate that led to the back garden and knocked on the back door. Within seconds, a very attractive young woman in a satin negligee threw it open and glared at her before asking abruptly, 'Who the hell are you?'

Just as her aunt had warned her, Sophie quickly found out that Celia's nature didn't match her looks. But all the same she had no wish to get off to a bad start so she flashed her a friendly smile.

'I'm Sophie, Mrs Springs' niece. Didn't the doctor tell you that I'd be cleaning for you until she's recovered from her fall?'

'Yes . . . I think he did now that I come to think about it,'

Celia replied as she eyed her up and down. 'But I was expecting someone a little older.'

'Well, it doesn't really matter how old I am as long as you're satisfied with my work, does it? So . . . shall I make a start then?'

Celia stood aside grudgingly and as Sophie entered the kitchen she looked around. Her heart sank; the whole place looked as if a tornado had swept through it and she wondered how long it would take to put it to rights. The sink was overflowing with dirty pots as was every single work surface including the table, and there were unwashed clothes strewn everywhere.

'I don't suppose you'd have time to do a little washing for me, would you?' The request came out more as a command as Celia nodded towards a twin-tub washing machine housed in one corner. 'I'm afraid Adam is running out of clean shirts and I have to go out so I won't have time to wash them myself. Speaking of which, I'd better get ready. I'm going to be late at this rate.'

She sashayed from the room as Sophie continued to look around in dismay, wondering where to start, but after a few seconds she rolled her sleeves up. Standing there looking at it wouldn't get it done so first she would tackle the dirty pots.

Almost an hour later, Celia reappeared. She was wearing a beautiful dress that was cinched in tight at the waist, with a billowing skirt. It was very flattering and although Sophie had already decided that she wasn't going to like the woman any more than her aunt did, she had to admit that she looked absolutely stunning. Not that Sophie would tell her so. She could see that Celia was vain enough as it was.

Already the sink and every single work surface had been cleared and wiped down and there wasn't a dirty pot in sight. If Celia noticed she didn't bother to comment and Sophie felt her blood start to boil.

'Right, I dare say you'll be gone before I get back,' Celia informed her coldly. '*Do* make sure that the house is cleaned properly. I do so hate shoddy work.'

Sophie swallowed the hasty retort that sprang to her lips, very aware of the fact that her hair, which she had tied back into a ponytail, was beginning to escape into damp little curls in the heat and that Celia would never be seen dead in the cheap off-the-peg dress that she herself was wearing.

Jamming the pipe onto the hot tap she began to fill the washing machine and when she next looked round Celia had gone without so much as a by your leave.

She shook her head in bewilderment. Over the last week she had met Adam Bannerman every day when he visited her aunt and in that time she'd come to the conclusion that he was a very kind, caring man. So what the hell had he ever seen in Celia? Looks, she supposed, and found herself pitying him as she tipped some Omo washing powder into the water and rammed the first of the dirty washing into the machine.

For the next half an hour she didn't think of anything but getting the washing done and pegged out onto the line where it flapped softly in the warm breeze. It was nearing lunchtime when she wiped the sweat from her brow and stood back to view the kitchen with satisfaction. The whole room was gleaming like a new pin. Just the rest of the house to tackle now, she thought, then sighed. If the rest of it turned out to be in the same state as the kitchen she might very well find herself there until bedtime. Crossing the beautiful parquet floor in the hall she opened the first door that she came to and found herself in the lounge. She looked around with envy. It was a truly beautiful room and to her relief she saw that while it was untidy it was nowhere near as bad as the kitchen had been. In no time at all she had that room gleaming too and she was just about to make her way upstairs when the front door opened and the doctor appeared.

'Hello Sophie. You found us all right, then?'

'Yes thanks.' He looked so genuinely pleased to see her that she felt herself blushing like a schoolgirl. 'I was . . . just about to make a start on the bedroom.'

'*Bedrooms* I'm afraid,' he told her apologetically. 'I've been doing a lot of the night calls and Celia was complaining that I wake her up when I come back in, so I've been sleeping in the small room for the past few nights. But don't worry. I've kept it tidy so there shouldn't be too much for you to do in there.'

'It doesn't matter. That's what I'm here for,' she replied.

'Right. Well, I suggest before you do any more you

have a tea break. I've no doubt you've earned it. As you've probably discovered, my wife isn't the tidiest of creatures.'

A refusal hovered on her lips but then as she saw him watching her she smiled and nodded. 'A cup of tea would go down nicely,' she admitted shyly.

'Good. Come along and I'll put the kettle on.'

She followed him into the kitchen noting the way he looked round appreciatively. 'Goodness me, someone's been busy. And is that my shirts I see flapping on the line out there? Thanks, Sophie. I was going to try and do them myself tonight after work.'

She felt herself warming to him as she slid onto a chair and watched him fill the kettle at the deep sink that was now snow-white.

'I'll probably have time to iron some for you before I go,' she told him but he shook his head.

'No you will not. You've done more than a fair day's work already. I'll do them myself tonight. Well . . . what I should say is, I'll do them after a fashion. I'm afraid I tend to put more creases in when I'm ironing than I take out.' His laugh was so infectious that she found herself relaxing a little. She had never been on her own with him before but as she was fast discovering he was remarkably easy to talk to.

One cup of tea turned into two as they talked of this and that. They discussed the blocks of flats springing up here and there and the new motorways that were being carved out of the countryside. He even confided his opinion about Nelson Mandela, much in the news of late after being imprisoned for life for treason. But eventually Sophie pushed her mug away and rose reluctantly.

'I'd best get on then,' she told him and he watched her as she walked from the room. With a little shock he realised that he had shared more of a conversation with Sophie in a few short minutes than he had with his own wife in months and the realisation was tinged with sadness. All Celia ever tended to talk about, when she did talk to him at all that was, was the latest fashions and where she would be going that day. Sighing heavily he carried the empty mugs to the sink and rinsed them before getting ready to leave.

'I'll see you on Thursday, Sophie. If today hasn't put you off that is,' he shouted up the stairs.

Her head appeared over the banister and she smiled at him. 'You'll see me on Thursday.'

He smiled back before letting himself out, looking forward to it already.

Sophie arrived home to find her aunt sitting in the yard sipping lemonade with Flo, her neighbour. Flo was a kindly soul as Sophie had discovered during her short stay, though she had yet to see her without the scarf that she always wore wrapped around her head, turban-style, with a single metal curler poking out of the front. This, added to the voluminous wraparound floral apron and down-at-heel slippers that she always wore, made her look a comical sight. Sophie found it impossible to even begin to guess her age and wondered what she would look like with her hair let loose.

'Ah, so there you are. I was just beginnin' to get worried about yer. How did it go?' her aunt asked anxiously.

'Fine.' Sophie propped the bicycle against the coal house door as Rachel came hurtling towards her.

'Schweeties?' she demanded and after fumbling in the pocket of her dress, Sophie produced a lollipop that had the child beaming from ear to ear.

'Has she been all right?' Sophie smiled as Rachel turned her attention to her treat and toddled contentedly away.

'Good as the day is long. I'll tell yer, that little 'un is an angel,' Philly replied as she stared at the child affectionately. 'But now, come on. Tell me all about it. Did yer get to meet Miss High an' Mighty?'

'I certainly did,' Sophie giggled. 'And you weren't exaggerating when you told me what she was like. She's very . . . confident, isn't she?'

'Huh! That's an understatement if ever I heard one.' Philly's face darkened now. 'Too bloody vain for her own good that one is, if you ask me. What the doctor ever saw in her apart from a pretty face is beyond me. Still, I suppose it's none o' my business. I just think he could have done so much better fer himself, that's all.'

At that moment they heard footsteps in the entry and when the doctor came through the gate Philly went as red as a brick.

'Oh . . . hello, lad. We was just talkin' about you.'

'Were you really? It was all good I hope?'

Philly was so embarrassed that she could scarcely answer him. 'Oh yes it was all . . .' Eager to change the subject she stopped mid-flow and demanded, 'What you doin' here anyway?'

'Charming. I'll go away if that's how you feel.'

'No, lad, no, don't do that. I didn't mean it in that way.' Philly was even more flustered now.

Luckily, Flo chose that moment to stand up and the tense moment was gone. 'Right, here's me sittin' here like a lady o' leisure an' I've got dinners to cook. My Derek will be home in the blink of an eye an' he won't take kindly to me havin' no snap on the table.' She flashed them all a friendly smile then disappeared into the kitchen door opposite Philly's.

'Actually, I just popped in because I was passing to make sure that you were all right,' the doctor informed Philly.

'Right as ninepence,' she assured him.

'Good.' He now turned his attention to Sophie and said, 'Thanks for all your hard work today. And especially for ironing those shirts. I just called in at home to pick something up and saw them all done. I must admit ironing isn't my favourite pastime and I really wasn't looking forward to tackling them tonight. I'm afraid I've got rather used to Mrs Springs here spoiling me.'

Philly looked as proud as a peacock at the compliment. 'I told yer she was a good gel, didn't I?'

Hearing the note of pride in her voice he nodded in

agreement. 'You certainly did and I don't mind telling you she's worked like a Trojan today.'

'Well, don't get too used to it. It's only till this is healed up an' then you'll be stuck wi' me again,' Philly informed him as she leaned forward and tapped at her ankle.

'I can think of a lot worse things than that.' He nodded a farewell and after closing the gate behind him he walked away down the entry.

'Looks like you've scored points there,' Philly remarked and watched with amusement as Sophie in her turn became all flustered and fled into the kitchen.

Once alone again the smile slid from Philly's face. Why couldn't he have met someone like her Sophie instead of that stuck-up little madam he had married, she wondered? She could see him and Sophie together, somehow. Not that seeing would make any difference. He was a married man and that was an end to it. It was a bloody shame though! And then there was Rachel to worry about. What was it about the child's circumstances that Sophie wasn't telling her? She hadn't been lying when she'd told Sophie that the child had been as good as gold. What she *had* refrained from telling her was that the child had been asking for her mammy for most of the day.

Chapter Twenty

'Will you be visiting the house tonight, darling?' Anxious eyes fixed on Ben's rigid back as he stared from the fourth-floor window down onto the holidaymakers streaming past the hotel in the street below.

'I will, and there had better be some change in Tilly. Otherwise I may have to take action.'

His terse reply made her heart hammer. 'You don't mean Dr—'

'Of course I do,' he snapped. 'What choice will she have left me? If she hasn't conformed by now I think it's safe to say she's highly unlikely to, and I don't need to spell out what could happen to us if she escaped and spilled the beans, do I?'

Amanda's lip trembled although she could see the truth in what he said. 'But it's so—'

'All right then, you come up with another solution!' he stormed.

Her hands trembled as she lit a cigarette and pulled on it deeply. It wasn't like Ben to snap at her. In fact, she could count on one hand the times he had done so before. Still, she consoled herself, *he has been under a lot of pressure recently, what with Tilly refusing to cooperate and Sophie doing a disappearing act like that.* And then on top of everything there was the new girl up on the fifth floor to worry about. She had only arrived yesterday and ever since they'd shown her into what had been Tilly's old room she had done nothing but cry. *Perhaps Mrs G was right and it was time for them to retire?* As she thought of the bank book tucked safely away in the hotel safe her eyes lit up with greed. *No . . . perhaps not just yet. Up until Tilly and Sophie arrived everything had run like clockwork and soon things would settle down again. Wouldn't they?* Rising from the bed she went to stand close behind him, gently stroking his back. When there was no reaction whatsoever she frowned through a haze of cigarette smoke and strode away, slamming herself down onto her dressing-table stool.

'You don't usually take your bad moods out on me,' she whined like a petulant child.

Deeply exasperated, Ben sighed as he turned to face her. 'Do you have *any* idea at all what could happen if either of those broads decides to blab to the police, Mother? Why – they'd be down on us like a ton of bricks and I somehow don't think prison life would suit you, do you?'

Drawing deeply on her cigarette again she pondered what he had said before replying, 'Very well. Go and do whatever needs to be done but . . . be careful, Ben.'

His mouth set in a grim line, he nodded before disappearing through the door.

Once left to her own devices again, Amanda took up her hairbrush and began to tug it gently through her blond hair. *I really must get to the hairdresser's this week*, she thought to herself, pushing thoughts of the predicament they found themselves in to the back of her mind. *It really does need a trim . . . and is that another grey hair I can see there?*

Mrs G, who had come to stand in the doorway, entered the room. She took the brush from Amanda's hand and laid it down before leading Amanda to the bed. 'It's time you had a little lie-down now,' she encouraged her softly. 'You know it don't do you no good to go getting yourself all upset.'

The woman looked up at her trustingly and almost before her head had hit the pillow her eyes had fluttered shut.

With tears streaming down her face Mrs G watched her and her face creased with sorrow. 'Oh dear God – where is it all going to end?' she whispered but only silence answered her.

'Look, Tilly, *please*. The boss is due any minute an' if you ain't cleaned yerself up I can't be responsible fer what he might do.'

Seemingly oblivious to anything that Carol was saying, Tilly lay on the dirty eiderdown, her eyes staring blankly up at the ceiling.

Fraught with frustration, Carol flung herself away from the bed and began to pace up and down the confines of the small room. She had tried everything she could to get Tilly to comply with her wishes but it was just as if she was banging her head against a brick wall. It seemed that even Walter could not frighten the girl and now she was at her wits' end. Ben could arrive at any second and if the mood he had been in the last time he'd called round was anything to go by she guessed that he was very near the end of his patience. On top of that one of her girls had been diagnosed with a dose that very morning so all in all she wasn't having the best of days.

Realising that her words were falling on deaf ears she wearily left the room. She had done all she could. It was up to Ben now.

As she reached the bottom of the stairs she heard the key turn in the lock and Ben appeared with a face like thunder.

'Any change?' He thumbed towards the ceiling and when she shook her head he brushed past her into the kitchen where he snatched up the phone.

Realising his intentions she gushed, 'Ben listen . . . I think I know who yer callin', but couldn't you give me just a bit more time?'

'You're not going soft on me are you, Carol?'

'No, no of course I'm not,' she babbled. 'It's just—'

'There are no *justs* about it. You should know that by now. A madame who can't keep her girls in line is about as much use as an umbrella in a snowstorm to me.'

Deeply ashamed of her show of sympathy she hung her head. He was right: she was at risk of turning soft and if that happened she might as well retire right now. She closed the door softly behind her as he lifted the receiver to his ear. Tilly's fate was all in the lap of the gods now and there was nothing more she could do about it.

An hour later, Ben's car cruised past the luxurious houses overlooking the sea in Lytham-St-Anne's. Keeping his eyes fixed firmly on the road he looked neither to left nor right. He didn't relish the meeting ahead but felt he was left with no choice now. Tilly was becoming a liability. She would have to be dealt with.

Once the houses were left behind he kept to the sea road and hurtled past the sand dunes. Very soon high brick walls came into view and he found himself shivering despite the heat of the day.

This was it, Hatter's Hall, a home for the mentally ill, aptly named; the wealthy man who had once owned it had also owned a string of hat factories in the Midlands. The man had been known to be something of a recluse and following his death the Hall had stood empty for some years until Dr Thackeray had bought it and had it converted into a private nursing home.

Seconds later, Ben pulled up outside huge metal gates that were kept securely locked and almost immediately a bald-headed, round-shouldered man appeared from a small box-like structure at the side of them. As he peered through the intricate wrought-iron work at him, Ben was reminded of a little monkey.

Winding down the car window, he snapped, 'Ben Lewis to see Dr Thackeray.'

The little man nodded, then lifting an enormous bunch of keys dangling from his belt he proceeded to unlock the gates.

'In you go, sir.'

Ben nodded his thanks before roaring through the gates as a feeling of apprehension settled around him like a cloud. He could never visit this place without having nightmares about it for weeks afterwards, probably due to the fact that his mother had once spent some time incarcerated in a similar place in America.

As he negotiated the long drive leading to the Hall he passed emerald-green lawns and flowerbeds ablaze with coloured blooms. And then as he rounded a bend there it was in front of him, a cold forbidding-looking place that could strike terror into the bravest of hearts. Ben could imagine that at one time the great rambling manor house might have been beautiful, but now with metal bars fixed tight to each of its upper windows it looked exactly what it was: a prison for unfortunates.

He shuddered yet again; it was rumoured that at night the cries of the inmates rang on the air. Hence, the building was shunned by the locals, and he could well understand why.

Struggling to compose himself he slewed the car to a halt in front of enormous oak doors that had withstood the test of the sand and sea. Once outside on the gravel he looked around him. Although it was a beautiful day there was not a single soul to be seen within the grounds, save for the old man who had let him in at the gate. After climbing three wide concrete steps he rapped sharply with the huge brass doorknocker.

Footsteps immediately sounded from within and seconds later a middle-aged woman who he saw at a glance would never win any prizes in a beauty competition opened the door. Her faded hair was tied severely back into a bun, giving her eyes a slightly oriental slant, and a nurse's cap was perched on the back of her head.

'Yes!'

Ensuring that his voice betrayed no hint of his reaction to the place, Ben told her, 'Mr Ben Lewis to see Dr Thackeray.'

'Do you have an appointment?'

'No, but tell him I'm here and I'm sure he'll see me.' Ben knew that the doctor would be too afraid not to.

Sniffing her disapproval, the nurse allowed him to step past her into the entrance foyer, which was immaculately clean. 'Wait there. I'll see if Dr Thackeray is available.' She walked away with a rustle of starched uniform, her back so stiff that Ben wondered if she had a broom handle stuck up it, before disappearing into a doorway at the end of a long hallway.

He stood there, nervously rubbing his hands together and feeling for all the world like a naughty schoolboy who was due in to see the headmaster as his eyes flicked around the imposing entrance hall. The walls were decorated in a soft gold colour and cream damask drapes hung at the windows. He could have imagined he was entering a hotel.

Seconds later the woman reappeared looking as if she was sucking on a wasp.

'Follow me,' she ordered brusquely. 'The doctor will see you now – but I have to warn you that he is due to see a patient in fifteen minutes so I shall have to ask you to keep your meeting brief.'

Ben resisted the childish urge to stick his tongue out as he followed her back along the corridor, which smelt faintly of stale disinfectant and something he couldn't quite put his finger on.

When they came to the doorway of a luxuriously furnished day room she gestured towards a door in a far corner. 'You'll find Dr Thackeray in his office.' Sniffing her disapproval she flounced away, her footsteps echoing hollowly on the cold tiled floor.

Ben started across the room taking in the rich leather chesterfield settees that were set here and there with little ornate tables to the side of them. This was the room where the visitors were shown when visiting the private patients. The windows stretched all along one wall covered in floor-to-ceiling drapes topped off with elaborate swags and tails that spoke of splendour from a bygone age. Through the windows, yet more flowerbeds were visible and he realised that the whole place had been designed to give an air of peace and tranquillity. Unfortunately,

Ben knew that not all of the Hall was up to this high standard. He tapped at a panelled door and instantly a voice shouted, 'Enter.'

After closing the door behind him, Ben looked across at Dr Thackeray who rose from his desk and with hand outstretched hurried to greet him.

'Ben, this is an . . . unexpected pleasure. What can I do for you?' Despite the warmth of the doctor's greeting his voice was laced with fear and slowly Ben's courage returned. He shook his hand firmly before settling into the chair that the doctor pointed to.

Dr Thackeray was known to be a pillar of society in the community. He had run his private clinic for the mentally ill for many years, during which time he had become a very wealthy man. But Ben happened to know that much more went on behind closed doors than people knew about. And there was much more to Dr Thackeray if it came to that, which he had discovered some years ago when the doctor had become a regular visitor to his brothel in Back Street.

He now watched the portly man approach a filing cabinet from which he took a bottle of whisky and two crystal glasses. 'You'll join me in a drink, Ben?' He peered at him enquiringly through a great bush of greying hair that was long overdue for a haircut.

Ben accepted and watched the doctor's hand shake as he tipped a generous measure into each glass before handing one to Ben.

'So . . . I assume there is some reason for this unexpected

visit?' The doctor drained his glass in one, keeping a watchful eye on Ben, who slowly nodded, knowing only too well that he had the whip hand.

'I'm afraid I have a problem at one of your favourite haunts, William. But before I go into that, may I ask how you're enjoying your visits to my little establishment? Carol informs me that you've taken quite a shine to one of my new girls, Amy. I did think you'd like her, actually. You always did like the young broads, didn't you, William?'

By now the doctor's hand was shaking so much that he could barely hold his glass and he pulled at the neck of his shirt uncomfortably as if he couldn't breathe.

'I . . .' His voice trailed away as Ben looked on with amusement.

'And how is *Mrs* Thackeray? Keeping well I hope? Such a *lovely* woman, so I understand. A keen church-goer too, isn't she?'

'Look, Ben, don't play cat and mouse with me, please. Just tell me why you're here.'

'Very well. I have another young lady at the house who isn't . . . shall we say, quite as pliable as Amy? Carol has done her best with her, to be fair, but now she's becoming a problem.'

William Thackeray, who was quite aware of what went on on the fourth floor of Ben's hotel, scowled. 'Still pregnant is she?'

'No, thankfully she gave birth and that side of it has all been dealt with very satisfactorily. However, after her transfer to the house she became very difficult. She refuses to eat or even wash and I fear if I leave her there much longer she'll die. Obviously should that happen there it would be very difficult for me, whereas if it were to happen *here* . . .'

He deliberately refrained from telling the doctor the whole story for fear of him not taking her in; he undoubtedly would refuse to do so if he were to find out about either Rachel or Sophie. Ben was aware that, just like the hotel, Hatter's Hall held secrets. Many of the patients admitted there with mental illnesses came with the blessing of loving relations who were only too happy to pay vast sums of money to see their loved ones restored to health again. But others, many of whom had arrived some years ago, had been placed there by wealthy families whose daughters had strayed from the straight and narrow and found themselves pregnant out of wedlock. Far better they be locked away for ever than bring shame on their families.

And so the poor forsaken souls had been interred in Hatter's Hall where they had remained until they became as mad as the genuinely ill inmates around them, abandoned and forgotten, as Dr Thackeray grew rich. Ben, of course, was always more than happy to find doting families for the offspring that the unfortunate girls eventually gave birth to and so between the two of them they had a very lucrative sideline going.

Now the doctor strummed his fingers on the highly polished mahogany desk as he frowned.

'And what is there in this for me?'

Ben chuckled, 'Why, I would have thought that was more than obvious, William. Should Tilly escape she could blow the whistle on us all and everything we've worked for would come crashing down around us like a pack o' playing cards. All it's gonna cost you to keep her here is a room and enough drugs to keep her quiet, then you can go on enjoying the pleasures of Amy and any other little broad who takes your fancy at the house.'

Hearing the veiled threat in Ben's voice, the doctor sighed, knowing he was beaten. 'When would you want her transferred here?'

'Tonight I think.'

'And are you quite sure no one will come asking questions about her?'

'*Quite* sure.'

'Very well then. I shall have a room prepared and I'll meet you at the house at, shall we say, ten o'clock?'

Ben nodded with satisfaction as he drained his glass and rose from the chair. 'Until then.' He smiled as he departed, leaving the doctor looking thoughtful as he watched him go.

Minutes later the doctor rang a bell on his desk and the nurse who had just shown Ben out appeared as if out of thin air.

'Yes, Dr Thackeray?'

'We shall have a new patient arriving late this evening, Nurse Miller. I will be admitting her to the West Wing, hopefully into one of the wards. But just in case she should prove to be difficult I'd like you to prepare one of the padded cells, and we might need a straitjacket.'

'Very well, Doctor, I'll see to it straight away. May I ask the name of the patient?'

'It's a young female, Nurse Miller, by the name of Tilly. She has been causing certain problems for my friend and will be staying indefinitely . . . And there will be no visitors.'

'I *quite* understand, sir.' She backed from the room with a smile on her face. *Another one for the wacky wing then*, she thought. Very few people even knew that this part of the home existed, for it was locked to all except those who had been given the doctor's express permission to enter there.

The nurse's eyes glittered with sadistic anticipation. Another nice young one, eh? Just as she liked them.

When Dr Thackeray arrived at the house that night he found Carol hovering nervously by the door. Walter and Ben were deep in conversation further down the hallway and the sound of a Beatles song was floating on the air.

As soon as Ben spotted the doctor he stopped talking abruptly and came towards him. At that moment a young girl appeared out of a downstairs room tightly gripping the hand of an older man. In his other hand he held a large glass of wine, which slopped over the side of the glass onto the carpet as she dragged him, giggling, towards the stairs.

Ben waited until they had disappeared into one of the rooms on the first-floor landing before turning his attention back to the doctor. 'Do you have everything you need?'

Grim-faced, the doctor nodded curtly as he raised his black bag.

'Good, then we may as well go and get this over with.' His eyes shot a warning at Carol as they started up the stairs. He'd never known her do it before, yet she had pleaded with him right up to the second the doctor had arrived to give her just another few days to try and bend Tilly to their will. As far as he was concerned, Tilly had been given more than enough chances already and now he just wanted shot of her. He made a mental note to keep a close eye on Carol in the future. She would be no good to him as a madame for his girls if she was starting to go soft on him.

'Shall I come up with you?' she asked nervously.

He paused to look back at her and when he answered his voice dripped pure venom. 'I think the good doctor and I are more than capable of taking care of this, thank you. I suggest you go and check that all is well with the rest of the girls. After all, that *is* what I pay you for, isn't it?'

Painfully aware that she was skating on very thin ice, Carol scuttled away like a frightened rabbit.

By the time they reached the landing where Tilly was imprisoned, the doctor was out of breath.

'Too much good living, eh, William?' Ben said with

amusement. 'Perhaps it's time to cut down on the booze and cigarettes?' All the time he was talking he was going through a large bunch of keys until he came to the one that would unlock the door to Tilly's room. The smell when he opened it had the doctor reeling backwards with his face wrinkled in distaste.

'I did warn you that she wouldn't wash, didn't I?' Ben told him grimly as the doctor hastily pressed a handkerchief to his nose.

Snapping on the light they looked towards the bed where Tilly was sitting cross-legged, staring at them from dull, defiant eyes.

As the doctor snapped his case open and took from it a syringe that he had all ready, Tilly's brows drew together in a frown. 'What yer thinkin' o' doin' wi' that?'

'It's all right, my dear. You just lie there and you won't feel a thing,' he murmured reassuringly as he fired a small amount of liquid from the needle into the air.

'*Fuck off!* You ain't comin' near me wi' that,' Tilly screeched as she sat up and swung her legs over the side of the bed. Dizziness swept over her in a wave. Days of going without food had weakened her and she knew that her strength would be no match for theirs.

'Please . . . NO!' She began to cry pitifully as they approached the bed but Ben merely caught her arm in a tight grip and yanked her sleeve up.

As she felt the prick of the needle hot tears began to slide down her cheeks. 'Rachel . . . RACHEL . . .'

'Who is Rachel?' The doctor stared at Ben but he

dismissed his question with a wave of his hand as he watched Tilly's eyes glaze over.

'Probably just someone she once knew.' Even as he spoke, Tilly slipped sideways onto the bed and he smiled with satisfaction. Walter, who had been waiting on the landing outside, appeared in the doorway and Ben nodded at him.

'Right, Walter. She's quiet as a lamb now. Get her downstairs into the car for us, would you?'

Never one to waste words, Walter scooped Tilly into his arms as if she weighed no more than a feather. The silent procession then left the room and made its way down the stairs.

As they disappeared through the front door with Tilly's inert body dangling from Walter's arms, Carol pressed herself further back into the shadows in the dimly lit hallway and stifled a sob.

What was happening was wrong! Every instinct she had screamed out against it, yet what could she do?

With her fist jammed tight in her mouth she watched Walter throw Tilly none too gently onto the back seat of the doctor's car, which was parked at the kerb. When Ben got into the front seat at the side of the doctor, Walter came back into the house as the car roared away. It was then that an idea occurred to her and before she could give herself time to change her mind she confronted Walter.

'All done then?' Her voice was falsely unconcerned as he nodded solemnly. 'Good, then if you don't mind I'm going up fer a lie-down. I really do have the most dreadful bleedin' headache. It's probably all the stress o' that little minx brought it on. You can cope down here, can't yer, Walter?'

Another nod was her answer as he glared at her suspiciously.

Sweeping past him she started to climb the stairs. 'I'll see yer in the mornin' then. An' make sure no one leaves wi'out payin'.'

Once inside her room she snatched a light jacket from her wardrobe and draped it round her shoulders before tiptoeing back across the landing. Peering down into the gloomy hallway she smiled with satisfaction when she saw that it was deserted. Holding her breath she crept down the stairs and softly lifted the catch on the door then silently she slipped out into the darkness and hurried away down the deserted street.

Walter shrank back into the shadows of an abandoned warehouse as he watched her go, then as the sound of her footsteps died away his lips set in a grim line and, keeping to the shadows, he followed her.

Mrs G was sitting with her feet up listening to the radio and enjoying a glass of sherry when a tap came to the kitchen window. She started before cautiously approaching the door. Plucking up her courage she threw it open and stared out into the darkened yard.

'Who's there?' she hissed, then almost jumped out of her skin when Carol suddenly stepped into the light spilling from the doorway.

'God above! You almost scared the life out of me,' she gasped as she clutched at her heart.

Carol pushed past her and once in the kitchen she looked around fearfully before asking, 'Are we alone?'

'Well, of course we are. I can't see anybody else here, can you?'

Ignoring the note of disapproval in the older woman's voice, Carol began to babble. 'Look, Mrs G. I know you ain't got no time fer me an' that's yer choice. But I can't think o' no one else to turn to.'

Tight-lipped, Mrs G waited for her to go on; she didn't have to wait long.

'It's about a young girl you had stayin' here. Tilly was her name. Do yer remember her?'

'Of course I do. I am not quite senile yet, you know. But what about her?'

'They've took her away tonight to Hatter's Hall.' Carol's voice was laced with fear. 'Ben an' the doctor, that is. An' we both know what will happen to her now, don't we? She'll never see daylight again an' in a few years' time she'll be as loony as the rest of o' the poor sods locked away there. But the thing is, Tilly has a child an' it ain't right.'

Mrs G's eyes almost popped out of her head. 'What do you mean – she has a child? The child was born here and Ben found it a family.'

'No, no. Not *that* child. It turns out she already had a child when she came here. A little girl by the name o' Rachel. It ain't right that she'll never see her mam again. Can't you do somethin', Mrs G?'

Ms G gulped deep in her throat as her heart began to pound. 'And just what is it you expect me to do? You know right well that I don't have any dealings with the things that go on here . . . *or* at your place for that matter.'

Carol wrung her hands and for the first time in all the years that she had known her, Mrs G realised that beneath her hard exterior she had a heart. As her voice softened she reached out to squeeze Carol's arm.

'Get yourself away, girl. I don't have to tell you what trouble you'll be in if Ben or Amanda find out you've been here. There's nothing you can do or I can for that matter, more's the pity. If the poor girl has gone to Hatter's Hall then we both know that the only way she's ever likely to come out of there is feet first in a box.'

'But she kept sayin' that someone called Sophie would find her,' Carol told her.

Mrs G frowned. 'That doesn't surprise me though there isn't much chance of it now. Sophie ran away just after Tilly had given birth. They were as thick as thieves though I never let Ben know that. He frowned on the girls getting too friendly with one another but there was no keeping those two apart. I didn't know Tilly had another child, though. God above. Whatever made her come here then?'

'She wanted to make a new life with Rachel after the new baby had been found a good home. She didn't feel that she'd be able to support two financially. Poor little sod.'

As footsteps sounded in the corridor outside, Mrs G urgently pushed Carol towards the door. 'Get yourself away and forget all about her. That's the best advice I can give you. Now go while you still can and make yourself scarce.'

As Carol disappeared into the yard, Mrs G forced a smile to her face as she greeted the woman who was just entering the kitchen. 'Hello, love. After a nightcap are you? Then sit yourself down in that chair there and I'll put some milk on to boil. I always think there's nothing like a good cup of Horlicks inside you to ensure a good night's sleep.'

Carol slipped stealthily away, unaware of Walter, who was watching her from the deep shadows outside the laundry door.

Chapter Twenty-one

Thursday morning dawned bright and clear, the start of another beautiful day, and as Sophie freewheeled down the Cock and Bear hill she found herself humming, although she stopped abruptly when she thought of Celia, who she prayed wouldn't be in when she got to the doctor's house. Her prayers were answered when she unlocked the door and only silence greeted her.

Going first to the kitchen she immediately wondered how anyone could possibly have got it into such a mess in such a short time. It had been spotless when she left only two days earlier yet now it looked like a bombsite again. Judging by the paraphernalia strewn across the table she guessed that wherever Celia had gone she must have left in a hurry. An open handbag with all manner of things spilling out of it was in the centre of the table surrounded by jars of face cream and various items of make-up. The sink was piled high yet again with dirty dishes, and the wash basket was overflowing.

Ah well, she thought to herself as she slung her cardigan

across the back of a chair, at least I won't have time to get bored. She'd been hoping to get home slightly earlier today as it was Rachel's second birthday but now she wasn't so sure that she would. Tilly had fully intended to be spending this special day with her and had talked about it so much that the date was engraved on Sophie's mind.

As she thought of Tilly now, Sophie's heart was heavy but then she smiled again as she recalled the excitement she had left back at the cottage. Aunt Philly had been baking all of the day before and the kitchen was full of treats including a birthday cake, which she had stayed up late the night before to ice. There was also all manner of cakes and cookies, not to mention jellies and trifles.

'There's enough here to feed an army let alone the few children from the village you've invited,' Sophie had teased her but Aunt Philly was enjoying herself.

'Better too much than not enough,' she had declared stoutly so in the end Sophie gave up and let her get on with it.

She began to collect the contents of Celia's bag together and as she was doing so a folded sheet of paper fell open. She lifted it, fully intending to return it to the bag, but the beginning of what appeared to be a letter caught her eye. *My dearest darling*, it began. Wrestling with her conscience she stood there until curiosity got the better of her and she read the rest. The instant she had she wished that she hadn't, for it was a love letter to Celia and it wasn't from her husband.

Jamming it deep into the bottom of the bag she paused as rage swept through her. What the hell was wrong with Celia? Adam Bannerman was one of the nicest men, if not *the* nicest, she had ever met so why was the stupid woman playing away?

Her eyes surveyed the room, taking in the expensive fittings and all the mod cons that he had provided for her. He must obviously adore her and worked all the hours that God sent to give her anything she desired. Surely she could see just how lucky she was?

Cramming the rest of the things haphazardly into the bag she flung it onto a chair and set about washing the mountain of pots piled in the sink, her mind working overtime. Stupid, *stupid* woman! Why, if she had a man like Adam Bannerman who loved her she would return his love . . . Her cheeks flamed as she tried to get a grip on herself. What was she thinking of? Adam was married and that was an end to it.

Her thoughts returned to 8 Claypit Cottages and her aunt. Every day saw an improvement in her now and Sophie decided that perhaps it would be a good thing when Philly was well enough to resume her duties for the doctor.

Within an hour she had the washing flapping on the clothes line and the kitchen was once again spotless, as was the lounge. She was in the process of making the bed in the spare bedroom, where the doctor was obviously still spending his nights, when his voice wafted up the stairs to her.

'Sophie, come on. I've brought us both a bit of dinner.'

She straightened her skirt and made her way downstairs to the kitchen where she found him unwrapping two steaming packets wrapped in newspaper.

'I hope you're hungry,' he greeted her cheerily, thinking how nice she looked in the blouse she was wearing. It was exactly the same colour blue as her eyes. 'I was passing the fish and chip shop and I just fancied some. You do like fish and chips, don't you?'

'Well, yes I do but you didn't need to bring me—'

'Oh, just come and eat them while they're nice and hot. You don't mind eating them out of the paper, do you? I always think they taste so much better that way.'

His cheerful mood was so infectious that she found herself smiling as she pulled a chair up to the table to join him.

'Someone sounds in a good mood today,' she commented as she blew on a chip.

'I suppose I am now that you come to mention it.' As he looked across at her he suddenly realised why. He'd been looking forward to seeing her and enjoying another chat. A rare thing in this house nowadays.

'Have you got anything nice planned for when you leave here?'

She grinned ruefully. 'It all depends what you mean by nice. It's Rachel's second birthday today and when I left home Aunt Philly had every available surface covered in jellies and cakes. She's doing a little party for her at teatime so no doubt we'll be surrounded by screaming children.'

'Lucky you. It sounds wonderful.'

Hearing the note of sadness that had crept into his voice she asked, 'Are you planning on having a family?' The minute the question had spilled from her lips she could have bitten her tongue out, but it was too late to take it back now.

'*I* am but I don't think Celia is too fond of the idea,' he confided, wondering why he found her so easy to talk to. 'Of course, she is a few years younger than me so she's got plenty of time to change her mind.'

Sophie doubted it after the letter she had read earlier in the morning but wisely said nothing. She could see the doctor making a wonderful father though. As colour washed across her cheeks at the thought she choked on the piece of fish she was just swallowing and in a second he was round the table and gently thumping her back. She felt as if her skin was on fire where he had touched it, which added even further to her confusion. What the hell was the matter with her anyway?

'Is that better?' His voice sounded full of concern as he handed her a glass of water and with her eyes watering she nodded in answer, feeling suddenly very foolish as she gulped at it.

The awkward moment passed when he sat back down and started to eat again. Glancing appreciatively round the kitchen he remarked, 'Everywhere looks really lovely.

You must take after your aunt for being a homemaker. She's a lovely woman, isn't she?'

Now it was her turn to smile as she nodded vigorously. 'She certainly is. I don't know what Rachel and I would have done without her if—' She stopped abruptly. There she went again; he was so easy to talk to that she'd almost said more than she wanted. If he had noticed he tactfully refrained from saying so.

'Did you hear the Pope ranting on about the contraceptive pill on the wireless last night?' he suddenly asked with a shake of his head. 'I think it's a good thing but he is obviously strongly opposed to it. Think of how many unwanted teenage pregnancies it could save and . . .' His eyes fell on Sophie's empty ring finger and now it was his turn to blush. Trust him to put his big foot in it. Funny though, now he came to think of it, Sophie didn't seem at all the sort of girl to be an unmarried mother. Celia was always complaining about the things he came out with when he was in the company of her friends. Not, in truth, that he had much in common with them. In fact, he didn't even like them that much. They all seemed to live off the backs of rich parents and he was sure that a hard day's work would have killed them. Still, he supposed that she was entitled to mix with who she wanted to. Just so long as she didn't expect him to join in. The few times that he had been in their company had almost ended in disaster and now he was more than happy to let her go her own way. Up to a point of course.

Frightened of putting his foot in it again he ate the rest of his meal in silence; afterwards he put the kettle on to boil and measured two spoonfuls of Camp coffee into two mugs.

'Have you got a busy afternoon ahead of you?' she asked, keen to break the silence stretching between them.

'Not too bad. I've got an antenatal clinic.' He cursed silently. There he went again. 'And then I've got a couple of home visits to do but once they're over hopefully I can knock off for the day.'

'Why don't you call into the party if you're done in time?' Stunned that she had asked, Sophie studiously avoided his eyes. What had made her ask that?

She was even more stunned when he instantly replied, 'I'd love to. If you're sure, that is? I used to be a dab hand at pass-the-parcel when I was a kid according to my mother so I might be able to help keep the littlies entertained if it gets too much for you.'

'You're on.' Suddenly she was glad she had asked and the easy atmosphere was restored again.

They carried their coffee out into the back garden and after sinking onto a bench, Sophie watched brightly coloured butterflies flitting from flower to flower with a look of contentment on her face. Unlike the house, the garden was beautifully kept and she asked curiously, 'Do you tend the garden yourself?'

He nodded eagerly. 'Yes I do, as a matter of fact. It's a bit of a passion of mine. I love to come out here and sit. You'd be surprised how relaxing it can be.'

'I wouldn't. I'm almost dropping off, it's so peaceful here. My mam always loved to spend time in the garden . . .'

Tears sprang to her eyes before she could stop them as painful memories flooded back and suddenly, flustered, she got to her feet. 'Anyway, I'd better get on. You don't pay me to sit about chatting and drinking coffee.' She was halfway up the path when she turned back. 'And by the way, thanks for dinner . . . Dr Bannerman.'

'Adam will do nicely.'

She gulped and hurried on. Adam. It sounded nice as she rolled it around her tongue.

She arrived back at her aunt's in the middle of the afternoon to organised chaos. Rachel was rampaging about the place red-faced with excitement and the downstairs of the cottage was full of balloons, not to mention food everywhere she looked. Aunt Philly was positively glowing and obviously enjoying herself immensely.

'I can't remember when I last had so much fun,' she giggled as Sophie stared around in amazement.

'But Aunt Philly, I thought this was supposed to be just a *little* party?'

'Well, yer know the sayin' – if a job's worth doin' it's worth doin' well. Now come on. Don't stand there gawpin'. The guests will be arrivin' any minute an' Rachel needs to get her new frock on. I stayed up half the night to get it finished.'

Sophie lifted a pretty white cotton dress covered in tiny pink rosebuds from the back of the chair and gazed at it admiringly. It really was beautiful and so well made that no one would have known it hadn't been bought from a shop. It had little puff sleeves and a broad sash in the same colour pink as the roses. The skirt was full and the yoke was intricately smocked. Once she'd slipped it over Rachel's head and tied her hair into pigtails with matching pink ribbons the little girl looked totally enchanting. As Sophie stood back with her aunt to admire her a wave of sadness washed over her. She wished that Tilly was there; she would have been so proud. Forcing herself to push the thoughts to the back of her mind she set to and helped her aunt with the finishing touches; shortly the first guests began to arrive, all looking very spick and span in their Sunday best.

Sophie herded them out into the garden and in no time at all their laughter pierced the quietness of the air and they all looked, as Aunt Philly put it, 'as if they had been dragged through a hedge backwards'.

After a time they all trooped back into the house to sample the treats that Philly had prepared for them and Sophie looked on in horror as her aunt's tidy little cottage began to resemble a battleground.

'Stop frettin'.' Philly was enjoying herself far too much to let little things like fairy cakes being trampled into her carpet worry her. 'We'll soon clean it up between us when they've all gone. An' just look at Rachel's face an' dare to tell me it ain't all been worth it. Why, she's beamin' like a Cheshire cat.'

As Sophie followed her aunt's eyes she was just in time

to see Rachel lift a dangerously full spoon of lime-green jelly to her lips, half of which ended up all down her chin and the front of her lovely new dress.

Philly laughed aloud at the horrified expression on Sophie's face. 'Kids are washable, yer know? Now come on, let's get these here parcels passed round, eh? I spent hours wrappin' the damn things up so I don't want 'em goin' to waste.'

Pass-the-parcel was followed by musical chairs and while Sophie was trying to keep some sort of organisation Adam walked into the thick of it. She eyed his smart suit with some trepidation but before she could comment he was joining in and enjoying himself almost as much as the children.

One little boy who had eaten more in an hour than Rachel ate in a whole week suddenly turned a sickly shade of green and Adam hoisted him into his arms and marched him away to the outside toilet.

Sophie followed them hesitantly to find the poor child hanging over the toilet heaving his heart up.

'You go back in.' Adam spoke across his shoulder. 'He'll be right as rain in a minute. It's nothing to worry about. He's just overloaded his tummy, but I'm sure he'll live.'

'But your lovely suit . . .'

'Huh! Don't worry about that. I do have more than one, you know? I can drop it into the dry cleaner's tomorrow and it will come back as good as new.'

Sophie reluctantly retraced her steps, and was amazed when Adam reappeared only minutes later with the culprit he had dragged off looking as right as ninepence. In no time at all the little boy was back in the thick of it again and Sophie couldn't help but smile when Lily, who had been doing her best to hide under the table, suddenly shot out and launched herself into her arms.

'I think I can safely say she's not enjoying herself much. Though I have to say she appears to be the only one who's not!' Adam chuckled as he watched the little dog try to burrow her head under Sophie's armpit.

'Well, she's not used to all this commotion,' Philly piped up as she came to stand beside them. 'Our lives were peaceful till this pair landed on me doorstep. I'd sooner have it as it is now though! There's never a dull moment wi' that little madam around.' As her eyes settled on Rachel they grew soft and Sophie felt a wave of love for the little woman wash over her. It was such a shame that she had never been able to have children of her own. She had the patience of a saint and deep down Sophie had to admit that her aunt was even better with Rachel than she was.

Once again the responsibility she had taken on weighed heavy on her. She was only eighteen years old and yet she had a child to care for, and was now having to live off the charity of an old aunt she had never even known existed until a short while ago. Admittedly, she had felt slightly better about it since she'd taken over her aunt's part-time cleaning job at the doctor's. But her aunt's ankle was improving with every day that passed and any day now Sophie expected her to say she was ready to do it herself again. When that day came she would have to think of going back to Blackpool to look for Tilly. The mere thought of returning there struck terror into her heart but she knew that she couldn't postpone it for much longer. She could never rest until she had done what she could to find out what had become of her friend.

She shuddered involuntarily. The money Tilly and her mother had given her was dwindling fast and she didn't want to scrounge off her aunt forever, but perhaps she could give some of it to Aunt Philly and ask her to look after Rachel while she went in search of Tilly. At least then she would know that Rachel was safe. Her thoughts moved on to Ben and despite the warmth of the late afternoon sun she shivered. Would he still be looking for her? And if he ever found her what would he do? What had he done to Tilly?

As yet another balloon popped, Lily began to tremble in her arms and her thoughts were dragged sharply back to the present.

'So . . . what do you think then? Your aunt's all for it.'

'Sorry?' As Sophie stared vacantly back at Adam he laughed. 'You haven't heard a word I've said, have you?'

'That's nothin' new,' Philly remarked. 'She's off wi' the fairies half the time but fer what my opinion's worth I think it's a grand idea an' I'm all for it.'

'I was just saying that I feel rather guilty for turning up without a present for Rachel,' Adam repeated for Sophie's benefit. 'And I wondered if you'd allow me to take you all to the zoo for the afternoon on Sunday to make up for it?'

'But won't Celia mind?' Sophie asked as she stared up at him. She thought she detected a rueful smile before he shook his head.

'She won't know about it till she gets back. I came home from work tonight to a note saying that she's finally gone away with a friend of hers for a holiday they had planned a couple of weeks back. So . . . seeing as I don't have to work this weekend for a change, what do you say? Twycross Zoo only opened last year and I've been meaning to go and have a look round. It's in Leicestershire so it won't take us long to get there and I'm sure Rachel would love it.'

Sophie frowned uncertainly. The offer was tempting but on the other hand it didn't feel right. Adam *was* married after all. And she *should* be thinking of returning to Blackpool.

Seeing her hesitation, her aunt butted in yet again. 'Oh, come on. What harm is there in it? It's about time yer learned to let yer hair down a bit. You're only a young woman an' yer should be gettin' out an' about a bit more. Ain't that right, Doctor?'

Adam refrained from answering though he was amazed that there wasn't a queue of young men waiting to take Sophie out. Admittedly, she wasn't the most beautiful girl he had ever seen; at least not on the outside. He had never seen her wear make-up and it was more than obvious that the latest fashions were low on her list of priorities, yet when she really smiled, which was not often, her whole face lit up and could brighten a room. For the most part, she looked as if she had the weight of the world on her shoulders and he wondered yet again what secrets she was keeping.

Who was Rachel to Sophie? He had already guessed that the child wasn't hers. If she were, Sophie would have been little more than sixteen when she'd had her and somehow he'd already surmised that Sophie wasn't that type of girl. So where was the child's mother and why was Sophie looking after her? And why did Sophie close up like a clam every time he asked about her past and where she had come from?

'Well, let's have an answer then. The poor bloke can't stand here all day waitin' fer you to make yer mind up, yer know. He's only askin' to take yer to the zoo, not to elope wi' him. I reckon it would be lovely meself. I could pack us all a picnic. It's been years since I visited a zoo.'

Sophie knew when she was beaten. After all – what harm could there be in it? It wasn't as if she were going on her own with him and postponing her search for Tilly for another day or two wouldn't make all that much difference.

'All right then. That would be lovely. Thank you . . . I'm sure Rachel will enjoy it.'

Her aunt smiled with satisfaction before scurrying away to break up a skirmish that had broken out in the back yard.

Soon after, mothers began to arrive to collect their

offspring and as they disappeared off down the entry one at a time things began to quieten down a little.

'Phew!' Philly wiped the sweat from her brow as she sank onto a chair. 'Put the kettle on, love. Me feet feel as if they don't belong to me.'

Sophie obediently bustled away to do as she was told as Adam began to collect the dirty pots and pile them into the sink. Rachel clambered onto Philly's lap and immediately dropped off into an exhausted, contented sleep.

Ten minutes later when Sophie went back into the room she found Philly sound asleep too and a wave of guilt washed over her. She still hadn't told her aunt of the circumstances that had led up to her parents' death, and being the kindly soul that she was the woman hadn't pressed her. But she would have to tell her everything, and soon. Philly deserved that much at least.

'Don't worry. It won't go to waste.' Adam's voice sliced into her thoughts, bringing her sharply back to the present and he grinned as he took one of the mugs from her hand. 'Come on, we'll go and drink it in the garden so we don't disturb them.'

Seconds later they sank gratefully onto the grass and Sophie looked at the flattened flower borders. 'Oh dear, look at Aunt Philly's lovely flowers, or perhaps should I say what's left of them? There can't be more than half a dozen still standing and she loves her garden.'

'Don't worry, it's not as bad as it looks,' he assured her kindly. 'After surgery tomorrow I'll pop into Cook's nurseries and pick up some bedding plants. Most of these can be salvaged, though. If we cut the fuchsias and the geraniums back they'll soon flower again so don't get worrying about it.'

'I can't ask you to do that, you've got enough to do.' Sophie was deeply embarrassed and wishing she hadn't mentioned it but he wouldn't be put off.

'It's no trouble at all. You know I love to potter about in the garden. Actually, I'll be at a bit of a loose end with Celia being away and it will give me something to do.'

They lapsed into a comfortable silence as they sipped at their tea and gazed contentedly across the fields that bordered her aunt's back fence. Deeply conscious of his closeness Sophie felt a stab of anger as she thought of his wife. Had Celia really gone away with a friend, or was she with the man who had written her the love letter she had accidentally come across earlier in the day? Adam was such a kind, lovely man. Good-looking too. She felt herself blush as the thought popped unbidden into her head and was glad that he was enjoying the view rather than looking at her. Curiously, she found herself wishing that they could just sit there like that forever.

Chapter Twenty-two

As moonlight spilled through the metal bars covering the window onto the cold linoleum floor, Tilly struggled to open her eyes. Her head felt as if it was too heavy for her body and every single limb ached. She supposed it was hardly surprising when she thought back to the tussle she'd had with Nurse Miller earlier in the day. Tilly sometimes wondered if the woman was a nurse or an all-in wrestler, for she seemed to enjoy nothing more than inflicting pain on the patients in the West Wing. If they could be termed patients, that was. The way Tilly saw it they were more like prisoners, locked away from the world and forgotten. When tears sprang to her eyes she angrily swiped them away. At least she was back on the ward, which was something. Most of her short stay had been spent locked in a padded cell laced tightly into a straitjacket. Now she was trying to control her temper to avoid the need to be banished there again, but it was hard.

Her eyes moved along the row of beds opposite. There

were four beds in all and each of them was occupied. In the one nearest to the window lay a painfully thin middle-aged woman by the name of Edna who Tilly had soon discovered was as nutty as a fruitcake. She had never so much as muttered one coherent word in all the time that Tilly had been there but spent her sad existence rocking a plastic doll to and fro in her arms or sleeping.

In the bed next to her was yet another woman who Tilly had at first taken to be quite old. On closer inspection, Tilly had realised that the woman was nowhere near as old as she appeared. She too seemed locked away in a world of her own, spending every waking minute walking between her bed and the tiny sink on the wall in the far corner where she constantly washed her hands over and over again until Tilly's nerves were so stretched that she felt she would scream. This obsession had earned her the nickname Washy from Nurse Miller.

The fourth woman, who slept in the bed next to Tilly's, was the only one with whom she had so far managed to hold any sort of a conversation. Tall and willowy, she was beautifully spoken and the way she carried herself spoke of good breeding. As yet, Tilly had been unable to gauge how old she might be but guessed that she might be somewhere in her mid thirties, though she had never dared to ask. Dotty, as Nurse Miller scathingly addressed her, was dumb when the nurse was present. Her eyes would stare blankly off into space and her jaw would hang slackly open but Tilly was beginning to suspect that this was merely for the nurse's benefit, for the second she had left the room Dotty would become quite lucid again.

Sensing that she was awake now, Tilly whispered into the darkness, 'Are you awake, Dotty?'

'Yes,' the hushed voice carried back to her. 'But keep your voice down otherwise Nurse Miller will be bearing down on us with hypodermics again.'

Tilly shuddered at the thought. She'd had so many injections lately that she was beginning to feel like a pincushion. Deep down she knew that many of them could have been avoided if she'd only done as she was told, but her frustration was growing with every day that passed. The door to the ward was kept tightly locked and the only time they were allowed to venture from the room was when Nurse Miller frogmarched them one at a time each morning from there to the bathroom. This, as Tilly had soon discovered, was yet another humiliation to be endured. But she didn't want to think about that now. Instead she muttered almost to herself, 'There *must* be a way out of here!'

'I used to think that too . . . but not any more.' The voice that answered her sent a shiver running up her spine. It was empty – without hope.

'How long have yer been here?'

'For years and years.'

Tilly shuddered again. 'But if you don't mind me saying . . . you don't seem to have a mental illness.'

'No, I don't. But what I *did* have was an unwanted pregnancy when I was in my teens.'

Tilly's breath caught in her throat. 'So how come you ended up here then? An' why are yer still here?'

'I ended up in here because the man I was in love with turned out to be married. When he discovered I was pregnant he couldn't get away from me quickly enough and my parents didn't want the shame of it becoming common knowledge. So . . . they put me in here and told me that as soon as the child was born they would fetch me out.'

'And?'

'They didn't . . .'

Tilly could hardly believe what she was hearing. This poor woman had been sentenced to a mental institution just because she had become pregnant out of wedlock.

'So just how long *have* yer been here then?'

A sigh from the darkness and then, 'I don't really know now. I used to try and count the days but I gave up doing that years ago.'

Tilly squeezed her eyes tight shut as the horror of what the woman had told her washed over her in waves. If Dotty had been kept locked up here for years, did that mean that she might be too? Tentatively she asked, 'Is yer name really Dotty?'

'No it isn't. But my real name isn't important any more. My family pay a ridiculous sum of money to Dr Thackeray to keep me here because they feel that this is the safest place for me. They think that if they let me out I might go and get pregnant again. Family and friends were told that I'd gone to work abroad and I've resigned myself to the fact that I won't ever get away now. You ought to do that too. Once you do it becomes a little easier.'

'Never!' As the word exploded from Tilly's mouth she began to tremble. There *must* be a way to get out of here. Rachel would be wondering where she had gone and Alfie would be looking for her too, not to mention Sophie. She was sure that Sophie would find her. She moved to sit on the edge of the metal bed for a while and waited for the dizziness to pass. Then she padded quietly across the cold floor and gazed through the metal bars that covered the bare windows. As she had discovered all too soon, there were no luxuries in the West Wing.

She could vaguely remember the night she had been brought here and being carried through a beautiful foyer and up a thickly carpeted staircase. She had felt as if she were viewing everything through a fog, for the injection that Dr Thackeray had administered to her in the house in Back Street still had her in its grip. Hence she had been unprotesting. Until the next morning, that was, when she had woken with a mouth feeling like the bottom of a birdcage to find herself locked in a padded cell. The second Nurse Miller had unlocked the door to silence her, Tilly had launched herself at her like a woman who truly was possessed. But all that had achieved was a black eye and yet another brutally administered injection.

Slowly she had come to realise that it was best to do as she was told. At least then she was allowed to stay on the ward with the other women. And while it wasn't much, it was certainly better than being locked up on her own for twenty-four hours a day.

With a heavy heart, she stood gazing over the high brick wall to the sea beyond. Half of the window was covered in ivy, which grew in wild profusion across the walls of the West Wing. The gardeners never got round to tending the gardens at the back of Hatter's Hall. They were unloved and unkempt, just like the prisoners locked within. She began to cry softly at the hopelessness of her situation and after a few moments a gentle hand settled on her arm, making her jump.

'Don't cry.'

She saw that it was Dotty and fell into her arms as the older woman gently stroked her hair.

'I have to get out.'

Hearing the desperation in her voice, Dotty nodded understandingly. 'I know how you feel. But you really don't make it easy for yourself. We've all learned in turn not to cross Nurse Miller. When she tells you to do something you do it. Then if she sees that you're cooperating she'll put you onto tablets to keep you quiet like the rest of us. They're certainly less painful than her injections, I can assure you.'

'But there's nothing *wrong* with me!'

'There's nothing wrong with me either,' Dotty pointed out. Her eyes went to the figures huddled in the other beds. 'I can't speak for those two, though I have to say I think they may have a real mental illness. Not that it matters. Someone wants them kept here for some reason and here they'll stay just as I have.'

Pulling away from her, Tilly began to pace up and down the middle of the ward like a caged animal as anger again replaced her distress.

'There *has* to be a way out,' she muttered, more to herself than anyone else.

Dotty shrugged. 'Well, if there is I've certainly never found it.'

'Where do you go each day when the nurses come for you?' Tilly suddenly demanded, stopping abruptly in front of her.

'To work in the kitchens. But don't think you'd get out of there. The nurses watch you like hawks, believe me, and the doors are all kept locked. It's better than being cooped up in here all day though.'

'Mmm.' Tilly's mind was working overtime now that the effects of the last injection were wearing off. 'So if I was good they might let me work there too?'

'There's every possibility,' Dotty admitted. 'Though there's no saying it would be in the kitchens. They could put you in the laundry room but that's kept locked too while you're in there.'

Tilly climbed back into her bed and pulled the thin blanket up to her chin and as she stared up at the cracked ceiling an idea began to form in her mind.

Sunday morning dawned bright and clear and, just as he'd promised, Adam turned up bright and early, looking very casual in an open-necked shirt and beige slacks.

He found Philly brushing Rachel's auburn curls and a basket packed with all manner of goodies waiting on the table for him. Philly, however, frowned as she pointed to it and asked, 'Would yer mind very much if I was to pass on the outin', love? This ankle has been givin' me gip all night long an' I've a mind to stay here an' keep it up while the little 'un's out o' the way fer an hour or two. I reckon I must have overdone it on the day o' the party.'

Adam's face instantly became concerned as he started towards her. 'It should be well on the mend now,' he commented. 'Let me take a look at it for you.'

'No, no, there's no need fer that, lad.' She waved aside his concerns. 'As I say, no doubt I've just overdone it. A couple of hours off it an' it'll be as good as new. You just get off an enjoy yerselves now an' leave me to a bit o' peace, eh?'

Sophie looked at her aunt. 'Look, we could always postpone the trip until you feel up to coming with us,' she suggested, but Philly laughed.

'Ain't no need fer that, love. To tell the truth, as much as I love havin' the little 'un here I ain't as young as I used to be an' I'd welcome a bit o' quiet time to meself. Now take that basket there an' have a good day. There should be enough in there to keep you going till tonight.'

When Sophie obediently lifted the basket she laughed. From the weight of it there would be enough food to feed a whole army.

'Well . . . if you're quite sure then.' Sophie felt torn between letting Rachel down and leaving her aunt alone but Adam took control of the situation when Philly lifted her foot onto a nearby stool and yawned.

'Come on,' he urged. 'Let's leave her in peace, eh? She looks worn out.'

'I am that, lad,' Philly sighed dramatically.

Adam now took the basket from Sophie and began to usher Sophie and Rachel towards the door. 'We'll see you later then,' he told her and she flashed him a weary smile.

'You will that. Now you have a good time an' take as long as yer like.'

The second that the door had closed behind them, Philly leaped from the chair and rushed across to the window like a spring chicken. Lifting the net curtain she chortled with glee as she saw Adam herding Sophie and Rachel into the car. She rubbed her hands together as a wide smile settled on her face and felt not a scrap of shame as she watched the car pull away from the kerb. Then, turning about, she called Lily to heel and set off for the garden with a spring in her step to plant some of the lovely flowers that Adam had bought her from the nursery.

The first part of the journey was made in silence apart from Rachel who was happily singing in the back seat. Sophie was already beginning to regret leaving her aunt and as if sensing her discomfort Adam asked, 'So how are you settling in Nuneaton?'

Sophie shrugged, 'It's very nice . . . though I will have to think of going back to Blackpool very soon.'

'Oh yes, and why's that? I was hoping that you'd be settling here. Your aunt certainly seems to be enjoying having you stay.'

She gulped deep in her throat before answering. How could she even begin to tell him without telling him too much?

'I . . . I have a friend there that I need to see,' she eventually told him lamely.

'And will you be coming back once you've seen this friend?'

When Sophie flushed and stared through the car window he frowned. Why was it he always got the feeling that something was deeply troubling Sophie, he wondered? As a thought occurred to him his frown deepened. Perhaps this friend was a man? Could he be Rachel's father? He dismissed the thought almost instantly. Rachel never called Sophie Mummy, and surely she would if she was Sophie's child? Deciding that it was really none of his business he hastily changed the subject and they went on their way.

By the time they arrived at the zoo, Rachel was almost beside herself with excitement. Twycross Zoo was a flat, sprawling place full of animals that the child had only ever seen in picture books before and she scampered from one enclosure to the next at such a pace that it was all Sophie and Adam could do to keep up with her.

'Monkeys,' she squealed with glee but before they could answer her she was off at a trot again.

After two hours of this the little girl began to tire and Adam spread a blanket beneath the branches of a great oak tree while Sophie began to unpack their picnic. It seemed that Aunt Philly had thought of everything. Adam eyed the ham sandwiches greedily and promptly tucked into the feast while Sophie poured out some lemonade, now slightly warm, into a plastic beaker for Rachel.

'I'll give your aunt her due, she's an excellent cook,' Adam remarked as he bit into a slice of home-made bacon and egg pie. Rachel was now running around in the sunshine again with a sandwich in one hand and a sausage roll in the other, her tiredness already forgotten. Another family was sitting on the grass not far away from them and Rachel had teamed up with their little boy, who looked to be about the same age as her. They also had a baby in a small pushchair and as the couple looked towards Sophie and Adam they grinned. 'Makes you wonder where they get their energy from, don't it?' the man commented.

Sophie laughed in reply and he went on, 'It's all right for you two. You've only got the one to tire you out. Wait until the next one comes along and then you'll know it!'

Sophie flushed furiously as she realised that the couple must think that she, Rachel and Adam were a family. She wondered if she should say something but one look at Adam, who was obviously greatly amused, made her clamp her mouth shut.

Seconds later, Rachel ran breathlessly back to them

for just enough time for Sophie to thrust an apple pie into her hand before scampering off again. Her little arms were tanned and chubby and despite the fact that her hair had now escaped from her ponytail and she was more than a little dishevelled she still looked adorable. Sophie's face became sad as a picture of Tilly flashed before her eyes. Oh, how she would have loved to see Rachel enjoying herself so much. But then she pulled herself together. She owed it to the child to make every moment special today.

'Right then,' Adam now said. 'I reckon it's time we made a visit to the elephant house. And we don't want to miss the Typhoo chimps having their tea party, do we? What do you say, Rachel?'

The little girl whooped with delight as he rose and swung her into his arms and now the smile was back on Sophie's face as she hastily repacked the basket.

An hour later she watched with amusement as Rachel licked away at an ice cream and giggled at the chimps' antics. They were all dressed in little outfits and Rachel was totally enthralled with them, so much so that they had a terrible job to get her away from the chimps' enclosure when the tea party was ended.

By teatime Rachel was exhausted and Adam carried her back to the car. By the time they reached the car park she was fast asleep on his shoulder and he smiled indulgently as he gently laid her across the back seat and tucked a blanket round her.

'I think you might have to put her to bed in her

clothes tonight,' he remarked. 'She's gone out like a light and I doubt you'll be able to wake her.'

'I think you could be right.' Sophie got into the front with him and they set off for home.

The day had proved to be such a great success that when he eventually drew the car to a halt late that afternoon, Sophie was feeling relaxed and almost happy again. Rachel was still curled up on the back seat fast asleep and Adam smiled as he looked down on her.

'I've really enjoyed myself,' he told Sophie softly. 'Perhaps we could do it again sometime?'

'We'll see.' Suddenly embarrassed, she climbed out of the car as Adam lifted Rachel from the back seat.

In seconds Philly appeared at the door to meet them with a wide smile on her face. 'Had a good day, have you?' she asked innocently.

'We've had a *wonderful* day,' Adam confirmed as Sophie stepped past him into the cottage. Once inside she took Rachel from his arms and almost apologetically she told him, 'I'd . . . better get her upstairs to bed then. Thank you for a lovely day.'

He watched her head towards the stairs door with a sinking feeling deep in the pit of his stomach. Just for a few hours he had been able to pretend that he was a part of a real family, for that's how it had felt with Sophie and Rachel. But now he would have to go back to an empty house and a spare bedroom.

Seeing the look on his face, Philly squeezed his arm gently. 'Would yer care to stay for a bite o' tea, lad?'

'What? Oh . . . no, no, thanks all the same. I'm afraid I made rather a pig of myself with that lovely picnic you packed us and I really ought to be getting back now.' He turned towards the door.

'Well, have it your own way then, lad. But I'll see you tomorrow anyway. I reckon as I'm fit enough to come back to work now.'

He smiled ruefully, thinking what a miraculous recovery she had made but knowing that it would be pointless to argue if Philly had made her mind up. 'In that case I'll wish you goodnight and I'll see you tomorrow, but don't get overdoing it again now. Luckily there shouldn't be too much to do with Celia being away.'

With a thoughtful look on her face she watched from the door as he drove away. And once again she found herself thinking, *What a damn shame.* He and Sophie looked so right together. Why couldn't he have met her before he met that stuck-up little wife of his? Sighing heavily, she went back into the cottage.

At almost that exact moment in Blackpool, Walter came across Carol heading towards the front door. 'Off somewhere nice, are you?' he asked and she almost jumped out of her skin.

'Oh . . . no, not really. I just need a few bits an' bobs from the shop,' she told him falteringly. 'I won't be long though. You can keep yer eye on things fer a while, can't yer?'

He nodded solemnly as she left. When she was outside

she breathed deeply, then after glancing back at the bleak façade of the house she hurried on her way. Back inside, Walter watched her through the window, teetering unsteadily on her ridiculously high-heeled shoes. He tapped his chin thoughtfully then turning to the phone he slowly lifted the receiver and dialled a number.

The seafront was alive with holidaymakers as Carol pushed her way through them with a deep frown on her face. Since the night Ben and the doctor had taken Tilly to Hatter's Hall she had barely slept, and when she did her dreams were filled with a little girl crying for her mother. She knew that what she was about to do would put herself in grave danger, but she was prepared to risk it to have a clear conscience again.

Eventually she paused breathlessly in front of the Ship Hotel. A family was just entering it and the lights in the dining room, which overlooked the street, were blazing out onto the pavement in the late afternoon.

Hitching her heavy breasts up she clutched her bag and walked round to the back entrance. If she had judged it rightly, she would find Mrs G busy in the kitchen preparing the evening meal for the guests. Her theory was proved to be right, for after letting herself in by the back gate, she peered in through the open kitchen door to see Mrs G bending into the oven to baste a large leg of lamb cooking in there. She waited for a moment so that she could be sure the woman was alone, then quickly went inside, making Mrs G start.

'Oh,' the older woman gasped. 'What you trying to do, girl? You could give a body a heart attack creeping up on them like that.'

'Sorry,' Carol's eyes nervously swept the room before coming back to rest on Mrs G. Quickly Carol told her, 'We've *got* to do something about Tilly. They've shut her up in Hatter's Hall an' you know as well as I do that she'll rot in that place if we don't get her out o' there. Couldn't you talk to Ben? Appeal to his better nature, like?'

'Huh! I doubt that would do much good,' Mrs G replied regretfully. 'And anyway, you should know by now that I don't get involved in that side of things. As far as I'm concerned the less I know about what goes on the better.'

Despite her harsh words she found herself staring at Carol curiously. The woman was obviously deeply distressed, which was evident from the way she was wringing her hands together. Could it be that there was a heart under all that paint and powder after all?

Glancing towards the door, she now hissed, 'Look, you must know what will happen if Ben or Amanda find you here. The best thing I can advise you to do is get yourself away and forget about Tilly.'

'But I can't.' Carol now had tears streaming down her cheeks, leaving ridges in her thick make-up. 'I've told you, Tilly had a little girl. Can you imagine how awful it must be fer the child not knowin' where her mammy is?'

'I can't see why it should bother you,' Mrs G pointed

out and now Carol shocked her when she confided, 'It bothers me because I had a child when I was young an' I gave it up fer adoption. Didn't have much choice at the end o' the day, did I? I mean, what could I have offered the poor little sod? But Tilly kept her child an' if the way she kept goin' on about her is anythin' to go by, she loved the kid. Can yer *really* live wi' yerself knowin' as you're the means o' keepin' 'em apart?'

'It's nothing to do with me what Ben an' Amanda get up to,' Mrs G spat back. 'And now if you don't mind I've got a meal to prepare for the guests, so I suggest you get back to where you came from and keep quiet. I've told you before that I can't help you and that's an end to it.'

She turned abruptly, trying to shut the sight of Carol's crestfallen face from her view as Carol walked despondently towards the door. After a few minutes she dared to look over her shoulder and when she found that she was alone again she breathed a sigh of relief and swallowed the tears that were threatening to choke her. There was nothing she could do to help Tilly. It was as simple as that, and the sooner Carol realised it and put thoughts of rescuing her from her mind, the safer it would be for all of them.

Even as she was sinking heavily onto a chair, Ben was standing outside the door in the hallway, his face sombre. Walter had been right to warn him that Carol might be paying Mrs G a visit and he had heard every single word she had said. The thing now was – what was he going to do about it? Carol was becoming a liability. Thrusting his hands down into his trouser pockets he moved away, deep in thought.

It was almost midnight that night when Ben burst unannounced into the brothel in Back Street. Walter was in the hall and an unspoken message seemed to pass between them as Walter jerked his head towards the kitchen door. Tight-lipped, Ben nodded and without a word carried on down the hallway.

When he entered, the tea that Carol was just raising to her lips slopped over the rim of her mug as she gaped at him in surprise. 'Why . . . hello, Ben. I wasn't expectin' you tonight.'

Did he imagine a trace of fear in her voice? Smiling at her disarmingly he then told her, 'There's something come up. Something I need your help with.'

'Oh yes, an' what would that be then?'

His voice was light as he answered, 'A new recruit for the house. I have to meet her tonight and I'd like you to come with me.'

'*Tonight!*' Now he could hear the fear in her voice. 'But why didn't you just bring her 'ere then? It's nearly bleedin' midnight.'

'Yeah, I'm quite aware o' that. But the thing is, she's only sixteen and I think she was a bit nervous of going off with me by herself, so I told her I'd bring you along. We don't have far to go though. We could be there and back in half an hour.'

As her brightly painted lips pursed across her tobacco-stained teeth, Ben looked away, stifling a shudder of revulsion. Carol was well past her prime, but after a long day she looked even worse than she normally did.

At the same time her mind was working overtime. Why would he want her to go with him simply to bring a new girl to the house? He had never asked her to do such a thing before, but then . . . She decided to give him the benefit of the doubt. If the girl was only sixteen, as he said, then she supposed she could understand her being nervous.

'All right then, I'll come wi' yer. But you'll have to hang on while I go up to me room to grab a cardigan. Yer know how nippy it gets here of a night.'

Leaving a trail of cheap perfume in her wake, she ran upstairs while he went to the front door to wait for her. Seconds later she clattered down again to join him, shouting over her shoulder, 'Hold the fort fer a while will yer, Walter. I won't be gone a tick.'

As the door slammed resoundingly behind Ben and Carol, Walter drew a deep breath.

Just as Carol had predicted the night had turned cold, particularly when they turned onto the seafront.

'Brrr . . . it's right what they say about the sea air bein' bracin', ain't it? How far have we got to go?' she asked.

'Not far,' he said shortly and for a while they walked on in silence. It was when the pier came into sight that he informed her, 'We're to meet her at the end of that.'

Carol's eyebrows rose into her peroxided hair. The pier

was in darkness and looked deserted, as were the streets, save for the few younger people who were still out and about.

'Bloody daft place to agree to meet if yer ask me,' she grumbled, but all the same she followed him as he crossed the road and started towards it. Once they were on it her high heels sounded on the wooden boards and she shuddered as she looked down through them and saw the sea crashing far below. The breeze had turned into a bitterly cold wind now and whipped her bleached hair into a tangled frenzy as they ventured further along. The sounds of Blackpool were fading into the distance and now all they could hear was the sea as it slapped against the pier.

'So where is she then?' Carol asked when they had walked almost half the length of it.

'I told her I'd meet her at the end.'

She frowned into the darkness as the first cold fingers of unease began to snake up her back. Peering ahead into the gloom all she could see were the cold metal railings that lined the pier. There was not a soul in sight. Pulling her thin cardigan more tightly across her sagging breasts she walked on and at last she saw the end of the pier ahead of them.

'So where the bleedin' hell is she?' she snorted with disgust and at that moment Ben suddenly rounded on her and slammed her against the railings.

Her eyes almost started from her head as she felt his weight pushing her top half over the cold metal rail. She wanted to scream but the unexpected attack had driven the air from her lungs and for now all she could do was stare back at him from fear-filled eyes. Far below she could hear the sea slapping wetly at the long metal struts that held up the pier but apart from that they might have been the only two people in the world. All at once the moon sailed from behind the clouds and glinted on something that Ben was holding in his hand. Her heart started to pound as she realised it was a knife. She began to push against him in a frenzied effort to get free but before she could regain her balance he suddenly raised his arm and she felt something cold slash across her throat. She opened her mouth to scream but only a strangled gurgle escaped her as she felt the warmth of the blood on her chest, and then slowly her legs began to give way.

Ben lunged at her again and she had the sensation of flying through the air as he heaved her across the side of the railings. Thankfully, she was already dead when she splashed into the cold waves below. He stood for some time, watching her still figure bobbing on the waves before it slowly sank from sight.

Pulling in great lungfuls of air he snatched up the knife that had clattered onto the cold metal boards then flung it as far out to sea as he could. That was one problem dispensed with; now all he had to do was find Sophie.

Chapter Twenty-three

As Tilly followed Nurse Miller obediently along the corridor to the bathroom the woman frowned. Tilly had been all sweetness and light to her from the second she had stepped into the ward that morning, which was certainly a first. Perhaps the stupid girl was finally getting to realise that her tantrums would get her nowhere after all?

'Strip off,' she ordered when the bathroom door was closed and securely locked behind them and much to her amazement Tilly began to do as she was told without a murmur.

The woman bent to turn the taps on, keeping a watchful eye on Tilly all the time, but she needn't have worried; Tilly merely smiled at her sweetly.

Once the bath was run she told her shortly, 'Get in!' and again Tilly immediately did as she was told. With a smirk of satisfaction the nurse watched Tilly slide into the bath. Crossing to the side of it she now lifted a flannel and began to rub it round Tilly's tender breasts.

Swallowing a feeling of revulsion, Tilly sat very still although her flesh was crawling at the woman's touch. So that's why she works so tirelessly in this godforsaken place, she found herself thinking. It's so she can have her way with all the young girls. Resisting the urge to smack her right between the eyes Tilly forced herself to look straight ahead. If this was what it would cost to be allowed down into the kitchen or the laundry room then she would endure it. As far as she could see, that might lead to her only possible means of escape.

'You've got a fair little figure on you, girl,' Nurse Miller commented.

Tilly smiled at her sweetly.

'Thank you. Nurse Miller, I was wondering . . . If I carry on behaving do you think I might be allowed to work downstairs in the kitchen or the laundry room with Dotty?'

The woman now dropped the flannel into the water and rose to her full height before glaring at Tilly suspiciously. 'That all depends,' she said cautiously. 'On how you behave and how *nice* you're prepared to be to me.'

Tilly gulped deep in her throat. She was going to be sick, she knew it, yet somehow she managed to keep her smile in place, though every instinct was urging her to lash out.

'Oh, I can be *very* nice when I want to be,' she managed to mutter and a smile broke out on the woman's face again.

'Good, good. I'm glad you've decided to see sense.

We'll have to see what we can do then, won't we? Now hop out and we'll get you dried off.'

Tilly clambered out of the bath and then stood as the woman began to dry her slowly with a rough white towel. When the indignity was over she yanked her clothes back on and sighed with relief.

'Right, we'll get you back to the ward then an' I might find you something extra nice for lunch seeing as how you've been such a good girl,' the nurse simpered.

'Thank you.' Tilly hovered as the woman unlocked the door then thankfully followed her back along the landing to her room. The second the door had closed behind her she sank onto the edge of her bed and began to tremble uncontrollably as tears slid down her face. She could still feel the woman's hands on her and again vomit rose in her throat. But then a picture of Rachel flashed in front of her eyes and she knew that she would do anything to be with her again. Anything at all.

'It says here that a woman's body was washed up on the beach this morning,' Amanda remarked to Mrs G as she peered at her over the top of the evening paper. 'Apparently she'd had her throat cut but as yet they haven't been able to identify the body. Ugh . . . it makes you shudder, doesn't it?'

Ben was in the middle of his breakfast and he kept his eyes fixed firmly on his plate as the interchange went on. The news that Carol's body had been found didn't much concern him; she would be just another face without a name, as most of the girls who worked at the brothel were. The only person who could have come forward to identify her was Walter, and he was too busy basking in the glory of becoming the new manager of the brothel to make waves. He swallowed a smirk of satisfaction.

'Any description of the woman?' Mrs G asked and again Amanda's head bent to the paper.

'Yes, there is actually. It says she was somewhere in her late forties to early fifties. Well built, with bleached blond hair. They're asking for anyone who might have any idea of who she might have been to come forward to help the police with their enquiries.'

If Ben had seen the look that flitted across Mrs G's face at that moment he might not have felt quite as smug as he did, for as Amanda read out the description of the murdered woman a picture of Carol's face flashed in front of her eyes and she found herself thinking, *Oh dear God. Please don't let my suspicions turn out to be true!*

It was a bright Monday morning when Philly propped her bicycle against the tree in the doctor's front garden and pottered to the front door. She knocked but when there was no reply she took out the spare key he had provided her with and let herself in. Humming merrily she walked into the kitchen only to stop abruptly when she saw the doctor sitting at the table with his face cupped in his hands. His hair was unbrushed and he hadn't shaved, but worse still he looked deathly pale.

'Why, lad. Yer look like death on legs. Are yer not feelin' so well then?' she exclaimed.

As if just becoming aware of her presence he started and she was concerned to see that his eyes, when he looked at her, were dull and blank.

'No, I'm not ill, Mrs Springs, it's just . . .' He swiped a hand distractedly through his hair and then suddenly his shoulders sagged as he pushed a letter towards her. 'I'd just got up this morning when this came through the post. You may as well read it. It will probably be common knowledge soon enough anyway.'

As Philly started to read her mouth fell into into a gape. When she had read it through she then reread it, as if the second reading would somehow change the words written on the page. She slowly placed it back on the table as she said softly, 'So she's left you then, lad.'

'Huh! Hasn't she just.' His voice was laced with bitterness. 'The stupid thing is, the writing was there on the wall and I was too stupid to see it. This Dennis that she's gone off with . . . she's been spending a tremendous amount of time with him lately. You'd think I would have cottoned onto the fact that they were having an affair, wouldn't you?'

'Well, yer know the old sayin', lad. There's none so blind as them that don't want to see. I know it must hurt but I'm goin' to say somethin' to you now an' I hope you'll take it the way that it's meant . . . The thing is, from where I'm standin' she might have done you a favour. Oh, I know you won't look at it that way right now, but ask yerself – were you *ever* really suited?'

He seemed to consider her words for a few minutes before slowly replying, 'I don't honestly suppose we were. I think Celia regretted marrying me within weeks of the wedding. I wasn't a party animal, you see, whereas she was. Oh, she liked to be able to say that she was married to a doctor, but after a while she realised that there was a lot more involved in being a doctor than just the title. The call outs for a start-off. She couldn't cope with them because they interfered with her social arrangements. I suppose that's where I went wrong, looking back. I encouraged her to go and enjoy herself without me rather than her miss out.'

'Whatever the reason, I shouldn't whip yerself. You're still a young man with your whole life in front of you,' Philly told him wisely. 'Once you get over this you'll pick yerself up an' carry on, you just see if you don't.' She had to resist the urge to hold him and comfort him, so it took her somewhat by surprise when he reached out to her. His arms were suddenly round her waist and his sobs echoed around the room as he buried his face in her apron and she stroked his hair gently.

'There, there, lad. That's it,' she soothed. 'You get it all out now, an' then you can go on.' And so she stood for some time while he did just that.

When his sobs finally subsided she waddled across to the sink to fill the kettle as she told him, 'Right, now what we're goin' to do is get somethin' to eat an' drink inside you. Then you're goin' to go up an' have a wash an' a shave. Would you like me to ring the surgery an' tell 'em you ain't comin' in today?'

'Yes, I think I would,' he replied gratefully. 'That is if you're sure you don't mind?'

'I wouldn't have offered if I did, would I?' she told him practically. 'Now come on, shape yerself up. No good ever come o' wallowin' in self-pity. You've had a bad shock, admittedly. But I'm a firm believer that everythin' happens fer a reason. Between you an' me I don't think you're the only one who has problems. There's somethin' troubling Sophie, I know it, but so far she's holdin' back from tellin' me what it is.'

'I've thought the same, actually,' he agreed and she was pleased to see that she'd managed to take his mind off his own problems. However, at that moment the kettle began to sing on the hob and she bustled away to mash the tea, so for now the subject was dropped.

Much later that evening as Sophie and Philly were sitting together in the cottage enjoying a cup of cocoa before retiring to bed, Philly told Sophie of the day's events.

Sophie's eyes grew sad as she thought of the pain Adam must be feeling, yet deep down she was ashamed to admit that she was glad that Celia had left him. To her mind Celia had never been good enough for him anyway. However, she didn't dwell on the news, for there was something uppermost in her mind now and she knew that she had to talk about it to her aunt while she felt she had the courage to carry her idea through.

Glancing at her from the corner of her eye she asked hesitantly, 'Do you think I could ask a *very* big favour of you, Aunt Philly?'

'Why, o' course you can, love. Ask away.'

'Well, the thing is, I need to go back to Blackpool for a time to look for my friend, Rachel's mother, and I was wondering . . . could you cope with Rachel for a while if I was to leave her here with you? I know it's a lot to ask but there are reasons why I don't want to take her with me. I'd be back as soon as I possibly could, I promise.'

Philly remained silent for a time before eventually saying, 'Couldn't you trust me to tell me what's going on, love?'

'Oh, it's not that I don't trust you,' Sophie hastened to assure her. 'I'd trust you with my life. It's just that the less you know, the safer you'll be. Please, Aunt Philly. I'm handling this the only way I know how.'

As her eyes filled with tears, her aunt slammed her mug down and put her arm round her. 'Don't get upset, love. I just thought that perhaps it would be a case of a trouble shared is a trouble halved?'

'Oh, Aunt Philly, I want to tell you all about it, I really do, but believe me . . . I can't.'

'That's good enough then. Yer old enough to know what yer doin'. An' as fer lookin' after Rachel, well, that goes wi'out sayin' that I will. I just hope you ain't puttin' yerself in any danger, that's all.'

'I'll be fine,' Sophie assured her tearfully.

'So, when were you thinkin' of goin'?'

'I thought tomorrow, seeing as you haven't got to go to Adam's again until later in the week.'

'Well, that needn't have been a problem, Flo next door would have looked after Rachel while I was gone. But it seems you're determined to go through with this so I dare say you may as well go and get it over with. But Sophie: be careful, won't you? I don't know what it is that you've got yourself tangled up in but it don't sound too healthy to my ears.'

'I'll be careful,' Sophie promised, though her stomach was churning at the thought of what might lie ahead of her.

The next day, shortly after lunch, Sophie set off after a tearful goodbye with Rachel and her aunt. Rachel had clung to her as if her life depended upon it and it had been all Sophie could do to make herself walk away from her. But now she was on the train and in less than three hours' time she would be back in Blackpool again. The thought brought her no joy. In fact, she had as yet no idea what she was going to do once she got there. She only knew that she had to at least try to discover what had become of her friend.

When the train drew into the station, Sophie got out onto the platform and looked around her. She felt no pleasure in finding herself back in what had until recently been her home town. In fact, she realised with a little shock that although she had only been away from Blackpool for a relatively short time she was already missing Nuneaton and its leafy green fields. Her resolve wavered but then she pulled herself together with an enormous effort and forced herself towards the street outside.

The way she saw it, there was only one person who could help her in her search and that was Mrs G. She had prayed that she would never have to see the Ship Hotel again, but now her need to find out what had become of her friend overcame her fear.

Eventually she found herself at the back gate to the hotel. Her heart was pounding, but resisting the urge to turn and run as far away from the place as she could she tentatively inched it open. The laundry door was tightly closed so she tiptoed round the corner until the kitchen door came in sight, hoping that Mrs G would be there.

Flattening herself against the wall she inched her way towards it and when she looked inside, sure enough, there was Mrs G pottering about as she prepared the evening meal for the guests.

'Pssst . . . Mrs G,' she hissed.

The poor woman almost jumped out of her skin and when she saw Sophie standing in the doorway she looked as if she had seen a ghost. Glancing apprehensively towards the door in the far wall she now hurried across to Sophie and joined her in the yard before whispering, 'What in God's name are you doing back here, girl? Didn't I tell you loud and clear to get away?'

'Yes, you did, Mrs G. And I *did* get away,' Sophie

whispered back. 'I took Rachel with me too . . . but I had to come back. That little girl asks for her mother almost every single night when I tuck her into bed. Can you just imagine how awful it must be for her not knowing where her mother is? Please, Mrs G, I'm begging you to help me. You're the only one who might be able to lead me to Tilly.'

As Sophie gathered the old woman's hands into her own Mrs G's eyes welled with tears and for a moment she allowed them to rest there, but then she suddenly tore them away as if she had been stung and took a step back. 'I *can't* help you,' she told her coldly. 'Now for everyone's sake just go away and forget you were ever here. It will be God help you if you don't.'

'And *why* will it be God help me?' This time Sophie was not prepared to leave without putting up a fight. 'Are you trying to tell me that Tilly is dead?'

'No, no.' Panic laced the old lady's voice now as she dug herself ever deeper into the trap Sophie had laid for her. 'I didn't say she was dead, did I?'

'Then tell me where she is, because as sure as God is my witness I'll not leave you alone until I find her. I . . . I'll go to the police if need be!'

Seeing the determination blazing in the young woman's eyes and realising that she meant what she said, Mrs G began to tremble. Looking fearfully across her shoulder again she then leaned forward and whispered, 'Try thirty-nine Back Street and ask for Carol. That's all I can do for you. Now please go.'

She hurried back into the kitchen with her heart pounding in her chest. If what she suspected was true, Sophie wouldn't find Carol there and with luck she would then give up her search when she hit a blank wall and return to wherever she had come from. Again she lifted the newspaper containing the news of the poor woman who had been washed up on the beach with her throat cut and shuddered. Every instinct she had screamed at her that this poor woman was Carol and yet her mind revolted at the thought. Surely Ben wouldn't resort to murder? She made the sign of the cross on her chest as she wondered where it was all going to end and then forced herself to carry on with the preparations for the evening meal.

Once outside the gate, Sophie leaned heavily against the wall as she sucked air into her lungs and allowed her heart to slow to a steadier rhythm. Thirty-nine Back Street, Mrs G had said, and yet as far Sophie knew that street consisted of nothing more than crumbling warehouses and near-derelict houses. The night was drawing in now and she was tired and hungry. She had only brought enough money with her to pay for her train fare and a little to spare; certainly nowhere near enough to stay in a bed and breakfast for the night. *Mrs McGregor.* The name flashed into her mind unexpectedly as she wondered what to do. She had no doubt at all that the kindly woman would put her up for the night, but would it be fair to just turn up on her doorstep out of the blue?

She decided that first of all she would make her way to Back Street and look for the house that Mrs G had told her about. Knowing the short cuts as well as she did she was there in no time at all; number 39, just like all the other houses in the street, looked unkempt and dirty. Curtains were drawn closely across the downstairs window and it was as she was studying them that she thought she detected a faint light shining from within. Her first instinct was to rap loudly on the door and demand to see Carol, whoever she might be, but then some other sense seemed to take over and instead she crossed the deserted street and shrank into the shadows of a doorway that had once been the entrance to a warehouse, where she waited.

Time passed painfully slowly and her stomach began to rumble with hunger as she thought of her aunt and Rachel back at home in the little cottage. She imagined they would have had their supper and Rachel would be all tucked up in bed by now. The thought had barely left her mind when a car cruised slowly past and stopped some way down the road. She heard the engine die and watched the lights go out; seconds later a well-dressed man stepped out of it and began to walk back in her direction. Retreating even further back into the shadows she watched him approaching on the other side of the road. When he came to number 39 he paused and looked furtively up and down the street, then climbing the two steps to the door he rapped on it sharply. The sound echoed in the deserted street.

Seconds later the door opened and light spilled out onto the pavement. A huge bear of a man stood aside to allow the visitor to enter; however it wasn't him that Sophie was watching but a small dark-haired girl, dressed in little more than her underwear, who hurried forward to greet him. Clapping her hand across her mouth, Sophie stifled a gasp as she saw yet another girl in an equal state of undress lead another man up the stairs that ran up opposite the open doorway behind them.

Not until the door had closed again did she allow herself to breathe as she tried to figure out what sort of a place it could be. And then as realisation dawned she did gasp. It was a *brothel* – there could be no other explanation for it, but why would Tilly be in there unless . . . unless Ben was holding her there against her will! Never for an instant would Sophie allow herself to believe that Tilly would have gone to a place like that of her own volition. She had come to know her too well in the time they had spent at the hotel together and she knew that Tilly was keen to turn her back on that way of life.

Wrapping her arms about herself she stood there in an agony of indecision. If what she suspected was true, and every instinct she had screamed at her that it was, then how could she just march up to the door and demand to speak to Carol? And who *was* Carol? Was she one of the girls that worked there; or the madame of the place perhaps? Deciding that she needed time to think this through she moved noiselessly from the shadows and began to make her way along the deserted street.

Without her even being aware of it, her footsteps led her in the direction of Mrs McGregor's. If she had brought enough money with her to stay in a hotel or a bed and breakfast for the night she would never have contemplated going back there, but as things stood she knew that it was either Mrs McGregor's or a night under the pier. She was the only person Sophie could think of who might be able to help her at the moment, and as she had no intention of returning to her aunt's until she knew what had become of Tilly, she felt that she had little choice but to throw herself on the kindly woman's mercy.

In no time at all she was standing at the bottom of the metal stairs that led to Mrs McGregor's flat in Waterloo Road. She climbed them slowly before tapping hesitantly at the door. Within seconds a light appeared through the glass and as it was inched open Mrs McGregor's face peered out at her.

'Why . . . Sophie! What a pleasant surprise!' The woman now flung the door wide open and as she caught Sophie's arm and began to haul her into the flat she looked over her shoulder. 'On your own then, are you, lass?'

'Yes, yes I am.'

The woman led her into the small cluttered living room.

After swiping the toys from a chair, Mrs McGregor gently pressed her down into it and suddenly Sophie's eyes flooded with tears and she buried her face in her hands.

'Why, lass; whatever is the matter? Nothing's happened to Rachel, has it?'

Sophie shook her head as she tried to compose herself. But somehow the tears wouldn't seem to stop as the events of the last few months caught up with her and all she could do was sob as Mrs McGregor looked helplessly on.

Eventually the woman moved towards the kitchen, glad that the children were all in bed so that she could get to the bottom of whatever was troubling Sophie. And she was determined to do so now, for hadn't she always sensed deep down that something was amiss since the day Tilly had left Rachel with her?

'Right young lady,' she stated with an air of authority, 'I'm going to make you a nice hot drink with a drop of brandy in it to calm you down and then you're going to tell me exactly what the hell is going on, so you are.'

Sophie hung her head. She had promised herself that she would never reveal to anyone what had gone on in the hotel or anything that had happened since, but suddenly the need to confide was strong and she could think of no one better than Mrs McGregor to confide in.

Chapter Twenty-four

'By 'eck, lad. You're up wi' the lark an' make no mistake. Come away in.' As Philly held the door wide, Adam strode past her and glanced round the room.

'No work today then?' she asked and he grinned as he shook his head.

'No, not today or for the rest of the week,' he told her. 'I decided to take a few days off so I thought rather than mope about the house I might take Sophie and Rachel out for the day somewhere. That's if she wants to come, of course.'

'Well, I've no doubt she'd have loved to had she been here, but she left yesterday,' Philly informed him.

As his eyes dropped to Rachel, who was playing on the floor with a dolly in front of the empty fire grate the smile slid from his face. 'What do you mean, she left? Where's she gone? And why is Rachel still here with you?'

Philly scratched her head before trying to explain, then steered him into the next room and in a low voice told him, 'I don't rightly know what's goin' on, an' that's the God's honest truth, lad. All I know is, Sophie seems to think that Tilly, that's Rachel's mother, is in some sort o' bother so she's gone back to Blackpool to try an' help her.'

'Whereabouts in Blackpool, and how long will she be gone?'

'I can't answer either o' them questions,' she told him truthfully. 'All I can tell yer is that she said she'd be back as quickly as she could.'

'I see.' His face was troubled now as he stared distractedly through the open window. 'You don't think she'll be in any danger, do you?' he asked eventually.

'That I can't say,' she told him solemnly, but then on a lighter note she added, 'You're lookin' brighter anyway. So that's somethin' to be grateful for at least.'

He smiled ruefully. 'The truth is, after you left the other day I got to thinking and a lot of what you had said made sense. Looking back I realised that Celia and I haven't had much of a marriage for some time, so I wrote to her, wished her all the best and told her that I'd be happy to go ahead with a divorce as soon as she was ready.'

'Well, fer what my opinion's worth I think you've done the right thing,' Philly muttered approvingly. 'Though I never expected you to get over it this quickly.'

As a flush rose to his cheeks and he hastily looked away, the reason why came to her in a flash, and if she wasn't very much mistaken it had something to do with

Sophie. She'd seen the way they looked at each other when they thought no one was looking. Sophie's eyes would light up when he walked into a room, and she'd observed how they seemed to be at ease in each other's company. Of course, until recently he had been a married man so knowing both of them as well as she did, they'd probably never acknowledged their feelings towards each other. But now? Well, what was to stop them when Sophie got home? She sniffed loudly to prevent her thoughts from going any further. What was she thinking of, matchmaking like that? She was probably barking up the wrong tree, and they probably had no other feelings for each other than those of friends . . . but oh, it would be nice if they did!

'Come along then.' Nurse Miller ushered Dotty and Tilly out onto the landing as Tilly flashed Dotty an excited smile. This would be the first day she had been allowed out of the ward except to visit the bathroom, and although she was only going to work in the kitchens, the way she saw it this might be the first step towards escaping. After all, they couldn't watch her for every single minute, could they?

At the end of the landing, Nurse Miller selected a key from the many that hung on a chain from the belt round her waist and unlocked the door. An uncarpeted staircase that led down to the back of the house fell away before them and they clattered down after her. At the bottom the woman unlocked another door and ushered them along a corridor that seemed to go on forever. Again they paused while she selected yet another key and after unlocking a door with a panel of glass in the top half of it Tilly was ushered into the most enormous kitchen she had ever seen. A long scrubbed table stood in the centre of the room; huge ovens stretched all along one wall, and on another was a row of deep stone sinks, where two women were standing peeling vegetables. They glanced briefly at Tilly from dull eyes before turning their attention back to what they were doing.

Tilly's eyes darted to two doors that obviously led to outside but her heart sank like a stone when she saw that they were securely locked and bolted. Bars were fitted to the windows and she knew instantly that even from here escape was not going to be easy.

Another nurse, as thin as Nurse Miller was stout, was sitting at the table idly flipping through a newspaper, but when they entered she instantly rose.

'You get about your business then,' she told Nurse Miller brusquely. 'I'll see to these two.'

Nurse Miller nodded before disappearing back the way they had come and as Tilly heard the door bang to behind her and the sound of the key turning in the lock the thin nurse's lips pursed into a straight line.

'Right, Dotty, you get cracking on the pastry.'

When Dotty pottered away to do as she was told, the nurse turned her attention to Tilly. She pointed to a sack in the far corner. 'You can start peeling the potatoes. And don't even *think* of trying any funny business. I have a whistle in my pocket and should I have to blow it for help it will be God help you.' Her eyes were as cold as ice. As Tilly walked towards the sack tears of frustration stung at her eyes and she found herself thinking, *Will I ever find a way out of here?*

By lunchtime the kitchen was like a furnace and Tilly was so hot and bothered that she thought she might collapse. The nurse had found her one job after another since the minute she had set foot in the room, without so much as one kind word. Now she dared to ask hesitantly, 'Couldn't we just have one of the doors open?'

A smile stretched the woman's face for the first time as she sneered, 'Oh yes, I'm *really* going to open a door for you, aren't I? I'd have to be as mad as a hatter to do that. Why, I've no doubt you'd be out of here like a shot if I did. Now get about your work and if I have any more of your complaining I'll see that you're kept in the ward from now on.'

Tilly gritted her teeth as she turned back to the table that she was scrubbing, but all the while her mind was working overtime. The nurse wasn't as far through as a line prop. If a couple of them were to set about her and take her by surprise she had no doubt that they could get the keys off her. Her eyes strayed to the other women working there. They were going about their jobs like automatons, their eyes dead and glazed with drugs. Would they help her, or were they so institutionalised that they no longer wanted to escape? She determined to ask Dotty as soon as they got back to the ward. One thing she was sure of, if she had to bear this for much longer she would soon be as mad as they appeared to be.

'Right, I think I might have come up with an idea that could get you into the house in Back Street without it looking suspicious,' Mrs McGregor told her in a hushed voice. The children were in the room and she had no wish for them to hear what she was saying. She'd spent the whole night tossing and turning following what Sophie had confided to her the night before. Now she hoped she had devised a plan. If Sophie would agree to it, that was. Seeing Sophie's eyes were tight on her, she began hesitantly, 'The way I see it there's only one way to go. If you just knock on the door demanding to see this Carol, whoever she might be, it will look suspicious, so it will, but if . . .'

'Yes . . . go on,' Sophie urged.

'Well . . . if you're right and this place really *is* a house of ill repute then you could pose as a prostitute who's looking for a job.'

She watched Sophie's eyes almost start out of her head and shrugged helplessly. 'That's about the best I can come up with, lass. Though you know I think you should just go to the police and have done with it. There's something bad going on here to my mind. Young lasses just disappearing into thin air to be sure. It don't bear thinking about.'

'I won't do that,' Sophie was adamant. 'I promised Tilly

that I would keep Rachel safe and if I went to the police the Welfare would be down on me faster than I could say Jack Robinson and Rachel would be taken into care.'

Seeing the truth in what Sophie said, Mrs McGregor shrugged. 'I can hear what you're saying, so I can. So what do you think of my idea? Doing it this way you would have a reason to ask to see this Carol.'

Sophie considered this plan as she looked thoughtfully across at the children.

'I suppose it *does* make more sense,' she admitted reluctantly.

'Good, good. Then I'll have to nip out and get you some different clothes,' Mrs McGregor said. 'Those you're wearing aren't nearly tarty enough to be sure.'

Despite the seriousness of the situation, Sophie found herself grinning.

'Even if I wanted to dress tarty, I don't have any spare money and I'm *certainly* not going to let you spend yours. Things are tight enough for you as it is.'

'Mmm,' Mrs McGregor eyed Sophie's skirt then suddenly she crossed over to her and began to fold it at the waistband until it was so short that Sophie felt embarrassed.

'Right, now come into the bedroom,' she ordered and somewhat reluctantly Sophie followed her.

'Sit down there.'

Sophie sat down on the dressing-table stool as Mrs McGregor took up a brush and began to backcomb her hair. She then pointed to the cardigan Sophie was wearing.

'Undo the buttons down to here,' she ordered, stabbing a finger at Sophie's small cleavage. 'And roll the sleeves up like this. Good, good, that's it. Now then . . .' After rummaging in a drawer she took out a make-up bag and tilting Sophie's chin she spat on a mascara block, and proceeded to work on Sophie's eyes. Next she added a liberal amount of blue eyeshadow before finishing the whole look off with bright red lipstick.

'There,' she said eventually with satisfaction as she stood back to survey her handiwork. 'What do you think?'

When Sophie turned to look in the mirror she gasped with horror. 'Why, I look like a . . . a . . .'

Mrs McGregor nodded. 'You look like a street girl and that's just what we want.'

'I suppose you're right,' Sophie agreed, sounding dismal.

'Now, there is one thing I have to tell you, Sophie,' Mrs McGregor told her. 'Should anything happen and you don't come back I need to know your aunt's address.'

'Very well.' Sophie decided that she could hardly argue. After all, if anything were to happen to her then Aunt Philly would be left to look after Rachel and at her age it wouldn't be fair on her, much as she adored the little girl.

Mrs McGregor was solemn-faced now as she muttered, 'Oh lass, I have to tell you I'm not happy about this at all. I feel as if I'm sending you into the lion's den. Were I a few years younger I'd go myself but I hardly think anyone would want to give me a job as a pro at my age, do you?'

Sophie squeezed her hand gratefully. 'I wouldn't want to put you in any danger,' she assured her. 'You have those little ones in there to look after. What troubles me is, if it is a brothel as I suspect and Tilly *is* there, why hasn't she gotten away before now? You know as well as I do how much she adored Rachel and the whole point of her giving her baby away was so that she could turn her back on that way of life. It just doesn't make any sense. They *must* be holding her there against her wishes.'

Mrs McGregor's head bobbed in agreement. 'You're right, though I still think we should go to the police and be done with it. Still, we'll try this first and then go from there if you're still sure you want to. That Ben wants shooting from where I'm standing, and that twisted mother of his, and the way I feel right now, were you to put a gun in my hand I'd be the one to do it.'

Sighing deeply, Sophie stood up and embraced the kindly woman in front of her. 'I dare say there's no time like the present so I'm going to get this over with. First of all, though, I'll give you my Aunt Philly's address. I'll also give you Adam's phone number. He's . . . a doctor my aunt cleans for. Do you think you could just give him a call and ask him to let my aunt know that I'm all right?'

Mrs McGregor noticed the hint of colour that had crept into Sophie's cheeks at the mention of the man's name and instantly knew, without being told, that he was someone of importance to Sophie. 'Of course I will, lass, and gladly,' she agreed. 'You just jot it down now and you can consider it done. But I warn you: if you're not back by tonight I *will* be involving the police. I don't like this set-up. I don't like it at all, and that's the truth.'

Sophie quickly wrote down her aunt's address and Adam's phone number then taking a deep breath she took one last glance in the mirror. 'My mother would have died a thousand deaths if she could have seen me done up like this,' she said quietly.

Mrs McGregor's heart went out to the girl, but before she could answer Sophie's chin came up and she told her, 'Right, wish me luck.'

'That goes without saying, lass.' And as Sophie headed for the door, a feeling of dread settled over Mrs McGregor like a heavy cloud and she found herself thinking, *I've a horrible feeling you're going to need it.*

Once again, Sophie found herself standing outside the house in Back Street. In the cold light of day it looked even more run-down than it had the night before and she had to suppress a shudder. But now she had come this far she had no intention of turning back, so before she lost her nerve she hurried to the door and rapped on it sharply. For a time there was nothing but silence but then eventually she heard footsteps shuffling towards the door. When it creaked open she found herself face to face with a bleary-eyed young woman who was dressed in a silk dressing gown and very little else.

'Yeah?'

'I er . . .' Sophie gulped. 'I was wondering if I could have a word with Carol please?'

'Huh! You'll be lucky,' the girl grunted. 'She's fucked off out of it. What did yer wanna see her for?'

'I was told that she might be able to give me a job. You know . . . on the game?'

'Ah!' The girl seemed to think for a moment and then holding the door wider she said, 'You'd berra come in then. Walter, that's our boss, is out at the minute but 'e shouldn't be long.'

Sophie stifled a gasp of amazement as she found herself in a luxuriously decorated hallway. The girl now took a deep drag of a cigarette before looking Sophie up and down and asking, 'So 'ow did yer 'ear about this place then?'

'Oh, you know,' Sophie lied glibly. 'Word gets around when you're on the street. That's why I'm here, 'cos I'm fed up of being on the street. At least you can get to see the clients in comfort here.'

The girl nodded before thumbing towards a door that led off the hallway. 'Yer can wait in there,' she told her abruptly. 'Walter shouldn't be too much longer. An' don't get worryin'. He's a fair enough boss an' bein' as he bats fer the other side he don't wanna sample the goods if yer know what I mean?'

'Oh . . . right.' Sophie was so horrified that words momentarily failed her but she managed to keep her smile in place as she entered the room the girl had directed her to. She saw at a glance that just like the hallway it was beautifully decorated and very luxuriously furnished. Velvet settees and chairs were placed strategically here and there and girls were lounging across them, smoking, reading magazines and chatting. They all looked towards her when she first entered but none of them spoke as she perched uncomfortably on the edge of the first chair she came to.

'I tell yer, he's a right sadistic old bastard. Comes in 'ere lookin' like butter wouldn't melt in 'is bleedin' mouth then belts the livin' daylight out of yer.'

Sophie looked out of the corner of her eye at a girl who was showing off a huge bruise on the top of her leg to the girl sitting next to her. She suppressed a shudder.

'Huh! An' him supposed to be a so-called pillar o' society an' all. I wonder what his clients would think of 'im if they knew what 'e were really like?' As the girl rattled on, Sophie had to force herself not to get up and run as far away from this place as she could. She felt as if she had stepped into hell but her need to find Tilly kept her glued to the seat as the nightmare went on.

At that moment, she caught sight of another young girl passing through the hallway and her heart began to hammer. It was Amy; she would have staked her life on it. Knowing that she would have to act quickly if she wanted to speak to her she suddenly asked, 'Is there a toilet I could use, please?'

The girl who had been showing her bruise off stopped talking abruptly and glanced towards her as Sophie quickly stood up.

'Yeah, there's one in the hall, second door on the right.'

'Thanks.' Sophie hurried out into the hall just in time to see the girl about to walk into what looked like a kitchen.

After glancing across her shoulder to make sure that no one else was about she hissed urgently, '*Amy.*'

The girl she had addressed slowly turned and Tilly's heart lurched as she saw that she had been right. It was Amy, but not the Amy that she remembered from the hotel. This pale girl looked as if her spirit had been broken; her eyes were dull and listless and there was a stoop to her shoulders. She stared uncomprehendingly back at Sophie for a while but then as recognition dawned her clenched fist flew to her mouth.

'*Sophie* . . . what are *you* doing here?'

Sophie was just about to answer when the front door suddenly swung open and a huge man appeared. He glared at the two girls before asking abruptly, 'So, what's goin' on here then? An' who are you?'

Amy scuttled away as fast as her legs would carry her as Sophie quickly regained her composure and told him, 'I . . . I heard you were looking for new girls to work here and I was just going to use the toilet while I was waiting for you.'

'Were yer now?' His voice expressed his suspicion and it was all Sophie could do to maintain her composure as she looked back at him.

'I'll go to the toilet and then perhaps we could have a chat?' she said brightly.

'Perhaps we could,' he answered. The second she was gone his ugly face creased into a frown. It had appeared that Sophie and Amy knew each other from the few seconds that he had seen them standing together, and the way Amy had hurried off went a long way to confirming his suspicions. But if that was the case, then just who the bloody hell was this girl who had turned up out of nowhere looking for a job? Ben had assured him that Amy knew no one and up until now it had seemed that he was right. Deciding to err on the side of caution he waited patiently until Sophie reappeared and then nodding towards a door he told her, 'We'll talk in there.'

Fixing a bright smile to her face she followed him into yet another room, set out much the same as the first room she had entered. Plush settees took up the majority of the floor space and in between them were little ornately carved tables with red-shaded lamps standing on them. When she had sat down he took a seat opposite her and asked, 'So, how did yer know about this place then?'

'Well, most of the girls that are on the game in Blackpool know about it,' Sophie lied.

'Mmm . . .'

She forced herself to sit there while he eyed her up and down; when she felt unable to bear his scrutiny a second longer she babbled, 'The thing is . . . I'm sick o' standin' on street corners. You've got a nice place here an' I'd like to be able to work in comfort.'

'Fair enough.'

She felt as if he was looking into her very soul and offered up a silent prayer that the interview might end soon. Her prayers were answered when he stood up abruptly and nodded. 'All right then, we'll give it a try. You'll pay me forty per cent of whatever you earn and for that you'll be supplied with a room where you can take your clients, unless you want to live in, that is?'

'Oh, no, no, that won't be necessary,' Sophie gushed as panic engulfed her.

'Be back here for nine o' clock tonight then,' he told her. 'Ain't no point in comin' much before that. The punters don't start to arrive till then and we'll give you a trial run.'

'Thanks.' Sophie breathed a sigh of relief as she followed him from the room, forcing herself not to look towards the door that Amy had disappeared through. If only she could get to speak to Amy tonight she might find out where Tilly was. For all she knew Tilly might even be here right now in this very building.

The thought made her heart pound even harder as he let her out onto the pavement without another word. Head held high she resisted the urge to run as she walked along the deserted street, very aware that he might be watching her from the window. It wasn't until she had turned a bend in the road that she allowed herself to let her breath out and now tears stung her eyes as a picture of Amy's pale face swam in front of her. What if Tilly was there too? Would she have been broken as Amy was? The thought was almost more than she could bear and yet as she thought of Tilly's strong nature she knew that it was highly unlikely. Nothing, not even a bully like Walter, would have kept Tilly away from Rachel, so where was she?

Straightening her shoulders she walked on. Tonight, if she could get to speak to Amy, she would have her answer.

Chapter Twenty-five

'So, is she safe then?' Philly couldn't keep the concern from her voice as she looked back at Adam who had just called in to deliver Mrs McGregor's message.

'Yes, from what I could gather,' he assured her. 'She said that she hoped Sophie would ring me later tonight or early tomorrow with more news.'

'But has she found Rachel's mother yet?'

He shook his head as he glanced at Rachel who was fast asleep on the settee with her teddy bear cuddled close against her. 'Not yet, apparently.'

'I see.' Philly's eyes followed his and as they came to rest on the little girl on the sofa she sighed deeply. If only she could shake off this terrible feeling of foreboding. Still, she reassured herself, Sophie was a sensible girl for her age, she wouldn't do anything that would put herself in danger . . . would she? She now looked back at Adam and saw the same concern she was feeling mirrored in his eyes.

'You care about Sophie, don't yer, lad?' The words were

out before she could stop them, but instead of hotly denying it as she'd expected him to, he nodded.

'Yes . . . I suppose I do. Though I wouldn't let myself admit it till Celia had left me.'

'Well, yer know what I once told yer, everythin' happens fer a reason. Let's just get her safely home an' then let things take their course, eh?'

He nodded solemnly before he left.

'Oh, dear Lord, I'm not too keen about you goin' back there again, to be sure I'm not,' Mrs McGregor fretted as Sophie hastily told her of what had gone on in the house. 'Are you quite sure that it was Amy you saw, lass?'

'Oh, yes, I'm absolutely sure.' Sophie gazed towards the window, as she tried to put her thoughts into some sort of order. 'I even got to speak to her very briefly. If Walter hadn't come in when he did I'd probably have discovered where Tilly was there and then. As it is I don't have any choice but to go back tonight if I want to find out what's become of her. But don't worry, I'll be very careful.'

'I don't like it.' Mrs McGregor began to pace up and down the room, setting Sophie's nerves even more on edge than they already were. Suddenly swinging about she declared, 'You *can't* go back there. It will be like walking into a pit of vipers. Let me call the police, lass, and have done with it once and for all.'

'We can't do that, you know we can't,' Sophie told her sharply then, her voice softening, she crossed to the woman and gently took her hands in hers. 'Please try not to worry,' she implored her. 'I'll be careful, I promise. If I can only get Tilly out of there I can take her back to my aunt's with me and we can put this whole mess behind us.'

'Well . . . if you're quite sure,' Mrs McGregor told her in an agony of indecision. 'But I'll tell you now to your face: if you're not back here tonight by midnight at the very latest I *shall* call the police whether you like it or not.'

'No, please don't call the police,' Sophie urged her. 'If by any chance I don't come back, call Adam. He'll come, I know he will, and then you have my permission to tell him the whole story and let him decide what's best to do.'

'As you will,' Mrs McGregor agreed and wrapping Sophie tightly in her arms she rocked her to and fro as she would one of her own children.

'So, you enjoyed your first day in the kitchens, did you?' Nurse Miller asked with a sneer as she escorted Dotty and Tilly back to their ward.

Tilly glared at her. She was hot and bothered as well as being worn out and totally disgruntled. Yet still she swallowed the hasty retort that sprang to her lips. Just because today hadn't presented an opportunity to escape didn't mean that tomorrow wouldn't. Surely they'd have to open the kitchen doors eventually?

Seeing the surly look on her face, Nurse Miller reached

out to stroke Tilly's arm possessively, making the girl's flesh crawl.

'I was thinking after I'd done the medicine rounds I might let you take a nice bath?' she told Tilly as if she were offering her some great favour. 'You must be feeling all hot and sweaty after being in the heat all day.'

Tilly swallowed the bile that rose in her throat as she thought of the feel of the woman's great ham hands on her body, but when she looked at her she smiled sweetly.

'That would be nice,' she simpered. 'I am a little hot an' bovvered as it happens.'

'Then in that case I'll see what I can do.'

Tilly's eyes dropped to the keys that dangled from the nurse's belt. Would she have the strength to overcome the woman if she were to take her by surprise when they were alone together in the bathroom? Seeing as Nurse Miller was almost double her size she doubted it. The woman was built like an Amazon, and even if she did manage it, would she be able to get through all the other locked doors before the alarm was raised? Sighing deeply, she began to climb the bare wooden stairs that led back to what she had come to look upon as her prison.

She was almost halfway up them when another idea occurred to her and the higher she climbed the more the idea took shape and the more excited she became. The success of what she planned to do would depend a lot on Dotty so she determined to talk to her about it the first second that they were alone.

It was a relief when Nurse Miller shepherded them into the ward and locked the door behind them, for now Tilly could put her plan to Dotty.

Catching hold of the woman's arm she dragged her towards the barred window, out of earshot of the other two women who were lying on their beds staring blankly off into space.

'Dotty, I think I've come up with a way to get us out of here,' she whispered urgently. 'But I need you to help me.'

Fear flashed into Dotty's eyes as she snatched her arm away and shook her head. 'There's *no* way out of here,' she hissed. 'Don't you think I discovered that years ago? You might just as well make your mind up to it. Us at this side of the home . . .' She spread her arms helplessly to encompass the other two souls lying on the bed. 'We're here till they carry us out feet first in a wooden box. The sooner you make your mind up to that the easier it will become for you.'

'No, you're wrong,' Tilly cried. 'Listen to me *please*. The way I see it there's probably not going to be anyone in the kitchen after they've given out the last drinks, and that's when Miller comes to check on us and turn the lights out. Now if you and I were to be lying in bed fully clothed we could attack her when she turned round to leave and catch her off guard. We could hit her with something and get her keys off her, then make for the kitchen . . . think of it, please, in just a few more hours we could be out of here.'

'Huh!' Dotty shook her head. 'And what do we do even if we *did* manage to make it out of the kitchen? The gates are kept locked and they have dogs patrolling at night.'

This was something that Tilly hadn't thought about and her face fell. But then she suddenly smiled again. 'We needn't make for the gate,' she exclaimed. 'There are trees growing all along the wall. We could climb one of them and get out that way.'

Dotty sighed, 'But you've seen the size of Nurse Miller. She's like a bear, bigger than both of us put together. You say we could hit her with something, but what? I can't see anything in here that would give nearly enough clout to knock her out, can you?'

Tilly's gaze followed Dotty's around the room and then suddenly she whooped with excitement as she thought of something. 'We could use this,' she cried, grabbing a large chamber pot from under the bed. It was a crude heavy affair and Tilly almost died a death of shame every night if she was forced to use it, but now suddenly she saw it as a possible means of assisting their escape. 'Oh, *please*, Dotty,' she implored. 'Won't you at least think about it? I've got a little girl waiting for me out there somewhere.'

'Then you're lucky, because I have no one,' Dotty told her quietly. 'Just what the hell would I do if we did get out? Where would I go?'

'You'd come with me,' Tilly replied without hesitation. 'We could go to the lady who used to look after my little girl for me and then we'd blow the whistle on this hell hole. Just think; it wouldn't be just *us* who were regaining our freedom. We'd be giving a life back to all the other poor buggers who've been rottin' in here fer years.'

Indecision played across the woman's features now as she looked into Tilly's expectant face but then finally she nodded slowly.

'Very well then, we'll try it. But God help us if we fail.'

'We won't fail,' Tilly laughed as she grabbed her hands and shook them up and down. And so they sank onto their beds to wish away the hours until they could make their escape.

Mrs McGregor stood back to eye Sophie. She had redone her make-up and backcombed her hair again, and now as darkness fell it was time for Sophie to return to Back Street.

'*Please* be careful, lass,' she implored as tears started to her eyes.

Sophie hugged her close, as if she could somehow draw the woman's strength into her. 'I will,' she promised. 'And don't worry. I should be back here for midnight at the very latest. If I'm not then you'll know that something is wrong. Once I've spoken to Amy and found out where Tilly is I shall be out of there like a shot. Believe me, all the tea in China wouldn't keep me in that place a second longer than I needed to be.'

'Well, just remember, if you're not back by midnight I shall be on the phone to this doctor friend of yours whether you like it or not,' Mrs McGregor warned her.

Sophie kissed her cheek affectionately and then with her heart in her mouth she set off yet again for the house in Back Street. A drizzly rain had started to fall and before Sophie had gone very far she was feeling wet and even more miserable than she had when she set off.

A tall dark-haired man in a smart suit arrived on the doorstep at almost the same time as Sophie did and so Walter admitted them at the same time with a surly nod to Sophie.

'Wait in there,' he told her brusquely, indicating the second sitting room. Sophie walked on down the hallway as Walter disappeared into the front lounge with the man.

When she first entered the dimly lit room it appeared at first glance that she was alone, but then she became aware of someone huddled deep into a chair set in the shadows in the bay window.

She moved hesitantly towards it and when Amy suddenly sat forward her heart skipped a beat. A look of pure joy lit her face but it was instantly washed away when Amy hissed fearfully, 'Sophie, get yourself away from here right now. They're on to you. Walter saw us together earlier on. He heard me call you by name and clocked onto the fact that we knew each other. He . . . he made me tell him who you were and he's phoned Ben . . .'

Sophie's hand flew to her mouth as she looked back

at the girl. Her face was a mass of livid bruises and one eye was almost completely closed. 'But . . . I can't just go and leave you here,' she stuttered. 'What's he done to you, Amy? And where's Tilly?'

'Don't waste time worrying about me and asking questions . . . *just go* while you still can!'

As some of Amy's panic transferred itself to Sophie she realised that she was in grave danger. Without another word she headed back towards the door. But she had barely gone halfway across the room when it swung open and Ben appeared with a smug grin on his face.

'Well, well, well. If it isn't my little Sophie,' he drawled in that broad American accent that still haunted her dreams. Her eyes darted from side to side as she cursed herself for a fool. How could she ever have been so stupid as to put herself in this position, she wondered?

Ben meantime was advancing on her and Amy had begun to cry. 'You've saved me the trouble of having to come and look for you,' he ground out; now the bantering tone was gone and his eyes were flashing with fury. 'Couldn't keep away from me, eh?'

Sophie's chin jutted with defiance as she stared back at him. 'Why don't you just stand aside and let me pass?'

'Oh, now I'm hardly going to do that, am I?' His tone was mocking as her hands clenched into fists. 'Let's just say I have other things in mind for you. You can join our little family here, can't she, Amy? Amy will tell you how good we are to our girls, won't you?'

When Amy hung her head, Sophie stared back at her

incredulously. 'Why have you stayed here? Surely you can't enjoy living in a place like this?'

Grabbing Amy's arm, Ben dragged the sleeve of her blouse up and nodded towards the pinpricks in the crook of her arm.

'Amy stays here because, shall we say, she's grown partial to a certain little habit that we can supply her with, isn't that so, Amy?'

'DRUGS! You've got her onto drugs?' Sophie was totally appalled.

'Don't knock it.' Ben grinned. 'I've no doubt at all that in a few weeks' time you'll be as hooked on them as she is, and once you are . . . Well, let's just say they're readily available here as Amy will tell you. You do as you're told and we won't keep you short.'

Sophie went to elbow her way past him but at that moment Walter appeared in the doorway and her heart plummeted as she saw the hypodermic syringe he was holding in his hand.

'Now then, I think it's time you had your first little taster, don't you?' Ben asked.

Suddenly he had her arms pinned to her sides and although she kicked and screamed her strength was no match for his. Even as she struggled, she felt the needle jab into a vein and then slowly the fight went out of her as she floated away on a cloud of warmth.

'Right, are yer ready?' Tilly whispered as she peered over the top of the bedclothes towards Dotty.

The woman nodded. 'Ready as I'll ever be, though I have to say I really can't see us pulling this off.'

Tilly gripped the handle of the large chamber pot, which was concealed beneath the blankets. 'Don't forget, moan an' act like yer in pain. Anythin' to distract her attention from me an' then I'll see to the rest.'

Dotty nodded as they settled down to wait. Eventually footsteps sounded in the corridor and they heard a key turning in the lock. Nurse Miller strode into the room with a face as dark as a thundercloud. It had been a very long day and now she was impatient to be away.

She nodded with satisfaction when she saw that they were all tucked up and then she came to stand at the side of Tilly's bed. Her voice softening now, she told her, 'Sorry I didn't manage to get time to give you another bath tonight. I've been busy but we'll make up for it tomorrow, eh?'

Tilly kept her eyes tightly closed as a shiver of revulsion worked its way through her. Thinking that she was asleep, Nurse Miller was just about to head towards the door again when a low moan from Dotty's bed made her pause. 'What's wrong with you then?' she barked as she made her way towards her. This was the opportunity that Tilly had been waiting for and now she slid silently from the bed and began to creep towards the nurse, who had her back to her as she stared down at Dotty's pale face.

'So what's the trouble?' Suddenly aware of a sound

behind her she turned just as Tilly lifted the large pot high and swung it towards her with all the force she could muster.

'What the—' There was no time to say any more, for suddenly the pot caught her a glancing blow to the side of her head and she felt darkness rushing towards her.

As she slid to the ground, Tilly dropped onto her knees and began to undo the chain of keys from her waist.

'Come on, Dotty,' she urged the terrified woman. 'We ain't got a second to lose. She could come round at any minute.'

The keys were in her hand now; she grabbed Dotty's hand and began to pull her towards the door.

'But . . . but what about the others?' Dotty fretted as Tilly hauled her along.

'Don't get worryin' about them fer now. We'll blow the whistle on this place as soon as we're out o' here an' then the coppers will come an' see to them.'

They were at the door now and Tilly glanced up and down the corridor before hastening along it. Once they came to the door that would lead them to the stairs she fumbled with the keys, trying first one then another in the lock until at last the door clicked open. Then they were speeding down the stairs as if the very hounds of hell were after them. At the door to the kitchen, Tilly stopped again and now with hands that seemed to have suddenly become all fingers and thumbs she again tried to find the right key. Dotty was standing so close that she could feel her hot breath on her cheek and her heart was pounding so fast that she herself was finding it difficult to breathe at all. At last the key slid into the lock and they heard it click. Now as it swung open they almost fell in their haste to get to the back door, for now that was the only barrier between them and their freedom. Again, Tilly began to insert the different keys into the lock as Dotty urged her, 'Come on, Tilly, *come on!*'

'I'm doin' me best,' she hissed breathlessly and suddenly she felt the key turn. The night air washed across her face like a salve. It was at that moment that the kitchen lights suddenly clicked on and all hell seemed to break loose as nurses in starched white uniforms spilled through the door and bore down on them.

'No, no!' Dotty began to fight as two nurses grabbed an arm each. Throwing herself in front of Tilly she shouted, 'Run, Tilly, run!'

Tilly hesitated for just a second but that was all the time it took for another two nurses to each grab one of her arms. '*Let me go, you bastards!*' she screamed and her cries echoed around the kitchen as tears of frustration stung her eyes. She had been so close to escaping but now the chance was being snatched away from her. All her scheming had failed and it was almost more than she could bear. She watched helplessly as the two nurses who had hold of Dotty dragged her kicking and screaming back the way they had come. They were almost at the door that led into the kitchen when Dotty suddenly collapsed. Caught off guard the nurses released their grip on her and Dotty fell heavily, cracking her head as she slumped to the floor like a wet rag. Tilly's cries stopped abruptly as she looked on in horror.

'What have you done to her?' With an enormous effort she somehow managed to wrench herself away from the women who had hold of her and before they could stop her she was running across the room with terror pumping blood through her veins. She knelt down at the side of Dotty and lifted the woman's head gently onto her lap as tears slid down her face.

'Oh, Dotty, I'm so sorry,' she sobbed. 'This is all my fault.'

Dotty's eyes flickered open and she smiled weakly up at her. 'Don't blame yourself,' she said softly. 'Y . . . you'll get to your little girl. You'll see . . .' Her eyes suddenly took on a glazed look and then as Tilly gently rocked her to and fro she went limp in her arms and a look of peace settled across her weary features.

'NO . . . NOOOOO!' Tilly's sobs bounced off the bleak whitewashed walls as she felt Dotty slip away from her but she had no time to ponder, for at that moment she became aware of someone standing close and as her head swivelled round she saw a nurse leering down at her, holding a syringe in her hand.

Tilly's anger dissipated as shock and despair washed over her. Dotty had been right all along – there was no way out of this place once you were in it, and now, because of her, Dotty was dead and somehow she was going to have to live with that knowledge.

She had been subjected to enough injections since

entering the home to know that within minutes of it being administered she would feel nothing. And nothing must surely be much less painful than the feelings ripping through her right now, she reasoned. Without argument or struggle of any kind she watched the nurse bear down on her and felt the sharp prick of the needle. Sure enough, within seconds the nurse's face became blurred and a warm sort of lethargy crept over her. She gave herself up to the feeling of calmness that was stealing over her as a picture of Rachel's smiling face danced in front of her tightly closed eyes.

Chapter Twenty-six

'I'll give it ten more minutes an' then I'm phonin' that doctor friend o' hers,' Mrs McGregor muttered to the empty room as she paced up and down it. Glancing at the clock she saw that it was now three minutes to midnight, which was just two minutes later than it had been the last time she'd looked at it. Crossing to the window, she lifted the net curtain yet again and peered down into the street below, praying for a sight of Sophie. But the street was almost deserted, save for the odd few teenagers still wandering about. Every instinct that she had was screaming at her that something was wrong. Sophie had promised to get back as soon as she had managed to speak to Amy and that had been hours ago, so where could she be?

Looking towards her coat hanging on a coat rack beside the entrance door she considered going round to the house in Back Street to look for the girl, but she dismissed that idea almost immediately. It would mean leaving the children in the flat alone and what would happen to them if *she* didn't come back? Then, despite all her promises to Sophie, she thought of phoning the police, but again she rejected the idea. There was only one thing she could do now and that was to ring Sophie's doctor friend. With shaking fingers she lifted the scrap of paper on which Sophie had scribbled his address and began to dial his number with shaking fingers. She had waited long enough.

The loud ringing of the phone pierced the air and as he dragged himself up onto his elbow from the depths of the bed, Adam cursed. He got out and after pulling his dressing gown on he fumbled his way to the door in the darkness. Who the hell would be ringing at this time of night, he wondered? Once down in the hallway he snatched the phone up and snapped, 'Hello.'

'Hello there. Is that Dr Adam Bannerman?'

'It is.' He waited for whoever it was to go on. The voice was vaguely familiar. And then it came to him like a flash. This sounded like the same woman who had phoned him to tell him that Sophie had arrived safely in Blackpool.

'I'm sorry to trouble you so late at night, Doctor. It's Mrs McGregor and the thing is . . . Sophie asked me to call you if she didn't come home tonight. I . . . have reason to believe that she might be in danger.'

As she went on Adam's face creased into a frown. 'And why would she be in danger?' He was trying desperately hard to keep the concern from his voice and was failing dismally.

'Look, lad. I know that this is a lot to ask, but do you think you could come to my flat? I promise I'll tell you everything when you arrive and then if you wish to involve the police so be it.'

He glanced at the clock on the wall and, wide awake now, he told her, 'I should be there in about three hours or so. Give me your address.' He hastily scribbled it down and after dragging on the nearest clothes to hand he hurried downstairs and out to his car. He was on his way, his heart thumping painfully in his chest. He had only known Sophie for a relatively short time but already he had come to realise that she was important to him. Perhaps that was why he had been able to accept Celia leaving him so easily? There was no time to analyse his feelings at the moment; somehow he just knew that if Sophie needed him he had to be there.

At three forty-five in the morning he drew the car to a screeching halt in the small yard in Waterloo Road. Seconds later he was clattering up the metal stairs to Mrs McGregor's flat. She was waiting for him at the top of them, looking as if she had the weight of the world on her shoulders and after hastily shaking his hand she ushered him inside.

'Right,' he told her with an air of authority in his voice. 'I think you'd better explain what's going on, don't you?'

'Aye lad, I think I should, for what's goin' on ain't right.' The distressed woman poured out the whole sorry tale just as Sophie had recounted it to her. 'And so do you see now why she felt she couldn't involve the police?' she finished breathlessly. 'The poor lass was terrified that the Welfare Department would become involved and take Rachel away.'

Adam scratched his head as he tried to digest what she had told him. 'So what you're telling me is that this here Ben, the American, is not only running a baby farm from the hotel, but he's then taking the girls to a brothel when they've given birth and forcing them to stay there?' he said incredulously.

'That's about the long an' the short of it. But what could have happened to Sophie? There's no way on this earth she would have stayed there willingly. She was just meaning to have a word with this here Amy to find out if Tilly was there and then she was planning to come back and blow the whistle on Ben to get the other girls out of there. So what do we do now? Should we go round there?'

Adam began to pace the room, just as she had done for most of the night, as his brain worked overtime. 'I need to think about this,' he said.

'You do that, lad. An' while you do I'll away an' put the kettle on. I've no doubt you wouldn't say no to a nice hot brew after your long journey.'

When she returned with a laden tray some minutes later she found Adam standing at the window, staring down into the deserted street below.

'You say the girls were staying at a hotel. Do you have the address of it?'

'Aye, I do, lad. As I told you, there was an old woman worked there in the kitchen as the cook. Mrs G, Sophie called her. Lived in by all accounts an' it seems to me like she had a soft spot for Sophie 'cos it was her who encouraged Sophie to get away.'

'Then if she worked in the kitchens, no doubt she'll be up with the lark and I think I should be speaking to her first,' Adam decided.

She nodded as she glanced at the clock. 'Happen you could be right. It's just after four o'clock now an' if the hotel is full o' guests, as I've no doubt it will be at this time o' year, then by the time you've had a drink an' got round there it'll be goin' on five an' I dare say she'll be puttin' in an appearance in the kitchen. Sophie told me that there's a back gate, so perhaps you'd be best to use that so as not to draw attention to yourself.'

As she spoke she was pouring the tea and Adam took a mug from her gratefully. Within minutes he had drained it and he handed it back to her before saying kindly, 'Look, Mrs McGregor. It's been an awfully long night for you. Why don't you go and try to catch a couple of hours' sleep? I'll take over now.'

'Eeh, lad. I couldn't,' she declared adamantly. 'Not till I know Sophie and Tilly are all right.'

'Very well then, have it your own way. I'll hang on for half an hour or so and then I'll get round there. I'll let you know the instant I have any news.'

'Thank you. I'll be waiting.' Her face broke into a worried smile as she thought what a lovely young man he was and for the next half an hour they fell silent as they willed the time to pass. When he eventually rose from his chair to leave she told him, 'You take care now, do you hear me? An' good luck, lad.'

He let himself out into the cold early morning. The salt air was heavy with the smell of the sea and brought him fully awake as he hurried down the steps to his car.

Fifteen minutes later he was parked at the back gates of the hotel, which to his relief he found were unlocked. He slipped through them and was disappointed as he felt his way along the wall to find the kitchen in darkness. The sky was lightening now as seagulls wheeled squawking in the sky above him. And then suddenly a light clicked on in the kitchen, chasing away the shadows in the yard as he crept forward to look through the window. An elderly grey-haired woman in a bright wraparound pinafore was filling a kettle at the sink and when he tapped on the window she almost dropped it in her surprise.

'Who in the name of God is that at this time of the morning?' she gasped as she hurried towards the door.

'Mrs G. I'm a friend of Sophie's,' he whispered through the door. '*Please* let me in. I need to talk to you urgently.'

Even from the other side of the glass he could see the colour drain from her face as her hand gripped her chin. For some moments she stood as if she had been cast in stone but then she suddenly disappeared from view and he heard her fumbling with the key in the lock. Seconds later the door swung open and she told him dully, 'You'd better come in.'

As he did so the woman sank down heavily onto a chair.

'It's Sophie, isn't it?' she asked. 'She's gone and got herself into bother, hasn't she?'

'Yes, I'm afraid I think she has,' he agreed. 'She could be in grave danger and I think you might be the only person able to help her.' Now as she stared back at him he began to tell her of the phone call he had received from Mrs McGregor and when he had finished her chin sank to her chest. For some moments it seemed that she wasn't going to speak to him but then finally she raised her head and told him, 'I told her to get away. *Why* wouldn't she listen to me? On the day she left here I thought, that's it then, she'll be safe now. And she would have been if she hadn't come back here looking for that damn Tilly.'

'I know all about the brothel in Back Street,' he told her. 'Is Tilly there too?'

Her lip trembled as she took a handkerchief from her pocket and mopped her face before telling him, 'No, she's not. She's been moved to Hatter's Hall. It's a mental home along the coast. That's where the girls who won't settle in the house end up.'

'Oh, my dear Lord.' Adam was unable to keep the contempt from his voice. 'Is this Ben even human? How could he have young girls locked up like that? And what about the babies the girls give birth to?'

'Oh, they go to good homes, you need have no fear of that. Most of them end up abroad. Back in America where Ben was born, usually.'

'Well, it's going to stop here,' Adam told her in a voice laden with contempt. 'What he's been doing is highly illegal. He must have made a fortune selling the babies, let alone what he makes from the girls in the brothel. I could call the man an animal but that would be an insult to animals.'

'So, what do you intend to do?' the old woman asked fearfully.

'I have little choice but to go to the police now.' Even as Adam spoke he was going towards the door.

She sighed, for hadn't she always known deep down that it would come to this one day? Especially when Carol went missing. Tears stung her eyes and she shuddered involuntarily as she thought back to the report of the unnamed woman who had been washed up on the beach with her throat cut.

She listened to his footsteps receding in the yard and once the gate had closed behind him she pulled herself painfully up from her seat and began to prepare a breakfast tray for Ben and his mother. Some inner voice was telling her that the little kingdom Ben and Amanda had built on tears was finally about to come crashing down around them just as she had always feared.

'Right, sir, I think our first stop should be the house in Back Street,' Inspector Grey informed Adam when Adam had finished telling him of all that had gone on. Then, turning back to the assembled officers, he told them, 'I want two cars round the front of the house and two out back. We'll all go in together when I blow the whistle. Is that clear? Meanwhile, Harrison, you can organise some cars to get out to Hatter's Hall, and we'll want some ambulances on standby at both places as well.'

'Yes, sir.' The policeman and the other officers all streamed outside to the waiting police cars.

It was now nearly eight o'clock in the morning and Adam's nerves were stretched to the limit. He had first spent a whole hour at the station telling his story to a police officer who had looked at him as if it was he that was mad. Then another hour had been spent while the police verified that he was a doctor and came up with a plan of action. And now at last something *was* going to be done and although he was light-headed with relief he was also terrified of what they might find when they got into the brothel. How would he feel if anything had happened to Sophie? Pushing the thought away, he followed the inspector grim-faced from the station.

The men were all in position in Back Street and Adam stood back with his heart in his throat as he waited for the whistle that would send them all surging forward. Although he was expecting it, when it finally came he started and watched helplessly as the police began to batter at the front door. It gave way within seconds as two enormous policemen rammed at it with a large battering ram; then they were streaming inside and screams rent the air and everything was pandemonium as lights clicked on and scantily clad girls ran shrieking through the house. He saw two officers flanking a great bear of a man drag him outside onto the pavement where they clapped handcuffs on him and slung him unceremoniously into the back of a waiting police car. And then Inspector Grey was beckoning to him. 'Come with us, Dr Bannerman, please. We'll need you to tell us if any of these girls is Sophie.'

Adam's lips tightened as he followed the police officer upstairs. Men were being led from rooms in handcuffs and escorted away as the policemen threw open one door after another. There was no sign of Sophie on either the ground floor or the first floor and he began to panic. What if she'd been moved to the mental home? What would they have done to her?

As these thoughts were racing through his mind a small dark-haired girl tentatively approached him.

'If you're looking for Sophie you'll probably find her up there,' she told him, pointing towards a narrow staircase that he hadn't noticed at the end of the first-floor landing.

'And you are?' the police officer barked at her.

'I'm Amy,' she replied, then allowed herself to be led away to one of the waiting ambulances.

Adam was already running towards the staircase with the police officer hot on his heels. They clattered up the narrow steps only to pause breathlessly when they reached the top as they looked along the length of bare wooden floorboards. Adam went one way as the police officer went the other and simultaneously they began to fling the doors open. It was the police officer who eventually came to one that was locked.

'I reckon this might be the one,' he called and by the time Adam had run to join him he was already throwing his weight at the door. Suddenly they heard the wood crack with the force of his shoulder against it and, as it flew inwards, Adam ran past him into the room. There she was, lying on a dirty mattress, looking for all the world as if she were dead. Adam flung himself down beside her and almost cried with relief when he took her wrist in his hand and found a pulse.

'She's alive,' he gasped. 'But we need to get her to a hospital. We don't know what they've pumped into her.'

'I'll get them to bring a stretcher up,' the police officer told him, but he was wasting his breath for Adam had already snatched Sophie into his arms and was making towards the door.

All the way to the hospital he prayed as he had never prayed before as he held tight to her hand. 'Please don't die, Sophie,' he muttered over and over again. '*Please* don't leave me because I don't know how I could go on without you.'

Even as Adam was speeding towards the hospital with Sophie, yet more police cars were heading towards Hatter's Hall and the Ship Hotel.

Inspector Grey strode into the luxuriously decorated foyer of the hotel and straight through it towards the kitchen where he found an old woman sitting at the table staring blankly off into space.

'Madam, I have a warrant here to search these premises,' he told her sternly. 'And I would like to speak to Mr Ben Lewis and Mrs Amanda Lewis.'

Dragging her attention to him with what was obviously an enormous effort she told him, 'I'm afraid you can't do that.'

'Are you saying they are not here?' he said with a frown.

'Oh, they're here all right. You'll find them in bed up on the fourth floor. But they won't be able to speak to you. You see . . . they're both dead. I killed them.'

'You did *what*?' The officer stared at her in open-mouthed horror.

'I said I killed them. I had to, don't you see? They couldn't help what they did and Amanda could never have stood being locked up in prison. It was better this way.'

Sinking down onto a chair opposite to her he now asked, 'But why would you do that? And what do you mean – they couldn't help what they did?'

'Exactly what I said. It wasn't their fault.'

When he stared at her uncomprehendingly she felt the time for explanations had come and slowly she began to tell him the whole sorry story. 'It was like this. When Amanda was just a young woman she met an American who was over here on holiday. I wasn't too concerned at first. I mean – everyone has a holiday romance at some time in their life, don't they? And usually when the holiday is over they burn out as quickly as they started. But it wasn't like that with Amanda. When Casey Lewis went back to the States she was like someone demented and in no time at all he was back again. They were totally besotted with one another and before I knew it she told me that they were going to be married.

'Three weeks later he had a ring on her finger and he took her back to America with him. Well, it was New York actually. Hell's Kitchen, not the best of neighbour-hoods from what Amanda wrote to me. Not that it mattered; as long as she could be with him I think she'd have been happy to live in a shed. But he didn't keep her short, though I got the impression he was a bit of a wheeler and dealer if you know what I mean? Fingers into all sorts of pies and not all of them honest. Anyway, that was the last I saw of her for some years and during that time she had Ben. Oh, she always kept in touch with letters or such and I accepted it because she seemed to be happy. But then she wrote to tell me that Casey, her husband, had died and not long after that she turns up back here out of the blue with Ben. She was a nervous wreck, that's the only way I can describe her when she first came back, but that wasn't the worst of it. I soon realised that this obsession she'd had with Casey had transferred itself to Ben. She could hardly bear to let him out of her sight and I started to get worried. Ben was just fifteen at the time, a very impressionable age. Soon after that she bought this hotel and I came here to work for them in the kitchen, and here I've been ever since.'

She paused here to swipe a tear from the end of her nose before going on. 'As time passed things between her and Ben got even more unhealthy. He wasn't allowed to have any friends whatsoever, especially girlfriends. He wasn't allowed to go out or do anything at all without her. Truthfully, it didn't seem to trouble him and that in itself gave me cause for concern. At fifteen years old he was still sleeping in the same room as his mother and although he had his own single bed in there I felt it wasn't right.

'A few months passed and he left the school Amanda had managed to get him into when they first came home, then they both cleared off to America again for a couple of months and left me to run this place on my own. Amanda said they needed a holiday. When they came back they had a young American girl in tow and that's when it started. The girl was pregnant and once she'd given birth an American couple came and took the baby away. I was horrified and threatened to leave but they promised me it would never happen again and so against my better judgement I stayed. Shortly afterwards Ben started to bring other young girls who had got themselves into trouble here to stay and I tried to put my foot down. I knew what was going on without a word being said, but what could I have done about it without shopping Amanda and Ben to the police? Amanda was still, shall we say, not herself. She had been diagnosed as a manic depressive and was living on her nerves. Sometimes days would pass and she wouldn't even venture out of her room and only Ben seemed to be able to keep her calm.

'What I will say in my own defence is that I had no idea about the other racket they were running, the brothel I mean, until three or four years ago. I just thought the girls were having their babies and then clearing off back to wherever they'd come from. When I did find out about it I went mad. I even went to see Carol, she was the madame of the brothel until recently, and I threatened to blow the whistle on what was going on. By the way . . . while we're talking of Carol I ought to mention that I think the body washed up on the beach with its throat cut not so long back was hers. She got too close to Sophie for comfort and I've an idea Ben did away with her. Funny that . . . until she came to see me about Tilly I had no time for her, but after that I realised she had a heart and I looked at her differently.'

By now the inspector's face was ghastly pale as he tried to take in what she was telling him. 'But . . . but *why* have you stood by them all these years,' he eventually managed to stutter, 'knowing what was going on?'

'Because . . .' she told him with a wry smile, 'blood is thicker than water. Amanda was my daughter and I worshipped the very ground she walked on. A lot of what's happened is my own fault because she was my only one and I spoiled her rotten as a child. I couldn't see it at the time, of course. I had her late in life, and not long after that I lost my husband so she was all I had left. She was, shall we say, always a little *strange*, but I closed my eyes to any wrong in her. Oh, she appeared very calm and sophisticated to the outside world, but truthfully she lived on her nerves and pills, hence the obsession with keeping Ben in her sight every spare minute of the day.

'When they first came back from America, Ben started calling me Mrs G. G is for Grandma, you see? I loved him more than life itself but as he grew older I saw flaws in his character too. Just as I had once clung to Amanda I now saw Ben and Amanda clinging to each other and I knew it was my fault. Almost as if history was repeating itself. He told me that he was going to earn enough money to buy them somewhere nice to live in the country and that as soon as he had enough they would sell the hotel and move away, but he was driven by greed. Every single time a young girl came to stay he promised me that this would be the last but then another one would appear and I began to feel powerless to stop it. I can't even count how many times I've threatened to go but then when it came to it I just couldn't bring myself to leave them to fend for themselves.

'I only found out about the other business, Hatter's Hall, I mean, a few months ago when Cathy, one of the young girls we had staying here, died giving birth to her baby. Ben informed me that he was going to bury her body there and I realised something underhand was going on there too.'

'My God.' The inspector rose unsteadily from his seat. He had been in the police force for many years and in that time had seen and heard things that had made his blood run cold, but never had he heard a tale quite as disturbing as the one she was telling him now.

'Perhaps you could take us to Ben and your daughter?' he suggested now as he nodded at a pale-faced officer standing behind them. Without argument she rose from her seat and Inspector Grey and the officer silently followed her from the room.

Once they were on the fourth-floor landing she stopped outside a door and with her hand on the handle she turned to tell them, 'They're in here. You'll find they look very peaceful; they wouldn't have felt a thing. I put rat poison in their tea this morning and brought it up to them with lots of sugar to disguise the taste. Then they lay back down and just never woke up.'

The policemen followed her into a room in which stood two beds side by side, on each a body: one of a young handsome man and the other of an attractive middle-aged woman. Inspector Grey had to suppress a shudder and it was all he could do to pull himself together enough to read her rights to her.

'You do realise that you'll be tried for murder, don't you?' he eventually told her in a low voice, and with no trace of fear or regret she solemnly nodded before replying.

'Yes I know I will, but I simply did what had to be done. It was all getting out of hand and hopefully this will be the end of it.'

Crossing to the beds she gently pulled the sheets across their faces as tears slithered down her wrinkled old cheeks.

Chapter Twenty-seven

Half an hour later, while Mrs G was being taken to the cells at the local police station for further questioning, Inspector Grey's car drew to a halt outside the gates of Hatter's Hall. The gate man was standing to one side; his face deathly pale as the officer flashed his ID card at him and drove on past to the Hall. There seemed to be policemen swarming everywhere as the car drew to a halt as well as three ambulances that were waiting on the drive with their doors open.

'Sir.' The grim-faced officer he had sent on before him was waiting for him in the luxurious foyer.

'So what's going on here then?' the inspector barked without preamble. It was turning out to be a long day and it was beginning to tell on him.

'You wouldn't believe it, sir,' the officer told him with a shake of his head. 'The private patients are living the life of Riley, by all accounts. Waited on hand and foot. But the back of the home . . . well. It's like walkin' back into the dark ages, sir. They've got people locked up for days at a time like animals. They're that drugged, half of them, that the poor sods don't even seem to know what time of day it is.' Even as he spoke an ambulance man came towards them leading an elderly lady who had a blanket draped round her shoulders.

Inspector Grey shook his head in dismay as the officer went on. 'We've kept Dr Thackeray in his office, sir, until you got here. I thought you would want to interview him yourself.'

'Too damn right I do,' the inspector replied but the words had barely left his lips when a young policeman came running down the corridor towards them.

'Sir, sir.' His voice was laden with panic. 'It's Dr Thackeray. He's been pacin' up an' down the room like someone demented an' then suddenly he clutched at his chest an' just went down like a ninepin. I can't wake him, sir.'

'Get an ambulance man in to him straight away,' the inspector ordered and a young officer standing by the door shot outside with a speed that would have done justice to a whippet.

When he flew past them again moments later with an ambulance man hot on his heels Inspector Grey scratched his head in bewilderment. 'To think,' he declared, 'that all this has been goin' on right under our bloody noses for years an' we had no idea of it.'

At that moment another two ambulance men were descending the stairs carrying a stretcher bearing a red-haired girl, who looked for all the world as if she was dead.

'We found the poor soul locked in a padded cell,' one of the ambulance men explained as he saw the inspector's eyes on the girl. 'We're taking her to the hospital to get her checked over.'

Inspector Grey frowned as he continued to stare at the girl. Hadn't Dr Bannerman said that his friend, Sophie Winters, had gotten herself into the predicament she had been in because she was looking for her friend Tilly, who had red hair? The girl on the stretcher certainly looked to be about the right age.

'What's that girl's name?' he now demanded of the ambulance man at the front of the stretcher.

'I've no idea, guv,' he told him. 'Some o'your lot are questionin' a Nurse Miller up there.' He nodded back across his shoulder. 'Seems she were the one in charge of all the poor buggers in the wing where we found this one.'

'I see, carry on.' The inspector now turned and made for Dr Thackeray's office. Once in the doorway he paused to look down on the ambulance man who was leaning across the doctor's inert figure on the floor. After a moment the man rose and gravely shook his head.

'I'm afraid there's nothing I can do for him. He's gone,' he informed the inspector. 'Looks like a massive heart attack to me.'

The inspector thumped the desk in his frustration, setting the inkpots dancing. 'Can you believe it?' he cried. 'It seems that all the ones responsible for these rackets are dropping like flies.' Then he snapped to the waiting officer, 'Have that Nurse Miller taken down to the station and make sure that the rest of the people who were locked in that wing are taken to the hospital, would you? I'm going back to the station.'

'Yes, sir.' The young officer scooted away as the inspector cast a last withering look at the body on the floor before leaving.

Sophie had the sensation of floating. She was in a warm dark place where nothing mattered any more. Not her parents' death or the circumstances that had led up to it, not Tilly's disappearance . . . nothing. But now there was a light at the end of what appeared to be a long dark tunnel and her mind was playing funny tricks on her. Words kept repeating in her mind. '*Please don't leave me because I don't know how I could go on without you.*'

She could have sworn that Adam had said them, but why would he say that to her? She must have imagined it. But oh, if only he had said them, for she knew now without a shadow of a doubt that she loved him. She had known for some time but what good would it do?

The light was getting closer now and she felt a surge of anger. Why wouldn't it go away and leave her in peace? It was nice here in the dark. But no, it was coming closer and closer and now she was aware of a terrible pain in her head and she was feeling sick. She could hear someone moaning and realised with a little shock that it was her. Someone was holding her hand and she gripped the fingers tightly. And then she was blinking as her eyes struggled to open.

'It's all right, Sophie. You're going to be fine. I'm here.'

The voice seemed to be coming from a long way away but it was Adam's voice, she was sure of it. A woman's face bending over her swam into focus and panic engulfed her. It was a nurse, but why would she be back in the hospital? She had lost the baby some time ago.

The nurse smiled at her kindly. 'That's right, my dear, just take it slowly now. You've been drugged but once the effects have worn off you're going to be just fine. Isn't she, Doctor?'

With a great effort, Sophie managed to turn her head and there was Adam. He was the one holding her hand but she hardly dared to believe it.

'T . . . Tilly . . .'

'It's all right,' he soothed. 'Tilly is fine. In fact I think she's in the very next ward. It's all over now, Sophie. Everything is going to be all right. You just rest now and concentrate on getting well. I'll be here when you wake up, I promise.'

Now that Adam was there she wanted to stay awake, but the darkness was closing in on her again and within minutes she was fast asleep again.

The next time she woke up it was dark outside. The ward was so quiet that she could have heard a pin drop but she saw Adam dozing in the chair at the side of her bed. Apart from still having a mild headache and slight nausea she felt much better now although she ached everywhere.

'Adam.'

His eyes started open and suddenly he was leaning over her. 'Welcome back to the land of the living.' He gently squeezed her hand. 'How are you feeling now?'

'Better,' she whispered. 'But what's happened?'

Settling himself onto the side of the bed he slowly began to tell her of what had gone on since the night before.

'So Tilly really is safe then?' she asked when he'd finished.

'She certainly is,' he told her with obvious delight. 'In fact from what I'm hearing, she's causing havoc in the ward next door. You should be able to see her tomorrow, all being well.'

'Thank God.' She smiled up at him, setting his heart racing, but then as a thought suddenly occurred to her the smile slid from her face and she asked, 'What about Celia?'

'Well, Sophie, the thing is . . .' He struggled for a way to explain then deciding that he might as well just come out with it, he blurted, 'In actual fact, Celia has left me. Gone off with one of her so-called men friends.'

'Adam, I'm so sorry.'

To her surprise he laughed. 'Don't be. Now that I've had time to come to terms with it, it's almost a relief. Let's face it, ours was hardly what you could term as a marriage made in heaven, was it? But anyway . . . I ought to be going now. Mrs McGregor has kindly offered to put me up for the night, what's left of it. I shall be back first thing in the morning though. Is there anything you need me to bring in?'

'Just yourself,' she told him and then felt the colour flood into her cheeks. What was she thinking of, saying things like that to him?

She needn't have worried, for he gave her a broad smile as he stood up and stretched painfully. 'Right then, you try and rest now, eh? And please try to keep out of mischief. When I think of how all this mess might have ended up it makes my blood run cold. Whyever you tried to sort it all out yourself is a mystery to me. But still – all's well that ends well. We'll talk more tomorrow when you're feeling more chipper.'

He gave her hand a final gentle squeeze and she watched him walk away, never taking her eyes off him until the double doors at the end of the ward had closed behind him. Only then did she allow herself to look about her. Rows of beds stretched away on either side of her and in the middle of the ward, a nurse was bent over a desk writing by the light of a dull lamp.

What was it Adam had said? That Tilly might be in the very next ward? She was all right. She was *really* all right. A little bubble of excitement began to grow in her stomach as she thought of Rachel. Once she and Tilly got out of here she could reunite them. She could imagine their faces when they saw one another; suddenly it had all been worth it and she could hardly wait for the morning to come.

The police arrived early the next day to interview her and she was shocked when they told her of all that had gone on. So both Ben and his mother were dead? She could hardly believe it, especially when the policeman informed her that it had been Mrs G who had killed them. Fancy her being Ben's grandmother! And to think that poor Tilly had been locked away in a madhouse. Just the thought of what Tilly must have been forced to endure sent shudders up her spine. As if the poor girl hadn't already gone through enough. But she wouldn't dwell on bad things. At least now they were both safe and with luck later in the day they would be allowed to see each other.

Not long after the police had left, the doctors did their rounds of the wards and Sophie was relieved when they told her that as long as she felt well enough she could be discharged the next day. They assured her that there should be no lasting effects from her ordeal although they would like to keep her in for just one more night for observation to be sure. She realised then how very lucky she had been but she also realised that things might have turned out totally differently if Adam hadn't come when he had. *Adam.* Just his name caused her to break out in goose bumps.

'There now, that's good news, isn't it?' The sister beamed at her as she tucked the blankets around her legs, bringing her thoughts sharply back to the present. 'Seems you're the heroine of the hour from what's being said, my dear. I've had to send that handsome young man of yours packing already this morning. I've told him to come back at visiting time, which he wasn't too pleased about. Still, he did leave you a beautiful bunch of flowers. One of the nurses is just putting them in water for you now.'

'Oh no, you've got it wrong,' Sophie started to tell her. 'Adam isn't my—' Her words fell on deaf ears, for the sister was already moving briskly away just as a nurse approached the bed with the most enormous vase of flowers Sophie had ever seen.

Smiling, she placed them on Sophie's locker then hurried off as Sophie stared at them in total confusion.

After dinner, which consisted of an overcooked concoction of boiled cabbage and beef, the sister allowed her to get out of bed and after a couple of laps of the ward, Sophie felt her strength returning. 'When can I go and see my friend in the next ward?' she dared to ask the nurse and the woman smiled at her as she hurried by with a bedpan in each hand.

'Sister's just told me that as soon as I've emptied these I'm to show you into the day room an' your friend will come to you there,' she informed her.

Minutes later Sophie was shown into a small room at the end of the ward, full of nothing but hard-backed chairs and a small table laden with magazines. She began to get nervous but then suddenly the door swung open; Tilly almost exploded into the room and they were in each other's arms laughing and crying all at the same time.

'Aw, Sophie. I don't know how I'm ever gonna thank yer enough fer gettin' me out o' that hell hole,' she sobbed as she clung to her friend. 'But never mind about that fer now – 'ow's my Rachel . . . an' Alfie?'

'Rachel is fine. She's with my Aunt Philly back in Nuneaton, no doubt being spoiled rotten,' Sophie assured her. 'And Alfie . . .' When her voice trailed away and she dropped her eyes, Tilly took a deep breath.

'He's done a runner on me, ain't 'e?' she asked dully.

Sophie nodded miserably; there was no easy way to tell her.

'Aw well,' Tilly sighed. 'It don't come as no big surprise if I'm to be honest. I've had a lot o' time to think while I were locked away an' lookin' back I reckon he only went out wiv me in the first place 'cos I kept him in beer money. I've only meself to blame at the end o' the day. I were so desperate for a happy-ever-after endin' that I pinned all me hopes on the first bloke to show me a bit of attention when I got 'ere. But I've still got Rachel though, ain't I? An' that's the most important thing. I gave a statement to the police this mornin'. What do yer reckon to all that's gone on though, eh? And what about you? How are you doin' an' what about your baby?'

'I lost the baby,' Sophie told her gently. 'It was on the day I ran from the hotel.'

'Cor blimey!'

They now sank down onto two chairs with their hands

clasped tight and for the next hour they talked through the things that had happened to them since they had last met.

'But what happened to Cathy and Amy?' Sophie asked at one point of the conversation and now Tilly's eyes welled with tears.

'Amy's in that ward there wiv me. She's gonna be all right. But Cathy – she didn't make it. The coppers told me she died givin' birth in the hotel an' then that bastard Ben buried her body at the back o' Hatter's Hall. Apparently, she weren't the only one either. They've discovered some more unmarked graves at the back o' the home. They reckon as they're gonna start diggin' 'em up soon so as the poor sods can be identified an' buried proper like.'

'Ugh!' Sophie shuddered at the thought. 'I still can't take it all in.' She shook her head in wonder. 'And Mrs G! I never dreamed that she was any relation to Ben and his mother though looking back we should have guessed the way she defended them all the time and wouldn't have a bad word said against them. It's sad how it's all ended up though, isn't it?'

'Huh! I don't bloody think so.' Tilly tossed her fiery red curls indignantly. 'I reckon the whole bloody lot of 'em got what were comin' to 'em. What were she thinkin' of, lettin' Ben an' his mother carry on like that? I just hope that the little 'un I gave up will be well cared for by the couple that took 'im, that's all.' Tilly's voice was now loaded with regret and fear. 'The coppers told me that they're goin' to try an' trace the babies that were sold but they ain't holdin' out much hope. They'll have left the country an' be long gone by now.'

'Well, at least you've still got Rachel,' Sophie pointed out. 'And I think she'll go mad with delight when she finally sees you again. She's been a little angel but not a day has gone by when she hasn't asked for you, particularly at bedtime.'

'Then I have a lot o' makin' up to do to her, don't I?' Tilly reflected pensively. 'An' yer can bet yer bottom dollar I won't be doin' nothin' to risk us bein' parted ever again. But that's enough about me fer now. Who's this here doctor that come to yer rescue, eh? Sounds like he's a bit keen to me.'

'Don't be so silly,' Sophie mumbled as colour flooded into her cheeks. 'Adam and I are just friends. My aunt cleans for him and—'

'Yeah, yeah! So yer say, but if he's just a friend why 'ave yer gone beetroot at the mention of his name then?'

Sophie had no time to reply, for at that very moment the door swung open and the very person they had been talking about came into the room with Mrs McGregor close behind him.

'You're looking more your old self today.' Adam smiled at Sophie. 'And this must be the infamous Tilly?'

'Yer right there,' Tilly beamed as she shook his hand and then Mrs McGregor caught her in a bear hug.

'Eeh, you pair have near turned me grey overnight, so you have,' she scolded but despite her words her eyes were shining. 'I've had your aunt on the phone, Sophie,' she told her over Tilly's shoulder. 'She says as soon as you're well enough you're to take Tilly back to Nuneaton with you and she can stay with her for the time being.'

'Well, that's solved one problem then,' Tilly remarked gleefully. 'I was wonderin' where I was goin' to stay till I got meself sorted out.'

Her eyes now moved to Adam, who was watching Sophie intently, and a grin spread across her face. Just friends were they? Well, time would tell.

Chapter Twenty-eight

'Right, now you both be sure to keep in touch, do you hear me? And try to keep yourselves out of trouble please.'

Sophie grinned at Mrs McGregor as she loaded the small bag Sophie had arrived with into the back seat of the car with Tilly.

They were going home and Tilly was nearly beside herself with excitement. In just a few short hours she would see Rachel again and after their enforced separation she could hardly wait. Sophie was sitting next to Adam in the front seat and after they had waved goodbye to Mrs McGregor she turned her attention back to them.

Adam had been marvellous to both of them over the last few days. He had sat in at every police interview and shown nothing but kindness, although she had a sneaky feeling that his feelings for Sophie went beyond that because every time he looked at her his face would soften. As far as Tilly was concerned a blind man on a galloping horse could have seen that they were just perfect for each other, but it seemed that as yet they hadn't realised it. Or, if they had, they'd chosen to ignore it. *It's early days yet though*, she comforted herself and settling back in the seat she thought about Rachel waiting for her back in Nuneaton.

The journey seemed to take forever but at last the car turned into a lane that Sophie informed her led down to her aunt's cottage. Tilly sat forward, impatiently peering over Sophie's shoulder, and then they were pulling up in front of a little terraced cottage whose door was flung open and there was Rachel in an elderly lady's arms. The woman placed the child gently on the ground and the second Tilly climbed from the car the child flew to her with a scream of pure delight: 'Mammy, Mammy!'

Aunt Philly meanwhile had run up to the car and was now clasping Sophie to her as tears streamed down her face. 'Eeh, but you've put years on me,' she scolded. 'I once told yer I were at heaven's door, but I reckon over the last few days I've gone a few steps closer. Whyever did yer have to try to tackle it all on yer own, love? I'd never have slept a wink had I known what you were mixed up in.'

'I'm sorry, Aunt Philly,' Sophie said soberly. 'I don't think I quite understood what a hornet's nest I was stepping into myself. Still, it's all over now and I'll introduce you to Tilly if she ever gets to put Rachel down.'

They all laughed as they looked towards the mother and child who were ecstatic to be together again. Aunt Philly then turned to Adam and told him, 'And you, lad. Why, I dread to think how this might all have turned out if you hadn't taken the law into your own hands when you did.'

He shrugged self-consciously as Sophie nodded in agreement, but then the mood was broken when her aunt started to usher them all into the cottage. 'Come on,' she ordered. 'I've got you all a meal ready an' it's right welcome you are, Tilly. It'll be a bit of a squeeze, I warn you, but I've no doubt we'll manage.'

'Thank you, Mrs Springs.'

'Now now. Let's start as we mean to go on, eh? There'll be no "Mrs Springs" here. It will be Philly, or Aunt Philly if you don't mind.' They exchanged a glance and both knew in that moment that they were going to get on like a house on fire. And so, with Rachel still clutched tightly in her arms, Tilly entered what was to be her temporary new home for the first time.

They had all eaten and darkness was falling across the village when Adam finally, reluctantly, rose from his seat.

'I ought to be off,' he told them regretfully. 'I'm due back at work tomorrow and my partner, Dr Beech, might not be too pleased if I turn up late the first day.'

'Thanks again, lad,' Philly told him sincerely.

'Anyone would have done the same,' he replied, but she shook her head.

'Anyone wouldn't, an' from now on I'm in your debt.'

'Nonsense.' Inclining his head towards Tilly and Sophie he followed her to the door where he said, 'Actually, I was glad to be away for a few days. While I was gone,

Celia was going to collect the rest of her things from the house. She's agreed to a divorce so when I get back she will have taken everything and then we can get it over with.'

'Yes, well, yer know what they say, when one door shuts another one opens,' Philly informed him wisely and she was amused to see the look of longing in his eyes as he glanced back at Sophie. She hoped romance would now blossom; they had both been through an awful lot in different ways and they were overdue a little bit of happiness.

Tilly had now been living with Philly for two weeks and, as Philly put it, she was beginning to get some roses back in her cheeks. But the same could not be said for Sophie, for strangely she seemed to have slipped into a deep melancholy and Adam didn't seem much happier. When he had first brought the girls home following their ordeal, Philly had harboured high hopes that Sophie and Adam might get together. But now she was beginning to think that she must have misjudged their feelings and they seemed to be avoiding each other.

'I don't know, it hardly seems worth me comin',' she grumbled to him one bright sunny afternoon as she wheeled her bicycle to the front gate. She had cleaned the house from top to bottom in less than two hours, because, as she had pointed out, since Celia had left the place didn't seem to get untidy any more. 'What if I just came once a week from now on to tidy up an' do yer washin' an' ironin'?' she suggested as he followed her onto the pavement.

'No. Let's just keep things as they are for now,' he pleaded then flushed as she raised her eyebrows. 'The thing is . . . it's nice to have someone to talk to on the days that you're here when I come home for my lunch.'

'As you will, lad,' Philly agreed. Sensing his loneliness, she asked, 'Why don't yer call round to our place tonight fer a bit o' tea when you've finished surgery?'

He seemed to be wrestling with himself before he finally answered, 'Thanks Philly, but no. I think you're already bulging at the seams without another visitor.'

Philly threw back her head and laughed. 'Well, I suppose yer could say we are a bit cramped. But I'll tell yer somethin', I ain't never been happier. The more the merrier, that's what I say. Tilly is a right little live wire. Rough on the outside but she's got a heart o' gold underneath. But what's happened has knocked the stuffin' out of my Sophie. Poor girl. I think everything that she's gone through over the last few months has finally caught up with her. She's taken a little job in the village shop, yer know? Only five hours a day, but she's an independent little bugger an' insists on payin' her way. Tilly is goin' fer an interview an' all fer the night shift at Courtaulds. That way either me or Sophie will always be there to keep an eye out fer Rachel.'

'Good.' He sounded genuinely pleased that things were working out for them. By now Philly was clambering onto her bike and he watched with amusement as she started off.

'Don't forget what I said now,' she threw over her shoulder. 'If yer should decide to change yer mind there'll be more than enough cottage pie for another mouth this evening.'

'Thanks, Philly.' He watched till she had turned a bend in the road before slowly making his way back into the empty house.

When Philly wheeled her bicycle up the entry that divided the small cottages and entered by the back gate she saw that Tilly and Rachel were playing in the garden with Lily. The little dog instantly hurtled towards her owner and began to lick any part of her that she could reach as Tilly hurried down the garden path.

'Oh, come an' sit down, Philly,' she urged her. 'You must be worn out bikin' in this hot weather. Come an' sit here in the shade an' I'll go an' get yer a nice cool drink.'

Philly smiled as Tilly took the bicycle and leaned it against the outhouse door before hurrying away into the kitchen. She had known the girl for a relatively short time, but already she was beginning to dread the day when she would leave her. The council had interviewed her and her name was now on the council list, which meant that she might be offered a little house at any time now. She had also had a visit from the Welfare Department, but thankfully that had gone well, for they could see how much Tilly and Rachel adored each other.

They had accepted the fact that both Tilly and Sophie had been led to believe that Ben's mother was connected with their department and that the babies would be going to legitimate homes and so had decided that no further action would be taken. It was now in the hands of the police who had also paid Tilly and Sophie numerous visits over the last few weeks as they prepared the case for court. Philly had refused to have a newspaper in the house, because the story seemed to be plastered all across the front of every one and she knew that Sophie was already at the limit of her endurance.

Now that Philly knew the full story, she couldn't help but have mixed feelings about Mrs G and found it hard to feel sorry for the woman. After all, as she saw it, it was the way she had spoiled her daughter shamelessly in the first place that had led to the whole sorry situation.

At that moment, Tilly appeared with a glass of lemonade in her hand and Philly took it gratefully as she watched Rachel trot off down the garden with Lily again.

'Sophie still at work is she?' she asked and was concerned when Tilly nodded with a sober expression on her face.

'Yes she is, she's due back any minute now but . . . Well, the thing is, we had a good long talk this mornin' an' I reckon she's beginnin' to miss Blackpool. Well, not Blackpool exactly, but her brothers. She's on about goin' back to see them. She still misses her mam summat rotten.'

'I see.' Philly couldn't prevent her voice from trembling. She'd known since the moment Sophie had come

452

back that the girl was troubled and she supposed deep down that she could understand her need to see what was left of her family. After all, her brothers were all she had left now apart from herself. Even so, she knew that if Sophie should decide to stay with them she would miss her dreadfully.

The urge came on her to cry but she resisted it. Here she'd been thinking that Sophie and Adam might get together when all the time Sophie had been planning to leave. Still, no doubt she would keep in touch and she still had Tilly and Rachel, for the time being at least. At that moment the topic of their conversation appeared through the gate and the instant Sophie looked at her aunt she knew that Tilly had told her about her proposed trip.

'So yer off to see yer brothers then, are yer, love?' Philly said softly.

Sophie nodded. 'I hope you don't mind, Aunt Philly? You've been so good to me, I don't know what I'd have done without you over the last few months, but the thing is—'

'The thing is, yer missin' what's left of your family,' Philly finished her sentence for her. 'But you shouldn't feel bad about that. It's understandable after what you've been through an' no doubt they'll be worried sick about you by now. I dare say your name will have been plastered all over the papers in Blackpool the same as it has here so it's only right that you should go an' put their minds at rest. When were yer thinkin' o' goin?'

'I just spoke to Mrs Burton in the shop and she said she'd be quite happy to let Tilly take my job. That would save her having to walk all the way into town to do a night shift and she's prepared to let Tilly take Rachel with her if need be.'

'There'll be no need fer her to do that if I'm here to watch her,' Philly declared indignantly.

'In that case I thought I might go early next week,' Sophie told her quietly.

'An' will yer be comin' back?'

Sophie's head drooped. 'I honestly don't know yet. It will all depend on what reaction I get from my brothers when I get there. But I'll always stay in touch, I promise.'

The next instant they were wrapped in each other's arms and Philly felt as if her heart would break. Sophie would leave a great gap in her life but it wouldn't be right for her to stand in the girl's way. 'Just remember, you'll always have a home here waiting for you no matter what,' she whispered into her sweet-smelling hair and then they clung together as Tilly looked sadly on.

It was a total surprise when Adam arrived that evening. Having earlier turned down her invitation to have tea with them, Philly hadn't been expecting him, but she was delighted to see him all the same.

'Why, this is a nice surprise,' she greeted him, then, 'Tilly, set another place at the table fer the doctor would yer, love?'

Tilly grinned before pottering away to do as she was

told with a broad smile on her face. Sophie was in the kitchen, just lifting the cottage pie from the oven when Tilly told her, 'Adam's turned up, an' if I'm any judge it ain't just the meal he's come for.'

'Don't be so silly,' Sophie snapped as her eyes flashed with annoyance. 'I really don't know how you've got it into your head that there's anything other than friendship between us, I really don't.'

'Have it yer own way then,' Tilly retorted cheekily. 'But I still say that that bloke is smitten wiv yer. An' yer could do a lot worse fer yourself so just think on what I've said. I'll tell yer now, I wish it were me he had eyes for. He's a bit of all right he is.'

'Oh Tilly. You're a hopeless romantic, you really are,' Sophie hissed, but she was smiling again, for she could never stay annoyed with Tilly for long.

Soon after when they were all seated at the table, Philly told Adam of Sophie's impending departure. He listened solemnly and made no comment, but did she see a look of sadness flash briefly in his eyes? She sighed. Young people were so hard to understand nowadays. But she was a great believer that what was meant to be would be so she wisely didn't comment and the conversation turned to other things.

After the meal, Tilly dragged a loudly protesting Rachel off for a bath and Philly rose to retire to the front room to put her feet up and read the newspaper. 'Leave the pots till later,' she told Sophie and Adam but they both shook their heads.

'No, it's all right. You go and sit down and I'll see to the clearing away and the washing-up,' Sophie told her.

'And I'll give you a hand,' Adam chipped in. 'It's the least I can do after that lovely meal. It isn't often I get to have anything home-cooked. Though I think I must have put at least half a stone on with all that bread and butter pudding I ate.'

'Yer can thank Sophie fer that,' Philly told him. 'She's a right handy little cook,' and with that she left them to it with a cheeky twinkle in her eye.

For a time the atmosphere between them was strained but as Sophie washed the pots and he dried them it gradually became more relaxed until he eventually said quietly, 'Would you like me to come with you when you go back to Blackpool, Sophie? I mean, it isn't going to be easy facing your brothers after everything that's gone on.'

She smiled at him sadly, noting the way a lock of hair had slipped over his forehead and resisting the urge to brush it away. 'I appreciate the offer, Adam, but to be honest, I think this is something I should do on my own.'

He nodded in understanding and again a silence stretched between them until he broke it when he suddenly said, 'I hope things turn out all right for you, Sophie.'

Her hands became still as she looked up at him from dull eyes. Time and time again she had thought back to the night he had rescued her from the house in Back Street when she had heard him say, *Please don't leave me because I don't know how I could go on without you.* She found herself blushing hotly as she lowered her eyes once more to the steaming soapy water. What was the matter with her? Just because he had said he'd miss her didn't mean he was in love with her. It was just her being silly and reading more into it than he had actually intended. After all, what would a man like him ever see in her after being married to a woman as beautiful as Celia? Adam looked on her as a friend, and anything more than that was just wishful thinking on her part.

It suddenly hit her with a little shock that he was one of the reasons she wanted to leave. Every time she saw him it was almost painful, for she knew that she had feelings for him that he could never return. So perhaps it would be for the best all round once she was gone? She could try to put her life back together again then and forget all about him. Even as the thought occurred she knew deep down that this was going to prove much easier said than done.

With the washing-up all finished and the pots returned to their rightful place, they strolled out into the garden and sat down on the bench overlooking the fields that backed onto the end of Philly's garden. It was an idyllic evening. The sun was just sinking on the horizon and the sky looked like a canvas that had been painted with soft colour. All they could hear was the lowing of the cattle in the field and birdsong.

'Will you be glad to get back to the hustle and bustle of town life?' Adam asked. 'You must have felt as if you'd been stuck out in the back of beyond here.'

'Actually, I shall miss this little cottage, and Aunt Philly,' Sophie told him truthfully. 'She's been an absolute godsend to me over the last few months. In fact, I don't know what I would have done without her . . . or you for that matter. I shall never be able to thank you enough, Adam. If you hadn't come to Blackpool when you did . . . well, I just shudder to think what might have happened to me – and Tilly if it comes to that.'

He shrugged and then unable to hold it back for a moment longer he blurted out, 'I would have gone to the ends of the earth for you, Sophie.'

Her head snapped round and now she was staring at him incredulously as she stuttered, 'Wh . . . what do you mean?'

It was his turn to blush now as he answered, 'I know I probably shouldn't be saying this right now, not until my divorce has come through at least and that could be some time away. But the thing is, I have feelings for you and if you *should* decide to come back from Blackpool and you don't mind waiting . . . I was hoping that one day you might return my feelings.'

'Oh.' She was so astounded that for now it was all she could think of to say.

Spurred on by the fact that she hadn't rejected him he hesitantly went on, 'I can understand your need to go back to your home town, but I'd like it if you'd at least consider it. I wouldn't push you into anything, I promise, and I'd be happy to wait for as long as it took. But the thing is, I want to marry you, Sophie, as soon as I'm free. This all must sound totally ridiculous to you because we haven't known each other for long, but I think I fell in love with you the very first moment I clapped eyes on you. I realise now that's why I could accept Celia leaving me so easily. So what do you say? Will you wait for me until my divorce has come through and marry me?'

'Of course I'll wait, and I'd be proud to be your wife.' She was crying now as a look of pure joy spread across his face and he clasped her hands in his. 'I love you too. That's one reason I wanted to leave, because I never thought you would feel the same about me.'

His arms were suddenly round her and she had the strangest feeling of coming home.

'I think this trip might prove to be a bit of an ordeal for you,' he told her, and she nodded through the tears that were sparkling in her eyes.

'It probably will be. But at least I'll know now that I have something to go on for. If you're here waiting for me, I mean.'

'Oh, I'll be here waiting all right,' he whispered, but then there was no more time for words as his lips closed over hers. She gave herself up to the sheer joy of his nearness and suddenly there was light again at the end of a long dark tunnel.

Epilogue

It was the night before Sophie was to return to her home town and her emotions were mixed. Philly had been like a cat that had got the cream ever since Sophie and Adam had told her of their love for one another. But now Sophie's feelings of elation were being consumed by apprehension as the time to leave drew closer. Her bag was packed at the side of the door and her train ticket was booked for three o'clock the following day. She was standing at the window in the small front room waiting for Adam to arrive and Tilly had a broad grin on her face as she brushed Rachel's hair before tucking her into bed.

'I don't know. Yer like a cat on hot bricks,' she teased. 'Anyone would think yer hadn't seen him fer a month instead o' just last night. Talk about bein' lovesick.'

Sophie smiled back at her as Tilly swept Rachel into her arms and after Sophie had planted an affectionate kiss on the child's cheek, Tilly carried her off to bed. Tilly had been really brave although Sophie was very aware that she still pined and fretted every single day for the baby she had given up.

Her thoughts now went back to the baby she herself had lost and tears pricked at the back of her eyes. As yet she still hadn't told Adam or her Aunt Philly about the night her father had raped her and the knowledge she had kept to herself was hanging over her like a great black cloud. Perhaps she should tell them tonight and get it over with? At least that way there would be no secrets between them. And she owed it to both of them to be honest.

At that moment, Aunt Philly came into the room and dropped onto the settee just as Adam's car pulled up outside and instantly she hurried to the door to admit him. The second that he got out of the car she saw by the look on his face that something was wrong, so she stood aside and said nothing as he came past her into the room.

Philly was the first to speak when she asked him, 'What's wrong wi' your face then, lad? Yer look like you've lost a bob an' found sixpence.'

'Actually, Philly, I've just had a phone call from Inspector Grey in Blackpool. He rang to tell me that Mrs G won't be standing trial for the murder of Ben and his mother after all. She died peacefully in her sleep last night in custody.'

Sophie bit down on her bottom lip as Philly gasped but then she said quietly, 'Perhaps it's just as well. She was an old lady and somehow I can't see how she would have coped locked up in prison.'

'There is that to it,' he agreed sadly. 'Let's just hope that this will be an end to the whole sorry mess, eh?'

Deep down Sophie wondered if there would ever be an end to it. She knew that the things she had endured over the last few months would haunt her for the rest of her life; so many deaths and so much pain and unhappiness. Now she felt the time was right to be totally truthful to both her aunt and Adam.

'Adam, sit down, would you? I have something to tell you.' When her aunt went to rise, Sophie motioned her back into her seat. 'No, this is something you should hear too, Aunt Philly,' she told her solemnly then taking a deep breath she went on, 'The fact is . . . there is still one thing that I haven't confided to either of you about and it's eating me away. You see . . .' She stopped momentarily to swallow the huge lump that had formed in her throat before going on. 'It all started one night when my father came home from the pub. He'd had a lot to drink and I had fallen asleep at the side of the fire in the kitchen.' Slowly she forced herself to tell them everything. She left out nothing and by the time the tale was told it was hard to tell who was the paler of the two listeners.

It was Philly who finally broke the silence when she rose painfully from her chair and took Sophie into a loving embrace. 'Eeh, fer such a thing to happen,' she muttered brokenly as she rocked Sophie to and fro. 'And to think you've kept all this locked away inside you for all this time.' She now stepped back and discreetly moved towards the door. 'I'm goin' to go an' put the kettle on an' give you pair a bit o' privacy.'

Once the door had closed behind her, Adam gently took her hands in his and she saw that his cheeks were wet with tears. 'Oh, Sophie, I don't know what to say . . .'

'You don't have to say anything,' she told him quietly. 'I just didn't want there to be any secrets between us.' Deep inside she had dreaded Adam's reaction but now as she saw that he was attaching none of the blame for what had happened to her she felt as if a great weight had been lifted off her shoulders.

'We can go on from here,' he told her and she prayed with all her heart that he was right.

Sleep eluded her that night when she finally went to bed. She had given her slightly larger room to Tilly and Rachel and had moved into the small boxroom. She could hear their gentle snores now through the wall; not that it worried her. It was comforting to know that they were close by and all safe and sound.

When her thoughts turned back to Adam a warm glow started in the pit of her stomach and slowly spread through her. Already she was looking forward to the day when they would be married. They had agreed that they both wanted it to be a very low-key affair and the only thing that spoiled it was the knowledge that her mother wouldn't be there to share it. As a little girl, Sophie had always dreamed of shopping for her wedding dress with her mother, but that couldn't happen now. Still, she tried to console herself, that will probably be a few years away. Before they could do anything they had to wait for Adam's divorce to come through and then she would probably go to choose her dress with Aunt Philly. First of all, though, she had to face her brothers.

The first light of day was painting the sky before she finally drifted off into an uneasy doze and even then it was filled with nightmares. She was back in the brothel in Back Street and Walter was advancing on her with a needle in his hand. And now she was in back in the hotel again watching Tilly's baby being taken away. Her mother was there too, but the faster Sophie walked towards her the further away her mother seemed to get. At this point she started awake in a cold sweat with tears running down her face.

She got out of bed and padded along the landing to the bathroom. It would be no use trying to drift off again, she was too afraid that the nightmares might recur, so she decided that she might as well get washed and dressed.

By the time Tilly came down the stairs with Rachel in her arms, Sophie had the breakfast all ready on the table. 'Crikey, talk about an early bird,' Tilly said sleepily. 'What time did you get up?'

'Oh, I couldn't sleep,' Sophie told her airily and then they both sat down to their first cup of tea of the day.

'So, how are yer feelin'?' Tilly asked through a mouthful of hot buttered toast.

'A bit mixed,' Sophie admitted. 'Obviously I'm looking

forward to seeing my brothers again, though I think it will be a bit of a shock when I turn up on their doorsteps. They haven't heard a peep out of me since the night I left home apart from the one letter that I sent to Brian shortly after I got here, telling him that I was safe and well. They must have been shocked to see all the reports in the newspapers about what's gone on. But it's going to be strange going back without my mum being there any more.'

Tilly looked at her sympathetically. By now Philly had joined them and as she looked towards the window she frowned. 'Would yer just look at that weather,' she grumbled. The rain was lashing against the windows and the sky was heavy and overcast. Just like my mood, Sophie found herself thinking.

By mid-morning there was no sign of the rain ceasing, as they all sat in the small middle room that served as a dining room enjoying a coffee break.

'The Blue Lagoon will be overflowin' at this rate,' Philly remarked. 'An' it's comin' down so fast it will be playin' havoc wi' them new plants I put in.'

Tilly and Sophie exchanged an amused smile but had no time to reply, for just then there was a knock at the front door.

'That'll be Adam,' Philly said as she rose from her seat and pottered towards the door that led into the small front room. 'You two stay where you are. I'll go an' let him in.'

The girls turned their attention back to Rachel who was happily scribbling away in a colouring book with some crayons that Philly had bought her. It was when they heard the woman exclaim that they quickly looked towards each other, puzzled. They rose from the table in unison and had just started towards the door when Philly appeared. Her face was chalk-white and she was crying and laughing all at the same time as she stared towards them.

'My God, yer look like you've seen a bloody ghost,' Tilly exclaimed in her usual forthright manner.

Philly laughed through her tears then turning her attention to Sophie she told her, 'I think I just have. You'd better sit down, love. There's someone here to see yer an' I think it's goin' to come as a bit of a shock.'

Totally bewildered, Sophie slowly sank back into her chair. Who would be coming to see her? She hardly knew anyone hereabouts apart from Adam. She didn't have long to wait before she found out, because at that moment a face appeared over Philly's shoulder and her hands flew to her mouth as shock jolted through her. And then suddenly she was out of her seat and flying towards the visitor as she cried, 'Oh . . . *Mam*!'

She was terrified that the vision would vanish into thin air and she would wake again to find that she'd just had another nightmare. But no, she was in her mother's arms now; she could feel her, solid and warm, and smell that special smell that had always belonged to her alone.

And then the room was swaying and if the woman hadn't held tight to her she would have slithered to the floor. Sally pressed her down onto a chair and told her,

'Put your head between your knees for a minute, love, there's a good girl.'

Finally the dizziness passed and now the questions came, 'But, Mam . . . I . . . thought you were dead. It said in the papers that you'd taken an overdose. I came to visit your grave . . . I . . . I don't understand.'

Philly had gone to fetch a glass of brandy, which she now pressed into Sophie's hand. 'Get that down yer,' she ordered, 'an' then happen your mam will explain.'

Sophie gulped at the liquid, coughing and spluttering as it burned its way down her throat and into her stomach, and now she saw that Matthew was there too and if she was asleep she prayed that she would never have to wake up again as he smiled at her.

At last her mother asked her gently, 'Can we go somewhere private?'

'O' course yer can.' Philly began to herd them towards the front room. 'You've both got a lot o' catchin' up to do so we'll all leave yer in peace. You just take as long as yer like now. Meantime I'll get to know our Matthew here.'

Once the door had closed behind her, Sally drew Sophie to the settee and when they had sat down she slowly began to explain. 'I did take an overdose, love. But Matthew found me in time. They rushed me off to the hospital and pumped my stomach. Once I was well enough to be let out I was arrested for your father's murder and they locked me up.' She shuddered as she remembered what she could of that terrible time before going on. 'I stabbed him, you know? I couldn't cope with what he had done to you and when I confronted him about it he started to hit me and something just snapped . . . Anyway, I eventually went to trial but they let me off on the grounds of diminished responsibility. It was splashed all across the papers for a time and I was terrified that you'd read it and worry yourself sick.'

Sophie slowly shook her head. 'We didn't get to see the newspapers at the hotel, apart from the odd ones left lying about that we managed to smuggle up to our rooms. But, oh Mam, to think you've been through all this . . .' She stared at her mother and realised with a start that she appeared to have shrunk. She had been frail for many years following her stroke but now she looked so fragile that Sophie imagined she might snap in two.

Seeing the distress on her daughter's face, Sally went on, 'I was on the verge of a nervous breakdown by then and I don't remember much after that for some time except that I was put into another hospital. A mental hospital . . . and for months I didn't even know who I was. I suppose it was my way of shutting out everything that had happened. But then, one night, Mattie visited me and started to read out a piece from the newspaper with *your* name in it. It was about all that dreadful business you got mixed up in. From then on I started to come back to life, or at least that's how it felt. When they finally discharged me from the hospital, Mattie took me to live with him and Becky, his new wife. I was beside myself with worry and had no idea where you could be. So in the end Mattie went to the police and they told us where to find you. And well . . . here I am.'

'B . . . but the grave? I went there. I saw your name on it.'

'Yes, you saw the name Winters – but that was your father. At least . . . Oh, Sophie, there's something else I *have* to tell you. I've died a thousand deaths ever since the night you left home because I wasn't completely honest with you then.'

Seeing the bewilderment on Sophie's face, Sally forced herself to go on as shame washed over her. 'The thing is – Bill, your dad, *wasn't* your dad, love. What I omitted to explain was that the man I had the affair with was your real father. That's why Bill never took to you. On the night he died he told me that he'd known you weren't his from the moment he set eyes on you.'

'Oh!' Sophie was struck dumb as emotions coursed through her. So at least she hadn't been raped by her *real* father then? Somehow the knowledge made what had happened fractionally easier to bear.

'I lost the baby,' she told her mother eventually and Sally nodded.

'I know you did, love. The police told us everything. I'm so very sorry. How am I *ever* going to make it up to you? You've been through so much and it's all my fault.'

'No, no, it isn't,' Sophie cried as she shook her mother's hands up and down. 'It's all in the past now and we can start to put it behind us and try to get on with our lives again.'

At that moment, Adam came into the room, having found the front door swinging open, and he looked about in bewilderment as Sophie rushed towards him with an expression of joy on her face. He had always thought that she was pretty, but now she looked positively beautiful.

'Oh, Adam, you're never going to believe what's happened! I won't be going to Blackpool after all . . . come and meet my mam.'

'Your *mam*?' Now it was Adam's turn to look shocked as he noticed the woman sitting on the settee. Sophie laughed up into his face and slowly began to explain.

The next hour took on an unreal quality as Sophie gradually came to realise that the nightmare was really, finally all over. Philly couldn't stop smiling as she fussed over the niece she had never thought to see again and the atmosphere was light. Sally was still weak and tired, however, after her long illness, so after lunch, Philly insisted that she should go up to her room and have a rest while Tilly and Rachel entertained Matthew, who hadn't stopped smiling since the second he had set eyes on Sophie.

Now, Adam took Sophie's hand and led her out into the garden where he told her, 'Your mother and your brother can stay at my house tonight. There's more than enough room, in fact I'm rattling around like a pea in a pod now so they can stay as long as they like. I dare say you won't want them to be going back too soon, will you?'

'No I won't.' Sophie laughed, still hardly able to take in the latest developments, and then she suddenly looked up at the sky, which was now a cloudless blue, and said incredulously, 'Oh, look, it's stopped raining and the sun has come out again.'

Following her eyes, he smiled. 'Sophie Winters.' He now took her hands in his and turned her to face him. 'I promise you that from now on you're going to see *nothing* but sunshine.' And as his lips pressed down on hers she knew that he was right and all was well with the world.